Rescuing Casey

Rescuing Casey

Delta Force Heroes

Book 7

By Susan Stoker

Edited by Kelli Collins
Cover Design by AURA Design Group
Manufactured in the United States

Table of Contents

Chapter One

CASEY SHEA SHIVERED. It was ridiculous that she was cold. Costa Rica had an average temperature of eighty degrees with humidity levels hovering around eighty-five to ninety percent. She should be sweating her ass off, but several factors were working against her.

First, the darkness. The pit she'd been thrown into was pitch black. Whatever her kidnappers had used to cover it was absolutely impenetrable. Not even the smallest sliver of sunlight made its way through the darkness.

Second, she was dehydrated and hungry. She'd been using her bra to try to filter the water that dripped down the sides of her prison, but the few drops weren't enough.

Third, she was stressed.

She'd done everything her brother had taught her. She'd kept calm. Thought positively. And did her best not to give in to despair.

But she was getting desperate.

Casey forced herself to get up and pace the small

prison. She knew exactly how many steps it was to get from one side to the other. Four. Four steps forward, four steps backward. Two steps wide. That's it.

She'd tried to climb out of the hole, with no success. The sides of her prison were too unstable. She'd only ended up bringing more dirt down on her head. The top of the hole was only a few feet above her arms when she stretched them over her head, but the pit may as well have been forty feet deep, for all the good her efforts did. She couldn't climb out, didn't have enough wood planks to stand on to reach the top, and whatever they'd covered the hole with, it had taken the three kidnappers a long time to carefully conceal her tomb.

The smell of decay and rot had been overwhelming when she'd first been dumped down into the hole, but she was so used to it now, she barely noticed. This had probably been where the villagers had put the parts of the animals they didn't eat or use when they were done with them. There were bones under the liquid at her feet, but since Casey couldn't see them, she had no idea what kinds of animals they might've been from.

She didn't know how long it had been since she was separated from her students, but it was too long. Before that, they'd been doing all right, keeping calm and rationing the food and water they'd been given. One of their kidnappers had told them they were being held for ransom, but Casey wasn't sure she believed him.

Astrid might be ransomed—she was the daughter of a Danish ambassador—but Casey and the others? No way. She wasn't anyone special. And she didn't think Jaylyn or Kristina's families had money either.

The girls had been doing great on the research trip. Getting along and excitedly waking each morning to head out into the jungle to find more bugs to examine. Not every school trip went so well. Differing personalities and dealing with the culture and climate of Costa Rica sometimes brought out the worst in her students. But not Jaylyn, Kristina, and Astrid. They all got along very well, considering their differences.

Astrid came from money, lots of it. Jaylyn was attending the University of Florida on a full academic scholarship. Kristina was more of a party girl, president of her sorority, and barely squeaking by Casey's class with a B-minus average.

On the surface, they shouldn't have gotten along as well as they had, but with Casey's guidance and their busy schedule, they'd been doing well. But Casey'd had to step up her leadership game when they'd been kidnapped. She knew that, without her, things would have likely already gone south between the three women. There were signs of dissension before she'd been separated from them, and Casey prayed they were holding on, and remembering what she'd tried to teach them in the short time they'd had together after being snatched.

Casey stopped and looked upward. She couldn't see anything, but that didn't make her stop glancing up every couple seconds in case there was sudden light peeking into the hole. She was breathing hard after only ten trips back and forth across the small area. She eased back to the corner she'd been using as her sleeping space and sat on her butt. She'd been surprised to find a few planks of wood at the bottom of the hole, and she'd stacked them on top of one another, giving her a raised platform that was just above the water pooled all around her.

Her hiking pants were soaked. As were her feet in her all-terrain Gore-Tex boots. They were supposed to be waterproof, but standing in water twenty-four seven was no match for the material. It had been inevitable it would eventually fail, and her wool socks and nylon liners were now soaked.

Still, Casey tried to stay positive. Her brother would come. He was a badass Special Forces soldier. He'd always been protective of her. When they were young, they'd played soldier for hours together. When she got older and started dating, he was the one who'd warned her dates to treat her right. After he'd joined the Army and had gone through Special Forces training, he'd come home and taught her how to shoot, fight, and what to do if she was ever taken hostage.

She'd laughed at that last one, and had protested that she'd never be in a situation where she'd need to know the psychological tricks kidnappers tried to use, and how she could turn those tricks around on them, but Aspen had simply shaken his head and told her that she never knew what the future would bring.

Casey sighed and rested her head against the mud and clay behind her. Her hair was covered with dirt and probably well on its way to becoming dreadlocks. Every inch of her was caked with mud. She'd welcomed it at first, knowing it might keep the kidnappers away if they decided they wanted to sexually assault her, but now she'd give anything to be clean.

She longed to lay down flat. The only way she'd been able to sleep was sitting up. Her back throbbed and she'd been having weird dreams about her bed at home.

"I need you, Aspen," she whispered, despite knowing the words were ridiculous. He couldn't hear her. No one could. Her voice was useless; she'd screamed for help so long when she'd first been dumped in the hole, it was now ruined. The dehydration, unsanitary conditions, and humid conditions had all worked together to keep her almost mute.

As if her words had magic powers, Casey suddenly heard shouting high above her head.

Then gunshots.

And more shouting.

It was the first time she'd heard anything since she'd been dumped deep in the ground.

She quickly stood and looked upward, praying for a miracle.

"I'm here! Someone come and get me," she croaked as loud as she could.

It might have been minutes, or maybe hours, but eventually the gunshots stopped, as did the shouting...and Casey was left in her silent, dark tomb once again.

She hadn't allowed herself to cry. Not once since the ordeal had begun.

But knowing rescue had been imminent, only to slip through her hands like the dirt when she'd tried to climb out of her hole, Casey sank back down on the planks of wood and sobbed.

No tears fell from her eyes, as her body didn't have any extra fluid to produce them.

She was going to die there, and no one would ever find her body.

"I'm sorry, Asp," she croaked between the heaving of her chest. "I'm so sorry."

TROY "BEATLE" LENNON'S entire focus was on the radio

sitting on the table in front of him. Blade paced back and forth behind the table, too agitated to sit. The rest of the Delta team was either sitting or standing around the small room. They were in Costa Rica, but had been denied permission to head into the jungle to rescue Blade's sister and the other women because the Danish Special Forces group, the Huntsmen Corps, had beaten them into the country.

Blade had wanted to say "fuck you" to the Costa Rican government, but Ghost had put his foot down and ordered the team to stand down and wait.

The Huntsmen Corps was the Danish equivalent to the Deltas. They'd been mobilized by the Danish government after Ambassador Jepsen had notified them about the kidnapping of his daughter. No one knew exactly when the group of students and their teacher had been taken, but by Blade's estimate, it had been at least a week and a half ago.

The Costa Rican government had said they'd received an anonymous tip about four American women being held in a village deep in the jungle. So when the Huntsmen arrived, they'd immediately headed to the reported location.

The Deltas could do nothing but wait while the rescue attempt went down.

They'd been receiving regular updates from the captain of the Huntsmen, but it had been fifteen minutes since the last one, and everyone's nerves were shot.

The last they'd heard was that the camp had been found and they were moving in.

"Fuck," Blade said, breaking the silence. "Why are we just standing here? We should've gone with them."

"Easy, man," Ghost said quietly. "You know why."

"I don't give a fuck about politics! My *sister* is out there, Ghost. She needs me!"

The leader of the Deltas looked up at his friend. "And she'll get you. I know more than most how someone can be affected after being held hostage. She's going to need your support, Blade. It's better that you aren't a major part of her memories in the jungle."

Beatle clenched his hands into fists in his lap. He knew what Ghost was talking about.

"I thought Rayne was doing better." Truck said what they all were thinking.

"She is," Ghost said immediately. "But her counselor told me that part of the reason she doesn't want to get married is because of what happened to her."

"I thought she was resisting because she didn't want to do it while Mary was sick?" Fletch asked.

"That was her original excuse," Ghost agreed. "But when Mary got better, she came up with another excuse. Then another. It's a trust issue. I don't give a fuck if we ever get married. All I want is Rayne to know deep down in her gut that she's safe. That I'll *keep* her safe.

She's going to carry the scars of being kidnapped in Egypt for a long time. In a way, I think it would've been easier if I hadn't been smack dab in the middle of it. Her bad memories of what almost happened to her are all mixed up with her feeling of relief when I showed up out of nowhere. I hate being connected in any way to that prick who almost raped her."

Ghost paused, then looked at Blade. "All I'm saying is, when the Huntsmen get her out of the jungle, you can be there for her in a way that isn't tainted with the actual kidnapping. You can be her rock. You know as well as I do that sometimes when a victim's family sees them when they're at rock bottom, it doesn't go well in the long run."

"Fuck!" Blade swore again and resumed his pacing.

The radio crackled on the table and all the men's attentions were immediately focused on the small black box.

"Hunter One to base."

"This is base. Continue Hunter One."

Beatle held his breath. They weren't authorized to use the secure channel, and could do nothing but listen as the outcome of the raid on the kidnappers' lair was finally revealed.

"Three packages secured. Repeat. Three packages secured."

If possible, the tension in the room increased tenfold

with those words.

"Confirmed," the voice with the Costa Rican accent said. "Location of the fourth package?"

"Unknown at this time," was the response from the Danish Special Forces soldier.

"Come on," Beatle said under his breath. "Who's missing?"

"ETA on your return?"

"Twenty-four hours," the soldier said. "Packages are in bad shape. Our speed will be compromised. Two casualties on our side as well. Verify rendezvous?"

"Dammit," Hollywood said harshly, pounding a fist on the table. "Ask who's missing."

As if his words were heard by base operations, the next question made every Delta Force soldier around the table hold his breath.

"ID on the missing package?"

There was a long pause before the Danish solider answered. A period of time where the United States soldiers listening in the small room each felt as if they'd aged ten years waiting for the answer.

"The oldest. The packages said it was removed from the area a week ago."

Before Blade could react to the news that his sister was still missing, Ghost stood and headed for the door. He turned to look at his team. "Politics be damned. One of our own is missing, and we aren't leaving this country until we get her back."

Beatle followed his teammates out of the room, all the while his mind spinning. The only picture he'd seen of Casey Shea had been the one Blade had shared with the team. It was a couple years old, taken at Christmas.

She'd been standing next to Blade and had him in a headlock. The soldier had obviously let her get the drop on him, because at over six-three, there was no way she'd be able to actually overpower him. It was the absolute joy in Casey's eyes that Beatle couldn't get out of his mind.

She was smiling so big, he thought for sure she'd been laughing when the picture had been taken. She wore a pair of jeans that were molded to her long legs. The shirt she was wearing had dipped over a shoulder, exposing the red bra strap underneath it. Her feet were bare, her toes painted the same bright red as her lingerie.

Her dirty-blonde hair was bunched on top of her head in a messy bun, making it impossible for Beatle to tell how long it really was. Her green eyes were staring straight at the camera...and she looked absolutely adorable.

Beatle didn't believe in love at first sight, but he couldn't deny he'd felt a jolt in his belly after seeing that picture. He was immediately attracted to not only her looks, but what he imagined was her carefree, happy personality as well.

And that was what worried Beatle the most. They'd rescued plenty of people in the past, and the thought of the happy woman in Blade's photo being changed by the violence she'd experienced ate at him.

Casey Shea didn't deserve whatever had happened to her. Not that anyone did, but the cheerful, laughing sister of one of his best friends definitely did not.

Hold on, Casey, Beatle thought. *We're comin' for you. Just hold on.*

Chapter Two

AS IT TURNED out, the Deltas weren't heading for Casey…at least not for a few days. They had run into obstacle after obstacle in their quest to search for Blade's sister.

They'd essentially been held captive in the hotel by the Costa Rican Army until the Huntsmen had returned. Then Ghost had insisted on sitting in on the interviews with the college students so they could get as much intel as possible before heading out.

As much as Beatle hated the delay, he couldn't deny the information had been useful.

Blade hadn't taken the news that they wouldn't immediately be heading out into the jungle to find his sister nearly as well. He'd had to be sedated so he wouldn't hurt himself any more than he already had. Punching walls wasn't exactly good for a person.

While Coach and Truck had stayed with Blade at the hotel, Ghost, Beatle, Fletch, and Hollywood had been allowed to listen to the interviews.

They'd been led to a room with a two-way mirror

where they could observe. Beatle had wanted to be able to ask questions, but the ambassador had denied access to his daughter to anyone other than the Danish soldiers who had rescued her. And since Astrid refused to be separated from Jaylyn and Kristina, they were all interviewed together.

"What happened?" the soldier in charge of interviewing them had asked bluntly.

It took a while for the girls to tell their story, but eventually they did.

They'd all been in the jungle looking for a new species of ant when the kidnappers came out of nowhere. They threw them into the back of a truck and driven for hours. During that time, apparently, Casey had instructed the girls to stay calm, to believe that they'd be missed and someone would come for them. She'd further told them to take things one day at a time, one minute at a time if needed, and to always find something positive about the situation.

At hearing that, Ghost had murmured, "Smart. Blade must've taught her that."

Beatle silently agreed. He'd had a long talk with his friend, and Blade had recounted how he'd lectured his sister about how to psychologically stay strong in a situation just like the one she'd found herself in.

The kidnapped girls continued to tell their tale, about how they'd been driven into the jungle and had arrived at what they'd thought was a village. It had been dark, so they couldn't really describe anything about it. That wasn't exactly necessary, as the Huntsmen had confirmed the girls had been held captive in a village in the middle of the jungle.

The girls went on to explain how Casey had been their leader, keeping them calm, making sure everyone had enough to eat and drink, and generally ensuring their spirits remained high.

After several days of captivity, one of their kidnappers had arrived and said that Casey's ransom had been paid, and he dragged her away. The girls hadn't seen her again, and had assumed she was safe, probably back in the United States. It had taken a bit of prodding by the soldier questioning them, but eventually the girls admitted that after Casey had left, they hadn't done as well. They'd begun to bicker and fight, and they'd been on the verge of seriously turning against one another when the Danish soldiers had arrived.

They looked guilty about that, but had been reassured it was normal. That many times, in stressful situations like they'd been in, relationships broke down and things got tense.

The interviewer asked more questions, but Ghost had heard enough. The four Deltas had left and Ghost had asked permission to enter the jungle, and the camp where Casey had last been seen, to begin the search for her.

Permission had been denied. It was the Costa Rican government's belief that the professor was dead, and they didn't want armed soldiers creeping around, possibly shooting innocent people while they went on a futile mission.

It took three more days, but eventually the government had conceded after pressure from the President of the United States, and grudgingly given the Deltas permission for their search-and-rescue mission.

By the time they left the town of San José for the jungle, it had been four days since the other women had been rescued. No one had heard anything about Casey Shea for almost twelve days. She could be anywhere by now, and every Delta knew it. She could have been smuggled into Mexico and into the sex trade.

Or she could've been shot as soon as she was separated from the others, her body dumped in the jungle somewhere, to become food for all of the various insects and animals the country was notorious for. The chance of them finding her—alive or dead—was extremely low.

But no one was going to give up. This was Blade's sister. She was theirs. And she was out there...somewhere.

HOURS LATER, AFTER being dropped off at the rendez-vous point by the chopper on loan from the Costa Rican government, the seven-man Delta team spread out without a word as they made their way through the jungle. Beatle was paired with Blade. As they headed toward the last known location of his sister, Blade talked about her.

In a low voice, he told Beatle how Casey loved Chinese food.

How, when she was little, she was always digging in the dirt behind their house, trying to find a new species of bug.

How she'd refused to go to prom her senior year because there was a documentary that night on television about ants in Central America.

How proud he was of her when she'd gotten her PhD. She'd been working toward her Master's degree and PhD at the same time, and had recently received her Doctorate. She'd been at the university for years, studying, teaching, and taking classes. She was young to already have her PhD, but from what Beatle understood, she'd worked her ass off doing everything possible to get it done as soon as she could.

Beatle let his friend talk and soaked up every piece of information about Casey he could. After several hours, it was as if he knew Casey as well as her brother did.

They were taking a break when Blade put his hand on Beatle's shoulder and said urgently, "I heard what Ghost said a couple days ago. The last thing I want is to hurt my relationship with my sister. When we find her, I want you to stay by her side."

"Blade, I—"

He cut him off. "I don't want her to suffer negative consequences because I'm here. It'll kill me, but I'm going to do my best to stay in the background on this."

"Don't you think that'll hurt her more?" Beatle asked. "I mean, seeing you, her brother, and not having you comfort her?"

Blade shook his head. "No. I mean, I'll be there for her, but I don't want the sight of me to bring back bad memories. I'll take point on our return or something. *Please*, Beatle."

Beatle looked at his friend and teammate. They'd been trained to be one hundred percent honest in all things with each other. Their lives depended on it. "I'm attracted to her," he confessed. "I don't know what it is, but the second I saw that picture you showed us, I wanted to get to know her better. And with you talking about her all afternoon..." His voice trailed off. It sounded insane, but it was what it was.

Blade eyed him for a long moment then nodded. "Good."

"Good?"

"Yeah. Look…I have no problem with her hooking up with you. I know some men have some sort of dumbass bro code where they think it's not cool to date their friends' sisters, but not me. I'd get down on my knees and thank my lucky stars if Casey ended up with you. I guess you're really the only single one left on our team, other than me. We all know Truck is hung up on Mary, so he doesn't count. I know you, Beatle. I know all your good and bad points. If you and my sister fell in love, I'd get to see her more. I'd know she was protected. But, you know what the odds of that happening are…right? She's been out here for a long time…she might not be the sister I remember. She might resent me for not finding her earlier. She might've been raped. I just…"

It was Beatle's turn to put his hand on his friend's shoulder. "If she's anything like you, she'll get through this. She will."

Blade closed his eyes, but nodded. Then he took a deep breath. "She's out here," he whispered. "I don't know how I know it, but I do. I know what the odds are of her being alive, but I don't give a shit. She's waiting on us to find her."

Beatle nodded. "Then that's what we'll do."

Without another word, the two men silently moved forward with the rest of their team. The only evidence that they'd been there were two butterflies who were startled off a branch and lifted into the dense, humid air.

TEN HOURS LATER, the team lay on their bellies in the Costa Rican jungle. Their fingers were on the trigger guards of their rifles as their gazes roamed the deserted camp in front of them.

They'd reached the coordinates where the Huntsmen Corps had rescued the college students. They'd spread out and surrounded what was left of the hideout.

"Ghost?" Hollywood asked almost silently.

They were all wearing earpieces and could communicate with each other up to a couple miles apart.

"Nobody moves," Ghost ordered. "This could be a trap."

"It's deserted," Fletch insisted.

"Or maybe they're waiting for someone to show back up looking for Casey," Ghost returned. "I said, hold tight."

Beatle ground his teeth together, but did as he was ordered. His eyes scanned the part of the camp that he could see. His mind going a million miles an hour. It was wrong. He couldn't put his finger on what was bothering him, but this wasn't what he'd expected to see when they'd arrived at the location.

Instead of a hastily erected tent camp, the structures that were still standing looked semi-permanent. He could see a wooden floor in one of the circular huts. There were fire pits scattered around and even what looked like a large common-area tent. Why would guerilla kidnappers have such a permanent outpost?

He wasn't surprised to see a few dead bodies here and there. It was likely they were the result of the rescue mission done by the Huntsmen. There were a number of huts smoldering, as if they'd caught fire days ago when the raid had happened, but generally the majority of the village was still standing. For the most part, it looked as if the residents had just stepped away for a moment.

"Hollywood, you and Fletch start clearing from the far end. Me, Truck, and Coach will slowly work our way toward you from this side. Blade and Beatle, you guys do the same from yours. We'll meet in the middle. If you come across hostiles, make the kill quietly if at all possible. The last thing we want is to announce our presence and have everyone in a five-mile radius on our asses."

Beatle internally nodded. They'd been over the plan more than once, but Ghost repeating it was standard operating procedure.

"And make sure you turn on your cameras," Ghost added.

Scowling, Beatle flipped on the tiny camera located at the base of his throat. They'd been added to their uniforms and SOP after a team of Special Forces soldiers had murdered a group of civilians in the Middle East while on patrol. They'd claimed it was self-defense, but the investigation had been brutal for all involved because it had been impossible to gather evidence from the scene after the fact...and not only because all the witnesses were killed.

The cameras obviously weren't foolproof. If they had the desire, they could go in and destroy the rest of the village, burn all the huts to the ground, kill anyone they came in contact with, *then* start their cameras, claiming they'd come upon the village and found everyone dead and all the structures burning. But no one on the team would even consider doing that. They were honorable men, and even if their actions could be questioned later, they always did everything by the book.

But because of past violations by men who were supposed to be on the side of right and good, Ghost and his teammates each wore a small camera. It worked much like the dash-cams on police cars. They were required to turn them on before any sort of op...just in case. Big Brother was always watching.

Quietly and deadly, Beatle made his way toward the first hut, fully prepared to kill anyone he came across with the sharp six-inch KA-BAR in his hand.

Within minutes, all seven Delta men stood together in the center of the abandoned village.

"Is anyone else's 'what the fuck' meter pegged?" Hollywood asked gruffly.

"Yeah, something's off. Way off," Coach agreed.

"This wasn't a temporary asshole kidnapper's hideout." Ghost said what they were all thinking.

"Nope. By the look of the few dead bodies that are still recognizable, this was a native village," Fletch agreed. "I'm guessing there was some resistance when the Danes entered the village, but it was quickly squelched, either because they grabbed the girls and got out, or because the villagers realized they were out of their depth."

"So where's Casey?" Blade asked, looking frustrated and heartbroken all at the same time.

"According to the Huntsmen, the hut where the girls were being held was over there," Ghost said, pointing at one of the small structures.

The team made their way over and examined it. There were a few marks on the wall to one side, as if the girls had been keeping track of how long they'd been held captive. There was a pair of socks sitting forlornly across the room, as if one of the women had taken them off to dry before the rescue happened and hadn't been able to retrieve them.

A bucket lay on its side nearby, the smell coming from it letting the men know exactly what its purpose had been.

"Spread out," Ghost ordered. "There has to be some clue as to what they did with our target."

"She's not a fucking target," Blade growled. "Her name is Casey."

"Sorry, Blade," Ghost apologized immediately. "I didn't mean anything by it."

Blade took a deep breath, then nodded.

"Keep your eyes peeled," Ghost said. "Anything, no matter how small, could be a clue."

Hollywood, Ghost, Fletch, Coach, and Truck disappeared into the village and jungle surrounding it within seconds.

Beatle stood stock still, his gaze sweeping the area around the hut where the other women had been held.

"What are you seeing?" Blade asked softly.

"I don't know."

Seconds went by, then Blade said, "Talk to me."

"There's a clue here...I can feel it. It's like my subconscious recognized it when I saw it, but I can't put my finger on it."

Beatle closed his eyes for a moment, then opened them again. When he looked around, all he saw was jungle, the huts all around them, a couple smoldering, others perfectly fine, and the ashes of the abandoned fires. What had he seen that had caused this feeling?

He stepped to the side and put his back to the jungle and examined what was left of the village. It looked to have been a fairly large community. There were at least thirty huts, which meant there had been probably around a hundred people living there. Most likely more.

A hundred people living in the middle of the jungle. That meant organization. This wasn't a nomadic village. They were established. Settled. So where did they all go? And why?

Beatle glanced around again, seeing what he hadn't bothered to take note of before—the paths leading off into the jungle at various places.

"Look, Blade." He gestured to one of the paths with his chin.

"What am I looking at?"

"It's a path. Maybe to a water source. Or a bathroom."

"And?"

Beatle turned to look at his friend. "I don't know. But my gut is screaming. Look, the girls said it themselves, they were hanging in there until Casey was taken away. We both know there wasn't any ransom requested, so why did they separate her?"

Blade stood straighter. "Because she was older. More experienced. Their leader."

"Yeah. Take away the leader and the group falls into

chaos. But why would their kidnappers want that? I mean, wouldn't it have been better to have the group calm and cooperative?"

"No clue," Blade said. "Honestly, I don't really care right now. I just want to find my sister. When they took her away from the girls, wouldn't they just stash her in another hut?"

"Maybe the natives were getting restless. Didn't want the *gringas* in their village anymore," Beatle surmised.

Blade looked pensive, but not convinced. "Maybe."

"If they didn't have any other hut to put her in, maybe they improvised."

"Why wouldn't they just kill her?"

Beatle could tell it hurt his friend to ask. This kind of back and forth with the questions was something they did all the time when trying to come up with answers. It was just one technique the team used. "Maybe they did. But then they'd have to put the body somewhere. They couldn't just leave her on the outskirts of the village. It would attract predators. Or maybe there were some people in the village who didn't know about the women being held here, so they had to keep it on the down-low."

"So they needed to stash her someplace."

"Right. But maybe whoever kidnapped them in the first place had a use for her. Didn't want to kill her.

Wanted to separate her from the others for another reason."

"Yeah, all right," Blade said, sounding more optimistic. "So he took her into the jungle, and would *still* need to stash her somewhere."

"Probably using the paths," Beatle agreed.

Blade reached up and pressed the button in his ear. "Beatle and I have a theory." Then he proceeded to tell his teammates what they'd deduced. "Search each and every path leading away from the village. Anything that looks like it could hide a person, check it."

With a renewed sense of purpose, Blade and Beatle each turned their back on the village and took a path leading deeper into the jungle.

The hair on the back of Beatle's neck was standing straight up, but he didn't know if it was because they were close to finding Casey, or if it was because danger was waiting for them in the jungle. He hoped it was the former, but he knew the possibility of the latter was more likely. Pulling his KA-BAR from its sheath, he kept one eye on his surroundings and the other on the jungle floor.

I'm coming for you, Casey. Just hang on.

Chapter Three

CASEY SUCKED THE scant moisture from the underside of her bra desperately. The half swallow of liquid she'd collected since the last time she'd checked her makeshift filter wasn't enough. Wasn't nearly enough.

She was dying. She could live without food for a long time, but not without water. The irony of it was that she stood ankle deep in liquid, but none of it drinkable.

Water had trickled into her prison fairly regularly at first. She'd heard it dripping down the wall. Always coming from the same place. She'd been cautious at first, not sure she should risk drinking the liquid leaking into the hole she was in. But when no one appeared to give her sustenance like they'd been doing when she was in the hut with her students, she'd made the filter with her bra.

It had worked surprisingly well. She managed to wedge it into the side of the hole and catch the water with the cup. She'd then licked the filtered water as it had seeped through the material of the bra. It wasn't exactly clean, but at least she didn't have to lick the mud off the walls.

But recently her water source had dried up. Casey had no concept of time in the darkness of her prison, but assumed it had been several days. Whereas before the water had been a fairly steady stream, now it was barely a trickle.

She'd spoken with her brother once about a time he'd been held hostage in the desert in the Middle East. He hadn't been held long, thank God, but he'd told her about how helpless he'd felt, and how miserable the conditions were, though at no time had he allowed himself to believe he would die there. That had been the key to him overcoming the horrific circumstances, and the torture his captors had put him and his team through. He'd stressed that over and over. That mental toughness was the best thing she could use to help herself.

But Casey wasn't that strong.

She almost thought that torture and rape would've been better than this.

Being buried alive and slowly dying of lack of water.

She could drink the putrid mess at her feet, but it would do her more harm than good, give her diarrhea, thus making her lose more liquid from inside her body, not to mention having to stand in the mess.

She hadn't had to pee in quite a while, which she knew wasn't a good sign. She was getting just enough water through her bra filter to keep her alive, but she'd begun to think she might as well stop trying.

Casey blinked, trying in vain to see any kind of light, without success. Pulling her feet up out of the brackish water at the bottom of the hole, she grabbed hold of them with her arms. Laying her head on her bent knees, she closed her eyes. Maybe she could fall asleep and just not wake up.

She was tired. So tired.

Aspen wasn't coming for her. She had to stop kidding herself. She hadn't heard any kind of noise above her head in what seemed like forever, not since the gunshots. She was in the middle of a jungle in Costa Rica. Buried deep in the ground in a tomb. No one was ever going to find her.

BEATLE TROMPED DOWN another trail that led out of the village into the jungle. He stopped in his tracks, shuddering, when he came upon a huge spider web in his path. There was nothing he liked less than bugs. Growing up poor, he'd always found cockroaches, ants, and insects in his house. He would wake up to them crawling on his face. They freaked him out back then, and they continued to freak him out today.

But he had more on his mind than creepy-crawly bugs at the moment. Using his rifle to break up the web, he strode past it and continued scanning the jungle floor. He was more than aware of every second that passed. He somehow knew, deep in his gut, that time was running out for Casey.

She'd been missing far too long. If she was out here, he needed to find her. Now.

Walking up to another abandoned well, Beatle leaned over. Shining a light downward, he saw water glistening at the bottom of the ten-foot hole. No Casey.

There was a green rubber thing hanging over the edge of the well, one end resting toward the bottom, near the water. At first he thought it was just another vine, but upon closer inspection he realized it was a hose. Beatle followed it with his eyes as it disappeared into the jungle. He reached down and pulled. It gave slightly, but was apparently attached to something on the other end. He dropped it and shook his head. The residents of the village might not have running water in their homes, but they certainly were inventive when it came to collecting water as easily as possible.

Sighing, he turned his back to the water source and trudged toward the village. He had bigger things to worry about than investigating how Costa Rican natives jerry-rigged wells to give them a primitive source of indoor plumbing.

Beatle knew the others hadn't had any luck finding Blade's sister, either. They were each reporting their lack of success through the radio in his ear.

He was halfway back to the village when something made him look to his left. He stopped in his tracks and blinked.

Tilting his head, he tried to tell himself what he was seeing was nothing more than an animal trail…but it wasn't.

Beatle reached out and tugged on the leafy branches blocking the slight path, expecting resistance. There was none.

The branches weren't attached to anything.

His heart rate immediately sped up.

Why would there be branches strategically placed across this path if there wasn't something—or some-one—at the other end that a villager didn't want anyone to find?

Easily removing the other branches in his way, which also weren't attached to anything, Beatle took large strides through the thick underbrush. He came to a halt at what he assumed was the end of the trail.

He stared at the thick wood planks at his feet. There were three boards in a row that seemed to have been recently placed out here in the jungle. There were dark green vines woven together across their surface, and others strewn haphazardly on top, as if to try to make them more unnoticeable to the eye. Or to hide the fact that there might be something underneath the wood.

He knew without a doubt he'd found Casey Shea.

Whether she was alive or dead remained to be seen.

He fell to his knees by the wood and vines and pressed his finger to the comm unit at his ear. "I found her. Southeast of the last hut. Take the path on the left, halfway down there's a barely distinguishable footpath to the right."

Knowing he couldn't wait for his team, Beatle got to work cutting the vines away from the long, heavy wood boards.

"Casey? Are you there? Hang on, sweetheart, I'll have you out of there in a couple minutes."

Beatle had no idea if she could hear him, or if she was even conscious, but the words just fell out of his mouth without thought. The need to hold her and let her know she wasn't alone anymore, urgent inside him.

He brought the palm of his hand down hard on the wooden planks keeping him from her. "Hear me, sweetheart? I'm here, and I'm going to get you out."

CASEY JERKED IN fright as something loud sounded over her head. She tilted her chin up as if she could magically see whatever it was that had made the noise. Of course, she still saw nothing. The darkness complete in her dungeon.

But the darkness suddenly seemed to lighten when she heard the first words, other than her own, since she'd been tossed inside the pit however long ago.

"I'm here, and I'm going to get you out."

A whimper escaped her. Words wouldn't come, her throat hurt too much to attempt it.

As adrenaline surged through her veins, Casey managed to stand on the platform she'd made. Keeping her head tilted up, she turned and faced the dirt wall. Raising her arms, she rested them on the wall above her head, reaching for whoever was above her. At that point, she didn't care if it was her brother or her kidnappers. She wanted out of the pit she was in. She'd do whatever they told her to, as long as they'd let her out.

Another whimper escaped as she waited.

BEATLE HAD FINISHED brushing the vines aside when he heard footsteps approaching quickly behind him. He didn't even turn around. He was too focused on getting to Casey.

Two pairs of hands grabbed the vines he'd just re-moved and pulled them farther out of his way, tossing them off to the side without a second glance. Beatle immediately reached for one of the boards, but it barely budged.

"This fucker is heavy," he said under his breath.

By that time, Beatle realized that all his teammates were there. Working as the team they were, everyone began to hoist together to remove the wood.

They tossed the first board out of the way, revealing a black tarp, with more dark-green vines keeping whatever was under it from sight. The stench of rotting animal began to seep upward, fouling the air around them. No one said a word, but Beatle saw Ghost give Fletch a worried glance, and his head tilted to the right in an unspoken command.

Fletch stood and took hold of Blade's arm. "Give them room to work."

As if in a trance, Blade allowed his friend to force him backwards a step.

Grimly, Beatle continued to the next board. *She's not dead, she's not dead.*

The words repeated over and over in his head.

The team worked together to remove the second board, tossing it next to the discarded vines and first board. Leaving the third wooden plank where it was, Beatle took out his knife and inhaled a deep breath before stretching forward and slowly slicing through the middle of the tarp, from one side to the other.

Once he'd created a large enough hole to see through, he impatiently shoved it out of his way and got down on his belly. He inched toward the gaping hole, part of his lower body resting on the remaining plank. He felt hands clamp onto his calves, holding him steady in case any dirt collapsed under his weight. Balancing himself with both hands on either side of the hole, he looked down.

The stench emanating from the pit was almost unbearable, but he breathed through his mouth, ignoring the smell. Beatle couldn't see more than a few feet down into the hole. It was deeper than he thought it would be. Reaching back, he held out his hand and ordered, "Flashlight."

Within seconds, a slender tubular object was placed in his hand. Without looking, he brought his arm forward, clicked on the button to turn on the light and shone it downward at the same time he asked, "Casey?"

The sight that greeted him about broke his heart.

"Is she there?" Blade asked, his voice breaking.

Without thought, Beatle inched forward, wanting to reach down into the hole and grab hold of the woman who'd somehow managed to impress him without ever meeting him in person. The hands at his calves pressed down harder, holding him tighter, making sure he didn't fall into the hole on top of her.

Ignoring his friend for the moment, Beatle called

out again, "Casey?"

She didn't answer or move.

"My name is Beatle. I'm here to take you home."

CASEY WAITED AS the noises above her head got louder and louder. She could hear voices, but not what they were saying.

But it didn't matter. All that mattered was getting out.

There was rustling over her head and, for the first time since she'd been thrown in the hole, she saw something other than blackness.

It was just a slight lightening of the dark, but even that hurt her eyes.

She was torn between wanting to keep her eyes open and finally see something again, and not hurting herself. Not hurting herself won out. She scrunched her eyes shut, but otherwise didn't move.

There was more rustling above her and the voices grew louder.

If she had any moisture left in her body, Casey knew she'd be crying with relief.

She knew the second the last barrier between her and the rest of the world was removed. She felt the air from her hole rush past her. Her hair rustled with the breeze. She had the thought that even the stagnant, fetid air wanted to escape the tomb it'd been in.

She heard her name being called from above. She'd never heard anything so amazing in all her life. She didn't recognize the voice, but it was deep and soothing. She could tell from just her name that whoever had said it was American, with a slight southern accent. The sound burrowed inside her wounded heart.

Casey knew she'd never forget the feeling of safety, of security, she felt at that moment, just from hearing her name come from the man's lips.

"Is she there?"

It was her brother. God! She knew he would come for her. She *knew* it.

"Casey? My name is Beatle. I'm here to take you home."

She hadn't moved a muscle, afraid she was hallucinating, but at hearing that southern drawl again, she reacted.

She inched one hand away from the wall and clenched it into a fist, then opened it and held it up as far as she could, standing on her tiptoes to try to get closer to the top of the hole. Then, she slowly opened her eyes a fraction of an inch and squinted upward. She couldn't make out anything other than a shadow above her, but the beckoning and welcome sunlight behind the man with the low, gravelly voice was one of the most beautiful things she'd ever seen.

"Help me," she said, not recognizing her own voice. It was barely a whisper, and came out more a croak than actual words.

"I've got you, Case. I'm not leaving without you."

The light hurt her eyes, even though she was squinting, so Casey shut them once more. But she smiled weakly up at the man who'd called himself Beatle. It was appropriate that a man with the name Beatle was rescuing an entomologist.

BEATLE FROZE AT the sight of Casey Shea smiling up at him. She was covered from head to toe with mud and muck. The stench emanating from the hole was making his eyes water, but somehow, after all she'd been through, Casey was smiling. At *him*.

God.

Right then, in the middle of a godforsaken jungle, smack dab in the midst of a rescue op, Beatle fell head over heels in love.

He'd been ready to be impressed by Casey. He already liked her, simply after hearing stories about her from her brother all day. But seeing that smile had sent him over the edge.

He'd do whatever it took to keep Casey safe from

here on out. Whatever made her happy, he'd bend over backwards to give her.

He'd never understood why good soldiers quit the Army. He'd asked a fellow Delta once why he was getting out, and the man had only smiled and told him, "When you meet a woman you love with every cell in your body, you'll know why."

At the time, he'd thought the man was insane for quitting what he'd spent a good chunk of his life training to do. But he finally understood. He'd quit on the spot if it meant making Casey happy.

"Beatle?" It was Blade.

Scooting back so his elbows rested on the remaining plank over the hole, he turned his head to look at Casey's brother. Knowing full well she could hear every word he said, Beatle kept his words upbeat and positive. "She's there, and she's conscious and talking."

"Fuck," Blade swore. He closed his eyes and leaned over, propping himself up with his hands on his knees. "Fuck!"

It was easy to see he was struggling for composure.

Beatle looked at Ghost. "I'm gonna need some rope." He didn't, but he motioned back to the village with his head.

Because they'd been working together so long, Ghost immediately understood his unspoken words. "Coach, can you help Blade go back to the village and see if you can find any rope?"

"Absolutely. Come on, Blade, the sooner we go, the sooner we can get your sister out of here," Coach said without pause. He'd also seen Beatle's nonverbal signal to get Blade away from the area while they pulled Casey out.

Without another word, Blade turned from the group and headed back down the slight path, Coach at his heels.

Beatle had a feeling Blade knew he was being sent on a fool's errand to keep him away from the reality of seeing his sister as she emerged from the hole, but he'd obviously taken Ghost's words to heart about being there when his sister was rescued, and what it might mean for her future recovery.

As soon as the men were out of hearing range, Ghost asked, "What are we dealing with, Beatle?"

"She's about four feet below the top of the hole. I think I can reach her if you guys hold my legs and pull us up once I have her."

"We could fashion a belay rope out of the vines around here," Hollywood said.

Beatle shook his head immediately. "No time. She needs to get out of there." He knew by the desperation in her actions his words were true.

Truck was already at his knees behind Beatle. "Do it. I'll make sure you don't fall in headfirst."

Beatle nodded and turned back to the hole—and froze as some of the dirt under him shifted. He looked at Ghost. "Once I have a hold of her, I'm not letting go. When I say pull, *pull*. Hard."

Ghost nodded. He kneeled down on one side of Beatle, and Hollywood and Fletch got down on the other side. Beatle felt their hands on his back, and he nodded.

He inched forward slowly so the edge of the board was at his waist. He jammed the flashlight under a strap at his shoulder. The light bounced crazily around the interior of the hole, but he didn't need it aimed directly at Casey to be able to see her.

She was still standing exactly as she'd been earlier. Both arms raised, head back…waiting. For him.

"Hey, Case. You ready to get out of there?"

She nodded.

"You heard me tell your brother to go get rope, right?"

Another nod.

"I don't think I need it. But he'll be back. You'll see him soon."

Her eyes opened into slits again. If he didn't already know she was blonde and had green eyes, Beatle wouldn't have been able to tell by looking at her now. The combination of dirt and lack of light prevented both, but the life he saw shining out of her eyes from deep inside her once again made his stomach clench.

"Thank you for sending him away," she croaked.

Beatle leaned down into the putrid-smelling hole and stretched out his arms. He felt hands tighten on his lower body and didn't feel a moment of fear that his friends would drop him. Compared to some of the life-or-death situations they'd faced together, this was child's play.

His fingertips brushed against hers and she startled so badly, she almost fell backwards off the boards stacked up in the bottom of the pit.

"Easy, Case."

She regained her balance and stood on her tiptoes once more. Her fingers grasped Beatle's. Hard. Her intense gaze met his.

If asked, Beatle never would've guessed she had the strength she did, but she grabbed hold of him as if he were her lifeline. Which he supposed he was.

He held her hands in his for a moment, assessing. Her skin was cold, but not frigid. He reached out his index finger and placed it on her wrist, feeling for her pulse. It was a little fast, but beat strongly through her veins.

"Here's what's going to happen. I'll hold on to you and as soon as you're ready, my team is going to pull us both up and out of here. It'll happen fast, and all you have to do is relax. I won't let go and I won't drop you.

Understand?"

She nodded.

"Ready?"

"Yes." It was more a puff of air than actual sound, but Beatle understood.

Turning his head back toward the hole, he said loudly, "Give me a couple more inches."

Immediately, he felt himself lowered closer to Casey.

His hands loosened around hers, but she didn't let go of him.

He stared into her eyes. "Let go, sweetheart."

She shook her head frantically.

Taking a moment, even though Beatle wanted to get both of them up into the fresh air as soon as possible, he said softly, so only she could hear him, "Trust me, Case. I'm not leaving. I'm going to grab hold of you under your arms so it doesn't hurt as much when we're pulled up. I'll do everything in my power to protect you from here on out. I'm going to make whoever did this to you pay." The last bit came out a bit harsher than he'd intended, but Casey didn't flinch away from the anger he knew was coming off him in waves.

"As long as you want me by your side, I'm there, Casey. In this hole. Out there in the jungle. Even back home. Whatever you need, I'll make sure you have it. Understand?"

Her pupils were big in her eyes as they slowly adjusted to the dim light coming from the hole above their heads. She nodded.

"Here's the deal," he said in the same quiet tone. "I admire the fuck out of you. Anyone else would've died in this hole. By all rights, you shouldn't be alive." His eyes flicked to the bra she'd attached to the side of the wall, before meeting hers again. "But not you. You're something special. No pressure, but you should know, I want to be in your life. Any way you'll let me."

She snorted at that. Beatle thought it was supposed to be a laugh, but she didn't have the strength to do it properly. He grinned. "I know, I'm insane. But how about we get out of this fucking hole, get you some water, and you can tell me how crazy I am later. Yeah?"

"Water," she croaked.

"Yeah, sweetheart. Water. Now, let go of my hands and let's get out of here."

"What the fuck are you waiting for?" Ghost called down impatiently.

Beatle couldn't help it. His smile grew. He had nothing to smile about, but hearing Ghost's pissed-off tone and seeing the answering humor in Casey's eyes had him fucking ecstatic. He hadn't lied to her. By all rights, she *should* be dead. But somehow, she'd survived. Held on. For him to find. She had one hell of an inner strength to still be alive.

Her hands loosened around his, and he didn't hesitate. Reaching down, his fingers wrapped around her back while his thumbs rested on the edges of her pectoral muscles. He easily lifted her off her feet.

He felt her hands weakly grip his biceps, but she otherwise hung limply in his hold, trusting him not to drop her and to get her out.

"Now!" he exclaimed loudly.

As soon as the word left his lips, Beatle felt himself moving upward. He held Casey tightly, making sure her body didn't brush against the edges of the hole as they moved.

She wasn't light, but she definitely wasn't heavy, either. In fact, from what he could estimate her height being, she should be much heavier. The urge to feed her, to help her back to a healthy body weight, almost overwhelmed him, but he had to deal with other things first.

As they neared the opening and the light got brighter, her eyes shut once more.

Truck and the others eased him over the edge and Beatle felt the plank of wood scrape against his belly. Before he even had to say anything, Ghost and Fletch were there, helping him take Casey's weight and easing her out of the hole.

Beatle didn't let go of her. He simply rolled with her until he was crouched above her on the ground. His hand moved of its own volition to her hair. He brushed the filthy strands out of her face, leaving his palm on the side of her head.

Her eyes squinted open once more and she gave him a small smile. "Hi," she croaked.

"Hi," he returned, but didn't smile. She was breaking his heart. And for someone whose enemies would've said didn't *have* a heart, that was something.

Beatle didn't look away from her, just as she kept her eyes on him. "Water," he ordered, and held out his free hand.

A canteen was placed in his hand and Beatle held it as someone unscrewed the cap. Once it was open, he took a sip to gauge how full it was so he didn't end up pouring the water all over Casey's face. Moving his hand so it was behind her neck, Beatle lifted her as gently as if she were a newborn babe. "Drink, sweetheart."

One of her hands came up to his holding the canteen, and she gripped his wrist. She didn't try to take the water from him, simply let him assist her.

If he hadn't already been in love with her, her trust would've done it.

She opened her mouth and Beatle placed the edge of the canteen against her dry, cracked lips. "Go easy," he warned. "You don't want to get sick."

She gave him a nod and he tipped the canteen.

The second the water hit her mouth, her eyes closed and she greedily swallowed. Her grip on his wrist tightened, but she didn't otherwise move. Beatle let her have a few sips, then lowered the container. She whimpered in protest, but didn't make any sudden movements to take control of the water.

"Let that settle, sweetheart. Then you can have some more."

"Do you want me to start an IV?" Truck asked quietly from beside them.

Beatle still didn't take his eyes off Casey's face. Her own had squinted open once more at the question. But again, she didn't answer, giving him the power to do what he thought was right.

After thinking about it for a moment, Beatle shook his head. "Not yet. She needs to get cleaned up first and we need to get out of here. Later, before we go to sleep, we'll do it. It can help hydrate her overnight."

Beatle would've loved nothing more than to do whatever it took to make the woman under him feel better, but his gut was screaming at him to get her away from this village. He didn't know why, as it seemed to be deserted, but he always trusted his instincts.

"More?" he asked.

Casey nodded eagerly, and he brought the container back up to her mouth. He let her have a few more sips before stopping her.

"Want to try sitting up?" Beatle asked softly.

Casey nodded once more, and Beatle put the canteen down next to them as he moved to her side. His knees touching her thigh, he slid one hand under her back and the other he placed at her hip. "Ready?"

"Yeah," she whispered.

Beatle slowly brought her to a sitting position and held his breath.

She once again gripped his arms and let him take her weight. The little color she had in her cheeks faded away and she weaved in his hold. But damn if she didn't take a deep breath and steady herself. After several moments, her fingers relaxed.

Before she could say anything, Beatle reached into one of the pockets on his vest and took out a pair of sunglasses. He slid them onto her face. "Better?"

"God, yes," she breathed.

He reached down and picked up the canteen and placed it in one of her hands. "Easy now. Small sips. Okay?"

"Okay."

Beatle sat back, keeping one hand at the small of Casey's back as she sipped from the canteen. They heard footsteps running back down the path and, even as Casey tensed against him, Beatle murmured, "It's okay. It's your brother and my teammate, Coach."

It was hard for Beatle to back away from Casey when Blade entered the small clearing, but he did. The other man immediately fell to his knees next to his sister and took her into his arms.

Brother and sister held on to one another almost desperately. Blade finally pulled back, cleared his throat twice as if trying to gather his composure, then said, "You smell like shit, sis."

She swallowed hard, obviously trying to gain control over her own emotions, and retorted, "Now you do too, asshole." She wiped the back of her hand down the vest he was wearing, smearing more mud on him.

"Fuck," Blade said softly, then took his sister into his arms again.

The rest of the team didn't move, simply stood there, giving the siblings their moment. After a couple minutes, Ghost cleared his throat and said, "We should get moving."

Blade pulled away from his sister and stood abruptly. "I'm gonna go recon the village one last time."

No one questioned the move, as they'd all seen the tears in Blade's eyes. Hollywood immediately volunteered to go with him.

Beatle scooted closer to the woman still sitting on the ground. "What do you think? Want to get out of here?"

She nodded vigorously and gently pushed the sunglasses, which had slipped, back up her nose.

Beatle held out his hand, palm up. "Come on, Casey Shea. Let's go home."

He couldn't deny the feeling of rightness when she placed her smaller palm against his own.

Chapter Four

CASEY WANTED NOTHING more than to sink to her knees, then fall face down in the middle of the jungle. But instead, she clenched her teeth and stared at the ground as she put one foot in front of the other.

She was miserable. Every muscle in her body hurt. She was dizzy and felt like she was going to keel over any second, but her desire to get as far away from her own version of hell was stronger than her desire to stop moving.

The thought of guzzling an entire canteen full of water was always at the forefront of her mind, but she knew the man who hadn't left her side for one second, Beatle, wouldn't allow that. He was right, she'd probably puke it all up, but fuck did she want to.

She hadn't ever seen anything as welcoming in her life as his face when he'd leaned into the hellhole where she'd been prisoner. His hair was shorn close to his head, but she could still see its auburn hue. His light brown eyes had felt like they'd pierced her soul when he'd looked at her and told her he was going to protect her and get her home.

He'd lifted her as if she weighed no more than a small child, when she knew that wasn't the case. Oh, she was well aware that she'd lost weight over the last couple of weeks, but she still wasn't a lightweight.

He'd treated her at turns like a long-lost friend, happy to see her again; a bodyguard who wanted to wrap her in cotton wool and not let anyone even look at her; and a disinterested bystander. That last one he wasn't pulling off as well, however. Whenever she got more than a couple steps away from him, he was there, holding her hand, wrapping her fingers around the belt at his back, or simply slowing his steps so he could reach out and grab her if she fell.

And she *had* fallen. Several times. Her feet didn't want to work right. She didn't want to even look at what shape they were in. They'd been waterlogged for so long, Casey knew they were bad. She'd read about trench foot, and had even warned her students before they'd been kidnapped about the importance of taking care of their feet and keeping them dry. She'd tripped so often because she couldn't really even *feel* her feet. They were numb. They felt swollen in her boots, but she hadn't risked taking them off for fear she wouldn't be able to get them on again.

Her legs weren't cooperating either. She'd tried to keep her muscles active, but there simply hadn't been room in the hole to move more than a couple steps at a time. She didn't want to slow the group down, but knew she was anyway.

Beatle had offered to carry her, more than once, but so far she'd refused. The last thing she wanted was to look weak in front of her brother and his friends. No, when they stopped, she'd collapse then. She wanted to get as far away from the village as possible.

"We need to split up," Truck said when they'd stopped for a break.

Casey knew they were only stopping on her behalf. These guys could go for days without needing a breather.

"I'm not sure—" Blade started, but was interrupted by Ghost.

"That's a good idea. We need to get to San José and arrange transport back to the States."

"What happened to the chopper that was supposed to pick us up?" Hollywood asked in a pissed-off tone.

"It's a no-go," Ghost bit out. "It was arranged, but something happened. I don't even know what, exactly. All I was told was that there were 'complications' and it would be delayed. I'm not sitting around with my thumb up my ass waiting for them to get their shit together."

"Fuck," Coach swore. "What about the Danes? Wouldn't they pick us up?"

"Yeah," Ghost answered. "If they hadn't already left the country."

"Dammit!" It was Blade who swore that time. "What the fuck? Seriously? This is bullshit!"

Ghost held up his hand to forestall any other complaints. He sent an apologetic look at Casey before continuing. "You all know as well as I do that no one thought we'd be successful. We were only allowed access to the jungle because the Costa Rican government didn't want any negative publicity. They rely on tourist dollars, and an American woman kidnapped and killed in their jungles wouldn't be good for them at all. They're keeping everything on the down-low."

"That doesn't make sense," Fletch grumbled. "The kidnapping wasn't a secret, the Danish ambassador made sure of that. Everyone already knows what happened down here."

"But not that anyone was killed," Ghost argued. "All they know is that a group of women, mostly American, were taken hostage and subsequently rescued. Look, we're all aware that the government doesn't want us tromping around out here any longer than we have to. I don't know what the holdup is, but I'm going to stay in communication with them and get us out of here as soon as possible. If we manage to hoof it to Guacalito before they get their shit together, fine, they can pick us up there."

No one said anything, and the silence lay thick in the air between the team members as they all digested Ghost's words.

Casey looked from one man to the next. All seven were big, buff, killing machines. She always knew what her brother was, he hadn't ever lied to her about what he did for a living. She knew he was a member of a Delta Force team, had even heard him talking about his teammates here and there. But she'd never met them in person.

But here in the middle of the jungle in Central America, she memorized each and every one of their faces. They'd come for her. From what it sounded like, the local government wasn't happy they were here, but they'd done it anyway. She had no idea if the Army knew about or sanctioned their rescue attempt, but it didn't matter.

Ghost, the leader, wasn't any taller or shorter than the others, but he exuded power. Every time he spoke, Casey wanted to immediately do whatever it was he'd ordered...and she wasn't even in the Army.

Fletch was a bit taller than Ghost, and more muscular. He'd rolled his sleeves up his arms as they'd walked and she could see colorful tattoos covering his wrists and forearms. If he hadn't been with the group when she'd been rescued, she might've been scared of him, but the friendly look in his eyes put her at ease. She'd learned through the men's talk as they'd walked that he had a young daughter named Annie.

Coach was tall and dark. His hair was cut close to his head, like that of the others, but his square jaw and crooked nose made him look more like a thug. But he'd quickly earned her respect when he'd done a damn good job of entertaining her by reciting logic puzzles. When she'd asked how in the world he remembered the long riddles, he'd simply shrugged and told her he had an eidetic memory.

Hollywood was beautiful. Almost too good looking to be a part of the team. Casey would've thought he was an actor playing a part if it wasn't for the way he was constantly on alert, watching for anything that might be a threat to the group.

Truck had worried her at first. He was huge, easily the tallest of the team, and his arms were about as wide as her waist. The scar on his face pulled his mouth down into a permanent frown, but once she got to know him a little better she realized that he clearly had a soft side. Besides Beatle, he was the one who was constantly asking if she was all right and making sure she was comfortable as they hiked through the jungle. She knew without a doubt if he realized how *not* all right she was, he'd be the first to halt their retreat for the night and insert the IV he'd wanted to put in when she'd first been removed from the hole.

And then there was Beatle. His name made her smile. She had no idea why his nickname was what it was, but a part of her wanted to believe it was fate. She studied bugs, and he was named after one.

She'd immediately felt comfortable and safe with him. She supposed she should be clinging to her brother, but for some reason, she was uneasy being around him out here. He was just Aspen to her, not a super soldier. She wanted, needed, to keep the big brother she teased and laughed with separate from her ordeal.

It also made no sense to her at the moment, but she couldn't deny her attraction to Beatle.

And it wasn't a physical attraction, at least not at the moment. Casey was perfectly aware of how awful she looked. She smelled, was covered in dirt and who knew what else, her hair was in knots on her head, and she had so much grime under her nails, she wasn't sure she'd ever be able to remove it all. She wasn't thinking about sex in the least. But somehow, Beatle had looked beyond all the dirt and grime and seen *her*.

The second she'd looked into his eyes, Casey had known everything was going to be all right. She figured it was because he'd been the one to rescue her. The first person she'd seen after being trapped deep in the ground. A psychologist somewhere would probably tell her it was a result of her captivity and being rescued, but Casey wasn't sure about that.

They had an emotional connection. She trusted him, and not just because he was on her brother's team. He'd been gentle with her, but she wasn't an idiot. She'd seen the anger simmering in his eyes when he'd talked about making someone pay for kidnapping her. She knew he'd probably killed before, and would again. But instead of that making her wary, it drew her closer to him. Like a moth to a flame. She almost needed that banked fury as much as she needed his gentleness. Needed to know if push came to shove, if her kidnappers popped up in the middle of the jungle to take her again, he'd be able to protect her as he claimed he would.

While she'd been thinking about the men around her, they'd obviously been planning their next steps. She'd missed most of the conversation, but blinked when she heard her brother say her name.

"Casey?"

She raised her eyebrows at him in question. Her voice was slowly returning now that she'd had water, but she wasn't willing to push it.

"Are you okay with all this?"

Embarrassed to admit she'd been daydreaming, she instinctively looked for Beatle.

He was standing a couple feet away, but as if he felt her gaze on him, he turned toward her. He immediately put his hand on the small of her back and asked,

"What's up?"

"I was just asking Casey if she was okay with every-thing."

Since she had no idea what was going on, she looked up at Beatle and willed him to understand what she was asking without words.

As if he really could read her mind, he summed up what she'd missed. "Your brother and Ghost are going to San José. They'll meet with the authorities and get clearance for all of us to leave the country. Blade has a copy of your birth certificate and—"

"You do?" Casey asked incredulously, turning to her brother.

"Yeah, sis. I wasn't sure what was going on down here, but assumed your passport and other identification would be gone. So I figured it would help speed up the process of getting the fuck out of Costa Rica if I brought a copy of your birth certificate with me."

"You didn't know if you'd find me though," she protested.

Casey felt Beatle take a step back as her brother moved into her space. "The fuck I didn't. I wasn't leaving this country without you."

Tears she hadn't been able to shed welled up in her eyes. She hadn't hydrated enough for them to actually fall, but they were there.

Blade took her in his arms once more. She wrapped

her own around his waist and gave him her weight. She was tired, so tired.

Once again, she felt a hand at her back, and knew it was Beatle. He continued the explanation. "Blade and Ghost will arrange things so there's a doctor waiting for us at the capital city. Hollywood, Fletch, and Coach are going to stay a couple miles ahead of us as we make our way to Guacalito, before we all go to San José. We'll stay in contact via radio. They'll make sure our route is clear."

Casey understood what Beatle was saying. In case any of the kidnappers were lying in wait, the other Deltas would take care of them. And if necessary, tell Beatle what spots to avoid.

"Me and Truck will stay with you," Beatle finished.

Casey let out the breath she'd been holding. She hadn't realized how important it was to be able to stay with Beatle. She let go of her brother and turned to face him. "How long?"

"How long will it take for us to get to Guacalito?" Beatle clarified.

Casey nodded.

"I don't know. It depends on you. If it was just us, even without the chopper, and if we were pushing it, we could probably make it by morning."

Casey's eyes got big and Beatle grinned. "Yeah, but now that you're safe, we don't have to go that fast."

"I want out of here."

"I know you do, Case, but you're also not at your best. I'm not going to make you sicker by pushing it. I could carry you, but we all agreed that it'd be better if you walked on your own two feet."

Casey's brows came down in question. It wasn't that she wanted to be carried for however many miles it was to Guacalito, but she wasn't sure what Beatle was saying.

One of his hands came up and his warm palm slid under her gnarly hair and cupped the back of her neck. She was sweaty, and couldn't believe he'd willingly, without any kind of sign he found her repulsive, put his hands on her like he was. "We figured you'd feel less like a victim if you found the strength to leave on your own. You didn't have a choice about being brought here, but you've got a choice about how you leave."

Casey thought about that for a second and realized Beatle was right. Suddenly she wanted to show her kidnappers that they hadn't broken her. She didn't need to be carried anywhere by anyone. Fuck them. She'd walk out of the jungle with her head held high.

"I'm walking," she informed Beatle.

A look of satisfaction—and pride?—moved across his features before he nodded. "Right. So, me and Truck will stay with you. And the others will do their thing. The second we get to Guacalito, we'll head to San José, and then home to the States."

Suddenly realizing she hadn't even thought about her students, Casey asked, "Astrid, Jaylyn, and Kristina are safe?"

"Yes. They're on their way back to Florida as we speak."

Sagging in relief, Casey nodded.

"So you're okay with all this?" Blade asked from her right.

Casey turned her head, aware of the slide of Beatle's fingers as they left her nape. She shivered in reaction, but did her best to hide it. "Yeah."

"You're okay with me not being with you?"

"You're always with me," she told her brother with conviction. "Every second those assholes had me, you were with me. So yeah, I'm okay with you going ahead and arranging things so I can get the fuck out of here. I have a feeling you'd get annoyed with my slow pace anyway. You're always bugging me to hurry up."

It was the most she'd said since being pulled out of the ground, and by the end of her little speech, her voice had turned raspy again, but she wanted to reassure her brother that she didn't mind if he wasn't by her side. She'd never tell him she didn't want him there, but it was true. Casey knew she'd only held up as well as she had so far because of adrenaline and a deep desire to get away from where she'd been held. She didn't want her strong, larger-than-life brother to see her weak.

As if he could read her mind, Blade merely nodded and tugged her into his arms for one last hug. "Stay strong, sis," he said softly. "I didn't come all the way down here for you to keel over now."

She smiled up at him, as she knew he wanted her to, and slugged him lightly on the arm. "Shut up," she complained. "You aren't getting rid of me that easily."

Blade took a deep breath and nodded at Beatle behind him. Casey felt the other man's hands grip both her biceps but didn't turn around to look at him. She felt the warmth from his body against her back as she watched the other five men get ready to hike out ahead of them.

"We'll check in every hour," Hollywood told Beatle and Truck.

"One click for all-clear and two for danger," Coach added. "If there's trouble, we'll switch to the emergency channel for details."

"Stay safe, guys," Truck said.

And just like that, Casey was alone in the jungle with Truck and Beatle.

She supposed she should've been nervous, but all she felt was relief. She sagged in Beatle's arms.

"Do you think you can continue on for a bit more?" Beatle asked from behind her.

Casey looked up and saw Truck standing in front of her. She should've felt smothered, with all the muscles and testosterone surrounding her, but instead it bolstered her flagging energy.

"Yeah."

Truck eyed her critically, then looked over her head at his teammate. "An hour, max," he said firmly.

Casey opened her mouth to protest, but closed it just as fast. An hour seemed like an eternity, the way she was feeling, but she could do it. Hell, she'd just survived essentially being buried alive. An hour-long stroll in the jungle was child's play.

The canteen she'd been drinking out of appeared in front of her. Without thought, Casey grabbed it and immediately brought it up to her mouth. She'd never turn down water again. Never.

Too soon, Beatle gently took it away from her and Casey resisted pouting like a six-year-old. She needed the water, yes, but Beatle was being smart, making sure she didn't get too much at a time.

She'd munched on a couple of granola bars earlier, and Beatle handed her another.

"You've done well in keeping food and water down, so we'll try one more. Your body is going to require lots of small meals rather than a few large ones for a while. One hour, Case. Then we'll stop for the night. I'll make you some dinner, see if I can't find someplace for you to clean up, and Truck'll get you settled with an IV. You'll feel like a new woman in the morning. Swear."

"A shower?" Casey asked, looking up at Beatle with big eyes behind the sunglasses she still wore.

Beatle chuckled, and for the first time since she'd met him, Casey could hear true humor in the sound. "You are such a girl," he teased. "I'm not sure about an actual shower, but hopefully we can find some water to clean up with, because sweetheart, you stink."

A bark of laughter escaped her mouth before she could call it back. It wasn't like he was saying anything that wasn't true. She *did* stink, but she teased right back, "You're not much of a gentleman for saying it out loud."

A finger came out and put pressure on her chin, lifting her face up to his. "I told you before that I wasn't leaving your side, Casey. And in case you didn't realize it, I stink too. Whatever funk was in that hole is all over me now, because of the way I've held you in my arms. So I'll be finding us both a place to get clean."

Casey blinked. Was he coming on to her? It was hard to tell. His face held no humor but she also didn't see any lust behind his eyes. It relieved her. If he was thinking sexual thoughts in this kind of situation, she didn't know that she wanted anything to do with him.

Again, proving he could read her easily, he dropped his finger and took a step away. "I might not leave your side, but I *am* a gentleman. I'd never do anything to make you uncomfortable. Besides, this fucking jungle is the last place I'd try to seduce you."

"But you *are* going to try to seduce me?" The question came out without thought. Her eyes swung to where Truck had been standing, only to see he'd moved away and was messing with one of the packs each of the Deltas had been wearing.

She felt Beatle's breath on her ear when he leaned into her and, without touching her, he said, "Oh yeah, sweetheart. There will be seduction in our future. When you're ready for me, I'll be there."

"I'm scared I might never be ready," she admitted softly.

"Did they touch you?" Beatle asked in a harsh tone. "Were you raped?"

Casey appreciated how he came right out and asked. He didn't beat around the bush nor look at her with pity. It made it easier to talk about what had happened.

"No. They pretty much left us alone. I thought for sure that would be the first thing that would happen, but the only interaction we had with anyone was when they brought food and water into the hut. When they took me away from the others after telling them my ransom had been paid, they immediately dumped me in that hole. No one said anything about what was going on, and no one touched me."

"Thank fuck," Beatle breathed. Then his intense gaze met hers once more. He reached out and slipped the sunglasses down her nose so he could see her eyes. "You're going to be fine, sweetheart. I won't lie though, the next few weeks are probably going to suck. Nightmares, flashbacks, feeling as if you're being watched…but you'll get through it. Wanna know how I know?"

"How?" she whispered, not able to look away from him. It was if he were a magnet and she a piece of steel.

"Because you're related to Blade. And he's the strongest son of a bitch I've ever met."

Casey's lips twitched. "Okay."

"Okay," he agreed. "So after you've visited with a counselor and worked through this shit in your head, I'll be there. Hell, I'll be there *while* you're doing that, but when you're ready—*really* ready—all you have to do is crook your finger and you'll have me at your mercy."

Casey smiled. The man in front of her would never be at *anyone's* mercy, but it was a nice thought.

"Yeah, sweetheart, you don't realize it yet, but you will. All you have to do is ask, and I'd move heaven and earth to do whatever it is you want and need."

Blinking in surprise—she'd never get used to the way he could seem to read her mind—Casey merely shook her head.

"So…ready to go find that shower or bath I promised?"

Casey nodded.

He pushed the sunglasses back up her nose and bent to grab his own pack. He shrugged it on, not taking his eyes from her. When he was ready, he reached for her hand and nodded at his friend. "Lead the way, Truck."

With a knowing smile, the larger man simply turned his back on them and they were off.

Casey felt like shit and wasn't sure she could make it to wherever Truck was leading them, but when Beatle squeezed her hand, she took a deep breath and shored up her flagging inner strength. She wasn't being held against her will. She wasn't buried in a hole. She was free and on her way home. She could do this.

"Strong as fucking steel," Beatle murmured from beside her.

As if his praise and pride were shots of adrenaline, Casey immediately felt better. Stronger. She could totally do an hour. Maybe two.

Chapter Five

THIRTY MINUTES LATER, Beatle knew Casey wasn't going to make it another minute. It really was amazing she'd managed to go as far as she had since leaving the village. They'd been taking it very slowly, in deference to her, but she needed to stop. She needed tending. She was limping badly and her movements were sluggish. He mentally cursed the Costa Rican government for denying them a helicopter. Truth of the matter was, Casey needed a hospital. Yes, she was strong, but no one could go through what she had and not need to see a doctor.

With merely a chin lift to his teammate, which Truck immediately understood, both men began to look for a place to camp for the night. It was early afternoon, but Casey's health was more important than going farther at the moment.

He turned Casey into him and, without protest, she gave him her body weight. They were chest to chest and she was panting as if they'd just run a marathon. Beatle wrapped his arms around her waist as she limply leaned against him. "Truck is going to find us a place to camp."

She nodded against his chest.

He grit his teeth together when she didn't resist. He instinctively knew that wasn't like her. That at full strength, Casey would insist she could keep going another ten miles. And that she probably *could*. But she was done.

He was impressed she'd made it *this* far. No way she should've been able to. Not after all she'd been through. As he stood in the middle of the jungle and waited for Truck to return after reconnoitering the area, he thought about her ordeal.

Something was off about it all. Nothing had happened the way they'd expected. After listening to the short interview with the other women, and hearing the bits and pieces of what Casey had said, this kidnapping was unlike any they'd ever been involved in before.

There were no ransom demands.

The ambassador only raised the alarm when he hadn't heard from his daughter. She'd been calling home every night, but when two days passed without a word, he knew something was wrong. If he hadn't acted immediately, it would've been a hell of a lot longer before anyone realized the women were missing.

The women weren't raped.

Beatle was relieved about that, but again, it wasn't normal. Rape was a common torture technique and tended to make women captives very compliant.

The established village they were found in.

Most experienced kidnappers either stayed on the move or had a heavily fortified compound they brought their victims to. Not a native village in the middle of the jungle.

The more Beatle thought about it, the more uneasy he got. They didn't even have any idea who'd kidnapped the students and Casey. The only thing the government had said was that they'd gotten an anonymous tip from someone in Guacalito about where they were being held. Nothing made sense.

Something niggled at the back of his mind, but before he could focus, Truck returned.

"There's a good spot about a hundred yards east of here."

"Water source?" Beatle asked softly. He wasn't positive, but he thought Casey had somehow managed to fall asleep standing up.

"Not much. There's a small stream. Looks like it probably feeds into one of the larger rivers in the area. It's not wide or deep enough for any kind of full-out bath, but we can use it for washing and refilling our water supply."

Nodding, Beatle leaned over and put an arm under Casey's knees. He lifted her into his arms without much effort. The thought that he wanted to put some meat on her bones flitted through his head once more.

"What?" Casey asked groggily, waking as she wrapped her arms around Beatle's neck.

"Shhhh. Truck found a good place to bunk down for the night. We'll be there in a jiffy."

"Ants," Casey murmured.

"What was that?" Beatle asked, leaning into her. Truck held branches away from him so they wouldn't smack into Casey as they walked.

"Make sure there isn't a bullet ant mound nearby," she told him.

"I don't particularly like any kind of bug," Beatle told her. "But why specifically should we be concerned about this bullet ant and where is it found?"

"The bullet ant has a sting that people say is as painful as being shot. Thus the name," Casey informed them. "The worker ants kinda resemble wasps. They like to build their colony at the base of a tree so the workers can forage for food in the leaves in the canopy."

"We've been bit by fire ants back in Texas, is it like that?" Truck asked.

Casey shook her head. "No. Worse. You did hear me say the pain is like being shot, right?"

Truck chuckled. "Yeah, sorry."

"I can tell you don't believe me, but I'm not lying," Casey insisted, sounding more awake.

"Oh, I believe you," Truck said quickly.

"Some people have described the pain from a bite as waves of burning, throbbing, all-consuming pain that can continue for up to twenty-four hours. I don't know about you, but I'm definitely not all that fired up about experiencing that. I think being kidnapped and buried alive is enough for one trip for me."

Beatle tightened his grip on the woman in his arms. He was thrilled her voice sounded better and she was talking more, but he didn't like hearing her talk about her ordeal so flippantly. But he kept his mouth shut. It was good she was joking about her experience. He and his teammates did that all the time in order to better deal with their emotions after a tough mission.

"I'll make sure we don't use trees to anchor the hammocks if there's an ant nest under it," Truck reassured her.

"Hammocks?" Casey asked, turning to look up at Beatle for an answer to her question.

"We aren't about to sleep on the ground, sweetheart," Beatle said.

"Smart man," she quipped. "Do you know how many species of ants and spiders there are in Costa Rica?"

"No, and I don't want to," he said quickly when she opened her mouth to respond.

She smiled up at him. Then the grin faded and she asked, "What about me?"

"What *about* you?" Beatle retorted.

"Where will I sleep?"

He didn't answer her for a long moment, confused about what she was asking. Then finally said, "In a hammock."

"Then what about you? Where will you sleep?"

"In a hammock," he repeated patiently, still confused.

Casey looked over at Truck, then up at Beatle again. "You brought one for me?"

Understanding dawned. "Yeah, Case. We always carry extras. We definitely have extra supplies since we were on a rescue mission."

"Oh."

"Yeah, oh. But make no mistake…if I did only have one, it'd be yours." Not giving her time to respond, Beatle stopped. "We're here. Do you think you can stand on your own for a bit while we get things set up?"

"I can help," she said.

"That's not what I asked," Beatle told her patiently.

Casey took a deep breath and let it out slowly. "Yeah, I can stand."

She didn't sound so sure. Beatle leaned over and gently placed her feet on the ground, then kept his hands on her hips, supporting her as she took her own weight.

He didn't miss the grimace on her face and knew he

needed to do something about her feet. He hadn't missed the fact that they were wet, and probably had been for a while.

"Thoughts on this spot?" he asked her, trying to take her mind off the pain of her body.

She looked around. They were in a small clearing surrounded by trees. There weren't any mounds to be seen and nothing that screamed, "Watch out! Scary bugs live here," but Casey was the expert.

She finally nodded. "Yeah, this looks good. Can't say there won't be any mammals wandering through, but that's not my area of expertise."

Beatle backed up slowly toward one of the trees on the outside of the area. "Yeah, there are a few trees close together we can use for the hammocks."

"Good."

He smiled. He heard the disappointment in her tone, but knew she wouldn't ask. He leaned close and whispered in her ear, "There isn't a lake or river nearby, but Truck assured me there *is* running water. A small stream just beyond the trees over there." He gestured to them with his chin. "I'll help you get clean later."

Casey tilted her head up. "Thanks."

He wanted to kiss her. Badly. But held back. He told her the jungle wasn't the place for seduction and that hadn't changed, but his feelings about her were. He could admire a woman's beauty from afar and not feel the urge to do anything about it, but give him a gutsy, strong-as-hell woman, even when out of her element, and he was a goner. "You don't have to thank me for providing you with your basic needs. Food. Water. Shelter. Safety. Or a place to wash up. It's my pleasure to provide them for you."

She raised an eyebrow. "That's awfully…philosophical of you."

He chuckled. "Yup. Now…think you can stand here for five minutes while I help Truck? And be honest."

Her mouth had opened to reply, but at the last part, she closed it again. Finally, she said, "I think so." She looked down at the ground. "I'm not standing over an ant mound, so even if I can't, I'll be okay hanging out here on the ground waiting for you."

"I'll be fast, sweetheart. I know you're hurting, tired, hungry, and thirsty. I'm going to take care of all those things for you. Five minutes. Yeah?"

He ignored the tears that welled in her eyes and waited for her acquiescence.

"Okay, Beatle. You go do your thing. I'll be right here."

Knowing if he took her in his arms again, he wouldn't let go, Beatle settled for running his hand over her head in a barely there caress and nodded.

Then he turned and headed for Truck. The sooner they got camp set up, the sooner he could get Casey settled, an IV hooked up, and take care of her feet.

CASEY SWAYED, BUT refused to sit. Five minutes. That's all she had to do. Hell, she'd walked for hours earlier. She could stand, no problem.

But it *was* a problem. Even though she couldn't feel her feet, she *could* feel her legs. And they hurt. Hell, everything hurt. But it was more than that. She was weak. The adrenaline of her rescue had long since worn off and the lack of food and water had caught up to her.

The granola bars she'd eaten earlier, along with the constant intake of water, had gone a long way toward making her feel not on the verge of death. But the week and a half she'd spent underground without real sleep, along with all the worry and stress she'd experienced, had caught up to her.

Just when she thought she was going to fall on her face, Beatle was there.

"Fuck, you're amazing," he said, then swung her up into his arms once more.

Casey regretted saying earlier that she wanted to walk out of the jungle. Suddenly she wanted nothing more than to have Beatle carry her out, just like this. But no, that wasn't fair to him, and she didn't want to be the weak damsel in distress. She'd stayed alive when she knew others would've died, so she could walk her own damn self out of the jungle.

But…Beatle's arms around her felt so good. Safe.

He leaned over and gently eased her onto a hammock. But it wasn't a flimsy piece of rope that closed around her and sagged when she was placed on it. This was a rope hammock, yes, but it was braced on either end by several sticks he'd obviously pilfered from the jungle floor, making it more of a flat bed.

"The wood makes it more stable," Beatle told her as she looked at the hammock with wide eyes. "I'll take them out when we go to bed, and get out the mosquito netting, but for now, it's better if you're not rolled up like a burrito in the ropes."

Casey chuckled at the imagery his words evoked.

He'd placed her so she was lying widthwise rather than lengthwise, with her hips on one side of the hammock and her head at the other.

She slowly relaxed back onto the ropes and groaned in appreciation. She took the sunglasses he'd given her off her face and carefully handed them back to him. After he tucked them away, she said, "You have no idea how good this feels. I haven't laid down, flat like this, since they threw me in that hole."

Beatle scowled, but didn't respond. Merely sat on a small folding stool—what else did they carry in those packs of theirs?—and went to work on her shoelaces. He propped her foot on his thigh and bent over her boot, concentrating solely on the laces in front of him. It took him a while to get the knots out of the first one.

"Why don't you just cut it off?" Casey asked.

"Because I don't have any extra laces in my pack. I've got some paracord, but it's easier to use these if at all possible."

He hadn't looked up while he'd explained, just kept his head down and concentrated on what he was doing. Within a couple minutes, he'd coaxed the waterlogged shoelace to cooperate and had loosened the boot enough to ease it off.

Casey sighed in relief as the pressure on her foot eased, but within seconds, grimaced at the pain of it instantly swelling.

Beatle reached for the top of her wool sock and looked up. "Ready?"

She shook her head but said, "Yeah."

He smiled at her.

"If you pass out from the smell of my stinky feet, don't blame me," Casey tried to tease.

"You haven't smelled mine after trekking through a desert in Iran for four days," he quipped.

"You mean Iraq, right?" Casey asked, propping herself up on shaking arms. She wanted to see the damage she'd done to her feet firsthand. "Iran isn't exactly welcoming to Americans."

Beatle merely looked at her with his eyebrows raised.

"Yeah, sorry. Iran. Right. Super-secret soldiers. Slipping into off-limit countries and doing your thing. Check."

He gave her a small twitch of his lips, then concentrated on her foot again. He eased both the sock and liner off at the same time.

Casey gasped at the first sight of her foot and tears immediately sprang to her eyes. Not because of the pain, she really couldn't feel much, but because of how horrible it looked.

There were a couple of blisters and open sores. She knew that was bad. Fungal infection had probably already started to set in. She knew she could lose her feet if they weren't dealt with. Immediately.

"It doesn't look that bad," Truck stated in a neutral tone from above her.

Casey hadn't heard him approach, and she stared at him in disbelief. "Are you high?"

"Not that I know of," was his comeback. "Seriously. Yeah, you've got a bit of cyanosis from poor circulation and they're a little stinky, but I think that blister is more from walking so long today in wet socks than anything else. And I'll treat that tropical ulcer with a nice cocktail included in your IV in a bit."

Casey shook her head. "You're insane." But she couldn't deny his words made her feel better.

Beatle had already started working on untying the second boot and had that one off, along with her other sock, before too long.

Staring down at her poor abused feet, Casey asked, "Am I going to lose them?"

Without missing a beat, Truck said, "Do you often lose your feet like you do your keys?"

Casey huffed out a chuckle. "That's not what I meant."

"He knows what you meant," Beatle said softly, picking up her right foot to get a look at the sole. "They aren't gangrenous yet, so there's no need for amputation. I'm not a doctor, but I agree with Truck. We'll treat them tonight, and I guarantee you'll feel a hundred percent better tomorrow. I wish you would've said something though. It looks like me and Truck will be carrying you out of the jungle after all."

"No!" Casey protested immediately. "I can walk. Please, I *need* to walk."

"She's as stubborn as Blade," Truck observed.

"I kept them dry for as long as I could," Casey told the men. "The Gore-Tex did pretty well at first, but they weren't meant to withstand being submerged day and night. The boards in the hole weren't long enough for me to lay down, and I'd fall asleep with them propped up out of the water, but when my legs relaxed they always fell back in."

Beatle put her foot back down on his thigh and ran the palms of his hands up and down her calves. He'd pushed up her pants, and the feel of his calloused hands on her sensitive skin made goosebumps break out on her arms.

"You did good, Case. Really fucking good. Now lie back and relax. You're done walking for at least the next twelve hours. We'll get dinner ready and Truck will prepare that IV. Tomorrow will be a completely different experience for you...you'll actually have to stop to pee if I read that three-bag-IV look in Truck's eyes correctly."

Casey glanced up at the big man. He did have an assessing look on his face. "Three bags?" she asked.

"Maybe four," Truck responded before turning away and stomping over to his pack.

She looked back down at Beatle. "Guess that bath is out, huh?"

The man at her feet shrugged. "A full-body one, yeah. Although I wouldn't have recommended you stripping all the way down anyway. Not here in the jungle so close to that village. But I've got something in mind I think you'll like."

"What?"

He grinned up at her, and Casey's eyes widened at the look of playfulness in his eyes. "You're just going to have to wait. But trust me, you're gonna like it."

"Beatle…you can't tease me like that!"

"Why not?" He'd stopped smiling, and the question came out as serious as she'd ever seen him.

"Because. I…"

She wasn't sure what she was going to say, but it was going to be something along the lines of how he didn't know her that well. Or that they'd just met, or something equally ridiculous, but she stopped herself from saying the words out loud. Not because those things weren't true, but because she didn't give a flying fuck about them. She liked Beatle. A lot. Respected him. Trusted him. He could tease her all he wanted. It made her feel normal. Not like she was a kidnapping victim escaping from the scene of her confinement.

"Because it's not nice to tease a woman who hasn't had chocolate in weeks."

He smiled then. A wide smile that didn't completely hide the relief in his eyes. Without a word, he carefully moved her feet from his thighs, leaving them dangling over the edge of the hammock, and scooted over far enough so he could reach his pack and drag it back to where he'd been sitting.

He returned to his little stool but before he did anything else, he placed her feet back on his thighs, then opened a flap on one side of the enormous backpack. He rummaged around for a moment before pulling out an MRE. He grabbed a huge-ass knife from a sheath at his waist and slit the plastic open. He pulled something out, but kept it hidden in his palm.

"Close your eyes."

"Why?" Casey asked suspiciously.

"Because you trust me," Beatle said, his brown eyes piercing in their intensity.

Without further protest, Casey did as he asked. She felt his thighs bunch under her feet as he leaned forward. He picked up one of her hands and placed something in it.

"You can look now," he told her.

Casey opened her eyes—and stared at the tiny Hershey's Kiss in the palm of her hand.

She gaped at it, then looked at Beatle. "What…how?"

He shrugged. "Some of the MREs have them inside as dessert. It's probably completely mush from being out here in the heat, though."

Casey's mouth began to water like one of Pavlov's dogs. Her hand shook with anticipation. She wanted to pop it in her mouth, foil and all, but managed to control herself. She reached for the tiny treat, then stopped with her hand in midair.

"What?" Beatle asked, immediately picking up on her hesitation. She had a feeling he didn't miss much.

"My hands are filthy."

Without speaking, he reached for the chocolate and

carefully plucked it from her hand and placed it on top of his backpack. Then he dug inside again. He opened the package of wet wipes he'd unearthed from his magic pack and reached for her hand.

Casey wasn't sure what to say, so she remained silent as he carefully cleaned her hand. He first wiped down her palm, then ran the cloth up each finger. He used the now extremely dirty wipe to get as much dirt and mud off the back of her hand as possible.

Then he put the used wipe down and pulled out a new one. He repeated his actions on her other hand. When Casey thought he was done, he surprised her by pulling out another clean cloth and starting on her first hand again. But this time his ministrations felt more intimate. It was no longer simply about cleaning the dirt off her hands. It seemed to her that, with each swipe, he was attempting to wipe away the bad memories that had caused her hands to be as filthy as they were. He was caressing each finger as he worked on attempting to remove the caked-in dirt under her nails. His thumbs massaged the palm of her hand even as he increased the pressure to thoroughly clean them.

After all was said and done, Beatle had used six wipes to get her hands to their current state. She could still see dirt under her nails, but she never would've thought she could be that clean without running water and a shit-ton of soap.

Without the care and reverence he'd used on *her*, Beatle used the wipes to clean his own hands. Then he reached for the piece of chocolate. He carefully tried to peel the foil off, but the chocolate was simply too melted for him to be successful.

"Trust me?" he asked once again.

Casey could only nod.

She watched as he used his now clean index finger to swipe as much of the soft, gooey chocolate off the foil as he could. He leaned forward and held it up to her.

Feeling lightheaded with emotion, Casey reached up and took hold of his wrist, steadying his hand. Then she picked up her head and opened her mouth.

Beatle's mouth opened and he licked his lips slowly as he watched her. She could see the pulse in his neck speed up.

She hadn't felt a sexual attraction to him before, but now was a whole different story.

The moment his finger entered her mouth, she closed her lips around it. Wrapping her tongue around his digit, she sucked the amazingly sweet treat from his skin.

His pupils dilated as she stared at him. The eroticism of what she was doing wasn't lost on her. When she thought she'd gotten all the chocolate, she tightened her lips around his finger and sucked. Hard.

"Fuuuck," Beatle swore, but he didn't pull his finger

out of her mouth.

With one last swipe of her tongue, Casey finally pulled back. The arm she'd used to prop herself up was shaking, and she knew it was only a matter of time before she couldn't hold her own body weight anymore.

Without taking his eyes from hers, Beatle brought his finger up to his own mouth and slowly pushed it inside.

Casey licked her lips.

The moment was so sensual, so spontaneous, she wasn't sure what to say or do.

But of course, Beatle made sure she didn't feel awkward. After he'd pulled his finger from his mouth, he said, "Now you can't say I'm not allowed to tease you because you haven't had chocolate in weeks."

She couldn't help the giggle that escaped her mouth. She was shocked at her actions, but Beatle didn't make her feel weird about whatever was happening between them.

"Ready for your IV?" Truck asked from behind the hammock.

Casey startled so badly she would've flipped herself right off the other side, but Beatle was there to steady her. "Easy, sweetheart."

"Sorry! You surprised me, Truck. Yeah, I'm ready. Fill me up, Scotty."

Truck chuckled. "I think you have the wrong show.

That's *Star Trek*. I think we're in the middle of a *Die Hard* movie or something."

"No way," Beatle told him. "I'm thinking *Rambo*, or even the latest *Jungle Book* movie…you know, when that guy kicked ass in the jungle?"

Casey grinned. Her brother's teammates were funny. She hadn't expected that. She wasn't sure what she'd expected, but it wasn't to be laughing hours after being rescued from a hole in the ground she thought would be her tomb.

"We need to turn you," Beatle said in a no-nonsense tone. "Put your head up at this end. That's it. No, scoot up farther. More… Casey, all the way."

She scowled up at Beatle as he finally leaned over her and put his hands under her armpits, much like he'd done when he'd lifted her out of the hole in the ground, and manhandled her into the position he wanted.

Her head was all the way at the top of the hammock, resting on one of the sticks he'd used to stabilize the ropes. It wasn't exactly the most comfortable position, but she certainly wasn't going to bitch. She was lying down, and it felt heavenly.

Truck kneeled on the ground next to her and got to work cleaning her inner elbow with an alcohol pad while Beatle moved farther down and started to doctor her feet.

Neither the needle going in her arm—third time

was the charm in her case; apparently, her veins weren't cooperating—nor the scrubbing of her feet felt great, but again, the last thing on her mind was complaining. The men were doing this to help her, not hurt her. She needed the fluids *and* her feet cleaned.

So she sucked it up and simply closed her eyes, appreciating the fact she could hear the cicadas in the background, a few birds chirping, and the wind through the leaves high above their heads.

She never realized when she fell asleep. One second she was thinking of how lucky she'd been, and the next she'd simply faded out.

Chapter Six

"**W**HAT DO YOU really think about her feet?" Beatle asked Truck after she fell asleep.

"I think she's very lucky, but they should heal remarkably fast with the antibiotics I included in her IV and after a night's rest. Not to mention bandaging them up before putting on *dry* socks tomorrow."

They were talking in low tones so as not to wake the obviously exhausted woman in front of them.

Beatle moved his little stool up from her feet to sit next to her. He leaned forward, resting his elbows on his knees, and stared at her as she slept. "I don't get it," he mused softly. "Why not kill her outright?"

Truck didn't miss a beat, knowing exactly what he was talking about. "It doesn't make sense," he agreed. "In almost every kidnapping case we've worked, the women were raped, and if someone was separated from the group, they were either murdered or tortured."

"Right. And these assholes didn't even *ask* for a ransom. So they essentially had free rein to torture and-or kill all the women." Beatle looked up at his friend. "So why didn't they?"

"Technically, she *was* tortured," Truck said dryly. "Throwing her into that pit then covering it with those boards wasn't humane."

"But *why*?" Beatle asked again.

"She's not exactly anyone important," Truck mused more to himself than his teammate.

Beatle was offended on Casey's behalf all the same. "She *is* important," he countered.

"I didn't mean it like that," Truck said, trying to mollify his friend. "All I meant is that it would make more sense to use Astrid, because as the daughter of an ambassador, she was more likely to get them whatever it was they wanted."

"You're right, but they didn't ask for anything," Beatle said, agitated.

"Maybe they knew Casey was the sister of a Special Forces soldier?"

"Maybe. But I don't think so. She didn't mention them asking about her family or anything like that," Beatle said, reaching out and using his index finger to brush a stray lock of dirty hair off her forehead.

"Could it have been random? Like the villagers were out hunting and came across the women and didn't like them in their jungle?" Truck asked.

"It's twenty miles to Guacalito," Beatle said, shaking his head. "If villagers were out hunting, they likely wouldn't have gone so close to Guacalito. It wasn't as if the women were miles from the town. It's even more unlikely the villagers would randomly decide to kidnap four women and bring them all the way back to their village to hold them prisoner."

"Not to mention, the girls said they were transported in a vehicle."

"Right. Speaking of which…where was it?"

Truck shrugged. "I'd guess whoever took them high-tailed it out of the area when the Huntsmen arrived, or even before that. I'd think they would've mentioned seeing someone fleeing in a truck otherwise."

Neither man said anything for several minutes.

"Dammit," Beatle swore. "Nothing about this makes sense."

Truck didn't respond.

"She's amazing, isn't she?" Beatle asked his friend, staring at a sleeping Casey. "I mean, many people think women in general are weak. That they can't handle stress. But she not only handled the situation she'd found herself in, she fucking beat it to a bloody pulp."

Truck chuckled. "I'd say all of our women are stronger than anyone in their lives ever gave them credit for. They're the epitome of Delta Force wives for sure."

Beatle looked up at that. "Wives?"

His friend looked discomfited for a moment, but quickly hid it. "Yeah…you know…the team's women.

Coach and Ghost aren't married, but you know what I mean."

Beatle narrowed his eyes at Truck before saying, "I thought I did, but now I'm not so sure."

"She was smart to try to keep her feet out of the water," Truck said, motioning to Casey with his chin.

Feeling frustrated that it seemed like his friend was keeping something from him, Beatle scowled at Truck for a minute before letting him change the subject. Something was up with him. He'd been acting evasive for the last couple months. Disappearing for days at a time and not telling anyone where he'd been, more attached to his phone, and generally not being as open as to what was going on in his personal life as he used to be. The man was entitled to his privacy, but it wasn't like Truck. Beatle worried about his friend a lot lately. He made a mental note to corner him and find out once and for all what the fuck was up when they got home.

"She was. Blade says she earned her PhD recently. Pretty impressive for someone as young as her."

"In bugs, right?"

Beatle chuckled. "Entomology. I think she'd take exception to you saying her degree was in 'bugs.'"

"I don't know. She seems to have a good sense of humor. Smart, brave, strong as hell...maybe I'll—"

"Shut it," Beatle told Truck, not letting him finish his thought. "She's spoken for."

"By you?" Truck pushed.

"Yes, dammit. By me."

"Blade might have something to say about that. She's his little sister," Truck warned.

"He's already given me his approval," Beatle told him.

"Really?"

"Really. And if I had a little sister, I'd feel just like he does. I'd be fucking ecstatic if you or Blade wanted her for your own. I know you guys. I know you'd never cheat on her. You'd treat her like gold, and you'd do anything possible to protect and take care of her. Just like he knows that about me."

Truck didn't respond.

Feeling a bit defensive about his affection for the woman softly snoring on the hammock between them, Beatle said a little belligerently, "What? You think it's too fast?"

"Absolutely not," Truck responded immediately. "When you know, you know. One day, one week, one year. Every relationship is different, and what works for one man doesn't necessarily work for another. But the question is...does she feel the same?"

Beatle looked closer at his friend. Truck was staring at Casey, but he didn't think he was seeing her. "I don't know what she feels. But there's definitely an attraction on both sides. It's not like I'm going to have sex with her in the middle of the fucking jungle. For one, she's still way too weak and recovering. For another, she needs to deal with the psychological shit I know she's got in her head from the kidnapping. Not to mention she currently lives in Florida and I'm in Texas."

"You gonna let all that stop you?" Truck asked.

"Fuck no. I'll give her some time and space if she needs it, but I'll be there, however I can be, reminding her that I'm on her side. That I want to be her everything. When the time is right, it'll be right. I won't rush her into sex, but I'm going to make sure she knows that I want her. All of her. The last thing I want is for her to think what I feel for her is pity or friendship or a weird psychological result of this rescue. She's going to know I want her as my woman. Just as I want to be her man."

Truck looked up at Beatle then. His blue eyes piercing in their intensity. "You might scare her away if you let her know straight out that she's it for you."

"Bullshit," Beatle returned. "She might not believe me at first, but I'll show her through my actions that I'm serious. I think it'd be more confusing to be by her side, helping her get over this bump in the road, if I just acted like a concerned friend. I'll wait for her to realize I'm it for her too, but I won't shy away from letting her know how I feel. I've never felt like this for any woman before in my life. She deserves to know that. To feel it to the marrow of her bones. If she's going to truly lean on me, let me in, she has to trust that I want to be there."

Beatle's voice had risen in his passion and Casey stirred between them. He put a hand on her forehead and caressed her temple with his thumb, as he said a little softer, "The thought of her not knowing how much I care about her and wondering where I stand in our relationship would be almost as painful as the bite from one of those bullet ants she was talking about earlier."

Beatle looked up and saw Truck staring off into space with an introspective look on his face, and was about to ask his friend what was bothering him, when Casey moaned under his hand. When he looked down at her, her green eyes were open and staring right at him.

"How long was I out?"

"Not long. Go back to sleep. I'm going to get your surprise ready, but it'll take a bit."

"I'm not sure I like surprises anymore," she mumbled, obviously still half-asleep.

His heart breaking for her, Beatle leaned in and kissed her forehead with a feather-light touch. "I'll see what I can do about that. This will be a good surprise, sweetheart."

"Promise?" she asked groggily.

"Promise."

"Mmm-kay."

And with that, she was asleep once more.

When Beatle looked up at Truck, the focused soldier was back.

"I'm going to do a short recon. I'll radio the others and let them know we've stopped for the night and, as long as things look clear, will be here until mid-morning. Yeah?"

"Yeah, that sounds perfect. Thanks, Truck."

The large man got up and straightened the vest he wore, checking to make sure his weapons were situated properly.

"Truck?"

"Yeah?"

"When you get back, can you help me with my surprise for Casey?"

"Of course. What do you need?"

Beatle told his teammate what he wanted to do, and was rewarded with a huge smile.

"She's gonna love that."

"I know."

Truck stared at his friend for a moment, then said, "She's a lucky woman."

"No," Beatle countered immediately. "I'm a lucky man. Even if she decides she doesn't feel for me the way I feel about her, I've had the privilege of getting to know her. Of helping her get through this experience."

"You're a hell of a man, Beatle. I'll let you know when I'm back so you don't shoot me."

The last was said with humor, but Beatle could tell it was forced. He didn't say anything other than, "I'd appreciate that."

After Truck left, Beatle sat and watched Casey sleep for ten minutes before he forced himself to get up and start getting things ready for her surprise.

An hour later, Truck had returned and seemed to be more himself. Beatle had everything set up. He hated to wake her, but wanted to get this done before it got dark.

Putting a hand on her shoulder, Beatle gently jostled her. "Casey, wake up."

One second she was asleep, and the next she was awake and seemingly fighting for her life. She jackknifed up and swung a fist at Beatle's face. He barely yanked his head back in time. She immediately rolled away from him and landed hard on the jungle floor. She was on her knees and crawling away before he made it around the hammock to her side.

"Casey. Calm. It's me, Beatle. You're safe."

She obviously didn't hear him in her panicked state, because she continued her mad scramble to get away from him. Truck moved to stand in front of her and block her retreat. When she ran headlong into his legs, she whimpered and turned onto her side, curling into a ball and covering her face and head with her arms to try to protect herself.

Beatle felt her terror as if he was the one experiencing it. He kneeled behind her and ran his hand over the back of her head, all the time murmuring softly, "It's okay, sweetheart. You're safe, I swear. Come on, wake up now. That's it. Take a deep breath. It's me, Beatle. You're here with me and Truck, you're okay."

She took a shuddering breath, then another, before she slowly opened her eyes and turned to stare up at Beatle. He knew the second awareness came back because she blinked and looked confused for a second, before mortification moved in and an embarrassed flush rose up her neck into her face.

"Shit. I'm sorry. I guess I—"

"It's fine," Beatle soothed, cutting off her unnecessary apology.

"It's not, I didn't—"

"I once tried to shank Truck when he woke me up on a mission," Beatle told her without embarrassment.

"It's true," Truck piped up. "There I was with this ugly-ass scar on my face, and he tried to put a matching one on the other side."

Casey looked up at them with wide eyes. "Really?"

"Really," Beatle confirmed. "We were all on edge with the mission, and poor Truck had the misfortune to be the one to wake me." He shrugged. "It happens. Come on, let me help you up."

He held out a hand to her, and was relieved when she immediately placed her small hand in his. He helped her sit up and Truck helped him pick her up. He brought her back to the hammock.

Casey looked down at the blood trickling from her inner arm and grimaced. "Looks like you get to use me as a pin cushion again," she told Truck after seeing where she'd torn out the IV he'd so painstakingly put in earlier.

"How do you feel?" he asked.

Casey shrugged.

"Right. I was going to suggest maybe we could leave it out, but with that underwhelming response, I think it should go back in," Truck said.

When she didn't protest, Beatle knew she felt worse than she was letting on. He helped her swing her legs back up onto the hammock and once again hauled her toward the end of the swinging contraption.

"Ready for your surprise, sweetheart?"

"Sure." She still sounded a bit wary.

Beatle gestured to the containers sitting around the hammock. "We always carry a few collapsible buckets just in case. I thought you might feel better if your hair was clean."

Casey looked around her in confusion. "My hair?"

"Yeah, I'm going to wash it for you."

Her eyes widened with eagerness and delight. "Really?"

"Really. Although I should warn you, I haven't done this before. I'm pretty sure I won't be asked to work in a beauty salon anytime soon."

"And you'd do this for *me*?"

Beatle leaned forward until they were almost nose to nose. "I'd do anything for you, Case. Now, I'm going to scoot you up a bit more until your neck is resting on the sticks there. It'll feel a little awkward at first, but Truck will make sure you're balanced and can relax. That'll leave your hair hanging over the edge of the hammock and the water dripping down won't get all over your clothes. Okay?"

"Okay," she said softly.

Beatle ignored the tears in her eyes, hoping they were a result of being happy and pleased, and not sad or frightened. He helped shift her until her head was in position. He nodded at Truck, who had his hand on her back under the ropes. He let go, and, when Casey didn't immediately protest the position or say she was uncomfortable, got to work on cleaning her arm and replacing the IV.

Beatle picked up the first bucket of water and carefully lifted it. "This might be a bit chilly," he told Casey, then he slowly poured the water over her head.

Casey's eyes closed and she sighed as the water from the stream cascaded through her hair. It took several rinses to get the worst of the gunk from the strands, but Beatle worked slowly, running his hand through her hair each time, squeezing the water out and making sure it got to every part of her head.

When the water ran relatively clear, he pulled his little stool over and sat.

"What are you doing now?" Casey asked quietly, her eyes still shut.

"Shhhhh," Beatle admonished, smiling. It was obvious she was enjoying the attention. And he was enjoying caring for her. More than he ever thought he would. He picked up the small bottle of shampoo he'd taken out of his pack and squeezed a healthy dollop into his hand. He slowly worked the soap into her hair and lathered it up.

Casey groaned, completely lost in the sensation.

She didn't even flinch when Truck growled after his fourth attempt to reinsert the IV. Beatle saw him move down to her hand to try that vein, but turned his attention back to Casey's hair. He massaged her head as he worked the lather through her silky strands.

Her eyes were still shut as his fingers moved to her nape and massaged the tight muscles there. Soap was dripping onto his lap, but Beatle ignored it. Nothing was more important than helping make his woman feel clean and whole again.

After several minutes of massaging and washing her

hair, he asked, "Ready for a rinse?"

She nodded and Beatle stood once more. He repeated his actions from before, this time making sure none of the suds dripped onto her face. When the water ran clear, he sat and picked up the small chamois he always carried. He dried her hair as well as he could with the cloth, then picked up a comb.

"This probably won't feel great," he told her reluctantly. "I wish I had a nice soft brush to use, but it would've taken up too much space in my pack."

She smiled, as he'd intended her to. The hand without the IV lifted as she said, "I can do it."

Beatle grabbed her hand, then kissed the palm and gently placed it back on her belly. "I got this, sweetheart. I'll be as gentle as I can."

"Do your worst," she told him. "I can take it."

"I know. You're amazing," he said, then got to work. It took quite a while, as her hair was thick and extremely tangled, but he went slow, as promised, and did his best not to pull on her scalp as he worked the comb through her hair.

Even after he'd taken out all the snarls, he ran the comb through her hair over and over. His hand followed, caressing the strands with each stroke. Beatle was surprised how much he enjoyed taking care of her in this way. It wasn't something he'd ever thought of doing for a woman before, but it was intimate. Cleaning her, grooming her.

And with each swipe of the comb, she groaned in delight. Her face was completely relaxed and her lips were curved up in a slight smile. Beatle made a vow right then and there to do this for her often in the future.

Her hair wasn't quite dry by the time he stopped, but it was close. Her dirty-blonde hair was highlighted with lighter strands. It was gorgeous.

Beatle leaned over and kissed her forehead once more and ran his index finger down her nose. "Are you asleep?" he asked quietly.

"No. I didn't want to sleep through a second of that. Thank you, Beatle. That was amazing."

Truck had long since moved to the other side of the clearing and out of earshot. He was giving them as much privacy as the situation allowed and Beatle appreciated it. "I liked that."

Her eyes opened and she peered up at him. "You did?"

"Yeah, sweetheart, I did."

"What's your name?" she asked out of the blue.

Beatle's brows came down in confusion. She didn't know his name? Had she hit her head at some point? He didn't think so. "Beatle."

She shook her head. "No, your real name."

Ah. "Troy."

"Troy what?" she pushed.

"Troy Lennon," he told her.

She smiled then. A full smile with all her teeth showing. "The nickname makes sense now. I thought maybe it was because you're afraid of bugs or something."

Beatle knew he was blushing, but didn't hide it from her. "Yeah, well...I can't say I'm that fond of them."

Her smile grew, if that was possible. "You're scared of little bugs!" she exclaimed. "A badass Delta Force soldier is scared of little teeny-tiny bugs! Classic."

Mock scowling, Beatle stood and hovered over her. "You were the one who informed us about ants whose bites hurt more than a bullet. And shall we talk about other teeny-tiny insects that, with one bite or sting, can render a man or woman completely helpless? Damn straight, I don't like bugs. I'd happily take on an armed man over an innocent yet deadly insect."

She was still smiling, but she nodded quickly. "I agree. How about this? I'll keep you safe from the bugs if you keep me safe from the armed men."

"Done," Beatle said almost before the last word came out of her mouth. Then he leaned forward and covered her lips with his.

It was an awkward angle, as he was standing over her backwards, but he swore he felt electricity shoot from his lips down to his toes when he brushed his tongue over her bottom lip.

Drawing back, Beatle brought this thumb up and caressed the lip he'd just touched with his tongue, feeling the wetness there. His dick had hardened to a painful level with the slight touch of his mouth on hers, but he ignored it and stood. "There's some water left over, want to use it to wash up?"

Casey looked somewhat stunned, but blinked and recovered. "Yes, please."

Beatle helped her sit up sideways on the hammock with her legs dangling over the side. "Don't wash the goo off your feet. I'll take care of them in the morning before we head out." He handed her the chamois cloth. "Use this. It absorbs water, so it'll feel rough against your skin, but it'll do the job. Here's the shampoo, you can use it as soap. Take your time and be careful with that IV. I'll be over there with Truck. If you need me, just yell."

When Casey nodded, Beatle couldn't resist running his hand over her now shiny, clean hair once more, then he forced himself to pick up the stool, turn from her, and head across the small clearing to where Truck was sitting. He sat with his back to Casey and began to chat with Truck about their plan of action for the next day.

CASEY SAT HOLDING the soap in one hand and the chamois in the other as she watched Beatle walk over to his teammate. She was having a hard time thinking at the moment. She'd been shocked that Beatle would offer to wash her hair for her, but stunned silly at how gentle and thorough he'd been.

Then when he'd spent all that time combing out the knots in her hair and gently caressing her as he did, she'd wanted nothing more than to cry. She couldn't remember the last time anyone had taken care of her like Beatle had.

She'd lived on her own since the age of eighteen, when she'd gone to college. She'd had boyfriends, but they were academic types, like her, not alpha like Beatle, by any stretch of the imagination. As a professor, she was always in charge of her classroom and students. She was responsible for Jaylyn, Kristina, and Astrid while on the research trip, and after they'd been kidnapped, she'd taken even more control.

Casey hadn't realized how good it would feel to let someone else take charge. To make the decisions. To care for her. Even now he was doing it. His back was turned, giving her as much privacy as he could. But she knew if she said even one word, he'd be right there at her side in seconds. It soothed her. Made her feel safe—and she hadn't felt safe for one second since she'd stepped off the plane in Costa Rica.

It wasn't that the country was that scary, but she was always aware of who was around them, and that every decision she made could affect the college students who were with her. But here, in the middle of the jungle, she didn't have to make any decisions. Everything was up to Beatle and Truck.

Moving slowly, Casey leaned over and dunked the chamois into the bucket of water and added a bit of the shampoo. Then she lathered it up and brought it to her face. She scrubbed her skin until she was sure she was clean. Then she repeated the process and washed her neck, arms, belly and breasts, under her arms, calves, and lastly, even went so far as to unbutton her pants and use the cloth to clean between her legs.

The only parts she couldn't wash while dressed were her thighs, but she figured those were the parts of her that were probably the cleanest. Sighing in relief, she looked over to where Beatle had been sitting as she fastened her pants—and froze.

His back was no longer to her.

Truck was nowhere to be seen, and Beatle had moved so that he was leaning against a tree. His muscular arms were crossed over his chest and he was staring at her with eyes so intense she wanted to look away, but couldn't.

Her gaze roamed the rest of him, and she had to admit she liked what she saw. He was taller than she was by a few inches. He almost looked short next to Truck, but then again, everyone seemed diminutive next to the huge man.

He was wearing black cargo pants, hiking boots, a long-sleeve olive-green shirt with a mesh vest over it. The vest had pockets that were filled with who knew what. Whatever a badass Delta Force soldier might need while on the run from bad guys in the jungle. His jaw was clenched as if he were fighting some deep emotion, and she could feel the piercing force of his gaze from all the way across the clearing.

Her stare swept down his body once more, taking in all that was Troy "Beatle" Lennon, and her lips parted in a small gasp when she came to his hips. He was aroused. The bulge in his pants was easy to see, even from where she sat. Surprised, she looked back up at his face. He didn't seem to be ashamed of his arousal at all. But he wasn't smug or gross about it either.

Her gaze went back up to his and, amazingly, Casey felt her nipples tighten under her shirt. It didn't help that she wasn't wearing a bra, the sensitive tips brushing against the harsh material of her shirt made her all the more aware of her arousal.

Without breaking eye contact, she leaned over and draped the chamois over the edge of the bucket of now soapy water.

As if her movements broke him from whatever

trance he'd been in, Beatle strode toward her.

"All done?" he asked in a husky voice.

Casey nodded.

Instead of reaching for the dirty water, Beatle leaned over, putting his hands on the ropes at her hips. Casey tilted her head but didn't move away from him. His face was inches from hers as he said fiercely, his southern accent more pronounced with the emotion he was feeling, "I will kill and die for the right to make you mine, and to be yours in return."

Then, without waiting for a response, he straightened, bent down and grabbed two of the buckets, and disappeared into the trees.

Casey inhaled a deep breath and closed her eyes. If he'd stopped at the first part of his declaration, she might've been annoyed. She wasn't a piece of meat to belong to anyone. But to have him as hers in return? Yeah, she could deal with that.

What in the world was going on? Was she dealing with some sort of hero worship since he'd saved her? When she got home, would she wonder what she was thinking being attracted to him in the slightest? And what about him? Was he caught up in the damsel-in-distress thing? She had no answers, only questions...and the lingering arousal singing through her veins.

She brought a hand up to her face to rub some of the stress away, but squeaked in pain when she pulled on the IV. Damn. She'd forgotten all about it.

But now that she *was* thinking about it, all the little aches and pains she'd been ignoring snuck up on her. Her arm throbbed where she'd been stuck so many times as Truck had tried to find a viable vein. Her feet hurt. The muscles in her legs were screaming at her. Her back felt like shit from not being able to lie down for so long. On top of it all, she had a headache.

Shifting in the hammock and wincing when it swayed under her, Casey struggled to pick up her feet and lie down. She'd just gotten her legs into the hammock when Beatle returned with Truck. They both had wet hair and it was obvious they'd used the soap and water source to clean themselves as best they could.

"I'm glad you're back," she said quietly, not one to hide her feelings.

"You okay?" Truck asked, reaching for her hand to check the IV.

She nodded. "It's getting dark."

"We were just through the trees," Truck told her. "We wouldn't have left you here all by yourself if we weren't nearby to hear if you needed assistance."

"I figured, it's just…I have a feeling I'm not going to do well in the dark for a while."

At her admission, Beatle approached the hammock. He ran his thumb along her forehead and asked, "Headache?"

She nodded.

"Food'll help." Then he turned and went to his never-ending backpack of goodness and brought out an MRE. He came back to her and squatted down. "It's not the best tasting, but it's fast and full of calories, which you need," he said as he opened the plastic pack of food and got busy preparing it. He ripped open a smaller pack and held something up to her.

Casey took the piece of pound cake and smiled. "Dessert first?"

"Absolutely. Gotta make sure you have room."

Taking a bite of the sweet treat, Casey moaned at the way her taste buds fired to life. She looked down at Beatle as she chewed and froze. She swallowed hard and asked, "What?"

He shook his head. "Nothing. Good?"

"Um hmm," she said while chewing another bite.

She'd finished the cake by the time the hot part of the meal was done cooking. He handed her the plastic pack along with a spoon. "Can you handle it?" he asked.

She nodded, but wondered what he'd do if she said no. Probably feed her, which, surprisingly, didn't seem all that weird.

She quickly ate the pasta meal, telling him between bites that it was one of the best things she'd ever tasted.

Truck had returned and heard her comment. "You *must* be hungry if that shit tastes good," he told her with a wink.

Casey realized at that moment she was enjoying herself. She shouldn't be. She was in pain, in the middle of a foreign country with no identification, and had no idea if her kidnappers were waiting in the darkness to snatch her up again. But sitting in the dim light, Casey had no fears.

If something happened, if someone sprang out of the trees, Beatle and Truck would protect her. So she winked back at Truck and finished shoveling the meal into her mouth.

Then she closed her eyes, enjoying the feeling of being full once more, and swayed. Suddenly she was exhausted. So tired she didn't think she'd be able to move even if she saw a new species of beetle crawl across her arm.

She felt movement around her and cracked her lids open to see Beatle draping something over the ropes holding the hammock. Mosquito netting. She'd had the same sort of setup in the camp with her students...but now it felt stifling. She felt closed in. Her breathing sped up and she closed her eyes once more, trying to force the claustrophobic feeling back.

The hammock swung and her body dipped.

Gasping, Casey's eyes popped open to see Beatle settling himself next to her.

"What are you doing?"

Instead of answering, Beatle looked up at Truck, who was changing the empty IV bag to a fresh one. "I'm thinking a bit of stronger painkiller would be welcome at this point."

"Beatle," Casey protested, pushing at his chest, trying to put some space between them.

He ignored her. "Oh, and would you take care of the sticks for me too?" he asked Truck, motioning to his feet.

"Troy Beatle Lennon," Casey said sternly, ignoring the way his eyebrows went up and Truck chuckled at the use of his full name. "You can't sleep here."

"Why not?" Beatle asked, shifting until she was lying mostly on top of him and partly on her side.

"Because."

He grinned. "That's not an answer, Case."

"Because we're all mushed together. And it's hot. And you won't be comfortable."

"I like being mushed together. And I don't care about the heat. And I'll be more comfortable with you in my arms than I would be sleeping on the ground next to you."

"Why would you sleep on the ground?" she asked, ignoring the tingles his other answers gave her. "You do know there are *bugs* down there, right?"

He ignored her bug remark and said, "Because I need to make sure you're okay. And I can't get to you quickly if I'm inside one of these things, even if I'm strung up right next to you. This way, I can monitor your heart rate and breathing throughout the night. If you're hurting, I can get Truck to add more painkillers to your IV."

Casey wasn't sure what to say to that. She didn't have to worry about it though, because Truck finished messing with her IV and pulled out the sticks at their feet. The hammock immediately collapsed around their waists and legs. She wiggled and hiked one leg up onto his thighs.

"Careful of your feet, sweetheart," Beatle said.

As soon as he finished speaking, Truck pulled the upper stick out of the ropes.

If Casey thought she and Beatle had been close before, it was nothing compared to what they were like now. Touching from chest to toes, she'd never been held as tightly to someone as Beatle was holding her at the moment.

It was his turn to wiggle, subtly shifting her next to him, and making her more comfortable in the process.

"I'll be over there," Truck said with a head jerk. "Yell if she needs anything."

"Thanks, Truck," Beatle told his friend quietly.

Then they were alone. As was usual in the jungle, one minute it was dusk, and the next it was pitch dark. She stiffened, the darkness reminding her of the hole she'd been in hours ago.

"My parents live in Tennessee. They have one of those authentic log cabins. You know, like you'd see in Colorado or something. They actually have to hand crank the logs every now and then to make sure they stay together. My mom is a self-professed book nerd. She reads voraciously. Every time I go home, she has a new author she's obsessed over. Her favorite thing to do is snuggle up with a fuzzy blanket and read while my dad watches whatever sport is in season on TV."

Casey knew what he was doing, and appreciated it more than he knew. "Do they get along?"

"My parents? Yeah. They've been married for thirty-five years. I'm not saying they don't argue or get pissed at each other, but at the end of the day, they always say they love each other. I always thought their kind of love was normal. I never even considered that others didn't have that, until high school, then I truly understood what other kids went through with nasty divorces and only having one parent. Going overseas and seeing the kinds of lives others lead has only made me appreciate them more."

"Do you have any siblings?" Casey asked, then yawned.

She felt Beatle's lips brush across her forehead and he tightened his arm around her. She placed her hand flat on his chest and heard the steady *thump-thump-*

thump of his heartbeat as he spoke.

"Nope. I didn't really miss them, but seeing how close you are to Blade makes me wish I had a little sister."

"Big brothers are a pain in the ass," she whispered, but smiled against his chest.

"I remember this one time when I was fifteen, I..."

Casey closed her eyes as she listened to Beatle's stories. She occasionally asked a question, but for the most part, she let his southern drawl comfort and relax her. She realized after a while that she didn't hurt anymore. Whatever painkiller Truck had added to her IV had worked wonders. She was comfortable for the first time in a long while, and more importantly, she felt safe.

Sighing once and nuzzling into the man at her side, Casey let herself drift off, secure in the knowledge that Beatle would protect her when she was asleep and vulnerable.

BEATLE KNEW THE second Casey fell asleep next to him. Every muscle in her body went limp, as if she'd been holding herself stiff for years. Her body melted even closer to his, and it was the most amazing feeling he'd ever had in his life.

He hadn't lied earlier when he'd told Casey he'd kill

or die for her. It was that simple…and that complicated.

They had a lot of hurdles ahead of them.

The least of which was getting out of the jungle and out of Costa Rica.

But beyond that was the niggling feeling that, even once they were back in the States, she wouldn't be safe. Her kidnapping wasn't normal. And not normal meant trouble. He didn't know where the danger lurked, but he knew it was out there waiting. For *his* woman.

No way in fuck was he going to let her be put in another situation like the one from which she'd just been rescued.

"Sleep well, sweetheart," he murmured, closing his eyes. He and Truck would catnap, but neither would sleep deeply. Not now. They'd trained their bodies to rest, but not go all the way under when they were in the middle of a mission. While their situation wasn't dire, as it sometimes was when working, they never took anything for granted. Until their feet touched Texas soil, they wouldn't let down their guard.

Especially not with the life of the woman in his arms at stake.

As the night sounds of the Costa Rican jungle serenaded him, Beatle planned for his and Casey's future in his head. First goal was getting her home. Then he'd worry about convincing her to spend the rest of her life with him.

Chapter Seven

THE NEXT MORNING, Beatle and Truck were all business. Casey woke when Beatle climbed out of the cocoon they'd slept in all night. She realized that she'd slept better than she had in years. Which was crazy. She was covered with sweat from sharing body heat with Beatle all night, and wasn't exactly out of danger, but she'd still slept like a log.

She figured the pain medicine Truck had administered had helped her sleep, but deep down, she knew even drugs wouldn't have kept her under if she hadn't felt safe.

When Beatle had rolled out of the hammock, he'd kissed her on the forehead and ordered her to stay put. So she had. She'd watched Beatle and his teammate quickly and efficiently pack up as much of the camp as they could while they ate a couple protein bars for breakfast.

She was more than ready to get up and stretch when Beatle walked over to her.

"Need some help?" he asked with a smile.

"Please. I feel like I'm a pupa ready to emerge from my cocoon."

"Apt description, Dr. Shea." He removed the mosquito netting from above her, folded it into a small square and put it on the ground next to the hammock. "I'll hold open the sides of the hammock. Slowly swing your legs out toward me then sit up. When you have your balance, I'll help you stand. Put your feet on the netting so they don't get dirty. Ready?"

Casey nodded and, when he flattened the hammock, she awkwardly moved until her legs were over the side as he'd instructed. Standing was tougher. Her muscles were stiff from the unaccustomed movement of the day before after so long being cooped up in the hole. Biting her lip to keep her groan from escaping, she stood on wobbly legs. The second she cleared the hammock, Beatle bent slightly in front of her and put both hands on her hips, steadying her.

"Okay?"

She nodded, even though she didn't feel okay.

"Truck!" Beatle bellowed. "Need those pills!" Then he turned back to Casey. "Easy, sweetheart. Getting up is always the hardest part."

"And you know this how?" she bit out, a bit harsher than she wanted to. "You ever been thrown in a hole then forced to hike for miles on numb feet?"

The second the words were out, she regretted them.

Beatle didn't deserve her anger.

"No," he said calmly. "But I *have* been captured by terrorists, tortured, then had to walk my ass through the desert to reach the extraction point."

Casey swallowed hard and forced herself to look at the man in front of her. "I'm sorry," she said between clenched teeth.

Beatle didn't look upset in the least. He reached up and ran his hand over her head. "You have nothing to be sorry about."

"I didn't mean to be a bitch."

Beatle huffed out a small laugh. "If that was you being a bitch, I don't think I have to worry about your temper in the future." Then he turned and held out a hand to Truck.

Casey didn't know how long the other man had been standing there, but figured he'd probably heard her awful words to his teammate. She dared to glance up at him and was surprised when he winked at her.

"Beatle's right. When you get moving, you'll feel better. Promise."

She nodded and looked back at Beatle. He kept one hand on her hip to steady her but was holding a canteen with the other. "Truck will take out your IV. It looks like it did the trick and you're no longer dehydrated. I recommend you take some painkillers this morning, and probably for the next few days."

Casey nodded and reached for the canteen. Truck handed her two white pills and she swallowed them without asking what they were. She trusted these men. If they thought she should take them, and that they'd help her, she'd do it.

When she'd swallowed the drugs, she handed the canteen back to Beatle. He straightened and, without warning, lifted her into his arms. Casey squealed and threw her arms around his neck for balance. "What are you doing?" she asked in a high-pitched voice she almost didn't recognize as her own.

"I'm assuming you need to visit the ladies' room?" he asked with a lift of one of his eyebrows.

Blushing, Casey realized that she did need to pee. Badly. She simply nodded.

Beatle returned her nod and strode into the jungle with her in his arms. If he thought she was going to—

Her thought was interrupted when he stopped next to a tall tree and asked, "This look okay? No weird creepy-crawlies to bite or sting you while you're doing your business?"

Casey looked down automatically. The area seemed clear of ant mounds and any spiders or snakes. So she nodded.

"Great. I'll be over there," Beatle said, pointing to a tree. "Just yell when you're done and I'll bring you back to camp."

She wanted to say she could get herself back, but that would be silly, considering she was barefoot. So she nodded and tried not to blush. It was stupid to be embarrassed about peeing. She'd seen him and Truck taking breaks the day before, stepping off the trail behind a tree to do their business. Heck, she and the girls had peed in the jungle all the time when they'd been researching...but this was different.

He was gone before she had a chance to say anything, and she quickly did what she had to do. It was crazy how long it had been since she'd had to pee. She'd been so dehydrated that her body had used every ounce of liquid in it. As embarrassing as it was to have to be carried to the restroom, simply having to pee meant she was getting back to normal, which was literally a miracle. She'd take it.

She called out to Beatle and he appeared within seconds. She appreciated him not making the situation weirder than it already was. By the time they'd gotten back to camp, Truck had cleared away the hammock she and Beatle had slept in and all that was left was the little stool, the square of netting, one of the collapsible buckets with water in it, and the chamois.

Beatle put her down next to the stool and said, "Sit."

Casey sat.

As she ate breakfast, another MRE, Beatle and

Truck worked on her feet. She'd been washed, massaged, dried, gooped up, and bandaged. She hadn't had such treatment since the last time she'd been to the spa. Then, while Truck took care of the water, Beatle had gently rolled a pair of his sock liners on her feet. They were way too big, but they were dry, and that was all that mattered.

He then pulled a pair of wool socks over them, also too big. The heel came to the back of her ankle. Beatle grimaced and said, "I know they don't fit all that great, but they're dry. Yours should be good by tomorrow, but we need to keep moving."

"I know. They'll be fine," Casey reassured him.

"You'll have to wear your own shoes, there's nothing I can do about that. They're still wet, but better than yesterday. The socks and liners should keep your feet dry though. Let me know if you feel any wetness on your feet today, or if they start hurting unbearably." He paused then and looked up at her. "I mean it, Case. If your feet are too painful to walk on, we'll figure something else out. The last thing you want to do is be stoic out here in regards to your feet. You could do irreparable damage to yourself if you don't speak up. Okay?"

"Okay," she agreed instantly. "I will. I promise."

"I wish the stupid chopper could pick us up," Beatle murmured as he bent and concentrated on getting her boots on over her feet.

"Did Ghost ever find out why it couldn't?" Casey asked.

"Not as far as I know," he grumbled. "Assholes."

After tying the second boot and making sure it wasn't too tight or loose on her foot, Beatle gripped her calves and looked up at her. "I'm serious about you speaking up if you're hurting, sweetheart. We aren't on the run from terrorists, and I don't think there will be any trouble as we make our way to Guacalito. There's no need to be a hero. If you need a break, say something. I'll be watching you, but I have a feeling you're really good at hiding your feelings and hurts. I'll probably annoy you with how many times I ask how you're doing, whether you're hungry, if you need a break or water. Bear with me, okay? This isn't a race. We'll get there when we get there."

Casey swallowed hard. His words meant everything. She relaxed her shoulders. Beatle admitting he didn't think they would be pursued lifted a load she hadn't realized she was carrying. She took a deep breath. "*You* might not be in any hurry, but I am. I think I've seen enough of the jungle for a while."

His lips quirked upward. "Understandable. Ready to see how well those feet feel?"

Casey nodded and Beatle stood. He took her hands in his and pulled her to her feet. She swayed for a moment, getting used to the boots once again. Then she dropped her hands and took a tentative step, expecting to feel pain, but amazingly, it wasn't too bad. She took another step. Then another. Then she walked around the small clearing.

Beatle and Truck watched from the sidelines, assessing her. She ended up back in front of Beatle. "I'm good."

"I know you are," was his response. He handed her a plastic package. Casey looked down at it then her eyes whipped back up to his. "Another pound cake?"

He shrugged. "You seemed to enjoy it last night. Figured it'd be a nice after-breakfast snack, better than a protein bar…although you'll be eating plenty of those too."

"You're going to be stuffing me with food all the time, aren't you?"

Beatle nodded. "Yup. You need the calories after what you've been through. Lots of small meals will work better than a couple of huge ones."

She smiled at the reminder. "Thank you."

"You're welcome." Then he surprised her by leaning forward and kissing her on the forehead gently. He held out a rubber band. "For your hair."

She took it without a word, still thinking about the kiss. It was a tender gesture. One that a man who'd been dating a woman for a long time would use. But it felt right—and that was what worried her. She could get used to his caring gestures, despite knowing it would hurt when he dropped her off at the airport and got back to his own life, just as she got back to hers.

Swallowing hard, Casey ate her cake as she watched the men finish getting ready to go. She had just put her hair up when Beatle came back and held out a small bottle.

"What's that?"

"Bug spray. I'll do you if you do me."

The words weren't meant to be sexual, but Casey's thighs clenched together just the same. She tried to cover up her inappropriate reaction by reaching for the canister. Beatle turned around so she could spray his back, and she was glad for the reprieve.

When she had finished covering him with the necessary protection, he took the bottle and said, "Close your eyes."

She did, expecting to feel the wetness from the spray on her face. Instead she heard the spray, but didn't feel anything for a second—then his wet fingers spread the liquid carefully on her face. It was intimate and once again, caring.

He carefully smeared the protection all over her face, neck, and ears, then told her to hold her breath. She did, and he proceeded to cover the rest of her clothes and body with the repellent.

"All done," he told her, and she opened her eyes. He

was tucking the bottle into a small pocket on his vest. He looked up and caught her eyes. "Ready?"

"More than," she replied.

Beatle held out his hand, palm up, without a word.

Casey had never felt as safe as she did when his fingers wrapped around hers. Without looking back, they were on their way, Beatle in front with Casey close behind him. Her hand was still in his, and Truck was bringing up the rear.

She'd heard the larger man talking on the radio earlier, and he'd confirmed that everything looked good between them and the other three men in the jungle. Ghost and her brother were well on their way to San José. Soon this whole thing would be a memory.

Casey knew she had lost her mind when she found herself wishing time would slow down. She had a feeling saying goodbye to Beatle would be harder than the trek she was about to take through the jungle.

Chapter Eight

T HE WALKING WAS slow that morning, but Beatle didn't mind. For once, he didn't feel as if he was on the run from anything or anyone. He kept a close eye on Casey and they took breaks at least twice an hour. At this rate, it would take forever to get back to Guacalito, but Beatle didn't want to do anything that might tax Casey too much. She'd already been through one hell of an ordeal.

He couldn't help but admire her. Even after she'd been thrown into that pit, she'd managed to be resourceful. He hadn't missed how she'd used her bra to filter water, or piled up the boards to get her feet and body out of the fluid at the bottom. He'd also noticed she'd done her damnedest to claw her way out, without success. But even if she had been able to get to the top of the hole, she wouldn't have been able to break through the boards, which had been tightly secured over the entrance with vines.

She would've died in another couple days if they hadn't found her.

Beatle tried to shove the depressing thoughts away. They *had* found her, and she was doing amazingly well. They'd all been prepared to carry her out of the jungle and to safety, but so far that hadn't been necessary. The overnight break had done wonders for her feet, as well as her overall health. She wasn't completely back to normal, but she was getting there.

"Oh! Watch out!" Casey cried.

Beatle froze, and had his pistol out and ready to use before the last word had escaped her lips.

"You almost stepped on it!" she continued.

Beatle looked down.

Casey pushed him out of the way and picked up some sort of creature from the forest floor. She stood and held it up for him to see—and Beatle couldn't help the involuntary step he took away from her, and the hideous thing she was holding.

Giggling, Casey said, "It won't hurt you, Beatle."

"What *is* that thing?" Truck asked, seeming more interested than disgusted.

"It's a Hercules beetle," she told him, stroking the head of the insect as if it were a pet hamster rather than a creepy-looking alien bug.

It was as big as her hand. It was sitting on the fleshy part of her thumb with its jaws opening and shutting as she ran a finger over the olive-green hard shell of its back. The mouth was shaped like a giant pincher. It looked like it could take her finger off with one chomp.

"Maybe you should put that down," Beatle said carefully, wanting to knock the insect out of her hand then stomp on it, squishing its guts all over the jungle floor.

"Seriously, it's harmless," she told him. "I know it looks like it would bite, but it only eats fresh and rotting fruit. It won't and can't hurt humans. Some people keep them for pets. I've heard they can even be trained to do little tricks."

Beatle shuddered. He couldn't imagine having one of those things in his house voluntarily. He forced himself to look away from the giant bug and instead looked at something more pleasing…Casey.

She was smiling and looked more relaxed than he'd seen her since he'd met her. Bugs really *were* her thing.

"We need to keep going," Truck said gently.

"Right," she agreed. Stepping to the side, she held her hand over a log on the ground and the beetle happily waddled off her thumb onto it. "I wish I had my camera," Casey said a little mournfully. "I took a bunch of pictures of these guys…before…but I have no idea where it or my notes are now.

"Actually, I think the government packed all your stuff and sent it home with the other women," Truck told her. "We don't know if they have your ID and passport, but we can get you out with the birth certificate Blade brought. Hopefully your camera is with your stuff though."

Casey brightened. "Really? Awesome! Maybe Astrid, Jaylyn, and Kristina can finish their research." Then her shoulders slumped and she added, "That is…if they're up to it."

Beatle couldn't stand her dejected look and put his hand on her shoulder. "I won't lie, they were pretty shaken up. But they weren't assaulted, and I think with some counseling, they'll be okay."

"Really?"

Beatle stared down into Casey's luminescent green eyes. "Really," he reassured her. Putting a hand under her elbow, he steered her back onto the slight trail they'd been following. He moved his hand down her arm until his fingers grasped hers once more.

They were silent for a good five minutes or so, before Beatle asked, "What got you interested in bugs?" He honestly wanted to know, but he also wanted to keep her mind occupied with something other than the heat and discomfort of hiking through the jungle.

"It was Aspen, actually."

"Blade?" Truck asked from behind them. "This I gotta hear."

Beatle heard the smile in her voice as she recounted the memory. "He was always doing stuff to try to gross me out, but when I was eight and he was ten, he brought home his class's cockroaches. I guess every kid had a chance to bring them home for a week to study them. They were required to do some sort of report on what they are and their activity. Anyway, he thought he'd be funny and he took one out and held it in my face, thinking I'd scream and run away. But I had the last laugh. The roach jumped off his hand and onto his face. *He* was the one who started jumping up and down and yelling hysterically. The bug crawled under his shirt, and he was hopping around, slapping at himself and crying, trying to get it off him."

Casey paused to chuckle, and Beatle swore the sound reverberated through his heart. He loved to hear her laugh. Seeing her happy and carefree was something he knew he'd strive to always give her…if he had that chance.

"What happened?" Truck asked.

"I saw the cockroach fall to the ground as he was hopping all over the place. I scooped it up, because I knew Mom would freak if she learned there was one loose in the house. I put it back in its container with the others, but didn't tell Aspen. He continued to cry and carry on for another ten minutes, sure he was gonna be eaten alive by the tiny little thing. I got sick of his caterwauling and finally told him I had caught the stupid thing."

"Let me guess, he never tried to freak you out with

another bug," Beatle said dryly.

"Of course not," Casey said smugly. "Not only that, but I blackmailed him. Told him I'd tell the girl he wanted to smooch all about how scared he was of a little bug if he didn't agree to take over my chores for the rest of the school year."

"And did he agree?" Truck asked.

"In a hot minute," she said with a smile.

"And what were your chores?" Beatle asked.

"Vacuuming once a week, putting the dishes in the dishwasher every night, and picking up dog poop."

Both Beatle and Truck chuckled.

"Yeah, he wasn't thrilled, but he did it without complaint. One thing about Aspen I've always admired is that when he says he's going to do something, he does it. Anyway, so throughout that week when he had those cockroaches, I watched them. They fascinated me. Did you know that a cockroach can live a week without its head? It breathes through little holes in its body. It only dies because it can't eat or drink. Oh, and they can hold their breath for forty minutes, so they can survive being submerged underwater for long periods of time."

"Oh my God. I'm hiring an exterminator the second I get home," Beatle muttered under his breath while suppressing a shudder.

He almost grinned when he heard Casey laugh at him. Almost.

"Cockroaches are believed to have originated more than two hundred and eighty *million* years ago. That's so amazing to me."

"Can we please stop talking about cockroaches?" Beatle pleaded.

"So…you don't want to know that I have five Madagascar hissing cockroaches as pets back home, do you?"

Beatle stopped walking altogether and turned to face Casey. "Please tell me that's a joke."

She was grinning from ear to ear, clearly enjoying his discomfort. "Nope."

Beatle closed his eyes and sighed. "Great. Just great."

"You re-thinking this, Beatle?" Truck teased.

"Fuck off," Beatle told his friend.

"They're really not that bad," Casey soothed. "They're fascinating. I love to hear their hiss, it's amazing."

Beatle could only shake his head in disbelief. He turned and continued walking.

"Anyway, so my fascination with bugs started with those cockroaches Aspen brought home. Now I get to share with others how interesting they are, and take trips to different countries and see the insects I study firsthand…although, maybe that last part isn't really a good thing."

Wanting to take her mind off what she'd been through and bring back the smile and giggles, Beatle

SUSAN STOKER

asked, "What do you see as we're walking?"

"What do you mean?" she asked from behind him.

"All I see is leaves, dirt, and places someone could jump out and ambush us. What do *you* see when you're here in the jungle?" he clarified.

Casey was quiet for a couple of minutes, and he was afraid he'd lost her to the horror she'd been through. He looked back and saw that, while she was walking slowly, she was looking around her as if she hadn't ever seen a forest before.

"Life," she said finally. "I see life."

"Show me," Beatle ordered.

"To your right, on that log, is a bunch of click beetles. Those are some of the bigger ones...around two or three inches. But they like to forage for food in the warmer climates of the jungle. See the holes near the base of that log over there?"

Beatle turned to see where she was indicating. He nodded when he saw what looked like a simple hole in the ground.

"That's a tarantula cave. They get a bad rap, as they're generally very shy and not aggressive at all toward humans. They hunt mostly at night. Crickets, bugs, and other smaller spiders. Costa Rica has some of the more interesting species of tarantula. The Bluefront, Zebra, and Tiger Rump are a few."

Beatle hurried them along, away from the hole. He

didn't like bugs, but he *really* didn't like spiders. He recalled the movie *Home Alone* and the way the one bad guy screamed when the tarantula was placed on his face. Yup, that would totally be him if he woke up and had one crawling on him. And he wouldn't even be embarrassed about it.

"Can you maybe point out some pretty things, sweetheart?" he begged.

"Look up," she said after a moment.

Beatle stopped their little procession and did as she asked.

"Costa Rica has around fifteen hundred different species of butterflies. But one of the most beautiful and well known is the Blue Morpho."

Beatle stared at the little flying creatures above their heads. The electric-blue wings of the butterflies were easy to see amongst the green backdrop of the canopy. He lowered his head and looked at Casey.

She had her head back and was staring up at the life swirling and whirling above them.

"Aren't they beautiful?" she asked.

"Beautiful," Beatle agreed, not taking his gaze from her face.

After a moment, she lowered her head and smiled at him. "See? Bugs aren't so bad."

"Humph," Beatle snorted. "How you doin'? You need to stop and rest for a bit?"

Casey shook her head. "I'm okay."

He didn't insult her by asking if she was sure. But he did look over her head at Truck, and gave him a meaningful look. The other Delta nodded gravely, telling him without words that he'd be sure to keep his eye on their charge.

"What about you?" Casey asked after they'd started walking again. "What made you want to join the Army?"

Beatle shrugged. "I'd like to say it was a love for my country, but that'd be a lie." He fell silent as he thought about his life before he'd joined the military. He guessed he'd been silent for a bit too long, because he felt Casey gently squeeze his fingers in support. Even that small gesture warmed his heart. He'd never met anyone as good as Casey. She hadn't carried on and bitched about the fact they had to walk out of the jungle. She hadn't been hysterical or inconsolable about what had happened to her, even though she had every right to be. She didn't complain about being hungry, thirsty, or in pain, but he knew she had to be feeling all three of those things.

"My folks didn't have a lot of money. We lived in a piece-of-shit apartment and many times went without a lot to eat in order to pay rent. My mom did what she could, but since she didn't have a GED or high school diploma, any jobs she could get were crap. My dad did his best, but he was gone a lot since he worked at a factory in the next town over."

Taking a deep breath, Beatle looked straight ahead as he told Casey his story. Truck knew it; the team had plenty of time to talk and learn about each other while on missions. "You talked about Blade bringing home cockroaches to study. Well, I didn't have to worry about bringing any home in a nice sterile, plastic container...they had free run of our apartment. It became a habit to pound my shoes on the floor every morning to dislodge any that had taken up residence there. Any food we accidentally left out was completely inedible by morning because of the roaches helping themselves to it."

Casey's hand shifted in his, and he felt her thumb brushing back and forth on the inside of his wrist. She was showing empathy, but he was afraid to turn around and look her in the eyes, not wanting to see pity.

"Anyway, I was working as many hours as possible by the time I was a sophomore. I wanted to help my folks in any way I could. I got a job as a busboy at a local restaurant. I'd go right after school and work until ten at night when they closed. Wages were shit, but every little bit helped. My grades sucked because I never had time to do any homework or study. I knew I wasn't going to get accepted to any university, and we didn't have the money for me to go anyway. So joining the military seemed like the best solution at the time."

"How'd you choose the Army over the other branches?" Casey asked softly.

"Honestly?" Beatle asked.

"Always."

"They offered me the most money."

She chuckled. "That actually makes sense."

"Yeah. And they offered me five thousand more in a signing bonus if I agreed to eight years instead of the usual four. I didn't even hesitate."

"Ask him what he did with all the money," Truck said.

When Beatle didn't immediately offer up the answer to Truck's statement, Casey squeezed his hand. "What'd you do with the money?" she asked.

Beatle shrugged. "Put a down payment on a new apartment for my folks, one in a better part of town. Paid the first two years' rent so they didn't have to worry about it."

"He still sends money home," Truck said quietly. "I met his parents a couple of years ago, and they told me they're doing fine now and don't need his money, but he refuses to stop sending it. Gave them the money for the down payment on their cabin in Tennessee too."

Beatle was embarrassed, but continued walking. "They worked their butts off to try to make my life happy when I was growing up. We might not have been rich, but I knew without a doubt my parents loved me and each other. It's the least I can do for them...let them have a life without so much worry. Now they can afford to go out to eat and not worry about what bill might not be paid if they splurge. They took care of me for eighteen years, now it's my turn to give back." He shrugged a little self-consciously. "It's what a kid should do for their parents."

Feeling ill at ease when no one said anything, Beatle hurried on. "Turns out, I was good at being a soldier. Much better than I was a student or busboy. I attended a mandatory information session about Delta Force and decided to go for it. And here I am," he finished somewhat lamely.

"Well, I for one am very glad you're here," Casey said softly, her thumb still moving back and forth over his skin.

Beatle smiled. "Me too," he whispered.

Just then, the radio in his ear sprang to life. Beatle stopped abruptly and put a hand up to his ear to try to make sense of what Hollywood was yelling about.

"Ambush, ambush! One mile ahead of you. There's at least—"

The transmission cut off, but not before Beatle heard a hail of gunfire over the radio. The sound of the weapons firing echoed through the forest as well. He whipped around to look at Truck. The other man had pulled out his rifle and was standing right at Casey's back.

Casey's eyes were wide and scared as she looked from Beatle to Truck. "That sounded really close. Are the others okay?"

Beatle held up a hand to forestall any more questions until he knew what the hell was going on with his teammates.

"Beatle, route to Guac is compromised. Repeat, compromised. They keep yelling to find the woman," Coach barked. "Did you hear me? They want Casey! Switch to Plan B. Head west toward the mountain. Toward Volcan Orosi. Then south along its outskirts. We'll meet up as soon as we can."

"Fuck," Truck swore.

"What?" Casey asked, sounding panicked.

Beatle dropped his hand from his ear and turned to face Casey. He untangled his fingers from hers and put both hands on her shoulders. "Change of plans. We can't go the direct route to Guacalito anymore."

"Why? What's wrong?" she asked, her face pale and pupils dilated.

"The guys ahead of us ran into a little trouble. We're just going to skirt around them and head west for a bit."

"But you said the town is south of here. There's nothing to the west except the mountains and more jungle. I don't want to be in the jungle anymore!" The last came out as more of a panicked whine than a statement, and he had a feeling she'd hate it if she knew it.

Beatle hated the fear on her face, and the fact that whoever was attacking his teammates were specifically looking for Casey made his skin crawl. There was no way in hell he was letting them get their hands on her again. He knew without a doubt she wouldn't survive a second round of captivity. Not if it was anything like the first. As he'd told her earlier, he'd kill or die to keep her safe and get her home. "I know, but you're gonna have to trust us on this, sweetheart. Trust *me*. I *will* get you home."

Beatle watched as Casey struggled with herself and her fears. Her hands came up and clenched the T-shirt at his waist. She was breathing hard, but kept her eyes on his. After a long moment—of which they didn't have—she nodded.

"Good. And this sucks, because you were doing so well, but we need to move fast right now."

"Okay, I can do it."

Beatle shook his head. "No, you're not at top strength yet." He glanced at Truck, who nodded. Beatle looked back down at Casey. "Truck is going to carry you for a while, until we're out of this immediate area.

"No, I can walk fast," she protested.

Beatle moved his hands from her shoulders to her

hips, mimicking her hold on him, and leaned in. He lay his sweaty forehead against hers and said softly, "Not as fast as we need to move. I have no doubt if you were at one hundred percent, you'd be able to outrun any asshole who dared look at you the wrong way. But you and I both know you're not strong enough yet. The last thing I want is for your feet to get worse, or you to pass out because of dehydration. Truck can carry you easily. I swear."

He could feel her trembling in his grasp, but he held her gaze steadily. He was aware of time passing and knew they had to get going. Now. But still he waited. He didn't want to force this woman, who'd been so brave, to do anything. It needed to be her decision. But if she didn't make it soon, he'd have no choice but to make it for her.

"Okay," she whispered.

Beatle shifted and gave her forehead a brief but heartfelt kiss, then looked up at Truck. "Let's go."

The larger man nodded and took two steps to Casey's side. He picked her up as if she didn't weigh more than a small child and nodded at his fellow Delta.

Without a word, Beatle slipped his rifle from his shoulder and held it at the ready as he made his way deeper into the jungle. He wasn't thinking about how long their supplies would last now that their trek would take longer. He wasn't thinking about his teammates, who were obviously under heavy fire.

No, his only thoughts were to keep Casey safe—and to wonder who the hell wanted her so badly they were ready to take on a fully armed team of Special Forces soldiers to get her back.

Chapter Nine

CASEY WASN'T SURE exactly what was going on, but she was scared out of her mind. She'd been frightened when she was first kidnapped, and of course when she'd been thrown into the deep, dank hole. But she'd thought she was fine after being rescued. In pain, yes. Thirsty and hungry, yes. But she'd never thought she'd be headed deeper into the jungle than she'd ever been before, on the run from an unknown threat.

It was scarier this time because she knew exactly what was in store for her if she was recaptured. She had no doubt whoever was after her would kill Truck and Beatle if they could. And that freaked her out even more.

She shifted her grip on Truck's neck and felt him adjust her to a more comfortable position in his arms. She was grateful he hadn't thrown her over his shoulder like a sack of potatoes, but honestly, while being carried like this might seem romantic and comfortable, it was anything but.

Her feet were numb from his tight grip under her

knees and her neck hurt from keeping her head twisted to the side to watch where they were going. She could've rested her head on Truck's shoulder, but that seemed weird.

He was completely solid under her, every muscle tense as he half-walked half-jogged through the forest. Casey had the chance to be up close and personal with the scar on his face she'd noticed back at camp, but hadn't really paid any attention to before.

It was nasty. Running the length of his cheek and down his neck. It was completely healed, but she could see the additional small round scars on either side of it, where staples or some bad stitches had once held the skin together. Not only that, but his nose had obviously been broken at some point, because it was frightfully crooked. His lips were pressed together in a thin line of concentration, and he didn't even seem to notice her scrutiny.

Casey might've been feeling many things, but fear of the man who held her tightly in her arms wasn't one of them.

She swallowed hard and readjusted her arms once more when her hands slipped on his slick neck. They were all wearing long-sleeve shirts and trousers. It was asinine to wear anything less in the middle of the jungle. It made the heat even more unbearable, but the sweat and stickiness was much preferable to being eaten alive by the mosquitos that thrived in the damp environment.

She was beginning to think Truck and Beatle were actually machines with skin stapled on, not completely human, and could keep up the insanely fast pace all day, when they came to a halt.

"We'll rest for a bit here," Beatle said, even as he kept his watchful eye on the jungle around them.

Truck leaned over and placed her on her feet, keeping his arm around her waist until he was sure she could stand by herself. He unclipped the canteen from around his waist and held it out to her.

Casey blinked at him. He'd offered her something to drink before taking anything himself. Which was crazy, because she wasn't the one who'd been burning calories by running through the jungle.

She shook her head. "No, you need it more than me."

Truck opened his mouth to respond, when Beatle spoke up. He held out his own canteen to her. "Here, use mine," he ordered.

Casey looked up at him. His forehead was covered in sweat and she could see the tracks where it had dripped down his temples. There were sweat marks around his neck and under his armpits. She knew from watching him jog in front of her for the last hour that his back was also soaked with sweat. Compared to him, she was as fresh as a daisy.

"Have you had your fill?" she asked, not reaching for the water.

In response, Beatle reached out, grabbed her hand and wrapped it around the canteen. "Drink, Casey. You need the water as badly as we do."

"But I haven't been the one jogging through the jungle," she protested.

Beatle leaned in so close she could see the individual hairs of his beard growing in. "True. But *you* were the one who not too long ago was in a hole in the ground with no fresh water. *Drink.*"

As if in a trance, Casey brought the canteen up to her mouth and took a swallow. It wasn't fresh, it tasted metallic and like the purification tablets he'd used to make sure it was safe to drink. It was also warm; it had been so long since she'd had anything cold to drink, she almost didn't remember how good it was. But she couldn't deny her thirst once she started.

She forced herself to stop, but Beatle merely put his hand on the bottom of the metal container. "Finish it."

"But—"

"All of it, Case. I can get more."

She didn't know where he would, but she did as ordered. She drank until the entire canteen was gone. She licked her lips to catch the stray droplets, and went to wipe her mouth on her sleeve. But Beatle stopped her. He ran his thumb over her bottom lip, collecting the missed beads of water there, and brought his hand up to his mouth without losing eye contact with her.

The move was sensual, and Casey wanted nothing more than to throw herself into his arms and beg him to kiss her, but within seconds, the moment disappeared when Beatle took the canteen from her and stalked back to his pack.

She would've been embarrassed about her attraction to him, except she knew without a doubt he liked her as much as she did him. She could see it in the way his eyes raked her body. How he took care of her. How his pupils had dilated when she'd licked her lips after drinking the water.

But he knew as well as she did that, in the middle of the jungle, while they were on the run from whoever wanted to make sure she didn't make it out of Costa Rica alive, wasn't the time or place to act on their attraction.

"We'll rest here for a couple of minutes, then get going again," Truck informed her. "If you need to use the ladies' room, do it now."

Right. Instead of being embarrassed, Casey simply nodded. This was her new reality. Just like drinking muddy water in that hole had been. She needed to do what was necessary to stay alive.

She looked around and headed for a large tree nearby. Feeling eyes on her, she turned and shivered when she saw Beatle looking at her. In that moment, she relaxed, not realizing how wound up she'd been until right then. But seeing how Beatle was watching over her, no matter what she was doing or where she was, made her understand that he'd been serious when he'd told her that he would do everything in his power to get her home.

If a bad guy burst through the trees at that moment, she knew without a doubt Beatle would take him down. It should've made her wary to be around him, knowing how lethal he was, but it did the opposite. His ability to deal with the violence that had wormed its way into her life was a balm to her soul.

She nodded at him and got a chin lift in return. He tapped on his wrist as well, telling her to hurry. She nodded again and disappeared around the tree.

Luckily, she was paying attention to what she was doing and didn't stand in the bullet ant mound to do her business. It looked like a bunch of mud wrapped around the base of the tree she'd chosen to do her business behind. At first glance, it appeared innocuous, but she knew from experience that, once disturbed, the ants would swarm, looking for whatever had dared to attack their colony.

She gave the mound a wide berth, making sure to be extra careful when choosing an appropriate place to pee. She finished quickly and took a moment to appreciate the beauty of the ants.

Casey had come to Costa Rica to research them. She and her students had spent hours in the jungle outside their camp near Guacalito, observing many different species of the formicidae family. Every colony behaved a little differently.

By far, her favorite ant was the leafcutter. Watching them scurry back and forth carrying three times their body weight in leaves was amazing. Not only that, but before they'd been kidnapped, she and the others had found a mound that was over eight feet wide. It was monstrous, and amazing to think it could contain more than seven million of the small creatures.

Casey knew the ants could be extremely destructive, both with their foraging of plants and by ruining infrastructure with their huge nests, but for the most part, they weren't aggressive. They could and would bite, but the result was usually only itchiness, and not all that painful.

Overhead, she heard the sounds of birds chirping and cicadas "singing." The wind rustled the leaves in the trees and she closed her eyes, soaking in the moment. She loved the jungle…at least, she had before her ordeal, and she really didn't want her unknown kidnappers to take that away from her.

Not sure how long she'd been standing there with her eyes closed, Casey took a deep breath and opened them, knowing she had to return to Truck and Beatle so they could get going again.

She gasped in surprise when she saw Beatle standing not too far from her. He looked relaxed enough, so she didn't think he'd come to find her because of imminent danger. He seemed more introspective as his penetrating gaze stayed glued on hers.

"Am I taking too long?" she asked quietly.

"No. I just wanted to make sure you were all right," he answered in a low, grumbly voice.

"What if I'd still been in the middle of...you know."

"Then I would've gone back to where I left Truck and pretended I didn't see you."

She liked how he didn't beat around the bush. The thought of him watching her do her business should've been uncomfortable, but for some reason, it wasn't. It was as if being here in the jungle together had reduced them to primitive roles. He was the protector, the leader, willing to do whatever it took to make sure she didn't come to harm. And she was...

Casey wasn't sure who she was. She didn't want to think of herself as the weak link, but she knew it was true. She knew about bugs, sure, but other than that, she didn't bring any other skills to the table. It was as if she were a toddler, completely dependent on Beatle and Truck to keep her safe and get her home.

She took a step toward Beatle, keeping her eyes on

his. Then, feeling bolder, took another. She continued until she was standing right in front of him. Without a word, he reached out and ran the backs of his fingers down her cheek with a feather-light touch.

The world seemed to drop away. It was just the two of them. They could've been standing in the middle of an eighteenth-century ballroom, for all she knew. She took a deep breath, then another.

His eyes flicked to her chest, then back up to her face. The glance was so fast, she would've missed it if she hadn't been watching him so closely. Her nipples immediately puckered under her shirt at the thought of him liking what he'd seen.

They were covered in sweat, not smelling or looking their best, but Casey had never felt so connected to another human being in all her life. Her hands came up and rested on the hard-as-rock muscles of his chest and she leaned against him.

The hand that had brushed against her cheek moved to the back of her head, and he shoved his fingers into her hair, dislodging the messy bun she'd put it in earlier that morning. Still without a word he tugged on the hair in his grasp, tilting her head back until her throat was exposed.

Casey's fingers curled into his pectoral muscles and she licked her lips.

"You have one chance to tell me you don't want

this," he warned her. His brown eyes looked black in the shadows of the trees.

Casey swallowed. This was the warrior she'd seen hints of. The conqueror, the badass Delta who took what he wanted. She could feel her pulse hammering in her neck and her breaths came out in small little puffs. "I want this," she said softly. "I want you."

The second the last word left her lips, his mouth was on hers, taking her as if he had every right. As if he'd fought a great battle and won her as a prize. As if she were the most precious thing in his life.

He didn't ease into the kiss. His tongue surged into her mouth and took what it wanted. When she tried to twine her tongue around his, he growled low in his throat and tugged on her hair, tilting her head back farther and asserting his control over her.

Casey acquiesced immediately, letting Beatle take what he wanted. And he wanted it all. He learned every inch of her mouth, tilting his head this way and that to make sure he'd tasted all of her. And she stood docile and willing in his arms, allowing him to devour her.

He pulled back way before she was ready, but Casey realized when he did that she was panting for air. Beatle didn't look at her, merely used the hand at her back to pull her close. She wrapped her own around his and clung to him. The hand at her hair relaxed but didn't pull away.

She could feel Beatle's heart racing and his quick breaths fluttering over her face. His cock was hard against her belly, but he made no move to thrust against her or otherwise make any move toward sating his obvious lust.

But he wasn't alone in his desire. Casey knew she was wet, and not from the tropical heat, which had reached its peak of the day. She was more turned on from a simple kiss—okay, maybe not so simple—than she'd been from foreplay with some of her previous partners.

She pressed against Beatle unconsciously, as if doing so would ease some of the sexual tension inside her.

It took several deep breaths, but he finally stepped away from her. His cheeks were flushed and she had a feeling his scratchy five o'clock shadow had made its mark on her face, but she didn't care.

"We need to keep moving," he said.

"Yeah, I know," Casey replied.

He looked deep into her eyes for another moment, then turned her so her back was to him. She was about to ask what he was doing when she felt his hands in her hair. Closing her eyes so she could memorize every second of this moment, Casey sighed when he gently pulled the rubber band out of her hair and did his best to fingercomb the tangled strands.

"Did I hurt you?" Beatle asked.

"No. It…it felt good."

He didn't respond, but she could feel the tension in his body relax a notch. He carefully bundled her hair into a ponytail and wrapped the rubber band around it. When he was done setting her hair to rights, he turned her again.

Casey let him move her where he wanted. She still felt a little drugged by his kiss and the way he'd felt against her.

"I'm not sure how much farther we're going today," Beatle said. "We've put some good distance between us and whoever ambushed the others, but I won't be comfortable until we're several more miles away."

"Okay," Casey said, nodding.

"You okay with Truck continuing to carry you?"

Casey looked up at the man who had somehow become the center of her world. She once again thought that maybe she felt this way because he'd been the first person she'd seen when she truly thought she was doing to die, but at the moment, she didn't care. She might have to go through therapy for the rest of her life when she got home to get over him, but home seemed like such a foreign concept right now, she dismissed the thought. For the moment, she was here, with Beatle, and she could tell by the passionate look in his eyes that he wanted her as much as she wanted him.

"It's not my favorite thing in the world, but it's obvious you guys can go much faster if I'm not fumbling along trying to follow you on my own two feet."

"I need both hands free to take out any threat that might show up unexpectedly."

Casey tilted her head at him in confusion for a moment, then realized why he was telling her that. "It's okay," she reassured him. "I'm all right with Truck."

"It's probably better anyway," he murmured, more to himself than to her. "If I had you in my arms, the only thing I'd be able to think about was laying you down and having my way with you." Then his eyes met hers again, and she felt the full force of his desire once more. "But mark my words, there will be a time when I do have you in my arms. I'll carry you to bed, and there'll be no escaping everything I have planned for you."

Casey's lips twitched, but she controlled the smile that wanted to come out. "I can't wait."

His nostrils flared, but he didn't respond verbally. Instead, he grabbed her hand and turned to head back toward where Truck waited for them. The big man didn't comment on the amount of time they'd been gone, and he had the decency to keep his thoughts about the beard burn on her face to himself. He merely shrugged his pack on and waited.

Beatle got himself sorted and gave Truck a chin lift. As if that was the cue he'd been waiting for, Truck came over to Casey.

"Ready?" he asked.

"Ready," she confirmed.

He bent over and picked her up as if her weight didn't even register. Before they'd gone two steps, Truck said, "There's a protein bar in my top left pocket. You need to eat."

Following the unspoken order, Casey reached in and grabbed the chewy bar. She'd never been a fan of protein bars. They had a weird consistency and took way too long to chew for her liking. But she consumed the calories without complaint, knowing the alternative, dying in a hole in the jungle, was way worse.

They hadn't been on their way for more than twenty minutes when Beatle came to a sudden halt. Casey felt Truck stiffen under her, immediately on alert.

Beatle gestured to the right, and he and Truck slowly eased to their left and behind a couple of large tree trunks.

Truck eased her down and set her on her feet. He and Beatle immediately shrugged off their packs and set them soundlessly on the ground. Then Beatle grabbed her hand and pulled her about twenty feet farther away from where they'd been walking.

He looked around the area and tugged her down until she was kneeling on the jungle floor.

"There's a group of people about a hundred yards to

our right. Truck and I are going to go and check them out."

Casey grabbed his arm and dug her blunt nails into his skin. "No, don't leave me here!"

Beatle took her face in his hands and forced her head up to his. "I'll be back."

Shaking her head violently, Casey pressed her lips together tightly. No, he couldn't leave her by herself. She'd die out here without him. She had no idea where they were. Couldn't make it back to Guacalito by herself.

"Shhhh, sweetheart, listen."

But she couldn't. The panic had risen in her until she couldn't hear or see anything other than being recaptured and thrown in another hole.

Then Beatle's lips were on hers.

She relaxed into his firm hold and allowed the pleasure of his touch to push back her panic attack.

Way before she was ready, he pulled away. "I. Will. Be. Back," he enunciated carefully. "Do you believe me?"

How could she not? The determination was clear to read in his eyes. But she also saw regret and frustration. He didn't want to leave her there any more than she wanted to be left. It was that knowledge that gave her the strength to nod and let go of his arms. She sat back on her heels and looked up at him.

"So fucking strong. Stay here. But if you hear anything, head that way," Beatle pointed behind her. "Just keep going as quietly as you can. I'll find you. Hear me? No matter where you go, I'll find you. Just stay safe. Okay?"

"Okay," she whispered. "You too."

He grinned then. "Piece of cake."

Then he was gone. One second he'd been squatting in front of her, and the next he'd disappeared.

Casey blinked. It was as if she'd conjured him in her mind. Was that it? Was she still in that hole and all this was a dream?

She pinched herself and winced at the pain in her arm. Nope, she wasn't dreaming.

She slowly stood and flattened her back against the tree trunk. She'd automatically checked for biting insects before she'd kneeled in the dirt and luckily hadn't spied any. Taking a deep breath, she tried to moderate her breathing.

It took a while, but she finally calmed down enough to think a little more clearly. Beatle wasn't going to leave her. Not when he and his team had gone to such great lengths to find her. She'd overreacted, and she vowed to try not to do that again.

How long she'd stood there giving herself a pep talk, Casey didn't know, but it seemed like forever. She knew time was skewed, especially since she was alone. Just when she was about to lose her mind, a scream sounded obscenely loud in the quiet jungle, then was abruptly cut off.

It sounded as if it was right next to her, and Casey realized whatever was happening was going on way too close. She walked as silently as she could to another tree, and hid behind that trunk. Then she did it again.

She slowly and carefully made her way from tree to tree in the direction Beatle had told her to go if she felt she was in danger.

She'd been hiding behind a tree for a minute or two when she heard something to her right. Thinking it was Beatle or Truck, she turned in that direction with a relieved smile.

But it wasn't either of the Deltas.

It was a man she recognized from when she and her students had first been taken.

She opened her mouth to scream, but the man was too fast. He was standing in front of her with a dirty hand clamped over her lips before a sound could escape.

Casey looked into his eyes and saw nothing but satisfaction.

In a heavy Spanish accent, he sneered, "*Hola*, professor. My boss has some unfinished business with you."

Chapter Ten

B EATLE WIPED THE blood off his KA-BAR knife and
looked around for Truck. They'd watched the
group of men for a while to see if they were going to be
a threat, and realized that yes, they were definitely
looking for Casey. It wasn't obvious if they were the
same group that had attacked the other team of Deltas,
but ultimately it didn't matter.

Through their quiet discussion, it was clear the men
were hunting for Casey, and knew they were headed for
Volcan Orosi. How the hell they'd known they'd
changed course and were headed for the mountain,
Beatle didn't know. But he wasn't going to let them get
their hands on Casey. No fucking way.

He'd heard them talking about how the boss had
promised the reward for whoever captured and brought
her back would be to get "first go" at her. She hadn't
been assaulted when she'd been taken the first time, but
it was obvious whoever wanted her, had changed their
mind.

Beatle had seen red, and the anger he'd been holding

back roared to life. The image of a broken Casey looking up at him with blank eyes haunted him. The kiss they'd shared had been more intense and intimate than anything he'd ever experienced. He hadn't meant to go all caveman on her, but he couldn't resist the urge to make sure she knew that even though Truck was the one carrying her, she was his. In every way.

He'd expected her to resist the over-the-top controlling way he'd taken her, but instead she'd melted in his arms. The hardest thing he'd ever had to do was pull away from her and keep walking, but if she was ever going to be safe, they needed to keep going.

Hearing the men laughing and joking about how they were going to violate her, and the enjoyment they'd take in her screams and pain, had flicked that deadly switch that existed inside every Special Forces soldier.

He'd nodded at Truck and they'd split up. They'd taken out two men before another Beatle had approached from behind turned at the last second. He'd been able to let out a bloodcurdling scream before Beatle had thrust his knife into his throat, ending the sound as abruptly as it had begun.

But the man's death scream had been enough to warn the others in the hunting party. They'd scattered, and Truck and Beatle had been tracking them down and taking them out one by one ever since.

But even as he absently wiped the blood off his

knife, Beatle was counting. One was missing. He looked around, scanning the jungle for any sign of the missing dead man walking.

Something made him turn toward where he'd left Casey. Maybe it was instinct, maybe it was something deeper, but suddenly he knew without a doubt the man they were hunting had found her.

A veil of red formed over Beatle's eyes as he and Truck stalked through the jungle. They were moving as fast as they could while still staying quiet. If he *had* found Casey, he wouldn't get far with her. Beatle would track him to the ends of the earth if he had to.

The sooner he found her, the less chance she'd be violated. Beatle wasn't sure if the man would be stupid enough to take the time to rape her in the jungle, knowing she wasn't alone, but if he'd hurt one hair on her head, he'd—

Beatle's thoughts cut off midstream when a loud scream echoed through the jungle, startling a few birds and sending them screeching upward. Without consulting Truck, knowing the other man was right on his heels, Beatle gave up all pretense of being stealthy and ran as fast as he could toward the sound.

Just when he was sure he was going to find Casey flat on her back on the ground, at the mercy of whoever had found her, he burst past a tree into a small clearing.

"Stop! Don't get near him!" Casey screamed as soon

as she saw them.

The man from the hunting party was standing between him and Casey, and Beatle wanted to rush up to him and slit his throat, but Casey's frantic words stopped him in his tracks.

The first thing he noticed was that she was holding her shirt closed with one hand. It had been ripped from the neck to the hem. He could see flashes of the pale skin of her belly, and it made him want to kill the man in front of her.

He watched from behind as the man undulated, slapping at his legs as he stood on one foot, then the other. It almost looked as if he and Casey were doing some complicated dance. When he'd shift to the right, Casey would lean to the left. When he stepped to the left, she made sure to take a big step to his right. She was clearly trying to stay out of arm's reach of the man. She was backed up against a large boulder, making it so she couldn't easily run away from the man. Beatle was confused, however, about why the man seemed more intent on hopping about than grabbing Casey again.

Beatle once more saw the fright in Casey's eyes, and the urge to kill the man who had torn her shirt rose hard and fast. He'd taken another step toward him when Casey yelled again, "No! Get back, Beatle! I mean it. *Look*."

She pointed to the man's legs.

Beatle saw what she meant then—and suppressed a shudder at seeing the ants swarming over the man's pants. Casey couldn't run away from the man because of the boulder behind her, and even bolting to one side was risky with the way the man was undulating and flailing about. She was trying to keep her eyes on the swarm of ants on the ground to make sure they didn't get anywhere near her. He figured if he'd been even a couple seconds later she would've made her move and gotten around him to flee.

He motioned to Truck to head to the right, and Beatle went to the left, making a wide circle around the whimpering man. The prospective kidnapper frantically continued to swat at his legs, trying to get the ants off him, but all that did was allow the insects to crawl onto his hands and arms.

The man suddenly screamed once more and took off running back the way Beatle and Truck had come.

They made it to Casey at the same time.

"Are you okay?" Beatle asked urgently.

Casey nodded, her eyes glued to where the man had disappeared. They could still hear him screaming and crying out in pain, but his cries were fading as he got farther and farther away.

Beatle put his finger under Casey's chin and lifted her head. "Are you okay, sweetheart? Did he hurt you?"

She shook her head, but clutched her tattered shirt

harder in her fist. Beatle's teeth ground together. He needed to examine her and see how much damage that asshole had done, but he needed answers first. "What happened?"

"I did what you said. When I heard you fighting with the men, I tried to get away from where it sounded like everyone was. But he found me."

"I gathered that, Case. What else?"

"Uh…" She looked down at her feet, then grabbed hold of Beatle with one hand and took a step to the side.

"Don't be afraid of me," he ordered gruffly, confused by her contradictory actions. "I'm not going to hurt you."

"Move, Truck," she said urgently.

Without asking why, Truck did as she asked, taking a step toward her.

"Look," she said, nodding to the jungle floor with her head.

Beatle looked down—and immediately saw what she was worried about.

Ants. A swarm of them. They weren't exactly moving their way, but they were way too close for comfort.

Making his decision, Beatle swung Casey up into his arms without a word. He took the long way around the clearing and the ants, and headed back to where they'd left their packs.

He didn't want Casey to see the aftermath of the

lopsided battle, but they did need to collect their supplies. Truck hurried ahead to clear the way of anyone they might've missed, but Beatle was fairly certain they'd killed everyone in the hunting party. That didn't mean there wouldn't be more people looking for them, but for now, they were safe.

Placing Casey back on her feet, Beatle ran his gaze over her. She was still clutching the sides of her shirt together, but there was a bit of color back in her cheeks. "What happened after he grabbed you?" Beatle asked as patiently as he could.

"He...he kept one hand over my mouth so I couldn't scream and backed me against a tree. He ripped my shirt open and said he..." She stopped and swallowed hard. Beatle had never been as proud of anyone as he was of Casey at that moment.

"He told me in broken English that he was going to rape me before he brought me to his boss. He was too busy mauling me to pay attention to his surroundings. I...I pushed him and caught him by surprise. I managed to shove him into another tree...and a bullet ant mound."

Beatle's eyes got round. "Those were *bullet* ants all over him?"

Casey nodded solemnly. "I haven't ever seen them in action, but the effect of him falling into their nest was almost immediate. He stood up within seconds, but it was too late. He let go of me when he fell, and I backed into that clearing and got trapped by that big rock. He followed me and was going to assault me, but then the ants started biting him."

She shuddered and her voice dropped to barely a whisper. "Intellectually, I knew the bites hurt, but I didn't truly understand how much."

Beatle kept his finger under her chin. "I'm so fucking proud of you, and I owe you an apology."

Her eyes came into focus and she looked at him in confusion. "For what?"

"I've been treating you like you're a damsel in distress. Someone who needs rescuing. But I underestimated you. You've been through hell, there's no doubt, but you have more strength running through your veins than I gave you credit for. You were in trouble but instead of giving up, or waiting for me and Truck to rush to your rescue like a helpless female, you used your head and saved yourself."

She shook her head, "No, Beatle, I—"

He moved his hands to her shoulders and interrupted her. "You were able to push the panic back and take stock of your situation. That takes an amazing amount of fortitude, sweetheart. Why do you think most men don't make it through Delta training? Yeah, many can't deal with the physical aspects of what they have to do, but it's more than that. I've seen professional soldiers freeze in situations not nearly as scary as what was happening to you. But you were able to think critically and come up with a solution to help you get away. And I should've known; you did the same thing in that fucking hole with your bra water filter. You would've died if you hadn't figured out a way to get water. I underestimated you, and I won't do it again. So, I'm sorry."

He could see his words were sinking in. The lost and frightened look eased from her face. She was still stressed and hurting, but the expression of horror over what she'd done was fading.

He continued. "I *also* have to admit that I wasn't sure about how painful that ant's bite could really be, but I believe you now. You're officially in charge of scoping out any area we decide to take a break in to make sure it's free of creepy-crawlies that'll hurt us. Okay?" He shuddered, thinking about accidentally tying his hammock on a tree covered in the bullet ants.

"Okay. I can do that," she said with only a hint of the terror she'd just experienced.

"Good. Now, will you let me take a look?" Beatle gestured to her chest with his head.

She stiffened. "I'm okay."

"I know this is hard, but I'm not going to cop a feel, sweetheart. I'm not doing this to get my jollies. I need to make sure you don't need any stitches or antibiotic cream. You know as well as I do that open wounds have a greater chance of being infected here in the jungle."

She stared up at him for a beat then dropped her arms.

Her shirt gaped open down the middle, but still covered her breasts. Moving slowly so as not to startle her, Beatle took hold of one side of her shirt and carefully peeled it back. He swallowed at the perfection of her breast. It was full and soft. They were definitely natural, hanging slightly on her chest instead of sitting unnaturally high, as silicone breasts tended to do. She had a large pink areola topped off with a dark mauve nipple. She turned her head to the side as his fingers brushed over the dark red spots the man's fingers had made when he'd harshly grabbed her.

Beatle's jaw hardened, but since she didn't have any open wounds, he carefully covered that breast back up and repeated his inspection on the other side of her chest. Her left looked similar to the right, except for four angry scratches above her nipple. Wishing the man had spent longer sitting in the bullet ant nest, Beatle covered her back up and called for Truck.

He knew the other Delta had been giving them privacy but Truck immediately appeared beside them. "She okay?"

"Yeah, mostly just bruises, but he got her with his fingernails. Got the antibiotic cream?"

Truck nodded and dug into a side pocket of his pack.

"You guys seriously have everything in there," Casey said in what Beatle knew was a forced lighthearted tone. She impressed him more and more with every minute he spent in her presence.

"Yeah well, you never know what you're going to need on a mission," Truck told her with a wink. He handed the small tube of cream to his teammate. "We need to get moving," he said, telling Beatle something he already knew.

"Give me four minutes," Beatle told his friend. Truck nodded and disappeared around the tree once more.

Without a word, Beatle pulled out a wet wipe and began to vigorously clean his hands. When he was done, he placed the used wipe into a pocket on his vest and opened the tube of cream. He squeezed a dollop onto his finger and turned to her. "Ready?" he asked softly.

Casey nodded and even reached for her ruined shirt herself. She peeled back the material, exposing herself to him.

The feeling of pride for her strength rose up in Beatle once more. He used his finger to lightly brush against the marks on her skin, coating the scratches with the ointment. The urge to lean forward and kiss her nipple was strong, but he suppressed it. The desire to kiss her there wasn't necessarily a sexual need. It was more of a tender gesture he ached to make.

He quickly finished, making sure the wounds were completely covered, then reached for the wet wipe he'd used earlier. He cleaned the rest of the ointment off his fingers before reaching into his pack once more.

"I don't have any extra buttons, but I can sew that closed for you."

Casey stared up at him in disbelief. "You carry a needle and thread with you?"

Beatle smiled for the first time since he'd been aware of the other men. "It's not for doing needlepoint projects in the jungle, sweetheart. Sometimes we have to sew each other up after a firefight. We all carry a set."

"Ah." Understanding lit her eyes.

"Hold still," Beatle told her, then leaned down and got to work with a quick and dirty repair of her shirt. Several minutes later, he stood. "There. It won't win any awards, but it'll keep the mosquitos off your beautiful skin."

Casey ran a hand down the middle of her shirt and stared up at Beatle. "Thank you."

"You're welcome. I would've let you wear one of mine, but you'd be swimming in it. Come on, my four minutes was over three minutes ago. Truck'll be chomping at the bit to get a move on."

He stopped in his tracks when he felt Casey's hand

on his arm. "I'm not sure that man'll die from those ant bites. He might wish he was dead, but unless he's highly allergic, he probably won't. A lot of natives go through a ceremony where they're bitten by bullet ants over and over to prove they're a man. I don't think he's from one of those tribes, but I don't know for sure."

"He's in no condition to do us any harm at the moment. My immediate concern is getting out of here. We'll deal with him later if we have to."

Casey nodded, then asked softly, "How'd they find us?"

"I have no idea," Beatle said. "But it doesn't matter. We're going to get to Guacalito and home, no matter what. With the three of us working together, we can do anything, right?"

She smiled then. A tentative movement of her lips, but Beatle would take it. Yes, he'd underestimated his woman, and he wouldn't do it again. She was nobody's damsel in distress. Dr. Shea was smart, beautiful, stubborn, and strong. He'd done her a disservice treating her any other way.

He'd wanted to carry her, but she refused. It bothered Beatle that she was obviously hurting yet still turned down his help. But he understood, especially after the attack. She wanted to take back some the helplessness she'd experienced over the last weeks. Wanted to show the world that she was strong and capable. But what she didn't believe was that he already thought that about her. She didn't need to prove herself to him.

Chapter Eleven

T HAT NIGHT, AS they made camp, Casey sat on the little stool Beatle had unearthed from his pack and tried not to think about how miserable she felt. They'd walked all day, trying to put as much distance from where they'd been attacked and where they'd spend the night.

She'd insisted on walking the rest of the day, forcing herself to ignore her aches and pains. And she had them. She'd never been as sore as she was right now.

Beatle had made sure she ate several protein bars over the course of the day and had been pressuring her to drink as much water as she could. But her stomach was finally rebelling. Just thinking about eating made her want to throw up.

She'd approved the area where they wanted to set up camp, there weren't any nests or mounds that she could see, and Beatle and Truck silently began to do their thing. They worked in tandem without talking. Each in charge of a different part of camp. Beatle set up the hammocks and began to get a meal put together. Truck headed for the stream they'd passed not long before to replenish their water and gather wood for a small fire.

She'd asked if she could help, but both men had shaken their heads and told her to relax on her stool. She was relieved, but irritated at the same time. Beatle had told her earlier that he didn't see her as a damsel in distress anymore, but she was feeling that way at the moment all the same.

Both Truck and Beatle kept shooting worried glances her way. Casey was trying to ignore them, but every time they looked at her, then at each other and communicated using their weird hand signals, it made her more and more frustrated.

Casey wanted to be home. Back in her own bed, safe in her apartment, not worrying about stepping on some sort of creature that would make her misery even worse. If she was going to barf, she wanted to do it in the privacy of her own bathroom and not in front of the man she had begun to have deep feelings for.

It was unfortunate that, in the midst of her own private pity party, Beatle wandered over and held out a plastic packet of food he'd heated, one of the MREs from his pack.

"Fettuccine with spinach and mushrooms," he told her with a smile. "Gourmet in the middle of the jungle, just for you."

"I'm not hungry," Casey told him quietly, wishing

he'd just leave her alone.

But he didn't. Instead, he crouched down and balanced on the balls of his feet in front of her, still holding the damn food out. The smell of the pasta made her want to hurl.

"Case, you need to eat. You need the calories."

"I don't like mushrooms or spinach," she said softly. It wasn't a lie. She knew she couldn't afford to be picky when they were in the middle of the jungle and on the run from some mysterious enemy who wanted her dead, but she was grumpy and didn't feel like choking down the meal right then.

"What's wrong?"

Casey wanted to burst out laughing at his question. Was he serious?

She glanced up at him and saw the concern clear on his face. He was looking at her as if he really cared, and he was definitely serious.

"Nothing," she told him and looked down at her hands in her lap.

"This isn't a situation where you can keep anything from me," Beatle said quietly. "If you're hurting, I need to know so I can do something about it. We still have a ways to go, and if you don't tell me what's wrong, it could affect me and Truck down the line."

Casey stared at her fingers. There was dirt under all ten of her fingernails. She figured it would be weeks before she was able to get it all out. Her nails were chipped and broken, and she had a feeling two would come all the way off eventually. She'd bent those nails all the way back the first time she'd tried to climb out of the hole she'd been in.

The unfairness of her situation hit her all at once.

Why? Why had this happened to her? She wasn't anyone special. She wasn't beautiful, hell, she wasn't even all that pretty. Back in Florida, she kept to herself. She didn't party every night. When she went out, she usually had a glass of wine or two, tops. She didn't have a lot of friends, mainly hung out with other teachers from the university. Why she'd been targeted was a mystery. Was it simply because she was American? Casey had no idea.

She'd come to Costa Rica to study ants, for God's sake! How had she ended up being kidnapped and running for her life through the jungle? It wasn't fair and it didn't make any sense.

"Casey?" Beatle asked gently.

Suddenly, everything was just too much. She was tired of all of it. She'd reached her breaking point, and unfortunately, Beatle was in her crosshairs.

"You want to know what's wrong?" she asked bitchily. "Where should I start? How about the fact that I was kidnapped? Then, not only was I kidnapped, I was singled out for some reason for special treatment and buried alive. But you got me out. Yay. Thanks. But now we're on the run from an unknown enemy and I'm scared to death they're going to get their hands on me again and do something worse than simply throw me into a hole."

Beatle didn't react other than to look back at Truck, who she hadn't heard approach. His look must've communicated something, because the other man came forward and took the MRE Beatle had been holding. He took a step away, but didn't go far.

Turning back to her, Beatle put his hands on Casey's knees and asked, "What else?"

Casey ground her teeth together so hard, they hurt. But she barely noticed the small pain over all the others. She let him have it.

"What else? How about *everything*? My feet hurt. At least I can feel them, but I'm not sure that's a good thing right about now. Every fucking muscle in my body hurts. Did you know your fingers had muscles? Well, they do, and mine hurt. Squatting to pee is like the most painful thing ever. Oh, and speaking of which, I don't have anything to wipe with after I go, and that makes me feel dirty, which is stupid because it's been so long since I've had a shower or bath, I shouldn't be able to feel dirtier than I actually am. I'm so disgusting right now I can barely stand myself. My shirt is covered in dirt and sweat, and now blood, which is just peachy, because I got gouged by that asshole back there, I had to show you my boobs, which in any other situation I would be glad to do, but not because you feel sorry for me, and to top it off, I'll probably end up with some sort of weird jungle disease as a result of him scratching me!"

She paused to take a breath then kept going. Now that she'd started, she couldn't seem to stop. "My head is pounding and I feel nauseous. I've been trying to eat and drink like you want me to, but I know if I put anything else in my mouth right now, I'm going to puke it all up. My teeth feel as if they're covered in fuzz because I haven't brushed them in who knows how long. I'm hurt that my students were picked up by those other soldiers and I was left behind. I'm scared of the dark now, I have a million mosquito bites that itch like crazy, and I just want to go *h-home*!"

Her voice cracked on the last word, and Casey was more than aware of how badly she was whining, but couldn't help it. Her eyes filled with tears and she squeezed them closed, willing them back. She bit her cracked bottom lip to try to regain her composure. She thought she'd done it, until she felt Beatle's hand brush over her hair in a tender caress.

That was the last straw. A sob escaped and the tears escaped her closed eyes and fell down her cheeks.

She felt Beatle moving in front of her and held on

tightly as he picked her up. His arm under her knees hurt, but she barely felt it amidst all her other complaints.

She sobbed as if her world was ending.

And it pretty much felt like it was.

Casey felt Beatle sit on something, then he was lying back, clutching her to him. She didn't tense up, didn't open her eyes to see what was happening. She was over it all. Done.

She felt the familiar feel of the hammock close around her and Beatle, but she still didn't open her eyes. Beatle shifted under her, getting comfortable, making sure *she* was comfy too.

He didn't tell her to shush. Didn't tell her everything would be okay. He simply rubbed her back and stroked her hair.

How long she cried in his arms, Casey had no idea, but eventually her tears tapered off and then stopped.

"Feel better?" he asked quietly.

Without picking it up from his shoulder, Casey shook her head.

"Feel worse?" he asked, and she could hear the humor loud and clear in his tone.

She shook her head again. "I'm not sure it's possible to feel worse than I do right now."

"Mmmm," Beatle said, still caressing her back.

"I'm sorry," she said softly.

"For what?"

"For turning into a raging bitch. You didn't deserve that."

"Was everything you said the truth?"

"Yeah."

"Then you have no need to apologize."

Casey sighed and lifted her head enough so she could see his eyes. "But you didn't deserve to be dumped on like that."

"Case, you've had a rough couple of weeks. You've held up extremely well. You don't have anything to apologize for."

"Aspen always said I was too whiny when we were growing up," she informed him.

"Yeah, well, I think any big brother would say that about their little sister. Cut yourself some slack, sweetheart."

They were quiet for a long while and Casey felt absolutely no need to move. In fact, she'd be happy if they never moved.

"I'm worried about you," Beatle said after a minute or two. "While you've done really well, I know your feet need more care than me and Truck can give them. I don't like that you're not hungry or thirsty. You should be both after how long you went without anything to eat and as little to drink as you had. I'm not surprised your muscles hurt, especially after being cooped up in that hole for as long as you were. I don't like that we don't know who is after you or why, either, but we don't have time to stop and try to figure it out right now. I'd do everything in my power to give you a hot bath with lots of soap, but that'll have to wait until we're back in civilization, I'm afraid."

"I'd kill someone for a bath," Casey mumbled.

Beatle squeezed her in reply.

"I'll try not to bring the bitch out again," she told him.

"Don't."

"What?" she asked, confused.

"If that was you being a bitch, I can handle it. Casey, I've already told you this, but you've held up so much better than I thought you would. Hell, you've held up so well, I'd forgotten exactly how much you've been through. I'm sorry for not recognizing you were nearing your breaking point. You were so brave and strong when we rescued you, I didn't pay close enough attention to see that you were experiencing delayed shock. You can't be expected to tromp through this jungle for days on end without a break. Especially not after what you've been through. I'm the one who's sorry for not looking past your strength and recognizing when you couldn't take any more. I know better."

"*We* know better," Truck added.

Casey startled so badly, if Beatle hadn't been holding her close, she would've fallen out of the hammock. She craned her head around and saw Truck sitting on the stool she'd been on earlier.

Truck shared a look with Beatle before saying, "Change of plans. Tomorrow, we're heading due west, straight for Guacalito. It's more important to get you to civilization and a doctor than it is to try to play hide-and-go-seek in the jungle."

"But, I can make it," Casey protested, even as part of her said there was no way in hell she could make one more day on the run.

"I'm sure if push came to shove, you could," Beatle soothed. "But you don't have to. Truck and I can take care of anyone else we might run into. It was second nature for us to automatically head farther away from our target in order to shake whoever was following us."

"But if we go back now, won't we run into more bad guys?"

"Maybe. Maybe not. But I'm going to radio the others in a second and they'll be on the lookout for them. They'll clear the area before we get there. Look at me," Beatle ordered.

Casey looked up at him.

"It's not good that you're nauseous, and not hungry or thirsty. It's not good that your feet hurt. I want to get those scratches deep-cleaned, and I just plain want to do everything in my power to make you feel safe again." He paused, then said, "Oh, and one more thing. There was no way I was going to leave this jungle without you. I would've done whatever I had to in order to find you and bring you home. I've done the former; it's time I get on with the latter."

Casey relaxed and put her head on Beatle's shoulder. "I'll eat the pasta. Just give me a bit, okay?"

"No rush, sweetheart," was his rumbled response.

They stayed in the hammock for a long time. Casey was aware of Truck moving around them, but not what he was doing. She didn't care. After a while, Beatle got out of the hammock. He took off her shoes and socks and doctored her feet as best he could. He strung up the mosquito netting so she didn't get any more bites.

Truck approached with a handful of pills. She didn't even ask what they were for. Merely took them without a word and choked them down. The water did threaten to come back up, but she managed to keep it down. She didn't miss the worried look on Truck's face though.

She just hoped whatever he'd given her would help with the pain throughout her body.

Casey got restless when the sun sank below the horizon, not liking the darkness that descended on their little corner of the world. The small fire didn't light up the area enough. Just when she thought she was going to scream, Beatle came over and climbed into the hammock with her.

"I can't do much about the night," he apologized.

"It's better when you're here," she told him honestly. "It's just when I'm alone that I start remembering the hole and imagining that I'm back there."

"Good. I also can't do anything about how I smell either," he joked. "I forgot to bring my Brut cologne."

Casey chuckled. "I can't tell the difference between your rankness and mine. It's fine," she said. After several minutes, she asked softly, "Are we really going straight to Guacalito?"

"Yeah."

"And it's okay?"

Knowing what she meant, Beatle replied, "It's okay. I can't say there aren't things we'll have to keep our eye on, but we need to get you out of here. Now is not the time to wander the jungle trying to ferret out the bad guys."

"Is that what we were doing?"

"Not us, but the others, yeah. We were just getting out of their way so they could hunt."

"Won't your boss, or commander, or whatever he's called, be mad that you didn't try to catch the bad guys?"

"Absolutely not. You held up so well and were so amazing as we set out that we all quickly forgot you'd been through something horrific. The mission isn't to figure out who and why right now. It's to get you out of here and home safely. Case. *You're* my mission."

She couldn't help but be hurt by his words. She didn't want to be a mission for him.

She'd told herself when she'd first been rescued not to fall for Beatle. That he'd rescued hundreds of people and what she was feeling was simply a result of being grateful he'd found her. "Okay," she whispered.

Obviously, some of her hurt came through with that one word, because Beatle said, "I didn't mean that the way it sounded."

"I know," she said woodenly, not believing her own words.

"Seriously. You are not simply a mission for me," Beatle insisted. "From the second I saw your picture, I wanted you. *You*, Casey. I was going to find you, or die trying. And if that doesn't convince you, maybe this will." He shifted her leg upward until her thigh was lying over his groin. "Does this feel like you're just a mission?"

Casey's eyes opened wide in the dark night, not that it helped her see anything. Beatle was hard under her leg. He shifted his hips and she couldn't help put press harder against his dick. She felt it twitch under her leg.

"We're both dirty as fuck. We smell like we've been rolling around in the dirt for days, which I suppose we sort of have. You're hurt and worried, and I don't give a fuck. Seeing you bare yourself for me earlier today would've been a dream come true if it wasn't for the situation. I've dreamed about you standing in front of me and slowly taking off your shirt while I watched. The thought of you standing before me wearing only a pair of panties, then sliding them down your long legs, is almost more than I can stand. All my cock wants to do is bury itself deep inside your hot, wet cunt." Beatle's voice had dropped, and he was practically whispering now. The desire was easy to hear in his voice.

"You are not a mission, sweetheart. I've never felt this way about anyone before. This isn't a result of me rescuing you. It's you. And me. I'm going to get you safely out of this jungle and back to the States because I want to explore whatever this is with you. You might not feel the same, but I aim to do what I can to try to make you come around to at least giving me a chance."

"It's not just you," Casey said, bravely shifting her leg to feel his erection once more. "I...want to explore whatever this is with you too. But...I'm not sure how it can work with you living in Texas and me in Florida."

"Thank fuck," Beatle breathed, then moved her leg off his hard cock. "We can figure out logistics later. First things first—getting out of this jungle. Tomorrow is gonna suck," he said bluntly. "We're gonna move hard and fast to get to Guacalito. From there, we'll meet up with the others and figure out our next steps and how to get to San José. The capital is bigger and it'll be easier for us to get lost in. We'll be able to blend in with the tourists better there than in one of the smaller cities."

"We won't have to walk there, will we?" Casey asked.

"To San José?" Beatle clarified.

Casey nodded.

He chuckled. "No. Hollywood or one of the others will get us a ride. We'll probably have to spend a bit of time in the capital, but if I know your brother and Ghost, they'll do whatever they can to get us clearance to leave as soon as possible. Unfortunately, the Costa Rican officials are going to want to talk to you. Since you were kidnapped on their soil, they'll at least go through the motions of trying to investigate. We haven't talked about exactly what happened yet, but I don't want you to worry about meeting with them."

"Will you..." Casey paused, then took a deep breath and continued. "Will you be there with me?"

"Absolutely. Nothing could keep me away."

"Because you want to know what happened?"

"Yes, but more importantly, I want to be there to support you while you recount it."

"Thanks," Casey whispered.

"You're welcome. Getting you to San José will also give me a chance to get you to a real doctor."

"I don't want to see a doctor here," Casey protested, then shuddered. "I just want to go home."

"I know. But I'll make sure whoever Ghost finds is on the up and up. I'm not going to let anyone do anything that will hurt you further."

Casey swallowed and the tears threatened again. She felt so...off. Crying wasn't like her. "Okay," she said softly.

"I know your life is in Florida," Beatle said, "but there are schools in Texas too."

Her breath hitched in her throat at his implication.

"I can't exactly change where I'm stationed, and that sucks, because I don't like that you'd have to be the one to sacrifice if things work out the way I want them to. We'll take it slow. Date long distance for a while. Talk every night via Skype and the phone. I'll take leave and come see you, and maybe you can make it out to Texas here and there too."

"I'd like that," Casey told him. It wasn't as if she'd thought they were going to land back in the States and immediately get married, but hadn't thought he'd come right out and say that he wanted to keep seeing her, either. Not after two days of knowing her.

"Sleep, Case," he ordered. "Tomorrow will be a long day. I'll give you as many painkillers as possible, but you're going to have to make yourself eat something in the morning. And drink throughout the day."

"I will," she told him. "I just had a momentary pity party. I'll be better tomorrow."

"Don't ever hide how you're feeling from me," Beatle said. "I want to know how you're really doing. I might not be able to do anything about it, but don't ever think that you're whining. Okay?"

"I'll try," she said.

"Good."

"Troy?" She didn't know why she'd used his real name, but it popped out.

"Yeah, sweetheart?"

She could hear the feeling in his words. He obviously liked it when she called him Troy. "Thank you for finding me."

"That's something you don't ever have to thank me for, Case. Now sleep."

BEATLE HELD CASEY tightly long after she fell into an exhausted and uneasy sleep. He and Truck had talked before he'd joined her in the hammock and agreed that they'd pushed her too hard. She wasn't strong enough to be tromping through the jungle. They'd misstepped there. Since she hadn't complained, they'd assumed she was fine. She wasn't.

He'd heard Truck talking to the rest of the team on the radio earlier. The plan was just as he'd told Casey. They'd turn and head in a straight line for Guacalito. If someone got in their way, they'd simply kill them. It was more important to get her back to the States than to search for her kidnappers.

But the feeling that he'd missed something nagged at Beatle. The entire kidnapping wasn't like anything they'd ever experienced before. Whoever had been the mastermind behind it was smart, but Beatle knew no one was perfect. The kidnapper had left breadcrumbs somewhere. They could be tracked.

But as he'd told the woman in his arms after her mini-breakdown, there was time to figure out the who and why later. His main concern was Casey.

He was more relieved than he could say that she seemed to want to see where a relationship between them could go when they got back to the States. They had a lot of hurdles ahead of them. He was stationed in Texas and her job was in Florida. He couldn't exactly up and move...unless he quit.

The thought of leaving his teammates hurt, but the thought of never seeing Casey again hurt more. He'd fallen hard and fast and wasn't ashamed to admit it. He'd seen how happy his teammates were with their women, and he wanted that for himself. With Casey.

She hadn't lied, they were both pretty rank, but it didn't matter. She was alive and in his arms; he didn't care what they smelled like. Beatle kissed Casey's forehead and closed his eyes.

His dreams were filled with horrific visions of finding Casey in the hole, but this time he'd been too late. Of her dying in his arms as they hiked through the jungle. Of her stepping into a bullet ant mound and screaming in pain.

After each vision, he jerked awake, only to find her sleeping safe and sound in his arms. Right there and then, in the middle of the Costa Rican jungle, Beatle vowed to figure out who had kidnapped her and the other women, and why.

"I'll make sure you always feel safe," he whispered.

He didn't sleep any more that night, simply held the amazing woman in his arms tightly and watched over her.

Chapter Twelve

THEY DIDN'T MAKE it to Guacalito the next day, but they made good progress. Casey knew both Beatle and Truck were keeping a close eye on her, making sure she was eating, drinking, and trying not to push her too hard. Which she appreciated more than she could say.

They'd camped for another night without any issues. Then they'd started out once more.

When they'd been walking for several hours, Beatle stopped them.

"We're close, sweetheart," he told her gently. "I'm going to scout ahead and meet up with Hollywood, Coach, and Fletch. Get the lay of the land.

The thought of seeing the town of Guacalito again made Casey's breath catch. She'd loved the little town when she'd first seen it. The people who lived there had welcomed them with open arms. They'd seen many researchers from the university over the years and liked the tourist dollars they brought with them.

The thought of any of the men or women she'd met betraying her...that hurt. Had one of the townspeople been behind their kidnapping? Someone who didn't like the Americans coming there? Something niggled at the back of Casey's mind. She tried to concentrate on whatever it was, but before she could bring it into focus, Beatle was speaking.

"Stay here with Truck, Case. I'll be back as soon as I can. I'll be in contact with him, so if you guys need to move, I'll find you. Okay?"

She nodded. "Okay. Go. Do your thing. The faster you meet up with your teammates, the faster I'll get that shower I've been dreaming about."

The smile that spread across Beatle's face was worth her forced lightheartedness. The truth was, she hated the jungle now. Everything about it. And she felt horrible about that. She'd spent her life wanting nothing more than to immerse herself in the sounds and smells of the jungle. Studying bugs meant everything to her. Still did. But now she'd have to change her focus from insects that thrived in the jungle, to those that lived elsewhere.

But being on edge, on the run, and having to make sure the creatures she'd once adored wouldn't kill any of them, had ruined her joy for the forest. The pain inside felt as if she'd lost a person she loved.

Pushing back her morose thoughts and vowing to speak to her friend, who happened to be a psychology professor, when she got back to Florida, Casey tried to smile at Beatle.

She must have been in her head for too long, because when she focused back on Beatle, his smile was gone. He leaned his forehead against hers and tenderly grasped the nape of her neck in his large hand. Her hands came up and clutched the sides of the vest he wore.

They didn't say anything, simply held on to each other. Finally, he pulled back and kissed her forehead tenderly. "I'll be back soon," he said, then turned and strode off into the jungle, disappearing within seconds.

Casey sighed and stared at where she'd last seen him. There was a lump in the back of her throat and she felt off-kilter. *He'll be back. You need to get a grip. In a few days, he's going to walk out of your life and there's no guarantee you'll ever see him again. He's just doing his job. This attraction is probably a result of the danger, stress, and adrenaline.*

As if he could read her mind, Truck said softly, interrupting her internal pity party, "I've never seen Beatle like this before."

Casey turned her head and looked at the large Delta Force soldier next to her. He gestured to the small stool Beatle had left.

Wanting more information about Beatle, but feeling shy, she asked, "Really?"

When she was seated, Truck sat on his own stool. "Really."

"Mmmm," Casey said. She liked Truck, but didn't

really know him all that well.

"You remind me of my Mary," he said out of the blue.

Casey's eyes widened. "Mary?"

"Yeah. She's literally one of the strongest women I know. But she's also stubborn. Doesn't like to accept help from anyone, least of all me. Even when she needs it, she fights me helping her."

Casey bit her lip. Yeah, that sounded a lot like her. She loved her parents, but they'd raised her to be a little *too* self-sufficient. She'd learned how to change a tire when she was twelve. She was driving herself to high school activities as soon as she had her license. Her mom did everything she could to make sure her daughter was independent.

Aspen had helped. He didn't coddle her, as some big brothers did to their little sisters. Oh, he'd protected her when a boy at school didn't take her refusal to date him well, but for the most part, he'd had his own stuff going on when they were teenagers.

It was hard for her to ask for help. Really hard. Besides, she knew a lot of people who had tough lives. Bad marriages, struggling to make ends meet, special needs children, chronic illnesses…the issues she had didn't come close to stacking up. So she'd learned to muddle along as well as she could on her own. There were times she ached to have someone to share her life with, but for the most part, she didn't mind being single. She had a good job, made decent money, and was content to hang out with and talk to the other professors at the university.

"I'm just used to doing things on my own," Casey said lamely, when the silence between her and Truck had gone on too long.

"So is Mary. But she's learning that it's okay to lean on someone else. That having someone help you doesn't mean you're weak. That the sharing of a burden actually makes you stronger in the long run."

"I'm glad she has that," Casey told Truck.

"Yeah. I'm doing what I can to break down her walls and let her see that her past doesn't have to define her future, and that the people around her love her and would move heaven and earth to be there for her."

"You included?"

"Especially me."

"You love her?"

"With all my heart."

"She love you?"

Truck hesitated, and Casey's heart broke for the giant man sitting next to her. It was more than obvious he wanted to say yes, but after a moment, he shrugged. "I'm not sure she even *likes* me all that much some days. But ultimately it doesn't matter. I'm going to do whatever it takes to make sure she's healthy. And if, after she gets that clean bill of health, she walks away, it'll hurt like nothing I've ever experienced before. But she'll be alive. The alternative is unacceptable."

Casey couldn't imagine anyone not liking Truck, but she had a feeling he was leaving out a lot. A thought struck her. "She's not rejecting you because of your scar, is she?" The question came out a bit more brusque than she wanted it to, but she couldn't help but feel pissed that the unknown Mary might reject the amazing man in front of her because of the gnarly scar that bisected his cheek and pulled his lips down into a perpetual frown.

Surprisingly, Truck smiled. "No, Casey. She doesn't give a shit about my scar. I think I annoy her just by being in the same room as her. But...I'm taking heart from the fact that she's slowly getting less and less prickly around me. I'm going to call that a win."

"I don't know your Mary, but I have to say, if *you* love her, she has to be worth the fight for her heart. She'll come around. How could she not? I haven't known you very long, and if I didn't feel the," she hesitated, trying to come up with the right word, "pull toward Beatle that I do, I'd probably do everything in my power to get you to notice me."

He chuckled. "Thanks. I needed to hear that. Anyway, as I was saying earlier, you remind me of her. You're both stubborn and think you can do everything, get through everything, on your own. There's nothing wrong with accepting help, Casey. Whether that's from Beatle, or your parents, or even from a shrink when you get home."

She flinched at the mention of the shrink.

"I know, you don't want to talk about what happened, but you need to. You have to. The Army hasn't always been proactive about getting soldiers help after they've been deployed, but they're getting better."

"I'll talk to Beatle."

"That's good, you should, but it's not the same as talking to a clinical psychologist. Someone who's trained on how to help you."

Casey thought about Truck's words. She knew he was right, and she'd even told herself the same thing earlier, but she hated the idea of even thinking about this country again once she'd left it. "Okay," she said softly.

"Think about it," Truck told her. "You work at a university, there has to be a medical facility on campus, right?"

She nodded.

"You might feel more comfortable talking to someone there. Or if you want to keep your work life separate from what happened, you can find someone at a nearby hospital. But the important thing is to talk about it with someone qualified to help you."

"The other girls will need help too."

"I agree. I think the ambassador was taking his daughter back to Denmark, but Kristina and Jaylyn will need help getting their lives back to normal too."

"I'll call them when I get back," Casey said immediately, her mind already whirling about how to help her students. "Maybe we can all go together for some sessions. I have a colleague at the university who teaches psychology. She's also licensed, and volunteers at the student health center anytime there's a suicide or other incident on campus."

"That sounds good," Truck agreed. "Just don't be too stubborn to get help," he implored. "Do it right away too. Sometimes the longer you wait, the worse you can get."

"I will. Thanks, Truck. I appreciate it."

"You're welcome. Now…you gonna be okay with a few days in San José?"

She looked over at him then. His blue eyes were piercing in their intensity. He was way too big to comfortably fit on the little stool, but he sat there, his knees up around his waist, waiting for her answer.

"Why wouldn't I be?"

"I don't know exactly how this is gonna go when we get there, but I suspect it'll be like what we've done in the past. We'll check into a hotel and wait for the authorities to get their shit together. That could take a day or a week, there's no telling."

"A week?" Casey gasped. The thought of having to stay in Costa Rica for another week made her skin crawl.

"Yeah, but I'm thinking it won't take that long this time."

"Why not?"

"Because your brother is there now, and he's probably crawled up their asses so far, they're gonna want to see the backside of *his* ass sooner rather than later."

Casey smiled. Aspen *could* be a pain if he wanted something.

"Anyway, so we'll spend a couple of days in the hotel, you'll be interviewed by the authorities, then we'll have to wait for clearance to leave the country. Hopefully they've got your passport, which will make things go quicker too."

"Will you guys… Never mind."

"Will we what?"

Casey bit her lip, then finally blurted, "Will you wait with me? Or do you have to get back to go on another mission?"

Truck leaned forward and put a hand on her knee. "We're not leaving until you do," he reassured her.

Casey let out the breath she'd been holding. Then she patted his hand and said flippantly, "Well, then, spending a few days in a hotel doesn't sound so bad. If they have hot water and a tub, I'll be golden."

Truck leaned back and shook his head. "Strong and stubborn," he murmured.

Casey blushed, knowing he'd seen right through her bravado.

"I'm proud of you," Truck said. "You went through something horrific and could've just laid down and died in that hole. But you didn't. You fought to live. Not only that, you tromped through this jungle as if you hadn't just been kidnapped. You helped me and Beatle figure out where to make camp when we were out of our element and didn't understand the threat from the insects all around us. You ever need anything, don't hesitate to contact me, okay?"

Casey nodded. "I think I might like to meet this Mary of yours."

Truck smiled again, one side of his mouth quirking up and the side with the scar stubbornly remaining still. "I think she'd like that too."

They fell silent then, each lost in their own thoughts. Casey knew her ordeal wasn't over, but for some reason, a little of the tension she'd been feeling rolled off her shoulders. Soon she'd be in the city, surrounded by Beatle, her brother, and the other Deltas. No one could steal her away with them around.

She refused to think about when she went home to Florida and the men returned to Texas. She'd cross that bridge when she got to it. One day at a time. That's all she had to do.

FIVE HOURS LATER, Casey could hardly believe she and Truck had been talking in the middle of the jungle earlier in the day, and now she was walking into a Sheraton hotel room just west of San José.

Beatle had reappeared and they'd immediately made their way toward Guacalito. Once they'd arrived, she'd been reintroduced to Hollywood, Coach, and Fletch, and they'd gotten into a helicopter. Casey hadn't asked any questions, but had held on to Beatle's hand tightly. He'd squeezed her hand several times, trying to reassure her. They'd landed at a military base of some sort near San José where the team leader named Ghost had been waiting for them.

They'd been allowed to leave without any issues, and had pulled up in front of the fancy American hotel chain. Even seeing the logo had made Casey feel better, safer.

Her brother had obviously been dealing with the logistics of the hotel because he was waiting when they entered the lobby. He'd hugged her tightly, handed her a bag with some clothes he'd gotten for her, gave Beatle a key, and then he'd led them to the elevators. All the other men had crammed into the small space and they'd traveled to the top floor. It made her feel better to see the men had entered rooms all around the one Beatle led her to. She was surrounded by them, which further helped her feelings of safety.

Casey stepped into the room and turned around to thank Beatle, but jerked in surprise when he followed her inside and shut the door behind them. He went past her and dropped his pack on the carpet.

He then went to the closet and opened it, looked under each of the two double beds and behind the curtains. Then he went past her and into the bathroom. After making sure they were the only two people in the room—at least that's what she assumed he was doing— he strode over to her and peeled the bag out of her grasp. He placed it inside the bathroom and put his hands on her shoulders.

"Bathroom is all yours. I'll be out here. Take your time."

"But I heard Ghost tell that military guy he could come here and interview me."

"He did," Beatle said. "But not until you're ready. You need to get clean. Then you need to be checked out by a doctor. Then you need to eat. By then, it'll be too late to talk to anyone tonight, and you need a good night's rest on a real mattress without having to worry about bugs."

Casey couldn't deal with the tender way Beatle was speaking to her, as if she were the most important thing in his life. It made her feel both good and worried at the same time that he'd feel differently once they were back home. "The chance there are bedbugs are higher here than in the States. Warmer climate, clients not as wealthy, hygiene not as valued..."

Beatle shuddered. "Let's not think about that. As much as I love that entomological brain of yours, Dr. Shea, at the moment, I've had all the bugs I can take."

She gave him a small grin.

"Right. Anyway, the shower's all yours. Take your time. I'm not going anywhere. You'll be safe to take as long as you want in there."

The thought of him having her back while she was naked and vulnerable made the tears she'd been holding at bay, since they'd walked out of the jungle into the town of Guacalito, threaten to spill down her cheeks. Casey held them back by pure stubbornness. Beatle had seen her cry way too much for her liking. She wanted to be strong...for him.

"Thanks," she said softly.

It was obvious he hadn't missed her attempt at controlling her emotions, but he didn't comment on it, which she appreciated. "There's soap, a razor, shampoo, and conditioner on the counter. I'll comb your hair for you when you come out, so don't worry about that.

There's also a toothbrush and toothpaste next to the sink." He leaned forward until all she could see was him. "Take. Your. Time. Don't worry about me. Don't worry about anyone coming into the room, because they absolutely will not. Don't worry about using all the hot water. You're safe here with me. Got it?"

The pesky tears were back, clogging her throat, making it impossible for her to say even one word. So she simply nodded.

Then, keeping eye contact with her, Beatle leaned forward, closing the distance between them. He brushed his lips across hers in a touch so feather light and sweet, it almost broke her. She hadn't brushed her teeth in weeks, she could smell the jungle funk wafting up from her clothes, and she knew she had a carpet of hair under her armpits and on her legs, but she also knew none of it mattered to Beatle.

He drew back, staring at her for a beat, as if making sure she was strong enough to shower without him, before nodding and turning her toward the bathroom. "I'll be right here," he repeated.

Casey walked into the luxurious bathroom and shut the door. Her finger hovered over the small lock in the doorknob for a second, before she turned toward the shower, deliberately not looking in the mirror. She felt awful enough as it was, the last thing she wanted to do was *see* how terrible she looked.

She grabbed the toothbrush and toothpaste deciding she'd try to scrape the fuzz off her teeth while standing under the running water. She didn't want to take a second longer than necessary to get clean.

Stripping off her clothes in disgust, she left them in a heap on the white tiled floor. She was about to step into the shower when her nerves got the best of her. She took a step to the door and turned the knob, cracking it open an inch.

Satisfied that Beatle would be able to hear her if something happened, she cranked on the water. Barely waiting for it to warm, she stepped under the spray. She stood under the water with her head back, eyes closed, for what seemed like forever. The warm water felt heavenly against her skin, and she could imagine the dirt and filth being washed away down the drain as she stood there.

BEATLE PACED THE hotel room in agitation. It had taken everything he had to leave Casey with Truck in the jungle while he went on ahead to make sure Guacalito was secure. The last thing they needed was another kidnapping attempt at the site of the first one.

Hollywood had been the first of his team to meet him, and had assured that they hadn't encountered any more resistance since the attack in the jungle.

But Beatle hadn't let his guard down. Someone wanted Casey badly enough to try to prevent her from making it out of the jungle alive. He was going to make sure they didn't succeed.

The trip to San José had been uneventful. Ghost and Blade had arranged for a military helicopter to pick them up, and they'd arrived at the capital within hours.

Officials had wanted to interview Casey right away, but Blade had put his foot down. It didn't matter; even if her brother hadn't intervened, Beatle would've. Casey needed to get her equilibrium back. Before she talked about her ordeal, she needed to be cleaned, doctored, and fed. Once she felt more like herself, it would be easier to talk about what had happened to her, he hoped.

Beatle was as interested to hear her entire story as everyone else, but his first priority was Casey. So here he was, pacing the carpet, wanting to be in the shower with her so bad he ached. Not so much for sexual reasons— though the desire was there—but to take care of her.

He'd heard her open the door and had looked over, expecting to see her standing in the doorway of the bathroom, ready to ask him something, but all he'd seen was the door open a crack. He wanted to think she felt safer with him in the room and the door cracked, so he could get to her faster if she needed him, but he shook his head. No, she'd probably done it to try to reduce the steam in the room. That's all.

He'd about convinced himself of that when he'd heard her first sobs. It took everything in him not to go to her. He wanted to take her in his arms and tell her she was safe, that everything would be all right, but he didn't. He stood stock still in the middle of the hotel room, his hands fisted, his nails biting into his palms as he listened to the woman who had somehow wormed her way into his heart, sob as if her life was over.

Truck had pulled him aside in Guacalito while they were waiting for the chopper and had given him some advice. Told him that Casey was like Mary, independent and stubborn. And she'd hate to be treated as if she was a weak kidnapping victim. He'd done a good job of treating her like a member of the team, because she was, but Truck warned him that he needed to continue to do that. Not to baby her. Support her, yes, but not treat her as if she was broken in any way.

Beatle had taken his friend's words to heart. He didn't know what was going on with him and Mary, but instinct told him that Truck was right. Casey would hate to be fussed over.

The way she'd fought crying in front of him before she'd entered the bathroom had solidified that.

But it killed him to allow her to cry by herself. *Killed.*

He was about to say fuck it and join her in the shower when he heard the water turn off. Not taking his eyes from the bathroom door, Beatle waited for Casey to appear. He needed to see for himself that she was okay.

It took a while, so long that once again he was tempted to go to her, but he stood steadfast.

He saw the door moving before he heard it. Then she was there.

God. Damn.

Beatle had been attracted to her even when she'd been covered in dirt and smelling like body odor in the jungle. He knew what she looked like, had seen the picture of her Blade had shared. But nothing had prepared him to see her fresh and clean from the shower.

A waft of air and steam from the bathroom brought her scent to where he was standing. His nostrils flared, as if that would help him inhale more of her smell.

She smelled *clean*. Nothing fancy. No overly scented soaps. No perfume. Just Casey.

Her hair shone under the lights. Even wet, it was several shades lighter than it had been in the jungle. She was wearing a T-shirt that looked a size or two too large for her slight frame. She'd most likely lost weight because of her ordeal, and her brother had estimated her size wrong. She had on a pair of gray cotton shorts that came down to her knees. He couldn't see her figure, but she was still the most beautiful woman he'd ever lain eyes on. She was upright, safe, healthy. It was a miracle.

Standing in the doorway, she bit her lip and looked up at him. "Sorry I took so long," she said quietly.

Her words broke the trance he was in. Beatle slowly walked toward her, not breaking eye contact as he did. He stopped two feet in front of her. "You're beautiful," he said softly.

A blush swept up her neck and gave her cheeks a healthy glow. She tucked a wet piece of hair behind her ear. "I think you've just been in the jungle too long."

Beatle reached out a hand, but stopped when it was a couple inches from her face. His hand was filthy. The dirt under his nails startling him. He dropped his hand.

"It's okay," she whispered. "You can touch me."

Beatle shook his head. "Not when I'm so dirty."

"Maybe after you shower?" she asked, a hopeful look in her eye.

"Absolutely. Go and sit," he ordered gruffly to try to hide how much he wanted her. "I'll be fast. Blade said he'd be coming over with the doctor. But don't answer the door until I'm out. Okay? Even if it's your brother."

"But...I trust Aspen. Don't you?"

Beatle reprimanded himself for the doubt his words had put in her eyes.

"With my life," he said immediately. "But I don't trust anyone else. Not even the doctor Ghost found to come check you out. I'd rather there be at least two of us present while he's looking you over."

"Do you think he'd try something?"

Beatle immediately shook his head. "It's not likely, but I'm not about to risk your well-being if I'm wrong. Five minutes, Case," he said in a low voice. "I'll be out before you know it."

She nodded. "I used most of the shampoo, but there's still lots of soap."

Beatle smiled. "That's so...girly of you," he teased. "To assume I'll be okay using plain ol' soap in my hair and not fancy shampoo."

Instead of blushing and apologizing, Casey rolled her eyes. "Whatever."

The urge to take her in his arms was almost overwhelming, and Beatle knew he needed to put some distance between them. Now wasn't the time or the place, and he was disgusting. He needed to clean up.

He took a step toward her. "Unless you want to get my stink on you, you'd better get out of the way." He mock frowned at her.

She giggled, the sound burrowing its way into his heart, and scooted out of the doorway. "You do your thing. I'll just be...over here."

Beatle watched as she headed for one of the beds. He waited until she was seated at the edge of the mattress. He couldn't help but stare at her.

"Go," she ordered. "Your stench is permeating the entire room." She waved a hand in front of her face like a fan.

Beatle winked at her and entered the steamy bathroom. He didn't bother shutting the door, leaving it standing wide open. He wanted to be able to get to Casey if she needed him.

Placing the last clean T-shirt he had in his pack and a clean pair of boxers on the counter, Beatle stripped and dropped his dirty clothes on top of her discarded ones. He'd arrange for them to be washed by the hotel later.

Without hesitation, Beatle stepped into the shower, his only thought to get clean and back to Casey.

Chapter Thirteen

CASEY TOOK A deep breath. The doctor had come and gone. He'd pronounced her still a bit dehydrated and malnourished as well as suffering from various cuts and bruises, thanks to her time in captivity and her trek through the jungle, but otherwise surprisingly healthy.

Whatever Truck and Beatle had put on her feet had done wonders. He'd prescribed some more antibiotics and an antifungal cream, but said they were well on their way to being healed.

All in all, it was amazing how well she was doing. Truck had said "strong and stubborn" under his breath when the doctor had expressed surprise at her condition, and Beatle had merely squeezed her hand to the point of almost pain.

Her brother had hugged her so hard, she thought he was going to break a rib, but he'd let go right before he'd really hurt her. "I love you, sis. You scared me. Don't do it again."

Casey had snorted. As if she'd gotten kidnapped on

purpose.

Ghost had escorted the doctor out of the room and then came back and stared at her with his hands on his hips.

"What?" she asked.

"You've got a choice," he informed her.

"No," Beatle broke in.

Ghost ignored him and kept his eyes on Casey. "As you're probably aware, the Costa Rican authorities are anxious to hear what you have to say about your abduction. They aren't happy Americans were kidnapped on their turf, especially when they've done all they can to curb the drug trade and increase tourism."

"Ghost, seriously, I don't think—"

"This isn't *your* choice," Ghost interrupted, turning to Beatle.

The two men glared at each other for a heartbeat until Casey said, "Beatle, it's okay. Go on, Ghost, what's my choice?"

"It looks like we'll be here for at least two nights. We'll leave the day after tomorrow, first thing." Ghost looked at his watch. "It's already seven at night, and you've had a long day. The authorities would like to talk to you tonight, but I can put them off until tomorrow if you want."

"Tomorrow," Beatle said, moving to Casey's side. "She needs to eat something. Then sleep."

Casey put her hand on Beatle's arm. "Tonight," she told Ghost, while looking up at Beatle.

His eyes immediately swung down to hers, the light brown almost obliterated by his huge pupils. "Case, it's—"

"I just want it done," she told him swiftly, trying to forestall his complaints. "The faster I tell them what they want to hear, the quicker I can try to move past this. Please?"

Beatle moved then, reaching for her. His thumb rested on the pulse at her neck and the rest of his fingers curled around her nape. As if he didn't give one shit that his teammates were there in the room listening, he said, "Are you sure, sweetheart? They can wait."

"I'm sure," she told him. Then, deciding if he wasn't hiding his attraction to her in front of his friends, she wouldn't either, she said, "If we have to spend another day here, I'd rather it be with you, and not thinking about what happened."

"Okay," he acquiesced. "But if I think it's too much, I'm going to stop the interview and we can do it tomorrow."

Casey didn't really like that, but appreciated why he was saying it. She vowed to do whatever was necessary to be unemotional and matter of fact about everything so he wouldn't feel the need to stop the questions. "Okay."

Beatle turned his head, but didn't remove his hand from Casey's neck. "Go ahead and call them, Ghost. But give us an hour. She needs to eat."

"Will do," his teammate said.

Casey didn't think Beatle was going to move from her side, but was surprised when, the second her brother stepped up to her, he took two steps backward. Blade took her into his arms, but Casey was more than aware of how close Beatle still was. He might've let her brother into her space, but he hadn't gone far. She felt warmth move through her. The longer she was around Beatle, the more she liked and respected him.

"I'm so glad you're all right, Casey," Blade said softly into her hair. "I'll call Mom and Bill tonight."

Bill was her dad, and Aspen's stepdad. He hadn't ever called the man anything but Bill. Even though her dad had been more of a father to Aspen than his own, no one complained about the moniker. Aspen was two years older than her, and the result of a whirlwind relationship their mom had had with a man who hadn't wanted anything to do with his son once he'd gone his separate way from their mother.

Luckily, she'd met and married Bill not long after breaking up with Aspen's father. Bill had raised Aspen as his own son, and never once complained about the fact they had different last names. Their mom had wanted to keep Aspen's last name as Carlisle, in case his father ever had a change of heart. He hadn't.

"Thanks," Casey told her brother. "Thank you for coming to find me."

"Always, Case. Always," Blade replied. Then he pulled back and cleared his throat. "See you downstairs."

One by one, the other Deltas left the room, until it was just her and Beatle once more.

He immediately came to her side. "Are you sure you're okay with this? It's all right if you wait until tomorrow. Sleep will do you good."

"I'm sure," Casey told him. "I really would just prefer to get it over and done with."

"Okay, sweetheart. But let me know if you need a break."

"I will."

He leaned forward and tilted her head down and kissed the top. "I need to feed you. What are you in the mood for?"

Casey hadn't thought much about food thus far. She'd been more concerned with getting out of the jungle alive, not stepping in any bullet ant mounds, and then getting clean. But now that Beatle mentioned food, her stomach growled with the thought. "A cheeseburger. And fries. And a soda."

Beatle frowned at the mention of the soft drink. "You need water, Case."

She sighed. "I know. If I promise to drink a whole glass, can I please have at least a sip of soda? I'm craving the carbonation."

"I'm such a pushover," Beatle complained. "This doesn't bode well for our relationship. Fine. Soda *and* a water."

Goosebumps broke out on her arms at his offhand words. He'd said it as if a relationship between them was a foregone conclusion. She'd somehow been afraid that all his words in the jungle were a result of the moment. But they were currently safe, and clean, and he still seemed to want to see her when they got back to the States.

She smiled. Huge. Then teased, "I think it bodes great for our relationship."

"You would. You got what you wanted," Beatle groused.

Feeling more like herself than she had in a very long time, Casey leaned forward and boldly kissed Beatle. It was a short kiss, merely a brush of her lips against his. "Thank you, Troy."

His hand caught the back of her head, preventing her from moving away from him after her kiss. "You're welcome, Casey." And then he slowly dropped his head.

Casey's eyes closed and she tilted her head in welcome. She'd been half hoping making the first move would encourage him. If she'd had any inclination how well her kiss would work, she would've done it way before now.

He kissed her as if it were the last kiss either of them would ever have. Passionate, possessive, and lengthy. It wasn't until her stomach growled that he pulled back. Once again, his brown irises were hard to make out because of the size of his dilated pupils. "I need to feed you," he said in a low, grumbly voice.

"Yeah," she agreed, but stared at his lips even as she licked her own.

"Fuck," he murmured, before dropping his mouth to hers again.

It was several minutes before he tore himself away from her once more. But this time, he actually backed away to the other side of the room. He shook his head. "You're addictive as hell, sweetheart."

"It's not me," she countered. "It's you."

Without another word, he picked up the phone and ordered room service for them both, offering a hundred-dollar bonus if they got the food to them in the next twenty minutes.

THE CHEESEBURGER THAT had been so delicious an hour earlier sat in her belly like a rock. Casey was at a table in a room at the hotel, sitting across from two

Costa Rican police officers. They had been polite enough, but it was more than obvious they were anxious to hear everything she had to say. She'd been adamant with Beatle that she wanted to get this over with, but now she wasn't so sure she wanted to talk about her experience at all. With anyone.

The longer she sat there silent, the harder it was to start talking. She swallowed hard and licked her lips. Then she took a sip of the water in front of her. She clasped her hands together, then flattened them on her shorts and tried to dry the sweat from her palms.

She made the mistake of looking up, and saw the impatient look on one of the police officer's faces before he looked away.

Shit. She couldn't do this.

Just when she was about to blurt out that she wanted to go back to the room, Beatle took her hand in his. He was sitting on one side of her, and his teammate, Coach, was on the other. Ghost, Blade, and Hollywood were standing behind her somewhere. Fletch and Truck weren't in the room; she had no idea where they were or what they were doing.

She felt a finger under her chin and almost rolled her eyes. Beatle loved to do that, but she obediently turned her head and met his gaze.

"Don't look at them. Tell *me* what happened."

Casey wasn't sure that was any better. But she closed

her eyes and took a deep breath. She felt Beatle take hold of her other hand as well. His thumbs rubbed over the backs of her hands and, amazingly, his touch helped calm her.

"We were at the research spot in the jungle we'd been using for several days. We'd found a leafcutter ant colony and had been studying it and taking pictures. Astrid had forgotten her notes from the day before, and she and Kristina had gone back to Guacalito to get them. I always made sure we traveled in pairs. Because, you know, it was safer."

Casey blew a huff of air out her nose. "Right. Safer. Anyway, they had been gone a long time and I was getting worried about them. So me and Jaylyn started back toward town to see what was taking them so long. I was walking behind Jaylyn, and saw two men approaching in front of us. I was smiling and calling out a greeting, when I saw the knife in one of their hands. Before I knew what was happening, there were men all around us. Yelling in Spanish and English. Telling us to shut up and no one would get hurt. They herded us away from the town and after walking only a short distance, we were inside a truck. Astrid and Kristina were there too, already tied up with their eyes covered.

"They blindfolded me and Jaylyn and they wouldn't tell us anything about what was happening. We drove for a while, then they forced us out and made us walk. I don't know how long we walked, but it seemed like a long time. We got to the village and they shoved us into a hut. They didn't bother to untie us or take off our blindfolds, but I managed to get Astrid to turn her back to me and I got the rope off. She helped get me free, then we untied the others. We looked around the hut but there was absolutely no way out. We even tried to dig, but they'd reinforced the outside with some sort of mesh or something, so we could only go so far."

When she took a breath, Beatle asked, "Did you hear them say anything about what they were going to do with you?"

"No."

Beatle squeezed her hands. "Close your eyes. Think, Casey. I know it's painful, but try to remember what you heard. Was anyone talking while you were in the truck? Did they talk about where you were going? What about when you got to the village? Did you hear any of the villagers talking?"

Casey squeezed her eyes shut and tried to think back. Without her knowing it, she began to tremble. The harder she tried to think, the more she shook. There was something there, but she couldn't remember. All she could think about was how scared she'd been. But the girls had needed her, so she'd sucked it up...

"It's okay, Case," she heard. "Open your eyes. Look at me."

She did as requested, and saw Beatle's beautiful brown eyes looking into hers. "That's it. We'll come back to it. What happened after you were in the hut?"

Feeling as if she'd dodged a bullet for some reason, she resumed telling her story. "We were in the hut for a while, and things were…okay. Not great, but they were bringing us food and water. Not a lot, but I divvied it up so we all got our fair share. The girls had stopped being so freaked out, and we were just waiting. No one had hurt us and we didn't really feel threatened. We were actually bored, if you can believe it. Then one day, that guy, the one from the jungle, with the ants, came to the hut and told me to get up. That my ransom had been paid and I was going home.

"I had no idea what he was talking about. I mean, we didn't even know they'd asked for ransom for us. I tried to reassure the girls that I'd make sure their ransoms were paid as soon as possible too, and I left."

Casey got quiet again, thinking about what she'd just said. "There wasn't any ransom paid, was there?" she asked Beatle.

"No, sweetheart. There wasn't ever a demand for one. When Astrid's dad didn't hear from his daughter, he started trying to locate her, and when he couldn't, got to work getting the Dutch Special Forces team down here to find her."

"So if we were in Costa Rica doing our research

without her, then no one would've known we were taken?" Casey asked, the realization of how lucky they'd all been sinking in.

"What happened after you were taken out of the hut?" Beatle asked, not answering her question.

He didn't need to. Casey knew exactly what would've happened if they'd all been nobodies. Eventually they would've been missed, but it would've been too late. Especially for her. Casey didn't know what had happened to the girls after she'd left the hut, but from the little she'd learned from Truck and Beatle as they went through the jungle, it wouldn't have turned out well for them either. She would've died in the hole in the ground and no one would have ever found her body. She shuddered and looked to her lap.

"You're safe," Beatle said softly from beside her. "I found you, you kicked the jungle's ass, and we're here in this luxury hotel waiting to go home. You're *safe*."

Casey nodded. She was. Beatle was right. So, she took a deep breath and continued her story. "They put a blindfold on me again, and I thought they were taking me back to the truck and I'd be driven back to Guacalito. Stupid me, I didn't even think about any other scenario. I was too focused on figuring out how to get the other girls freed too. I walked for a while, and I heard whispering around me, then the man who had gotten me from the hut stopped me. He tore off my blindfold, and I saw the hole there in front of me. I couldn't take my eyes off it. I should've looked around to see who else was there, but all I could think about was that damn hole. It took me a second to understand what was happening, and when I did, I fought. But it didn't do any good. They shoved me forward and I fell right into it. The breath was knocked out of me for a moment, and when I regained my senses, I looked up, only to see the hole above me being covered up. I—"

Casey massaged her temple, the headache seeming to come out of nowhere. There was something she needed to remember, but she couldn't. It was right there, but she couldn't bring it to the forefront of her mind. Something had happened while she was at the bottom of the hole looking up, but what? She remembered seeing the trees above her head and hearing voices, then it had gotten dark. What wasn't she remembering?

"Casey?" her brother asked from behind her.

His voice grounded her back to the present, and whatever it was she was trying to remember was gone.

"They covered the hole and it was pitch dark," Casey continued. "It took me a while to figure out there was water coming from somewhere above me. I tried to climb out, with no luck. But I used the random boards at my feet to make a perch for myself to get out of the water at the bottom the hole. You know about the bra water filter," she told Beatle with a pathetic attempt at a grin. He didn't smile back.

"Did you hear anything else while you were down there?"

"Not really," Casey told him. "I mean, I heard people talking every now and then. I tried to yell that I was there, for them to help me, but they either didn't hear or were ignoring me. I don't know how much time had gone by when I heard gunshots, I guess that was when the girls were rescued. I thought for sure they'd come and find me too, but after everything got quiet again, I figured I was a goner.

She looked up at Beatle. "How did you find me?"

"I don't know," he told her, not taking his gaze from hers. "A little bit of instinct, a little bit of a hunch, and a fuck of a lot of luck."

"You wear cameras, yes?" one of the police officers asked from across the table.

Casey startled at the voice. She hadn't even remembered they were in the room.

"Yes," Ghost replied. "We turned them on when we got close to the village."

"We would like copies," the other officer ordered.

"When we get home and get copies made, we will send them to you," Ghost reassured them. "The village was deserted when we got there. There was evidence the Danish Special Forces had, unfortunately, killed a few villagers in their rescue mission, as well as burned some huts, but nothing that spoke to a slaughter or wide-spread destruction of the entire village. I know you have no reason to believe us, but when you watch the videos, you'll see that the huts had been burning for several days by the time we got there, and the decomp of the bodies will also prove we weren't the ones who killed them."

"You were wearing a camera?" Casey asked Beatle, her eyes wide.

"Yeah."

"Was I...did you film me in the hole?" She absolutely didn't want to see that. Ever. In fact, she didn't want anyone else to see it either. The thought of someone seeing how low she'd sunk, literally, was horrifying. She knew she'd been close to dying. Had *wanted* to die.

Beatle took her face in his hands and said, "You didn't do anything wrong. In fact, you did everything right."

"I just...people will see me like that?"

"They'll see a miracle, Case. Just like I did. When I leaned into that hole and saw you looking back up at me, I swear to Christ I was looking at the most beautiful sight I'd ever seen in my life. You have nothing to be ashamed of. *Nothing.* With that said, the only people who will see that video are these officers here and my commander. The tapes are used to review *our* actions, not to judge anyone else who might be on them. Trust me."

Casey could only nod at the sincerity she saw in his eyes. She did trust him. How could she not? "Okay."

"Okay," Beatle echoed.

The rest of the meeting with the officers went fairly fast. Beatle described their encounter with the group of men who had been talking about their boss wanting to get her back. Coach added what his group had experienced, how they'd been shot at, and how they'd had to neutralize the men who were obviously looking for Casey and her rescuers.

When the officers were satisfied they'd heard everything, they all stood. Everyone shook hands and the officers said they would be in touch with Ghost.

Before she knew it, it was just her and the Deltas left in the room.

"You look exhausted," Blade told his sister. "Why don't you go up to sleep?"

She didn't want to go anywhere without Beatle, but forced herself to nod. In another day or so, she'd have no choice but to part with him. She couldn't spend the rest of her life glued to his side.

"I'll walk you up," Beatle told her. Then he turned to his friends. "Someone desperately wanted to find her out there. We can't leave her alone until we're out of this country."

"Agreed. We'll all go upstairs, and we can meet in the room next door to hers. That way we won't disturb her, and we'll be able to keep our eye on her," Hollywood said.

"That work?" Beatle asked her. "We'll keep the connecting door open just in case, but you'll still have your privacy."

Casey wanted to ask if he would be staying in her room, but chickened out. She didn't want to look weak in front of her brother, and, more importantly, didn't want to sound desperate in front of Beatle. "That'll be great. I'm looking forward to stretching out on that comfy mattress." She tried to say it nonchalantly, but wasn't sure she succeeded, especially with the side-eye Beatle gave her.

But he didn't call her on her fake bravado, simply clasped her hand in his and led the way out of the room. They all got in the elevator and went up to their floor. They reached the room she'd been in earlier and Beatle unlocked it. He put his hand on the small of her back to guide her inside. "Open the door," he told Coach with a chin lift. "I'll be there in a couple of minutes."

"Will do," Coach told him, moving to the room next door behind Hollywood.

"I'll grab Truck and Fletch," Blade said.

Ghost stood there looking at Casey for a long moment, then finally nodded at Beatle and followed Coach.

"Inside, Case," Beatle ordered.

She took a few steps inside the room, and he shut and locked the hotel door behind them.

He guided her to the bed, then grabbed a bottle of water he'd brought up earlier. He twisted off the cap and handed it to her. "Are you okay?"

"I'm good."

"Don't lie to me," he ordered as he paced in front of her.

Casey took the time to check him out. He cleaned up really well. He kept running a hand over his short reddish hair and even the look of concern on his face didn't diminish his good looks. He was wearing only a pair of shorts and a T-shirt, but his outfit in no way diminished the "don't fuck with me" look he carried like a second skin. Their clothes had been sent somewhere to the bowels of the hotel to be cleaned and the clerk had promised they'd be done in a couple of hours. Definitely by the time they needed to put them on in the morning.

Beatle's thigh muscles flexed with every step he took, and Casey couldn't help but stare. She'd been attracted to him when he'd been covered from head to toe with his gear in the jungle, but practically naked? He was even more handsome.

Casey flushed with shame. She shouldn't be thinking about him like that. Not when he was her brother's friend. A soldier who'd rescued her. He couldn't be anything else. He wouldn't want to be anything else.

But then she remembered his kisses. And the look of lust in his eyes.

She'd had a one-night stand back in college, and while it had been exciting at the time, it had left her feeling gross. She hadn't known anything about the guy she'd slept with, and for a long time afterward had avoided getting in any kind of relationship as a result of her guilty conscience.

She didn't want a one-night stand with Beatle, and didn't think that's what he wanted from her. Seeing him pace made her long-lost libido flare to life. She hadn't had a boyfriend in years, she'd been too busy getting her PhD and working. Maybe what she was feeling was simply a way to affirm that she was still alive, maybe it was a result of her feeling grateful he'd rescued her. But deep down, Casey knew neither of those things were true.

She wanted Troy "Beatle" Lennon. Bad.

She jerked out of her thoughts when he stopped and squatted in front of where she was sitting on the bed. "Don't lie to me," he repeated. "Are you okay after all that? It wasn't easy for you to go through it all. I know it wasn't."

"I'm okay," she told him immediately. "It wasn't easy, but you were there and I'm safe now. Go talk to your team." She kept her eyes on his by sheer force of will. All it had taken was one glance downward and seeing his knees spread apart, his inner thigh muscles straining with the squat, and she'd felt herself get wet. She needed some space from him. Space to try to control her out-of-control libido. "I'm going to crawl into bed and sleep."

He stared at her skeptically. Then finally, taking her at her word, said, "I'll be right next door. We all will. If you get nervous, frightened, or if anyone knocks on the door, you yell out and we'll come running. Okay?"

"Okay," she agreed.

Beatle didn't move for a heartbeat, then slowly stood. Casey tilted her head back, knowing if she didn't keep looking at him, his cock would be right at her eye level. She'd be at the perfect height to reach forward and pull down the elastic of his shorts and—

She swallowed hard and forced herself to ask, "Will you turn on the bathroom light before you go?"

His voice gentled and he ran the back of his hand down her cheek. "Of course. Climb in, sweetheart."

She did as he ordered, and held on to the comforter tightly. Casey wanted to ask if he was going to be sleeping in the room with her, but was too embarrassed. She was twenty-nine, for God's sake. She didn't need him to stay with her. The thought of being alone, like she'd been when she was in the hole, threatened her composure, but she gamely smiled up at Beatle.

He leaned over her, his fists on the mattress at her shoulders. "If you need me, I'm right next door."

"I'll be fine," she said firmly.

For a second, she thought he was going to call her on the lie, but he simply bent down, kissed her on the lips, then pulled back. "Good night, Case."

"Good night, Beatle. Thanks for…well…everything."

He didn't respond, but stood up and clicked off the light next to the bed.

Casey swallowed hard at the immediate sense of claustrophobia that tried to overwhelm her. It was if she were standing at the bottom of the hole once more, looking up as the men above her covered it.

Once more, something niggled at the back of her brain, but it was gone when she looked at Beatle.

He was studying her, and after a moment, he walked quickly to the bathroom and turned on the light, shutting the door halfway. Then he said softly, "There's no shame in admitting you need the light on, Case."

"Thanks," she murmured.

Then he went to the connecting door and paused, waiting for her to look at him. When she did, he pointed to himself, then at the next room.

Casey nodded, understanding and feeling comforted by the fact that, even if he wouldn't be in the same room as her, at least he'd be right next door.

Then he was gone. Casey could see the connecting door was cracked, not shut all the way, and she heard Beatle greet his teammates. She couldn't quite hear what they were talking about, but their voices soothed her nevertheless. If she could hear them, she wasn't alone.

She turned to her side and closed her eyes. Sleep. If she could go to sleep, then she wouldn't be scared.

Chapter Fourteen

B EATLE WAS TIRED. He wanted nothing more than to go back to Casey's room and crash. He and the others had gone over and over everything Casey had told them, and were no closer to coming up with answers as to who might have been behind the kidnapping than they were when they'd started two hours ago.

They were missing something. Something big, but no one could figure out what. They'd spent some time reviewing the tapes from their cameras to try to see if there was anything obvious they'd missed. If the threat was someone from Costa Rica, it would be better to find out now rather than waiting until they got home. But they hadn't caught anything that looked out of the ordinary. They'd have to review them more carefully once they were back in Texas. Maybe get their friend, Tex, who was a computer genius, or one of the techs at the post, to help scrutinize them.

Beatle had gotten up several times to check on Casey, and each time she'd been lying still under the covers. He hoped a good night's sleep would do wonders for her, both physically and mentally.

She hadn't hidden the fact that she was freaked out. Not even close. In situations like this in the past, he'd felt sorry for the rescuee, but that definitely wasn't what he was feeling for Casey.

"You really like her," Blade murmured. The other man had come to stand next to him at the connecting door.

Without taking his eyes from the woman sleeping on the bed, Beatle nodded. "I hope you were serious when you said you wouldn't mind if your sister got together with me."

"I was serious," Blade reassured him. "I know you, Beatle. And I've never seen you act like this with a woman before."

Beatle turned to his friend and teammate. "That's because I've never felt about a woman the way I do your sister. I don't know what it is, but I've fallen hard and fast for her."

"She lives in Florida."

Beatle ran a hand through his hair. "I know. Believe me, I've thought about nothing else *but* that."

"I'm not sure it's the best thing for her to go back there right now," Blade said. "I mean, someone was very determined she not get out of that jungle. They sent a dozen armed men to make sure of it. I'm not convinced she'll be safe once we leave here."

"What the hell is going on? From what she's said, she's simply a university professor. Who could want her that badly? And for what? To throw her in another hole? To torture her? There has to be a deeper reason for all this, Blade."

"I know. I *completely* agree. That's why I think we need to keep an eye on her until we figure it out. The last thing I want is some asshole getting his hands on her again. She's been handling everything pretty well. But if she gets snatched a second time, I think it'll break her, and she'll never be the little sister I know and love again."

Images of Casey lying on a bed, broken in body and spirit, flashed through Beatle's mind, and he flinched. His eyes sought her out for reassurance that she was safe.

"Here's the thing," Blade continued. "I know my sister. She doesn't like to be a burden. Not to anyone. She's not going to take kindly to being told she needs a babysitter. She's going to want to go back to Florida to check on her students. She's going to think she needs to get back to her life, and she'll pretend nothing happened."

"What do you suggest?" Beatle asked. He hated that he didn't know Casey well enough yet to be able to instinctively know how to handle her, but the fact of the matter was, he didn't. They hadn't known each other that long, even if the time they'd spent together had been intense and they'd gotten close as a result. Blade was her brother, he'd known her all her life. If anyone would know how to get her to do something, it would be him.

"She's not stupid," Blade said. "She's not going to risk her life just to defy me. But…I think she'd be more willing to listen if you brought it up."

Beatle sighed. Yeah, he thought that was what Blade was going to say. "We…I'm not sure I'll have that much sway."

"You will. You do," Blade insisted.

"I agree," Truck added quietly from behind them.

Beatle startled. He hadn't heard the other man approach. He'd been concentrating too hard on Casey's sleeping form.

"From the second you two met, there's been a connection. You can't deny it," Truck said.

"I'm *not* denying it," Beatle replied. "But there's a difference between having a connection, and her agreeing to come to Texas so we can look after her for an indeterminate period of time. What about her job? Her students? Her friends?"

"All good questions," Truck agreed. "But that woman is scared out of her freaking mind. It's easy to see. Blade said it himself, she's not stupid. Besides, it's not like you're going to tell her she can't ever go back to Florida. Talk to her, Beatle. She needs to hear everything we talked about tonight. I have a feeling she's the key to figuring all this out. But she's been through a lot, she needs time to feel safe, and to let her brain remember every detail. The smallest thing she saw or heard could be the solution to making her safe once and for all."

Beatle agreed. He'd seen the way Casey had furrowed her brow as if trying to remember something, but then when she'd been interrupted in her musings, whatever fleeting thought she'd had disappeared. "I'll do everything in my power to make her safe," he vowed.

"She said she had a colleague at the university, a psychologist," Truck said. "Maybe you could suggest flying her out to Texas?"

"Maybe," Beatle replied. "Although sometimes it's easier to talk to a stranger than a friend."

"Talk to her," Blade pressed. "Fletch said you guys could stay in his garage apartment. We can help look out for her easier there than at your place."

The more they talked about it, the more Beatle wanted Casey to return to Texas with him. It was insane. But it also felt right. They hadn't known each other long, but the time they *had* spent together had been intense. What was that movie? *Speed*? Where Sandra Bullock told Keanu Reeves's character that relationships that start under intense circumstances never lasted?

Fuck that shit.

"I'll do what I can," he told his friends. "And if for some reason she absolutely refuses to come to Texas, I'll go to Florida."

Silence met his pronouncement for a beat before Truck said, "But you won't have any backup. I'm not sure you can even get approved for leave for as long as it might take to figure all this out."

Beatle looked his friend in the eye. "I don't care. She's not safe. You both said it. I'm not forcing her to do anything she doesn't want to, and I'm not going to leave her vulnerable to be snatched again."

"If it comes down to that, I'll talk to the commander," Ghost said from behind them.

Beatle turned and saw Ghost and the rest of the team standing nearby. They'd obviously heard the entire conversation.

"I'd appreciate that."

Just then, a whimper came from the other room. Beatle was moving before his brain could kick in and assess the situation.

He was in Casey's room and at her side within seconds. But that was enough time for her to be lost in the nightmare she was having. She was thrashing on the bed, fighting the covers, desperately trying to escape.

"Shhhh, it's only a dream, you're safe," he murmured.

She didn't hear him. She thrashed harder, her legs flailing and her head whipping back and forth as if she were fighting someone who had hold of her.

"Casey," Beatle repeated, putting a hand on her shoulder.

Instead of calming her, his touch seemed to inflame her more. She jerked away from him and her eyes popped open. They were remote and unseeing, as if she were watching a movie only she could see. Or reliving the most terrifying moment of her life.

"No! Don't. Don't push me in there! I'll do whatever you want! Please, come back!" Then her back arched and she screamed as every muscle in her body tensed.

"Jesus Christ."

"Fuck."

"Those fucking bastards!"

Beatle tuned out the exclamations of his teammates and concentrated on Casey. Without thought, he did the only thing that seemed right in this case. He threw back the blankets and crawled into the bed with her. He murmured nonsense as he gathered her flailing body in his arms. He held her head to him and rocked back and forth.

She fought him at first, but slowly, she calmed. He could feel her pulse hammering under her skin, and the quick breaths that escaped her mouth were hot against his neck. But finally her eyes closed, and she grabbed hold of him as if she were never going to let go. She turned and went so far as to climb on top of him. Beatle eased onto his back to accommodate her. Casey shoved her arms underneath him and her knees came up. She huddled on top of him as if her life depended on him holding her.

Beatle swallowed hard and tightened his arms around her. One hand went to the back of her head, the other landed on the bare skin of her lower back. Her shirt had rucked up in her struggles, and the skin-on-skin contact made him almost dizzy.

"I'll stay," Truck informed Beatle and their other teammates quietly. "She's used to me being around."

Beatle's gaze swung to Blade. He'd said he was okay with him forming a relationship with Casey, but saying it and seeing his little sister in bed with him, on *top* of him, were two different things.

"Take care of her," Blade said softly, before turning and leaving the room.

Coach leaned down and pulled the comforter over Casey's back. She didn't fully wake, simply tried to burrow farther into Beatle.

Ghost and Hollywood each gave Beatle a chin lift before they headed for the connecting door.

"She needs to come to Texas," Fletch said, his jaw flexing in agitation. "She can't go back to Florida. She's got too much to deal with to be alone."

"I know," Beatle said softly, not wanting to wake the woman in his arms.

"You know Annie'll take her under her wing and make her forget all her troubles," Fletch said.

Beatle nodded. Yeah, Annie was incredible. It was as if she knew exactly what the vulnerable and wounded needed. She'd been amazing with Fish, the honorary member of their team. He was a relatively new addition to their group of friends, and he'd recently moved to Idaho. But at Fletch's wedding, Annie'd had the man wrapped around her little finger from the moment she'd met him. She did the same to Truck too. The first time she'd met him, she'd put her little hand on his scarred cheek and wanted to know if it had hurt. Yeah, Annie would be good for Casey.

And he couldn't help but admit that he wanted her to get to know the others as well. Rayne, Emily, Harley, Kassie, and even Mary would be good for her. "I'll do my best to convince her."

"You do that," Fletch said, then spun on his heel and left.

"As soon as we land, I'll call Harley and have her get in touch with Kassie, to see if they can't get her a few outfits from JCPenney. She'll need clothes."

"Thanks, Coach," Beatle told his friend.

"No thanks necessary. We take care of our own." And with that, Coach left the room, shutting the connecting door almost all the way.

Beatle closed his eyes and tried to memorize the way the woman in his arms felt. He didn't like that she was huddled on him, as if trying to protect herself, rather than lying relaxed and easy. But he could feel her bare stomach against his own. Both their shirts had twisted and pulled up. Her skin was damp with a sheen of sweat from her agitation. Beatle felt like an asshole when his mind immediately imagined them lying together like this after a long, sweaty lovemaking session.

"Are you okay? Can I get you anything?" Truck asked from the other bed. He'd stretched out on the second queen-size bed in the room, diagonally so he'd fit, and Beatle could feel his eyes on him.

"No. I think we're okay."

"You're good for her," Truck said. "I've never seen two people connect like the two of you have. I'd pay any amount of money for Mary to look at me the way Casey looks at you."

Beatle wasn't sure what to say. He couldn't exactly say that Mary would come around, because he wasn't sure she would. Truck and Mary definitely had an interesting dynamic. It was no secret that Truck loved the woman, but what *wasn't* as clear was how Mary felt about him in return.

His chance to probe into Truck's relationship with Rayne's best friend was lost when Truck said, "I'll make myself scarce in the morning so she won't feel awkward."

"Thanks, Truck. And…if you ever need anything…an ear or whatever, I've got your back."

"Appreciate it. But no worries. Mary might be stubborn, but I'm even more so. She'll come around. Eventually."

And with that, Truck turned on his side, putting his back to Beatle and Casey, giving them as much privacy as possible in the small room.

Beatle shifted, bunching the pillow under his head and getting more comfortable. Surprisingly, having her on top of him wasn't a hardship. He barely felt her weight; she was more like a weighted blanket than anything. He'd gotten so used to sleeping plastered to her as they'd made their way through the jungle that she just felt right in his arms.

She moaned a little in her throat and Beatle ran his fingers lightly through her clean blonde hair. "Shhhhh, sweetheart. I've got you. You're safe."

His words seemed to do the trick and she stilled.

Knowing he'd done that, made her relax and sleep peacefully after her nightmare, made his eyes burn. He'd never felt as much for someone else as he did for the woman in his arms. He couldn't live without her in his life. He simply couldn't.

Beatle didn't know how much time had passed, but

eventually his eyes got heavy and he felt himself falling into the abyss that was slumber. He turned his head and kissed Casey's temple, leaving his lips there on her skin as sleep finally overtook him.

CASEY CAME AWAKE slowly. She kept her eyes closed and tried to remember where she was. She'd never been so cozy in all her life, and she didn't remember her mattress ever being as comfortable as it was at that moment.

When the bedding under her moved, Casey almost leaped out of bed in fright. But suddenly she remembered everything. Costa Rica. Being kidnapped. Being in the hole. The dash through the jungle. Beatle.

Her eyes opened, and it took her a moment to understand what she was looking at. Beatle's jaw. Then she realized that she was lying on top of him. It seemed more intimate than when they'd slept together in the hammock in the jungle. There, she'd slept against him, but they'd been more side by side. Now, she was literally on top of him. She had to be squishing him, but he didn't seem to care. His breaths were slow and easy, and he was completely relaxed under her.

Casey didn't move a muscle. She liked this. A lot. She tried to remember anything about how they'd gotten in this position but couldn't. The last thing she recalled was lying in bed and staring at the connecting door to the other room.

"After you climbed on top of him, you slept like a log."

Casey inhaled sharply, but didn't jerk out of Beatle's arms. She recognized the voice. Truck. She lifted her gaze from Beatle's face to the bed next to them. Truck was lying on his back, one arm under his head, the other across his belly.

"I don't remember," she said softly, so as not to wake Beatle.

"You were having a nightmare. We all stormed in to kill whoever it was that had broken into your room to find no one here but you."

"I don't remember anything," Casey repeated.

"You thought you were in that hole again. And you fought like hell. Just as I'm sure you did when it actually happened."

She didn't answer this time. She *had* fought like hell. She'd done everything possible to get up and out of the hole after they threw her in. They'd thrown her away like she was a piece of garbage being disposed of.

"Our travel plans have been moved up," Truck told her. "I heard Ghost talking next door. We're leaving tonight. The fact that you spoke with the officers yesterday, and with a little help from a friend back in the States who has connections, we'll be out of here before the sun sets."

Casey sighed in relief. She couldn't wait to see the backside of Costa Rica.

"You have a decision to make," Truck went on, and her eyes went back to his face. "We need to know where to take you."

He paused, and Casey inhaled in surprise. She honestly hadn't really thought much beyond getting out of Costa Rica. But yeah, she supposed she should've thought about this before now.

"You of course can go home to Florida, but I don't recommend it. We don't know who kidnapped you in the first place. It might've been a random person from this country who thought he could make an easy buck, but the fact that none of you were actually ransomed makes that unlikely. And I think the fight in the jungle also clued you into the fact that whoever it is, really wants to make sure you don't escape their clutches."

"You said I had a decision. Where else would I go? Witness protection?"

Truck chuckled. "Nothing so dramatic. You can come to Texas with us. With Beatle."

Casey's eyes widened. "What?"

"Beatle's going to talk to you about this later today. He's going to suggest that you come with us. We'll keep you safe, Casey, have no doubt about that. But it has to be your decision. I wanted to give you a head's up so you could think about it. So you didn't feel blindsided."

Casey closed her eyes. Yeah, that's exactly how she felt. Blindsided. Go to Texas? She was ashamed to admit, even to herself, that she'd dreamed of Beatle asking her to go to Texas with him. Telling her he loved her and couldn't live without her. But that was fantasy. Of course he didn't love her.

And she had to go back to Florida, didn't she? Her job was there. Her apartment. Her life. She couldn't just…leave.

But that weird feeling was still there at the back of her mind. She wasn't safe. She remembered the man in the jungle, and how he'd threatened to violate her before giving her to his "boss." The person who wanted to make sure she never made it out of Costa Rica alive. Or at least not with her sanity intact.

Goosebumps broke out at that thought, and once again something pushed at her memory.

"Think about it," Truck said, breaking her out of her musings. "I'd love for you to meet my Mary."

And with that, the large man eased out of the bed and stood. Without another word, he headed for the connecting door and disappeared behind it.

Casey looked back at the man she was lying on top of. The room had lightened with the rising sun and this close, she could see that his five o'clock shadow had hints of red. His eyelashes were incredibly long, especially for a man. They were also tinted auburn. Her eyes traced the shape of his lips, his nose, even his cheekbones. He was good-looking, but in a rugged way. Not like his friend Hollywood, who was drop-dead gorgeous.

But Casey wasn't attracted to Hollywood at all. Nor any of Beatle's other friends. No, *he* was the one who made her tummy do summersaults and her pussy weep.

She scrunched her eyes closed. Darn it, she shouldn't be turned on. *How* could she be turned on? Her entire life was in upheaval. She needed to check on her students, make sure her parents knew she was alive and well, contact her friends and the dean at the university so they knew she was okay.

But somehow, lying in bed with Beatle—okay, *on* Beatle—made all those other things fade in importance. She was glad Truck had given her the head's up on the decision she had to make. Florida or Texas? She honestly wasn't sure what the right choice was. Texas would be smart, but she wasn't sure she could be around Beatle any longer and not act on her attraction to him. And if he disappeared, and let her brother stay by her side, it would hurt.

If they got back to the States and he realized that whatever feelings he might've had for her in Central American were a result of the adrenaline and excitement of the rescue, she'd never recover. Casey knew that about herself. But if she went to Florida and didn't even give them a chance, she knew she'd regret it. Not to mention the little detail that apparently someone wanted her dead.

She could go to Arizona and stay with her parents, but what if that put them in danger? Fuck, she was so confused.

Just then, someone dropped something next door, and Beatle moved so fast, Casey couldn't even begin to process what was going on. One second he was asleep, and the next he'd rolled until she was under him, his body covering hers.

"Shit, sorry," he muttered in a voice deep and gravelly from sleep. He eased up on his forearms above her. "Are you all right?"

"Yeah, I'm good."

His body slowly relaxed when no one came crashing into their room. "Sleep good?"

"Uh huh. You?"

"I don't think I've ever slept so well in my life."

Oh. My. God.

Casey swallowed hard and couldn't tear her gaze from his if her life depended on it.

"I like you in my arms. I could easily get addicted to it. To you."

Then, as if he hadn't just rocked her world, he rolled over and sat on the side of the bed. He looked back at her. His hand came up and brushed a lock of hair off her forehead with a touch so gentle and light, she almost didn't feel it. "Stay in bed, relax. I'm going to get up and see what our plans are for the day. I'll get some more shampoo and stuff for the bathroom and check on our clothes. You want anything specific for breakfast?"

She shook her head. "Surprise me."

"Anything you don't eat?" he asked.

"I'll be okay with anything but an MRE," she teased.

His eyes sparkled with humor. "You got it, sweetheart." Then he surprised the shit out of her when he leaned toward her again and shoved his hand under the back of her head. He lifted her at the same time he dropped his mouth to hers.

This was no gentle good-morning kiss. This was a claiming. A possessive, passionate, I-wish-I-could-stay-in-bed-all-day kiss. When he finally pulled back, Casey licked her lips, tasting him there.

"No MREs. Got it." He ran his thumb over her lips and took a deep breath. Then he moved, slowly and what looked like reluctantly, and stood. He strode to the bathroom without looking back.

Casey stayed on her back, looking up at the ceiling and trying to calm her racing heartbeat. The man was lethal, and in that instant, she made her decision.

She wanted to be wherever Beatle was.

So, Texas it was.

Chapter Fifteen

C ASEY FIGURED SHE should probably be nervous, but she wasn't. After a delicious breakfast of eggs, bacon, pancakes, and orange juice—oh my God, orange juice, she'd never tasted anything so good in all her life—Beatle had immediately sat her down to discuss their next steps. She was more grateful than she could express that Truck had given her a head's up as to what Beatle was going to talk to her about.

When she'd told him she'd like to go to Texas with him, she thought she'd seen relief on his face. Relief *and* desire. But she wasn't sure if she was just seeing what she so desperately wanted to, or if he really wanted her as much as she did him.

She knew she had a lot of people she needed to contact when she got back to the States, but she wasn't worried about it right then.

She spent her last day in Costa Rica safe and happy in the hotel. The air conditioning was kicking and Beatle stayed by her side all day. The other guys came in and out, and she'd learned a lot about them and the women in their lives as a result.

At one point, all eight of them sat down and played a rip-roaring funny game of Cards Against Humanity. Apparently, Hollywood had been talking to one of the employees and had mentioned that Casey was bored, and she'd unearthed the slightly scandalous game.

Casey had never laughed so hard in all her life. By the time they had to leave the hotel, she felt as if she'd known the Delta Force team for years.

So when they changed from the happy-go-lucky men she'd spent the afternoon with to the on-alert, deadly soldiers she knew them to be, she wasn't even fazed. In fact, she trusted them more than she had before.

Throughout their trip out of the hotel and to the private airport, Beatle was right next to her. His hand on her arm, or clutching hers, was comforting and reassuring. And when there was a slight problem at the airport, she didn't panic, merely did whatever Beatle told her to and put her life in his hands, again, with no hesitation.

She slept a little on the plane, with her head resting on Beatle's shoulder, his hand clutched in hers. The flight to Fort Hood Army Airfield took around six hours. The sun was just coming up over the Texas horizon when they landed. It took a bit to get the plane cleared, and Casey knew she still needed to meet with the team's commander, but she wasn't worried.

How could she be with Beatle and his teammates at her back? They'd proven time and time again that they had her best interests at heart, and that they'd keep her safe.

No, right then, she was less worried about her safety, leaving that to the man at her side, and more excited to meet the women she'd heard so much about in the last twelve hours or so.

But if she was being honest, the person she most wanted to meet was Annie. Fletch's daughter was seven, and if Casey believed everything he said about her, the cutest, smartest, most amazing child who had ever been born. She wanted to see the badass soldier with the little girl who obviously had him wrapped around her finger.

An hour after leaving the plane, and after a short talk with Beatle's commander, and after Ghost had turned over all the video footage from their time in the jungle, they were on their way to Fletch's house. Apparently, he had an apartment over his garage that she'd be staying in. Beatle said he'd take her to his place, but since Fletch's property had an extensive security system, it would be easier to keep her safe there.

Once again, Casey chickened out about asking if he'd be staying with her. She supposed she'd find out soon enough.

"What's going on in that head of yours?" Beatle

asked as Fletch drove them toward his house.

Casey shrugged.

"Are you worried?"

"A little. I mean, I have no idea if whoever tried to kill me down in Costa Rica will follow me to the States and try again. I don't know what's going to happen with my job. My parents are freaking out and are threatening to drive to Texas to see for themselves that I'm okay. I want your friends' women to like me, but since I haven't had many true friends in my life, I'm worried they might not. And if that isn't enough, I feel like I'm putting Fletch and his family in danger simply by being on his property."

Beatle didn't miss a beat as he addressed each of her concerns. "I hope whoever is after you *does* try to get to you while you're here. It'll make our job easier to find and stop them. But they aren't going to touch one hair on your head, that's my promise to you. Whatever happens with your job will happen. I'm not trying to be a dick about it, because I know it's important to you, but if the administrators can't cut you some slack and give you time off after what happened to you while on a school-sponsored trip, fuck them. There are other universities and other jobs. With your credentials, you can get another teaching position easily. And I don't blame your parents; if I had a child who'd been kidnapped and chased through the jungle, I'd want to see them in person to make sure they really were okay as well. They're welcome to come spend some time with you.

"And everyone is going to love you, Case. How could they not? I don't know why you haven't had any close friends in the past, but I have a feeling as soon as Kassie, Rayne, and the others set eyes on you, they're gonna adopt you as one of their own. I'm sure as hell going to do everything in my power to make that happen too. And you are absolutely not putting anyone in danger. Fletch was the one who volunteered to have you stay at his place. You aren't the first person, and you won't be the last, to take refuge there. If the shit hits the fan, both Emily and Annie know what to do. They'll be safe. Promise."

"Well. All right then," Casey said, a little dazed from all his rebuttals. "I might as well just turn off all the thoughts in my pretty little head and enjoy the ride, huh?"

Beatle smiled at her, and she thought she heard Fletch snort from the front seat, but she didn't take her eyes off of the man next to her to check.

Teasing with Beatle was new to her. Throughout their relationship, if you could call their time together a relationship, she'd been scared and freaked out. She was either crying in his arms or trying to hold herself together. But now that they were finally out of Central

America, she felt more like herself. Lighter. Safer.

He touched her nose with his pointer finger and grinned. "Yup. Exactly."

Casey rolled her eyes at him. Then leaned forward to talk to Fletch. "So...you and your wife are expecting?"

"Shit," Fletch grumbled, then looked at her through the rearview mirror. "You heard me talking to Em in the hotel, didn't you? I thought you were asleep."

Casey shrugged. "I wasn't."

"It's okay. It's a new thing. We haven't officially told anyone yet," Fletch informed her.

"It's about time," Beatle said with a smirk, leaning back and crossing his arms over his chest. "I mean, you're the one who's always talking about how hard you've been trying to knock her up."

"How far along is she?" Casey asked Fletch.

"Only about six weeks. I know people say you aren't supposed to announce anything until around three months, but we're both so excited we can't keep it to ourselves anymore. Besides, if something were to happen to our baby, I'd want our best friends to be there to support us both. I can't figure that telling everyone is a bad thing in any way."

"I'm surprised you didn't announce it from the rooftops when she was two days preggo," Beatle teased.

Fletch winked at Casey in the mirror and she stifled

a giggle. "Yeah, well, I can't help it if she's so irresistible I can't keep my hands off her. We haven't told anyone else yet, though, and no one other than me and her are supposed to know. I'd appreciate it if you kept the secret for a little longer. We're going to have a pregnancy reveal party next week. At least that's what she's calling it. I don't know why she doesn't just call everyone and tell them, but she insists this is the way it's done now."

Casey eyed Fletch. His eyes were on the road again, but the smile on his face contradicted his grumpy words. "You love it."

"I do, but if you tell her, I'll deny it," he told her.

Casey mimicked zipping her lips shut. "My lips are sealed."

"You get that present done for Annie?" Beatle asked.

"Yup. Emily is gonna kill me, but I can't frickin' wait to give it to her," Fletch said.

"What present?" Casey asked.

"Now that *is* a secret," Fletch told her.

"Awwwww, not fair," Casey grumbled. "I'm the one who's being hunted. I think I should know."

Casey felt a finger on her cheek and allowed Beatle to turn her to face him. His expression had lost all its good humor and he was serious as he said, "Don't, Case."

"Don't what?" she asked.

"Don't kid about what's happening to you. It's not

funny."

He was right. It wasn't. Casey immediately felt bad. "I'm sorry. But you should know, this is the real me. I tend to joke a lot to try to diffuse a situation. Especially when it's something happening to me. It makes me feel...I don't know...less stressed about it. Like, when our plane was delayed on the way to Central America, I joked that with our luck it was because we were being hijacked. Again, not funny, but sometimes by comparing what's currently happening to something more awful, my situation doesn't seem as bad."

"I can't stand the thought of something bad happening to you again, sweetheart. Even if you're just kidding."

"I'll try to curb it. But again, Beatle, it's just me."

He nodded and moved his hand to the back of her neck. Casey knew what was coming, and allowed him to pull her toward him. She braced herself with her palms on the seat between them.

Beatle touched his lips to hers and whispered, "I like 'just you,' Case. The more I learn, the more I like."

He let go of her neck and Casey stayed where she was for a beat before sitting back on her side of the seat.

"I called Emily and let her know when we were going to arrive," Fletch said from the front seat. "Annie was pretty excited to have another guest staying in 'her old house.'"

Casey looked at Beatle in confusion.

"She and Emily rented the apartment from Fletch. It's how they met," he explained.

"Ah. I'm looking forward to meeting your daughter," Casey told Fletch.

"And she's looking forward to meeting you," Fletch returned. "For the record, she's smart. Really smart. And being as smart as she is sometimes isn't conducive to being polite. She tends to say inappropriate stuff. I'd appreciate it if you didn't call her out on it. She doesn't mean to be rude, it's just how she is."

Casey blinked. "You think I'd be rude to your little girl?"

"No, but I didn't want you to take anything she might say too personally." His voice gentled. "She's my daughter, and I'll move heaven and earth to make sure she gets what she needs to grow up to be a confident woman who loves herself exactly how she is, no matter what society tries to tell her is appropriate, beautiful, or any other warped bullshit they try to shove down the public's throat."

"I understand," Casey told him. And she did. Her own father was pretty great, but she had a feeling Fletch would blow him out of the water. The little girl would have a hard time when she wanted to start dating. No one would be good enough for her in her daddy's eyes...as it should be.

"It's fine, Fletch," she told him. "I'm sure she'll be delightful."

"Delightful," Beatle snorted. "I'm not sure that's the right adjective."

Casey glared at him, which only made him chuckle. "You'll see," he said sagely. "You'll see."

Before too long, they'd pulled down a lengthy driveway. Casey saw a garage with a stairway along the side of it, then her attention was captured by the beautiful main house.

It was two stories and had a large wraparound porch, though what really caught her attention were the two people standing on the steps. The tall woman with brown hair had to be Emily, and the little dark-blonde-haired girl had to be Annie. But it was the sign the little girl was holding that made her eyes fill with tears.

Casey had been proud of how she'd been holding herself together recently. She'd never been a crier, but had felt like all she'd done was leak tears since she'd been rescued.

But seeing the bright pink sign with childish letters that had been painstakingly written by Annie almost did her in.

Welcome Home Casey
You'll be Safe Here

Casey had no idea what Fletch had told his wife, or

what she in turn had told Annie, but leave it to a kid to get right to the heart of the matter.

She felt Beatle take hold of her hand and squeeze lightly. Taking a deep breath, she looked over at the man next to her and gave him a small smile.

Fletch pulled right up to the house and stopped. He threw the vehicle in park and was out of the car before Casey could blink. He picked up his daughter and threw her over his shoulder, her sign falling harmlessly to the ground with his actions. She squealed in delight and laughed uproariously. He then leaned forward and tugged his wife around the back of her neck, much like Beatle always did to Casey, and pulled her to him, kissing her passionately and unapologetically.

"Let me down, Daddy!" Annie yelled.

Fletch pulled away from his wife and put his hand on her belly while he said something Casey couldn't hear.

"Ready?" Beatle asked quietly.

"Ready," Casey affirmed.

Beatle opened the door on his side of the car and tugged for her to follow. She scooted over the leather seat, all the while holding his hand. He helped her stand upright, and Casey was glad for his support when Annie careened into her. Her little arms went around her waist and squeezed.

Casey looked down in surprise at the affectionate

child. Some of her friends from work had kids, but none had ever greeted her like this, and she'd known some of them since they were infants.

"Oh. Hi, Annie," Casey said quietly.

The little girl looked up, her long hair brushing her butt. She had streaks of dirt on her face and her clothes were dusty, as if she'd been rolling around on the ground. But she didn't seem to notice or care.

"Hi! I'm so glad you're here. You're gonna be living in my old apartment. But there's more food there now than when I was there, so it's okay. You wanna play Army with me? You can be the damsel in distress and I'll be the soldier who saves you, just like my daddy did with you. Okay?"

Casey was taken aback by Annie's words. First, she hadn't ever met a girl who wanted to play "Army." She definitely didn't know the rules. But the fact that Annie wanted to be the one who saved the damsel was a little surprising.

On second thought, maybe it wasn't. Being the damsel in distress wasn't all that fun. Casey should know. So yeah, being the one with the gun and saving others sounded pretty darn good.

"I see how you are, squirt. Now that you have a new playmate, you don't even want to say hi to me."

Annie grinned, let go of Casey, and threw herself at Beatle. "Bug Man!! I missed you!"

Beatle picked Annie up and threw her high in the air. She shrieked in delight and when he caught her, demanded, "Do it again!"

So he did. Then he kissed her forehead and placed her feet back on the ground. "Why don't you let Casey get settled before you start bugging her to play with you?"

Annie pouted a little. "But I wanted to play with her now!"

Casey couldn't resist her cute little face. She squatted down, thankful for Beatle's steadying hand as she almost lost her balance. "I'd be happy to play with you later, Annie. But maybe not captive and savior, okay? That's a little too close to home for me right now."

"Close to home? But everything in my yard is close to the house."

Casey grinned, she couldn't help it. "Sorry, I meant, since it really happened to me, recently, it kinda hurts to think about it. I'm happy to play something else though."

The expression on Annie's face was a mixture of sorrow and sympathy. Casey had never seen such an empathetic child before. The little girl stepped forward and carefully wrapped her arms around Casey's neck. Surprised, Casey looked up at Beatle.

He simply nodded at her and held her steady with his hand on her shoulder.

"I'm sorry you were taken by bad guys," Annie said into Casey's ear. "I was stolded too and I was scared. But Daddy Fletch came and got me and Mommy, just like he did you." She pulled back and patted Casey's cheeks softly with her little hands. "Bug Man likes you. Mommy said Daddy told her. So at night, when you get scared, just crawl into his bed and he'll hold you tight and make the bad dreams go away."

Casey stared at the solemn little girl. "Is that what happened to you?"

Annie nodded. "I don't dream about the bad guy so much anymore, but Daddy says anytime I need him, he'll be there to protect me and hold me so the bad guy can't get me. I bet Bug Man will do the same for you."

Casey didn't take her gaze away from Annie's, but she felt Beatle crouch down next to them. "Of course I will," he said softly. "Just like your daddy did for you, Annie, I'll be there for Casey. Want to hear something cool?"

"What?" Annie asked, looking at Beatle but keeping her hands on Casey's face.

Casey tried to keep her cool, but Annie's innocent words struck her to her core. Beatle *had* done that for her. In the jungle, and in the hotel room the night before. When she'd had bad dreams, he was there to chase them away.

"Casey is a bug lady for real. She studies them. She

knows everything there is to know about bugs. Ants, ladybugs, fireflies, dragonflies...you name it, she can tell you about them. She even has five huge cockroaches as *pets*!"

This time when Annie looked at her, her eyes were wide with excitement instead of empathy. "Really?" she breathed.

"Really," Casey assured her.

"Cool!" Then she turned and ran back to her mom. "Mommy! Casey is a bug lady! She knows *everything* about them! I want a cockroach! I have to go catch some bugs so she can teach me!" And with that, Annie ran toward the side of the house and a large empty field, presumably to get some bugs.

Beatle helped Casey stand and smiled down at her. "You're going to have a class of one in a bit, sweetheart."

"Thank you," Casey told him.

"For what?"

"For bringing me here. For distracting her so I didn't have to be her damsel in distress. For doing what you do, keeping the world safe so children like her can be kids as long as possible."

"You're welcome," Beatle said. Then he brought his hands to her face and used his thumbs to brush against her cheeks. "She got you dirty," he told her as he concentrated on cleaning her face.

Casey smiled. "She *was* kinda dirty, huh?"

"I apologize for my daughter," Emily said from behind them.

Casey turned from Beatle and ran an arm over her face quickly then looked at the other woman. "It's okay, I wasn't complaining."

"She loves to play in the dirt. Lord knows I have no idea where that came from, as I can't stand dirt, but," Emily shrugged, "it makes her happy, so I won't stop her from doing it. Welcome home, Casey. I'm so glad you're all right and here with us."

"Me too," Casey said softly. Then Emily reached out, just like her daughter had, and gave her a genuine and heartfelt hug.

Casey smiled as she realized she'd been hugged more in the last week than she had in the last five years.

"Right," Emily said as she pulled back. "Fletch said that you didn't really have any clothes other than what you're wearing, so I called Kassie and she said she could pick up some stuff for you. She works at JCPenney and gets a wicked discount, and you know, their clothes are already always discounted, so they're super affordable. I just need to get back to her with your sizes and what you might like to wear. You know, if you're a jeans-and-T-shirt kinda gal, or if you like more formal stuff. Oh, and of course, what kinds of bras and panties you like. Lacey or cotton, thongs or granny panties. She can get whatever."

Casey's eyes about bugged out of her head. First, she was surprised someone she'd never met would offer to get her clothes, but second, there was no way she was going to talk about what kind of underwear she liked to wear in front of Beatle and Fletch.

"Thongs, definitely," Beatle commented from behind her.

Casey whipped her head around and, without thought, balled up a fist and hit him on the arm. "Not your decision," she huffed.

He froze for a moment and they stared at each other. Just when Casey was getting mortified that she'd *hit* Beatle, he threw back his head and laughed.

She heard Emily chuckling next to her. "Sorry," she said as she hooked her arm with Casey's. "I wasn't thinking. Shut up, Beatle, it wasn't *that* funny," she admonished. "Come on, we'll go inside and you can tell me, *in private*, what you want."

Before Emily dragged her off, Beatle said, "I'll be out here. I'll make sure the apartment has everything we need."

With one word, Beatle was able to calm the nerves Casey didn't even realize were still swimming in her belly.

Everything *we* need.

He wasn't going to leave her here by herself.

He was going to stay with her.

She smiled shyly at him and nodded.

As if they'd been together for years instead of mere days, Beatle read the relief in her eyes. Ignoring the fact that Emily was standing right there, he leaned in and kissed Casey on the lips. It was a short yet intimate caress.

"Let me know if you need me."

"I will."

And with one last touch of his hand on her biceps, Beatle turned and walked toward the garage with Fletch.

"Girrrrl," Emily breathed, "I can't *wait* to introduce you to the others. We have so much to talk about, but I promised not to pick at you for details until they could be here too."

Casey smiled at Emily. "I'm not sure I have a lot of details, but I'm thinking I could use some advice. I'm not sure I know what to do with a Delta Force soldier."

"Now *that* we can do," Emily told her with a broad grin. "Come on. Let's go find you something to eat. I'm sure you're tired too. You can rest while I write down your sizes and everything you need. You're in good hands with us, Casey."

Casey let herself be towed inside the big house and found that she couldn't stop smiling. She'd made the right decision to come to Texas. Absolutely.

Chapter Sixteen

B EATLE LOOKED OVER at Casey for what seemed like the hundredth time. She seemed to be holding up extremely well. She hadn't hesitated to go with Emily while he and Fletch had checked out the apartment over the garage to make sure it was ready for her.

By the time they'd gotten back to the house, Casey had given Emily her preferences and sizes for clothes and was taking a nap. He'd peeked in on her to make sure she was good, and found her sound asleep in one of the guest rooms. It had taken everything in him to shut the door and leave her alone.

Later, Kassie had arrived with the clothes and had blown off Casey's thanks. She was the proud new owner of three pairs of jeans, two long-sleeve T-shirts, two short-sleeve tees, four fancier blouses, two pairs of slacks, two pajama sets, and two pairs of black leggings. He'd caught sight of several pairs of lace undies and bras to match.

Seeing the underwear made him think back to the jungle, when he'd doctored the scratches on her chest.

And thinking about her tits made his dick lengthen in his jeans. He'd put on the performance of a lifetime and had pretended not to be at all interested in the clothes Kassie had brought, when in reality all he could think about was Casey standing in front of him wearing nothing but the bits of lace.

Casey had called her parents and talked them out of visiting, telling them Aspen was keeping his eye on her and that she was fine. She'd called Kristina, one of her students, and learned that Astrid had gone back to Denmark, but she and Jaylyn had appointments to talk to Doctor Santos, the psychology teacher Casey knew. She was currently on vacation, but was expected back the following week.

The haunted look in Casey's eyes had returned after talking to her student, and Beatle had wanted her to take a break from her calls, but she'd refused. She'd talked to her landlord, the dean from her university, her bank to cancel her old credit card and get a new one sent to her in Texas, and finally a neighbor, who promised to check in on her cockroaches.

Beatle had known Casey was at her breaking point. Dealing with the realities of her life and trying to get it put back together from hundreds of miles away was tough. Hearing time and time again that people hadn't thought she'd make it back alive after being kidnapped wasn't helping.

But Annie had come to the rescue. She'd collected quite the assortment of bugs from the yard, and she and Casey had spent hours discussing and learning about each one. By the time dinner was ready, Casey looked more at ease, although she still had dark circles under her eyes.

They were now sitting around the living room. Annie was watching television while the adults talked.

"After I talked to Fletch and he told me you were coming, I made sure the fridge was stocked in the apartment," Emily told Casey. "But if you need anything that's not out there, don't hesitate to let me know."

"Thanks. I appreciate it. I'm not sure how long I'll be here, but maybe I can make you guys dinner one night?"

Emily beamed. "I'd love that."

"We're going to see what we can do to get this cleared up for you sooner rather than later," Fletch said quietly. "Ghost is reviewing the tapes again to see if there's anything there, and if our commander gets any more information from the Costa Rican authorities, he'll pass it on."

Casey nodded. "Actually, I don't mind staying here. My dean said I could take the rest of the summer off with no problems. But what happens if we don't find any information about who the kidnapper was? I can't stay here forever."

"Why not?" Emily asked what Beatle was thinking.

"Uh…because I live in Florida. My job is there," Casey told her.

"But what if you come to like it here so much, you don't want to go back?" the other woman asked. "I know we just met, but I like you, Casey. I'm a pretty good judge of character, Annie's father notwithstanding. I'd hate to see you leave."

"Leave her alone," Fletch ordered gently. "She's been here for what, ten hours?"

Beatle tuned out the conversation between Fletch and his wife and kept his eyes on Casey. He wanted to plead with her to stay, just like Emily had done, but Fletch was right, it was too soon. She'd dealt with a lot of crap today. He needed to move slowly, let Casey feel comfortable here. Let her see what great friends Emily, Kassie, Harley, Rayne, and Mary could be. He was hoping that the longer she stayed, the higher the likelihood she would *want* to stay. He'd been thrilled to hear that her boss had given her the rest of the summer off.

Beatle was so busy trying to think about how to bring up the topic of her staying, he almost missed the way Casey flinched when the music in a dramatic scene in the cartoon Annie was watching suddenly rose in a cacophony of noise.

"Headache?" he asked softly.

"I'm okay," Casey said immediately.

"Case, we aren't in the middle of the jungle any-more. There's no reason to be a tough girl here."

She turned and glared at him. "I'm fine," she said between clenched teeth. "It's not like I'm covering up a gunshot wound or something. It's just a headache."

"Your head hurts?" Emily asked from across the way. "I've got some aspirin if you need it."

"No, I'm—"

"Thanks, Emily," Beatle interrupted. "I think, if it's okay, we're going to hit the sack."

He could feel Casey's eyes boring into the side of his head, and almost smiled. Almost. "I think I saw some pills in the medicine cabinet in the bathroom in the apartment, right?"

"Yup. It's fully stocked with just about everything you'd need," Fletch replied.

Beatle knew his friend was referring to the condoms he told him he'd stashed in the apartment earlier. If he had his way, they would come in extremely handy. But not tonight. Tonight, his girl had a headache and needed sleep.

He stood and held out a hand to Casey. She sighed, but did put her hand in his and let him help her up. He immediately wrapped an arm around her waist. He walked them over to Annie, who was still staring up at the television as if it held the meaning to life.

"See you tomorrow, squirt."

"Bye," she said distractedly, not looking away from the screen.

Beatle shook his head and turned to his friends. "Thanks for dinner. Fletch, the commander knows I won't be at PT in the morning. But I'll be in later."

"I'll remind him," Fletch assured Beatle.

"Thanks for organizing with Kassie to get me clothes," Casey told Emily. "I appreciate it. And I'll pay her back as soon as I can."

Emily waved her hand dismissively. "No need. And if you try, you'll just irritate us. Consider it a welcome-to-the-club gift."

"The club?" Casey asked, her brows drawing down in confusion.

"Yeah, the Delta—"

Fletch put his hand over his wife's mouth, cutting off her words. "Good night, guys. See you tomorrow."

Beatle gave his friend a chin lift in thanks. He was thrilled that Emily already thought of Casey as a Delta Force woman, but he knew he needed more time to convince Casey. He also knew she still thought he was with her because of some sort of psychological thing related to her rescue, but that wasn't it at all. He'd rescued hundreds of people, and hadn't ever had the kind of attraction to them that he did to Casey.

He steered her out of the main house and across the yard, pointing out the cameras as he went.

"Why so many?" Casey asked.

"Fletch has always had some, but after a misunderstanding with Emily that almost cost her life, and that of her daughter, he increased them. And after their wedding reception, when their presence paid off tenfold, he added a few more."

By the time they'd climbed the steps to the apartment and he had the door open, Casey had learned all about the attempted robbery at the wedding reception, and how easily all the Special Forces soldiers in attendance had crushed it. Not only that, but Fletch had hired contractors to make a panic room inside his house. He'd taught Annie the code word—red, of course—and anytime he or her mom said that word, she was to go inside without complaint and head to the safe room. It was equipped with anything the family might need in order to stay safe until the authorities could arrive. Televisions connected to the cameras on the property, phone lines that couldn't be tampered with from the outside, as well as food, water, and bedding.

"I guess I can't blame him for all the security," Casey commented as they entered the apartment.

Without another word, Beatle headed for the bathroom to get some aspirin. He came back and handed her two pills. She took them and washed them down with a swig of water without protest.

"You're exhausted," Beatle observed. "Why don't you go on to bed?"

She nodded and turned to the bedroom. Then she stopped and faced him once more.

Beatle waited patiently as she first looked at him, then at her feet, then at the wall next to her.

"What, sweetheart?"

"Are you staying?" she asked quietly, then bit her bottom lip while still looking everywhere but at him.

Beatle walked over to her until he was all the way in her personal space. He waited until she looked up at him.

"Do you want me to?"

It probably wasn't nice of him to push the issue. He could've just said that, yes, he was staying. That he had no intention of leaving her alone until she went back to Florida. But he needed to know the attraction he'd seen glimpses of in her eyes was still there. That the kisses they'd shared weren't simply spur-of-the-moment things when she'd been in danger.

Casey licked her lips and Beatle smothered a groan that threatened to escape his throat at the unintentionally sensual action.

"Yes."

"I can sleep out here," Beatle told her, gesturing toward the couch behind them.

She didn't take her gaze from his. "Will you…" She paused, then said quickly, her words strung together, "Sleepwithme?"

"Absolutely. There's nowhere I'd rather be. Go ahead and use the bathroom. Do your thing. I'll be in after a bit."

"Okay."

The relief in her eyes was almost painful to see, but Beatle didn't comment on it. Doing so felt as though it would be disrespectful, considering how well she was doing after her ordeal. He watched as she made her way to the bedroom, then when she came out a minute later with one of the pajama sets in her hand. She smiled shyly at him as she entered the bathroom and closed the door.

Only then did Beatle breathe normally again. He turned toward the kitchen and grabbed a bottle of water. He gulped it down as he tried to control his raging libido. He'd never been such a horndog before. He'd had relationships, but none had felt as intense as this one…and he and Casey weren't even having sex.

When he was away from her, he wanted to see her. When he was with her, he wanted to touch her. And when he was touching her, he wanted the right to slowly strip off all her clothes and taste every inch of her skin. It was a vicious circle, but one that made him feel more alive than he'd felt in a long time.

He loved his job with the team, but seeing his friends settle down one by one had been hard. Beatle went home to his small apartment by himself, and his friends all got to go home to women who loved them and were ecstatic to have them home.

He wasn't an idiot. He knew he and Casey had some pretty darn big hurdles to overcome before he could safely say they were a couple, but he hoped they could scale them.

Beatle made a mental note to talk to the commander about Casey seeing a psychologist from the post soon. He knew she had a co-worker who would gladly talk to her about what had happened, but she was in Florida. Casey needed someone here.

She also needed more of her own things. It was great that Kassie had gotten her some clothes, but she needed more than a few outfits. He knew she'd feel better if she had some of her own belongings. It would make Texas feel more like home.

"I'm done."

Casey's soft voice interrupted his musings, and Beatle turned.

He knew his mouth was hanging open, but he couldn't help it. She was absolutely beautiful. The light in the hall was off, but the light pink sleep shorts and spaghetti-strap top were easy to see. The top was loose on her frame, but Beatle could still see the swells of her breasts under the material. Her legs were long and lithe and his mind immediately went into the gutter. He could almost feel the soft skin of her inner thighs as they wrapped around his hips and squeezed him as he eased his cock inside her tight, hot body.

"I'll be in bed," she said, breaking into his fantasy.

Beatle had a feeling he was blushing, but he merely nodded at her, not quite ready to speak yet.

When she turned for the bedroom door, Beatle had to close his eyes, but it didn't block out the image that was already burned in his brain. The shorts she wore were tight and outlined her perfect curvy ass. She was beautiful. Softly rounded in the right places, and all woman. And Beatle wanted her. Badly. He could feel the blood beating through his cock like a heartbeat. He knew without a doubt if he ever had the chance to make love with Casey Shea, he wouldn't last longer than a minute, if the way he was feeling right now was any indication.

She wasn't even trying to entice him, and she'd snared him faster than any woman ever had before.

He hunched over a bit, trying to ease the pain of his intense hard-on and think about anything other than walking into the bedroom and stripping off her new pajama set and sinking into her body.

It took a couple of minutes, but finally Beatle could walk without limping. He went into the bathroom and brushed his teeth. Then he headed for the bedroom.

Casey was lying under the comforter and waiting for him with wide eyes. He'd half hoped she'd be asleep, but since it had only been a few minutes, that hope was silly.

He turned his back to her and took off his shirt. Then he unbuttoned his jeans and ordered his dick to behave and he shoved the material off his legs, leaving him in nothing but his boxers.

Without a word, he sat on the bed and swung his legs up and under the covers. He gathered Casey in his arms and inhaled deeply. Mistake.

The scent of whatever lotion Kassie had brought her filled his nostrils, and as if he hadn't already had a stern conversation with his dick, it filled with blood once more, readying itself to procreate.

"Thanks for leaving the door open," Casey told him.

"Of course. Is there enough light?" Beatle asked.

"I think so."

"I can turn on the hall light if you want me to."

She shook her head against his shoulder. "No. Don't go."

Fuck. As if he could go anywhere after hearing those two words leave her lips. "Is your head feeling any better?"

"A little."

"Good."

A minute or two passed, then she said, "This is weird. Why is this weird?"

"It's not weird," Beatle said immediately. "Relax."

"It seemed perfectly normal in Costa Rica, but now…it's weird."

Beatle rolled over until Casey was on her back and he hovered over her. His hands speared into her hair and he held her head still. He knew his erection was pressing into her hip, but he didn't care. "Down there, you were scared, and I helped make you feel safe. In the hotel, you'd had a bad dream, and I held you and you calmed. Now that you don't feel as if you're in immediate danger, your other senses can kick in. I hope to Christ you honestly don't feel as though this is weird, and it's really your body telling you other things."

"Like what?" she whispered.

"Like you're attracted to me. That you enjoy being in my arms not because I make you safe, but because you like me. Because I'll tell you right now, I'll lay it out, not that it's not obvious, I love holding you in my arms. Feeling you snuggle up into me. And, sweetheart, I've never been a snuggler. I've always preferred to have my space while sleeping. But since that first night with you in that hammock, plastered to your side, sweating with you in my arms, I've decided that there's no place I'd rather be than right here. With you."

He paused, staring down into Casey's wide green

eyes. "I'm not pressuring you for anything. If you truly feel too weird with this sleeping arrangement, I'll spend the night on the couch. But know that I love sleeping with you. And I truly mean that. *Sleeping*. I'm not saying I don't want more, eventually, but the when and if are completely up to you."

"You're truly not just saying that because you think I'm too weak to be able to sleep by myself?"

"Weak? Jesus, Casey. No. Weak is the last thing I think about when I think of you. I'm in awe of your strength."

"I don't feel very strong right now."

"Maybe not, but that doesn't mean you aren't."

"Hmmm. I *am* attracted to you. I think you know that."

"I guessed, but wasn't sure," Beatle told her honestly.

"I think that's part of it. I mean, friends just don't sleep together like this."

"*We* do," Beatle told her fiercely.

"But you're...you're aroused, Beatle," Casey said, her cheeks bright pink.

"I am. But that doesn't mean anything will happen between us until you're ready for it to happen."

"Can you even sleep like that?" Casey asked with a grimace.

Beatle chuckled. "Yeah, sweetheart. I can sleep. I feel

more relaxed here with you in my arms than if I were out on that lumpy couch. And don't worry about him," he lightly pressed his hips against her leg. "He'll calm down in a bit."

"It's not fair to you," Casey protested, still looking concerned.

Beatle smiled at her and turned back over until she was lying on her side next to him once more. They both shifted until they were comfortable, her palm pressed to his naked chest, his resting on the material of her sleep shorts at her hip. "It's not a matter of fair or not fair," he told her. "This is my normal state around you. Whether you're covered in dirt from head to toe, or fresh and clean from a shower. It's just you, Case."

"You're nuts," she told him.

"Probably," Beatle retorted. "Now hush and go to sleep."

Nothing felt as good as Casey relaxing fully against him.

Yeah, he was still hard, and he knew if she ever let him inside her, it would be an almost out-of-body experience for him, but still…having Casey trust him enough to let down her guard when she knew he wanted her was the most amazing feeling.

Beatle turned his head and kissed her forehead.

And smiled even wider when she unconsciously snuggled farther into his embrace.

Chapter Seventeen

T HE LAST WEEK and a half had been full of highs and lows for Casey.

Some of the highs included meeting all of the Delta Force women. She loved each and every one of them. Rayne was sweet and generous, offering to hang out with Casey whenever she wanted. Harley was beautiful. Tall and slender, but more than that, she was hilarious. She was super smart, and had spent one afternoon playing video games with her when the men were busy on the Army post.

Annie was also something else. She'd shown up every morning, bright and early, wanting to play. Emily finally had to forbid her to leave the house before nine in the morning, giving Casey time to wake up and have her coffee before being inundated with little-girl cheerfulness and energy…and bug questions.

Beatle was another high. He'd been true to his word and hadn't pressured her for anything more than she was ready to give him. Which so far had been only kisses and a little light petting when they went to bed. She wanted him, but her situation felt so up in the air, she didn't feel it was fair to either of them to start any kind of sexual relationship until she was surer of what was going on in her life.

The lows included a few email conversations with Doctor Santos. Her friend and fellow professor had been meeting daily with Jaylyn and Kristina. Casey had been emailing them herself, and knew they'd given Doctor Santos permission to talk to her about their experiences and counseling sessions. Marie had emailed Casey to report that the girls weren't doing well. Not sleeping, anxiety, night terrors, and no appetite.

She herself was seeing a doctor Beatle had recommended on post. It had been uncomfortable at first, but now that she felt more at ease with him, she was beginning to open up. She even admitted that there were some blanks in her memory, and he reassured her that once she felt safe enough, and more time had gone by, she'd most likely remember. He'd even offered to hypnotize her if she truly felt what she wasn't remembering was that important.

The other not-so-great thing happening was the videos of the jungle that each of the Delta men had taken hadn't been reviewed by the Army yet. Apparently, the techs on post were too busy and just hadn't been able to get to them.

Casey found she now had a morbid curiosity to

watch them. To see more of the village where she'd been held hostage. She certainly hadn't seen much of it when she was there.

Time seemed liked it was going by at the speed of light—the start of the fall semester at the university would be here before she knew it—but it was also going slow too. It felt as if she'd been in Fletch's small apartment forever. That she'd known the men and women in the Special Forces group her entire life.

Emily had broken down and told Casey about her pregnancy. She said she was just too excited and that she might as well spill the beans because everyone would know soon anyway. That very afternoon, she was having her "pregnancy reveal" party, although she wasn't advertising that was what it was. She'd used Casey's arrival as an excuse to hold a barbeque.

Casey had been helping her cook all morning. Emily had planned all sorts of finger foods. Deviled eggs, potato salad bites, mini corn dogs, caprese bites, fruit skewers, pesto pinwheels, and lots and lots of cookies.

She and Emily had been giggling all day about the announcement and what everyone would say and, as a result, Casey was almost as excited about the party as Emily was.

"Are you good?" Casey asked Emily when they'd plated the last of the cookies. The table in the dining area was filled to the brim with food. There were chairs set out all around the living room, and as soon as Fletch got home, he'd start up the grill in the backyard.

"Yeah. I appreciate your help so much. I don't know that I could've gotten it all done without you," Emily told her.

"Yeah, you would've...it might've taken longer though," Casey teased.

Emily sighed, but smiled all the same. She put her hand on her belly. "I hope this little guy doesn't make my life miserable."

"Uh...I don't know much about it, but isn't it early to know what gender your baby is?" Casey asked.

Emily laughed and nodded. "Yeah, but both me and Fletch have a feeling he's a boy. I've been calling him a boy from practically day one."

"Will you be disappointed if it's a girl?"

Emily shook her head. "Nope. Boy, girl, twins, whatever. It doesn't matter."

Casey smiled. "If Annie had her way, you'd have a dozen more. I've never seen a child want a sibling more than her."

"Right?" Emily said. "I felt bad about not telling her she's getting her greatest wish the moment me and Fletch found out, but I know the second she realizes she's going to be a big sister, she'll drive me crazy with questions. She's also the worst at anticipation. You should see her around Christmas. Lord."

Casey grinned. "She's amazing. You're very lucky."

"I know. Now…go get ready. Everyone will start arriving in about an hour," Emily informed her.

Casey wiped her hands once more and headed for the door. She walked across the driveway and yard to the apartment. When she reached the stairs leading up alongside the garage, she paused and looked up. The sky was a brilliant blue. She could hear birds singing and the remarkably loud sound of cicadas in the trees around them.

She vowed right then and there never to take her freedom for granted. There was a point not too long ago when she didn't know if she'd ever see the sky again. Standing in the yard of a family who was fast becoming close friends hadn't been something she ever would've predicted.

She shook herself out of her thoughts and hurried up the stairs. The cell phone Beatle had gotten for her was ringing when she unlocked the door, and Casey ran to the counter and clicked on the icon, hoping she wasn't too late.

"Hello?"

"Hello? Casey?"

"Marie?"

"Yeah, it's me. I'm so sorry to be bothering you. I just wanted to call and tell you in person how happy I am that you're okay. I mean, I know I said it in an email, but it's different hearing it out loud. You must be having such a hard time assimilating back into society after what happened."

Casey grimaced, and her friend's words made her feel guilty. Because honestly, she hadn't thought about what had happened to her all day. She and Emily had laughed, joked, and talked about normal girlfriend stuff.

"I'm doing okay, thanks. How'd you get this number?" Casey asked.

"From Jaylyn. She said she's called you a few times, and I asked if she'd give me your number so I could talk to you too."

Casey sat on the edge of the couch and nodded. "Yeah. I'm sorry to hear she and Kristina aren't coping very well with what happened to them."

"It's such a shame," Marie agreed sadly. "Jaylyn said the last time you talked to her, you asked if she remembered seeing or hearing anything out of the ordinary when you guys were first taken, or later when they were in the hut?"

"I did," Casey confirmed. "The men who rescued me have been trying to figure out who in the world would want to kidnap us, and we all agreed that maybe we heard or saw something, but with all the trauma we went through, maybe we've been blocking it."

"That's possible," Marie said. "The psychological damage the four of you suffered could definitely be blocking some of the details. Were you raped?"

Casey suppressed a gasp. Jeez, even the Deltas had been more tactful than Marie was being. And she was supposed to be her friend. "No," she responded a little curtly.

"Well, that's good," Marie said, oblivious to Casey's brusque response. "Jaylyn and Kristina say they weren't either. But isn't that weird? I mean, a bunch of women were kidnapped in South America and not raped? Maybe they just weren't attracted to you or something."

Casey's mouth hung open in shock. She didn't just say that. "You did *not* just say that," she told her colleague.

"Oh...sorry. I didn't mean to be insensitive," Marie said, sounding apologetic.

"Were you calling for a reason?" Casey asked, wanting nothing more than to hang up on the other woman.

"Yes, I was. It's the girls. You know I've been meeting with them every day to try to help them process what happened. We've talked, and think maybe some group sessions would do them good."

"Okaaaay," Casey said, not understanding what she had to do with Jaylyn and Kristina talking to the doctor together.

"With you, Casey," Marie elaborated. "You were their leader. They told me before you were separated, they were doing pretty well. Sharing food, their spirits were high that they'd be rescued. But when you were taken away, and they thought you'd been rescued and they were left behind, they fell apart. I think it would be a good idea if you joined us."

"Oh, well…yeah. I could do that. If you tell me when you're meeting, I could call in or something."

"No!" Marie exclaimed. Then, in a calmer voice, explained, "I don't think the phone will work. The girls need to see you. See for themselves that you're okay. And before you suggest it, Skype just isn't the same as seeing you in person, and being able to hug and touch. I think they really need to see you, in person, in front of them, to know for sure that you're all right. When are you coming home? You should be here among friends, anyway. It'll help you heal."

Casey thought that she was healing quite well as it was. "I'm doing okay. I'm seeing a psychologist here on the Army post. He's really helping."

"Really?"

"Yeah."

"What do you talk about?"

Casey actually took the phone off her ear and stared at it for a moment, as if she could figure out what the hell was going on. If she didn't know better, she'd think she was being punked or something. "I'm not going to tell you what I talk to my doctor about, Marie. I know we're friends and you're a psychologist, but that's not cool."

"I wasn't trying to be a bitch," Marie said a little defensively. "I just think the girls would be progressing better if you were all together. If you could talk about what happened with one another. Maybe whatever it is you think you've forgotten would come to you easier if you saw Jaylyn and Kristina. A reenactment might even help."

"A reenactment?" Casey asked in disbelief. She was more than done with the phone call. She'd been in such a good mood, and now she was irritated and grumpy. "I'm not going to fucking reenact being kidnapped, Marie. I can't believe you'd even suggest that!"

"You'd be surprised how cathartic it can be, Casey. It's obvious you're upset with me, but I honestly just want the best for you and the girls. I want you to get past what happened, and I'm interested in helping you do that. Not only that, but if you let me help you, maybe what you went through won't be in vain, and you can help other kidnap victims in the future recover from their experiences."

Casey simply shook her head. Marie didn't get it. "I'm willing to call in when you meet with Jaylyn and Kristina. Just let me know when."

"They'll be glad to hear that," Marie said. "I'll talk to them and we'll figure out a time. Please don't hesitate to call me if you remember anything you think will help the girls. They're scared someone will hunt them down, you know. Anything you remember that will reassure them they're safe would be a huge relief and a giant step forward in their healing process."

Casey nodded. She knew it would, because she felt the same way. "I will. If anything comes to mind, I'll let you know."

"I'm really glad you're okay. I can't wait for you to come home. We'll do lunch, okay?"

"Sure," Casey said, not really meaning it.

"Talk to you soon."

"Bye." Casey clicked off the phone and stared at it for a long moment. "What the hell just happened?" she asked aloud.

No one answered, which was good since she was alone in the apartment.

Casey closed her eyes and thought about the conversation she'd just had. Not only was it inappropriate, but it was weird as hell. She was friendly with Marie, but not *friends* with her. They saw each other at school functions, but hadn't really socialized much outside of work.

It was somewhat nice that the doctor was worried about her, but was she *too* worried? Why would she want her to come home if she was doing well where she was? Had her students told Marie more than the woman was letting on?

A part of Casey wanted to go back to Florida to check on Jaylyn and Kristina. But honestly, she couldn't really help them. They needed to keep seeing a psychologist. And why was Marie so interested in what she did or didn't remember about the kidnapping?

A shiver went up the back of Casey's neck. Could the doctor have ulterior motives? But what? It made no sense.

Just then, the door to the apartment opened and a male voice boomed through the room. "Casey?"

She jumped a foot and almost fell off the couch in her panic. She whipped her head to the door and saw Beatle standing there. The relief was so great, Casey felt lightheaded.

She felt his hands on her shoulders and relaxed into him. "You scared the shit out of me," she said softly.

"What's wrong?"

She looked into Beatle's worried brown eyes. "Nothing. You just scared me."

"Wrong. Try again. There's no way me walking in would scare you as badly as it did if something else wasn't up. I know you, Case. Talk to me."

"It's nothing. Just a weird phone call from Marie."

"Your psychologist friend? Weird how?"

"Just...weird. Can we drop it? I need to get ready. I haven't showered yet."

She could tell Beatle really didn't want to drop it,

but after a long look, he acquiesced. "Okay, but will you talk to me later? Tell me about what has you so rattled?"

That, she could do. "Yes."

"Good. Emily sent me up here to remind you that this thing is casual."

"I knew that," Casey said, confused. "Why would she send you to tell me something I already knew?"

She eyed Beatle—and was surprised to see a slight flush move up his neck. He brought a hand up and scrubbed over the short hair on his head. "Okay, I lied. She didn't. I just got back with Fletch and wanted to see you."

"You saw me this morning," Casey said.

"Yeah, but that was like, seven hours ago."

She knew the smile that spread across her face was probably goofy, but she didn't care. "You missed me," she whispered.

"Yeah, sweetheart. I missed you," Beatle agreed immediately.

Without thinking, Casey leaned forward and kissed him. She meant for it to be a light, isn't-that-sweet kind of kiss, but Beatle had different ideas. He immediately tipped them to the side and deepened the kiss.

He devoured her mouth as if it had been months since he'd seen her, rather than mere hours. But Casey didn't complain. The last ten days had been some of the best in her life. Because of Beatle. He made her feel pretty and strong. He'd invited her into his circle of friends without reservation. And when she'd needed his comfort and strength in the middle of the night, he'd been there with no strings attached.

She knew without a doubt he was attracted to her, but she hadn't felt ready to dive into any kind of relationship. But he'd slowly worn down her resistance, and right then, lying under him on the lumpy couch in his friend's apartment, Casey's libido flared to life.

She wanted him.

All of him.

As if he felt the momentous decision she'd just made in her mind, Beatle pulled back. His hand had snuck under her shirt and his fingers had been teasing her nipple through her bra, but he froze as he looked down at her. "What?"

"What, what?" Casey asked, trying for nonchalance.

"Something's wrong. What is it?"

"Nothing's wrong," she countered. "I think it's actually really right for once."

Beatle's pupils dilated and he licked his lips. "Tell me what that means," he ordered hoarsely.

"I want you, Beatle." It was hard to say the words, but he deserved them. He'd been more than patient with her. Hadn't ever made her feel as if she owed him anything. The more time she spent with him, the more he proved that he enjoyed being around her. That he honestly would wait as long as it took for her to want him back. And even if she'd decided she never wanted that, she knew down to her bones, he'd have never forced her.

Troy Lennon was a good man. To his core. And she wanted him. All of him. Now.

Instead of pouncing on her, which she'd hoped he'd do once she told him she returned his desire, he threw his head back and closed his eyes.

"Beatle?"

His head came back down and he had a grimace on his face. "Now, woman? You tell me I can have all of you *now*? When we have to go hobnob with our friends?"

She giggled. "Bad timing?"

"The worst," he agreed. Then leaned down and put his forehead on hers. "But you know what? I've waited this long, I can wait until tonight. You realize what you just gave me, right?" he asked.

Casey nodded.

"What? What did you give me?" Beatle asked.

"Me," Casey said simply. "I gave you me."

"Damn straight. And you'll get me in return. I know you didn't declare your love for me and insist that we run away to get married, but you need to know this isn't a fling for me. I'm in this for the long haul."

Casey nodded. She knew that. It had been one of

the things that had been holding her back. She hadn't been able to wrap her mind around how a relationship between them would work, with him here and her in Florida. But thanks to the call from Marie, she realized that she wasn't sure she wanted to go back to her job. Yes, she loved teaching, but like Beatle had said once upon a time, there were universities in Texas. Or even through the Internet. She could teach online and live wherever she wanted.

"I want to see what happens," she told him. "I've heard the others talk enough that I know being with an Army guy isn't the easiest thing in the world, but I'd like to try. If you would, that is."

"Fuck yeah," Beatle breathed before taking her mouth with his once again.

Casey wasn't sure how he managed it, but ten minutes later, he sat up with her in his arms and forced her to stand. "Shower, sweetheart. If I have you under me any longer, I won't be able to wait."

She eyed his lap and the erection that had been torturing her for the last ten minutes. "Are you gonna be able to walk?" she teased.

"I have no idea," he said, wrinkling his brow.

Casey couldn't help it, she laughed. Loudly.

When she got herself under control, she opened her eyes and saw Beatle smiling up at her with a goofy look on his face.

"What?"

"I love to see you laugh. I'd give everything I own to always see that beautiful smile on your face."

She sobered. "Beatle."

"No. No more sweetness. I can't take it. Go shower. I'll wait for you out here. We'll walk back over to the house together." He ran a finger up the outside of her arm. "Tonight, I'm making you mine."

"Only if I can make you mine," Casey retorted.

"I'm already yours," he responded. "Go."

In a trance, she did as he ordered.

Throughout her shower, she replayed his words.

I'm already yours.

How could she resist that?

She couldn't.

And she was done trying.

Chapter Eighteen

"**T**HANK YOU ALL for coming," Emily said later that night.

There were fifteen people sitting around staring up at their host, listening to whatever it was she wanted to say.

No one seemed to care that there wasn't really enough space for everyone in the living room. They were all just happy to be together, and it showed.

Casey smiled as she looked around the room.

Rayne and Ghost sat thigh to thigh on one side of the sofa, and Kassie and Hollywood sat on the other. Harley was sitting on Coach's lap in one of the big armchairs next to the sofa. Fletch was on the floor in front of the couch with Annie in front of *him*, leaning back against his chest.

She'd brought out a large, fancy-looking plastic box with an Army doll inside. She explained to everyone that she used to have two, but her bestest friend, Frankie, who was deaf and lived in California, had the other, and they played with them together over a special program on her iPad. After her explanation, she continued to play happily by herself until her mom started speaking.

Truck was hovering behind Mary, who was sitting on one of the chairs from the dining room table. Casey recognized the affectionate look in his eyes, as she'd seen the same look on Beatle's face for the last two weeks. It was obvious Truck more than cared about the woman, though Mary had done her best to put space between them as much as possible throughout the night.

But Casey had been watching her curiously. Mary might act like she didn't want Truck near her, but her eyes and nonverbal signals were saying something different. She couldn't take her gaze off the big man, and when Blade made a teasing comment about Truck's scar, Mary's face had turned hard and protective. She'd managed to control herself and not verbally berate Blade, but Casey could tell it took a lot of self-control.

The two men without women—Blade, and Rayne's brother, Chase—were leaning against a wall. Both had their arms crossed and looks of concentration and alertness on their faces. Casey had realized early on after moving into the apartment across the yard that all the Deltas were that way. Even the ones with women. They might be paying attention to their girlfriends or wives, but they were always aware of what was going on around them. Just in case.

Casey herself was standing nearby in the kitchen. She'd just finished a load of dishes, and Beatle had helped her. She'd been accepted as part of the group, but couldn't stand to just sit around and be idle. Emily had learned this about her quickly, and after a few protestations the first day or two, had let her do her thing.

Casey felt Beatle come up behind her and put his arms around her waist. She leaned back against him, letting him take her weight. She was feeling mellow and happy. And couldn't wait for Emily to break the news of her pregnancy to her friends.

"Hurry up! I want cake!" Hollywood joked.

Kassie elbowed him and said, "Shut it!"

Everyone laughed and Emily continued. "As you may or may not know, Fletch and I have been...er...working on Annie's request for a little brother or sister..."

"Oh my God!" Annie screamed, scrambling to her feet and jumping up and down. "Please say you're pregnant! Please say you're pregnant!"

"I'm pregnant," Emily told her daughter obediently.

The little girl ran toward her mom and threw her arms around her. "When?" she demanded, looking up into her face.

"It'll be a while. Seven or so more months," Emily told her, running a hand over her head.

"Yipee!" Annie squealed, then let go of her mom and did an impromptu weird little dance in the middle of the room.

Emily held up a hand to forestall her friends from getting up and congratulating her. She looked at her husband. "We don't know the gender yet, but if anyone has a pool going, we're guessing it's a boy."

"A brother!" Annie breathed, then immediately burst into tears.

Fletch got up and gathered his daughter into his arms and said worriedly, "Those are happy tears, right squirt?"

Annie looked up at her dad and wailed, "I really *really* wanted a little brother! Someone who would play Army with me!"

"We're not sure about that yet, squirt. It's too early. It might be a girl."

Annie shook her head vigorously. "I can't lie, I'd be a little sad if it's a girl, but I've been soooooo good. Santa's been watching me and he knows how good. I couldn't be any gooder!" The little girl's enthusiasm and earnestness was adorable.

Fletch simply shook his head and smiled at his daughter. "I'm afraid if it *is* a boy, by the time he's old enough to play, you might not want anything to do with him anymore," he told her.

"Nope. I don't care if I'm old. Like *thirty*. I'll always

want to play Army."

Casey felt Beatle's chest rumbling behind her with his silent laughter. He leaned forward. "If thirty is old, we're all doomed."

Casey smiled and nodded in agreement, not taking her eyes off the sweet scene in front of her.

"Well…since this seems to be the time to tell secrets, Harley and I have one of our own," Coach announced.

Everyone's heads swiveled to look at him. He hadn't moved from his slouch in the chair, and Harley was still perched on his lap. Coach had one arm around her waist and the other rested on her thigh. He reached over and picked up her hand, running his thumb over the ring on her left ring finger.

"This isn't an engagement ring. It's a wedding ring. We're married. We went and had a civil ceremony right after she healed from her accident. We decided we didn't want to wait."

"*Seriously?*" Rayne declared, standing up from the couch. "You got married and didn't tell us? That's not cool. Not cool at all! What about the party? You *are* going to have a party, aren't you?"

"Settle down, Mom," Harley teased. "Yes, we'll have a party. We've just been enjoying married life without the hoopla for a while."

"Anyone else want to tell any deep dark secrets?"

Rayne asked. "And before you ask, no, me and Ghost aren't married. I don't care if we were the first to get together. Me and Mary always said we would have a double wedding, so I'm waiting for her." She waved at her best friend with a big smile.

If Casey hadn't been standing behind Mary and Truck, she might've missed the subtle way Truck moved to her side and pressed his hand on Mary's upper back. Or the way Mary gripped the arm of the chair hard enough for her knuckles to turn white. Or how, after everyone's attention had turned to Fletch when he began talking, Truck leaned down and whispered something in Mary's ear, which made her look into his eyes and shake her head back and forth quickly.

Casey really wanted to know what was up with the two, especially after the things Truck had told her about "his Mary" when they were in Costa Rica, but Hollywood was speaking now.

"Actually, yeah, this seems as good a time as any—Kassie is pregnant too!"

The room exploded with congratulations. Everyone was smiling and happy, and Casey hadn't ever felt as much love in one place as she did in Fletch's living room right that moment.

"When are you due?" Emily asked her friend.

"Sooner than you," Kassie said. "Four and a half months."

"Holy shit! I can't believe you kept this from us that long!" Rayne exclaimed. "How come you aren't showing that much yet?"

Kassie shrugged. "I was worried about that too, but my doctor assures me it's normal. Babies grow at different rates. But she's doing fine."

Hollywood put a hand on his wife's belly, rubbing where his child was growing.

"She?" Mary asked.

"She," Kassie confirmed.

"I'm just so happy for us!" Emily exclaimed, making everyone laugh.

Fletch was still squatting by his daughter, and he turned to her and said, "Mom and I have a present for you, squirt."

"For me?" she asked, her eyes wide and excited in her little face.

"Yes. For you." Then Fletch picked Annie up and plunked her on his shoulders. Her little hands went under his chin to balance herself. "Me and the guys have been working on it for a while to make it perfect. Everyone, feel free to follow us on out," Fletch told his friends.

"What'd he get for her?" Casey asked, as Beatle steered her out along with everyone else.

"Wait and see," he told her mysteriously.

Sitting in front of the house was a huge box in camouflage wrapping paper. Annie's squeal when she saw the present was probably heard on the other side of the state. Fletch leaned over and placed his daughter's feet on the ground. She immediately ran to the box and started ripping off the paper.

Then, without waiting for her dad's help, she lifted the box, which didn't have a bottom to it, and revealed what was inside.

"I knew it!" she exclaimed. "I *knew* it! Thank you thank you thank you! My own tank!"

"Yup. Although there's rules as to when and where you can drive it," Fletch warned.

Annie's head bobbed up and down, but it was obvious she wasn't listening.

"Give it up," Hollywood told Fletch. "She's not gonna hear anything you tell her right now as it is. You charged up those batteries before you wrapped it?"

"Of course I did. You think she'd have the patience to wait to ride it?"

Coach and Truck helped Annie climb up and sit inside the small motorized vehicle, which looked exactly like a Sherman Tank.

Annie was zooming around the yard, pretending to shoot invisible enemies within minutes.

Casey looked up at Beatle. "A tank?"

He shrugged. "She saw a lame plastic version online one day and had to have it. Of course, it was thousands of dollars, and Fletch told her she had to earn the money for it herself. She did a damn good job too."

Casey saw the glint of mischievousness in Beatle's eyes. "With lots of help from her uncles, I'm sure."

"Of course," he said. "Although this one isn't like the one she saw. We all got to talking, and the one online was a piece of shit. So, we put our heads together and figured out how to modify one of those Barbie cars that are sold in stores. We used the motor, but that was about it. Every chance we had, we worked on it. There's a guy online who made one from scratch, and we ended up emailing him a lot to work out the kinks in our version, but I think overall, it ended up pretty darn cool."

"It did. It's super cool," Casey agreed. "So the money she earned went toward parts?"

"Yup. Although, I think Hollywood ended up basically paying for the damn thing. Annie learned pretty quickly that he'd pay her to leave him and Kassie alone so they could make out. She was always popping up where she was least wanted." Beatle chuckled.

Casey couldn't help but laugh along with him. She glanced at the adults watching Annie zoom around the driveway and yard. She was in her heyday, and the absolute joy coming from her was beautiful.

The love this group of men and women had for each other was addicting. And something Casey was beginning to want more than she'd ever wanted anything in her life. She'd thought that being kidnapped was the worst thing that could ever happen to her, and it was, but...it had brought her here.

Through her experience, she'd met Beatle, discovered that she had more inner strength than even she would've guessed, and had been embraced and welcomed by this small group of friends. She shouldn't be grateful for being snatched...but somehow, she still was.

As the sun set, the couples slowly began to disperse until it was just Casey and Beatle left.

Casey felt Beatle's hands begin to roam. He was leaning against the side of the house and she was resting against him. Annie was still driving her toy tank around the yard, but it was obvious she was winding down. She was exhausted, but pure adrenaline and excitement were keeping her going. Emily had gone inside to finish cleaning up then get off her feet, and Fletch was wrangling his daughter.

Warm breath hit Casey's neck as Beatle leaned into her. His hands skimmed up her body, brushing over the sides of her breasts as he went. "You ready to head up?"

Casey inhaled and immediately nodded. Yeah, she was more than ready.

Beatle grabbed her hand and made for the garage, giving Fletch a chin lift as he went. Casey would've giggled, but she was concentrating too hard on not tripping over her feet as she tried to keep up with Beatle's fast strides.

BEATLE DID HIS best not to break out into a run, dragging Casey behind him as he headed up the stairs to the apartment he'd been sharing with the woman he couldn't get out of his mind. He knew eventually he'd have to go back to his own apartment, but for now, he was content staying at Fletch's place. At least until Casey made a decision about where she wanted to live. Unlocking the door and stepping inside, he inhaled, loving the smell of Casey that permeated the air.

Her shampoo. Her lotion. Her.

She said it was plumeria, and he didn't have the first clue what that was. But he knew he'd forever associate the sweet floral scent with Casey. Forcing himself to slow down, Beatle dropped her hand and took a step away from her.

She looked up at him in confusion, but didn't move from the now closed and locked door. "Beatle?"

"Be sure, Casey," he said in a husky voice. "Don't go to bed with me if it's not something you want."

The shy smile that spread across her face nearly did him in. "I'm sure. Very sure."

He went to her then, taking her face in his hands

and leaning down to kiss her lightly before pulling back. "When this is all over, move in with me," he said. "I know I'm not being fair, asking you to give up everything while I seemingly give up nothing, but I swear to you, I'll always put you first in my life. I know the Army controls a lot of it, but I'll do everything in my power to make sure you know how much I understand what you're giving up, and if possible, I'll always put your needs above my own."

She shook her head. "I don't need that from you, Beatle. If a relationship between us is going to work out, one of us is going to have to move, and it just makes sense that it's me. I wouldn't want you leaving your team. You obviously care about each other, and I think that's part of what makes you work together so well. Besides...I like the girls. And I want to meet Annie's baby brother. And see her grow up. I like it here. More than I like my life in Florida, as pathetic as that is."

"Fuck," Beatle murmured. "How'd I get so lucky?"

"I think I'm the lucky one," Casey countered. "Now...are we going to get it on or stand here being mushy all night?"

He grinned. "Get it on, definitely." And with that, he put one hand on the small of her back and the other on the back of her head and pulled her to him. She met him halfway, standing on her tiptoes and immediately opening to him when he kissed her.

Without taking their mouths off each other, they disrobed as they went. Clothes went flying as they headed for the bedroom. Shoes kicked off, socks pulled off. Casey backed off momentarily to get her shirt over her head and Beatle did the same. Their mouths crashed together again and Casey continued her backward steps.

Beatle reached for her pants at the same time Casey fumbled with his belt and zipper. She would've tripped over her pants, now around her ankles, but Beatle simply picked her up so her feet were dangling inches off the ground.

He shuffled to the bed, kicking off his own pants in the process, and fell to the mattress with Casey under him. He immediately shifted to his back and smiled up at Casey as she sat up astride him.

His hands reverently smoothed up her sides. He'd touched her this way before, but never when she was wearing only her undies. Beatle's eyes went to the black lace bra she was wearing. It pushed up her tits, giving her ample cleavage. He appreciated the sight, but yearned to see her as bare as he had in the jungle.

"Take it off, sweetheart," he ordered.

With a grin, her hands immediately went behind her back and she unclasped the sexy undergarment. She coyly let the straps fall over her shoulders as she held the cups to her breasts. Beatle knew he was panting, but couldn't help it. His knees came up and he braced her back with them. His thumbs teased the elastic at her waist as he waited for her to bare herself to him.

In a move that would've rivaled the most professional stripper, she dropped her arms and slid the bra off at the same time. Beatle had no idea what she did with the lingerie, because all he could see were her fat little nipples, hard and begging for his touch.

"Come here," he said.

Casey immediately leaned over, offering herself to his eager mouth. Taking one breast in his hand, he squeezed it lightly and pulled her down until she was in reach. He blew on her, watching in fascination as her nipple tightened further. He wanted to continue to tease. To see what she liked and what turned her on, but he couldn't wait to taste her anymore.

He didn't start out gentle. No, instead of lightly licking and working his way up to pleasuring, he latched on to her breast and bit down at the same time he sucked. Hard.

Casey's back arched and she moaned. He was afraid he'd hurt her for a moment, until he felt her fingernails digging into his biceps. She held on to him as if she'd shatter into a million pieces if she didn't.

Practically mindless with lust, Beatle feasted on her tits. Between sucking, licking, and nibbling on her tender flesh, he told her how good she tasted and felt in his mouth. He told her how perfect she was, and how he'd wanted to worship her just like this ever since the hotel in Costa Rica. When her hips began to move over him, dry humping his abs, Beatle knew she was just as gone as he was.

He flipped them until she was lying under him. His knee went between her legs and even through her panties, he felt how wet she was against his bare skin.

Pressing upward, Beatle kissed her. With his tongue, he mimicked what he wanted to do with his cock. Casey wasn't a passive participant in their lovemaking by any means. Her hips undulated against his knee and her hands pulled him into her.

Her excitement and obvious arousal turned Beatle on even more. He sat up and kissed his way down her body. When he stopped above her pussy, she ran her hands over the short hair on his head.

Beatle took hold of the elastic of her lacy underwear and asked, "May I?"

"Please," she moaned.

Reverently, Beatle stripped her undies down over her hips, slowly exposing her feminine folds to his gaze. He stopped and licked his lips when the material bunched at her hips. Casey laughed and reached down to shove them the rest of the way off.

Beatle didn't know what he'd expected from their lovemaking. Oh, he knew they'd both be satisfied, but he hadn't known exactly how Casey would react to his excitement. Because he *was* excited. Extremely so.

But he shouldn't have worried. As soon as she kicked off her panties, she put her feet flat on the mattress and dropped her knees open, giving him complete access to her pussy.

Beatle managed a quick look up at her face to make sure she was as into this as he was, and saw her lick her lips in anticipation. Not needing any other reassurance, he placed his hands on her inner thighs, holding her open, and dropped his head.

His first taste of her tangy sweetness made precome ooze from the tip of his cock. He ignored his own body's needs and dove into the experience of eating Casey out. He licked. He sucked. He used his chin and the stubbly growth of his beard to arouse her. He fucked her with his tongue. He even used his finger to stimulate the nerves of her ass as he sucked on her clit.

And through it all, Casey moaned and thrashed in delight under him. There were times he had to use his forearm to hold her down so she didn't lose his mouth. He loved every second of it. Beatle had gone down on women before but most of them had just lain still under him. Occasionally moaning in delight and sometimes trying to direct him.

But that had been years ago. He hadn't been with a woman in longer than he could remember. And breaking his drought with Casey was so fucking erotic and exciting, he couldn't believe it.

Deciding he wasn't going to be able to hold back his own orgasm for long, Beatle got to work. His mouth closed over her clit, creating suction, and he used his tongue as a mini vibrator right over the bundle of nerves. At the same time, he eased two fingers inside her soaking-wet sheath, stimulating the nerves there as he did what he could to push her to, and over, the edge.

The combination of his tongue and fingers did their magic. Casey let out a small shriek and her legs clamped together around his head. Her hips lifted and her thighs trembled as a gush of wetness ran over his fingers. She came hard. Her whole body shook with it, and Beatle couldn't remember ever being as turned on as he was right that moment.

His cock had been leaking precome the entire time he'd been between her legs, and feeling her explode around and under him had been the sexiest thing he'd ever seen. He pulled his fingers out of her still-trembling body and whipped off his boxers in record time. Nudging her legs farther apart with his knees, he moved up her body. He grabbed the condom he'd managed to remove from his wallet before collapsing on the bed. He quickly smoothed it down his length and, without delay, pressed against her still-weeping opening.

"Yes, Beatle. Oh my God, yes," she moaned, lifting her hips to help his entry.

She was tight, and so fucking hot, but Beatle didn't hesitate. He pushed through her spasming muscles until he was flush against her ass. He could feel her wetness soak his balls, and he closed his eyes, willing himself to hold on for just another minute.

He felt Casey's small hand snake around the back of his neck, and she pulled him down to her. Without regard to the release he knew was all over his face, Casey kissed him. Hard. She shoved her tongue in his mouth and took control of the kiss.

Beatle was so turned on, so fucking excited and relieved she'd finally let him in, he started thrusting inside her even as they kissed. Pulling back with a gasp, Beatle tried to stop his hips, but couldn't. As if his cock had a mind of its own—and it was debatable at this time if it didn't—he pressed in and out of Casey's cunt as if he'd never get enough of her.

"I can't wait...fuck...you feel so good," he ground out, trying to think of baseball stats. But since he couldn't think of the name of one fucking player, he wasn't having any luck.

Casey wasn't helping. She brought her arms above her head and arched her back under him, stretching as if she were a cat lazing in the sun. "Fuck me, Beatle. Take what you need."

So he did. His head dropped and he held himself up with his hands on either side of her. His hips pistoned as his cock thrust in and out of her. The sounds their bodies were making would've been embarrassing if they weren't so fucking erotic. She was so wet, he slid in and out of her with ease. She felt so good around his dick, Beatle knew it was only a matter of time before he came.

He brought his eyes up to hers. "I'm going to come. You feel too good. I can't—" He groaned when Casey squeezed her inner muscles as he pressed in, making it harder for him to get inside. And tighter.

"Fuck, yeah. Do that again," he ordered as he pulled back.

She did.

With two more thrusts, Beatle knew he was done. He slammed into her as far as he could get, moving a hand down to her ass to open her up so he could get even farther inside. She tightened her Kegel muscles and it felt as though she were strangling his dick.

Nothing had ever felt so amazing in all his life. Beatle came.

His come spurted out of his dick so hard, he was afraid it would bust the condom. But he didn't care. His dick twitched once. Then twice. Then again and again. It felt as if he hadn't come in years, when he knew for a fact he'd jacked off in the shower just that morning as he'd thought about Casey.

Finally, when he thought he was done, Beatle let go of her ass and caught his body weight on his hands once more. He felt Casey's hand slip between their bodies and move downward.

He knew what she was doing, but his mind was having a hard time firing on all cylinders after the most intense orgasm he'd ever had in his life.

He felt her fingers brush against his lower body as she began to finger herself.

"You feel so good inside me," she told him, holding his gaze with her own as she flicked her clit.

Beatle could feel every twitch of her inner muscles on his softening cock. Not wanting to miss a second of what she was doing, he forced himself to his knees. He sat back and hauled her body up his thighs. Her pelvis was now tipped upward, and she was resting on her shoulder blades. He anchored her to him, making sure to keep his cock buried deep inside her body as she pleasured herself.

"Make yourself come," he ordered. "I want to watch."

Without protest, Casey's hand began to move faster over her sensitive clit.

Beatle's fingers flexed against her waist, but he kept his hands to himself. His eyes were glued between her legs and how she was pleasuring herself.

She wasn't being gentle, either. No soft strokes for her. She was using two fingers and rubbing her swollen clit as fast as she could. Beatle knew when she got close, he recognized the signs from when his face was between her legs, but this time he felt her trembles around his waist and on his cock.

"That's it, Case. Fuck yourself on my cock. Get yourself there. So fucking beautiful."

As soon as the last word was out of his mouth, she exploded in her second orgasm of the night. Sweat was beaded on her forehead and he could feel her damp skin under his hands at her waist. Her legs tightened around him and her inner muscles clenched down on him so hard, she pushed his now soft cock out of her body. Beatle felt a gush of her juices soak his thighs, and it was the most amazing feeling ever.

He might not have physically given her that second orgasm, but it was glorious to behold. Even more so because she trusted him enough to touch herself in front of him.

They sat like that for a long moment, Casey recovering from her orgasm, and Beatle simply enjoying the feel and sight of her lying naked and open on the bed in front of him.

Finally, she shifted and blushed as she looked up at him. "Should I be embarrassed?" she asked quietly.

"Fuck no," he told her immediately. "In fact, I think every lovemaking session of ours should end that way."

"I can't get off without direct stimulation to my clit. No offense to you and your cock," she teased, biting her lip.

"None taken. I have no problem making sure that beautiful little clit of yours is stimulated from here on out."

Her blush deepened as she admitted, "I have a vibrator back home that I usually use. Do you think…maybe we could experiment with one while you're inside me."

The image her words brought to his mind made Beatle groan. "Yeah, sweetheart. We can definitely do that. I need to go take care of this condom. Crawl under the covers while I'm gone, yeah?"

"Okay," she readily agreed.

Beatle helped her shift her body weight until he was out from under her. He stood and leaned over her when she was settled. Then he kissed her on the forehead and whispered, "I'll be right back."

When he returned to the bedroom, Casey hadn't moved. She still lay on her back right where he'd left her. He didn't bother to pull on his boxers, but scooted under the covers and gathered her into his arms like he'd done every night since he'd found her in the jungle.

Without hesitation, she assumed her normal position: cheek resting on his shoulder, hand on his chest, one leg hitched up over his thigh. The fact that they were both naked made the position all the more intimate.

"Thank you," Beatle said softly.

"For what?"

"For giving me you. I was serious earlier. I'll do everything in my power to keep you safe and happy. If I do something that irritates you, tell me. I'm not a mind reader, and the last thing I want to do is be a shitty boyfriend."

"I don't think you could be a shitty boyfriend if you tried," Casey said sleepily.

"I'm glad you think that, but it's not true," Beatle said dryly. "Just promise to tell me if something's bothering you. It doesn't matter if it's about me, your friends, your job, or anything else. Okay?"

"Okay. Beatle?"

"Yeah, sweetheart?" he said, repressing the chuckle. She really was cute when she was tired and exhausted from two orgasms.

"We didn't talk about my phone call."

Beatle stiffened, but kept up the soft brushing of her hair with his fingers, not wanting to do anything that would make her tense up.

"We'll talk tomorrow," he reassured her.

"Okay."

He turned his head and kissed her forehead in the same place he did every night. "Sleep well, beautiful."

"You too," she mumbled.

Beatle had been exhausted and completely relaxed a second ago. Now he was wired and anxious. He knew the woman in his arms well enough to know that if she'd brought up the call, she was worried about it.

He forced himself to relax. There wasn't anything he could do about it now. Besides, they were safe right where they were. Talking about the mysterious call could wait.

AT AN AIRPORT in Florida, three women were settling into their seats on the redeye flight to the Dallas/Fort Worth airport.

"You're sure it's okay that we're going out there?" Jaylyn asked. Then added, "Maybe I should just call her and let her know?"

"I'm positive," Doctor Marie Santos said. "And no, you shouldn't call her," she continued harshly, then tempered her tone. "When I talked to Casey, she told me when she spoke to you last time, it brought back lots of scary feelings for her. She asked me to tell you to hold off on any calls until she sees you in person again."

Jaylyn nodded her head, but still looked concerned.

"I'm nervous to see her," Kristina admitted. "I mean, the last time we saw her, we were in that hut, you know?"

The doctor patted the college student on the hand. "I know. It'll be fine. We'll all talk. Find out if anyone remembers anything out of the ordinary that you haven't already told the authorities. Once everything is out in the open between all of us, things will go back to normal."

"I'm sure you're right," Jaylyn said, closing her eyes and settling back in the narrow seat.

"Of course I am," Marie murmured under her breath.

"How do you know where she's staying?" Kristina asked.

"She told me, sweetheart," Marie answered. "Now, try to get some sleep. The next few days will probably be tough, but don't worry, I'll be here to walk you through everything."

"We're really lucky to have you helping us," Jaylyn said.

"Yeah. You've really gone above and beyond. Thank you," Kristina added.

Marie smiled at the girls, and then turned to look out the window of the plane. She'd actually gotten Casey's address from the dean. Marie had told the other woman she wanted to send Casey some flowers, to let her know she was thinking about her, and the dean gave it over without a second thought.

Marie turned her mind from the ignorant dean, and thought about her greatest achievement yet to come.

The paper she'd written about the psychological effects of kidnapping, and how the human mind was able to cope with such a horrific experience, was just about finished.

In a month or so, it'd be ready for publication.

It was too bad her main subject had been rescued.

She was supposed to die in that hole in the jungle, never to be found again.

If she had, the psychological stress the other students would've experienced would likely have been tenfold what it was now. Which would've made for a more robust academic discussion in her paper. But since Casey had managed to get herself rescued...

Marie still wasn't sure how that had come about; obviously, the locals she'd hired were incompetent. But now that Casey was alive, Marie needed to do what she could to get as much information from her and the girls as possible so she could weave it into her paper.

But more importantly, Marie had to make sure Casey didn't remember anything that would tie what had happened back to *her*. She'd been careful, but was now second-guessing if she'd been careful *enough*. The natives she'd hired had definitely been a bunch of idiots. There was no telling what they'd said within earshot of the girls.

She was fairly sure Jaylyn and Kristina didn't know anything about who was behind their kidnapping; she'd certainly grilled them long and hard. But she wasn't so sure about Casey. She had a bad feeling about her colleague.

There was no way she'd let the stupid bug teacher ruin her research.

If the university had let her run her experiment the way she'd wanted in the first place, none of this would've happened. It was all *their* fault! And Casey Shea's—for not dying the way she was supposed to.

But as long as she didn't remember anything that would lead back to her, Marie figured she could use Casey's experiences as a follow-up. Casey might have questions about the article Marie was going to publish, but she could simply tell her it was just a coincidence it included a lot of the things that had happened to her and the students she took with her to Costa Rica.

And if Casey was recovering as well as it sounded, that was a significant finding. Marie had to figure out why, and include that in her paper as well.

Closing her eyes and pretending to sleep as the plane took off, Marie ran through her plan in her mind once more. Casey was too polite to tell them to leave. Marie could use her concern for her precious students against the other teacher. As long as Casey didn't remember anything, she'd be fine. But if she did...Marie would have to make sure she couldn't expose her.

The most important thing was her research.

A grin spread across the older woman's face. She

knew some people thought she was too old to continue to teach, and that she should retire. But she'd show them. She'd publish her research and get the praise she was due.

Chapter Nineteen

T WO DAYS LATER, Casey woke up slowly to the most delicious feeling.

Beatle.

She smiled, but kept her eyes closed even as she arched into his touch.

His fingers were between her legs, slowly stroking her.

"Morning," she said lazily.

"Morning, sweetheart," he murmured. His fingers began to move faster, and harder, in just the right place. Before she had time to think, Casey was orgasming.

Beatle had woken her up this way the day before as well. Just like yesterday, when she'd stopped twitching and moaning, he brought his fingers up to his mouth. She loved the satisfied and content look in his eyes as he did it.

Unlike yesterday, when he pulled her out of bed and into the shower, today, he leaned forward and kissed her lightly. "Go back to sleep. It's still early. I have to go into work this morning."

"Mmm-kay."

"I'll be back at lunch. We'll make time to talk about that phone call the other day."

They hadn't had a chance because yesterday had been busy from the second they'd woken up until they went to bed. And once they'd gotten horizontal, talking had been the last thing on either of their minds.

"Okay," she repeated. Casey truly did want to talk to Beatle about her conversation with Marie Santos. It still wasn't sitting well with her, and she really wanted to get his take on it.

"You have an appointment with the psychologist this morning, right?" Beatle asked.

"Yeah. It's at nine."

"Blade said he'd take you. He'll be here at eight-thirty. That work for you?"

"That's great," she told him. He'd been adamant that if she needed to go anywhere, either him or one of the guys on the team would take her. She didn't know if it was because he really thought she was still in danger, or if he was simply trying to make her life easier. Eventually she'd have to go back to Florida and get her car and other stuff…if she really was moving to Texas, that is.

And she was ninety percent sure that was what she wanted to do. She'd fallen head over heels for Beatle, and it seemed as though he felt the same way about her.

It was impulsive, and maybe stupid, but it felt right. She didn't have to decide right this second though, she still had at least a month left of summer before she'd have to tell her dean one way or another.

"Are you guys going back over the tapes again this morning?" Casey asked. She knew the men on Beatle's team had already viewed them once, but hadn't seen anything out of the ordinary. Beatle had told her the village had been deserted, and the tapes hadn't shown them anything to make them think otherwise. No one had ducked behind a hut, and there weren't any revelations that would lead them to whoever had orchestrated the kidnapping in the first place.

"Yeah. I've got a funny feeling we're missing something." He leaned forward and ran his thumb over her forehead. "It's nothing for you to stress over," he said as he tried to smooth out the worry lines that appeared on her face.

"What do you want for lunch?" Casey asked, trying to change the subject and do as he requested, not worry.

"Anything works."

"Is it okay if Annie joins us?"

"Of course. You don't even have to ask."

Casey grinned mischievously. "I wasn't sure if you had…other plans…for your lunch hour."

"As much as I wish I could keep you naked and in this bed forever, even I know that isn't possible," Beatle teased back. "Besides, I've heard that anticipation is a great aphrodisiac."

Casey ran a finger down his side and over to his belly before he caught her hand in his. "Sleep, Case. I've set the alarm for seven to give you plenty of time to get ready and eat before your brother gets here."

"Thanks. Beatle?"

"Yeah, sweetheart?"

"I'm happy." There was so much more she wanted to say, but that would do for now.

His eyes sparkled as he smiled down at her. "Me too, sweetheart. Me too. See you later."

"Bye."

Beatle leaned forward and kissed her gently, lovingly, then he was gone.

An hour and a half later, the alarm went off and Casey grudgingly got up. She got up way earlier when she was teaching, but she'd gotten lazy in the last couple of weeks. Sleeping in was a luxury she enjoyed. Even when Beatle had to get up before her, she found that she had no problem falling back to sleep.

She got up, showered, dressed, and was eating breakfast when her phone rang.

Thinking it was her brother or Beatle, she was surprised to see Kristina's name pop up on the display.

"Hey, Kristina, what's up?"

"Hi, Dr. Shea. You have a minute?"

Casey looked at her watch. "I've got about fifteen of them."

"Oh, okay, um…"

Casey's brows came down in concern. It wasn't like Kristina to beat around the bush, and if she was calling this early, even though it was an hour later in Florida, something had to be up. "What's wrong?"

"Well, nothing's wrong," Kristina said. "I'm sorry to be calling. It's just that, we're here."

"Here?" Casey asked. "Where's here?"

"Texas. Killeen."

What the fuck? "What? Why?"

"Doctor Santos said that she thought it'd be good for us all to have some sessions together. That you'd help me and Jaylyn cope with what happened."

Casey's hand clenched into a fist. She'd told Marie that she'd talk with the girls, but over the phone. And they'd come all the way to Texas? Was she crazy?

"When did you get here?" she asked Kristina.

"Yesterday morning. I wanted to call you right away and let you know we were here, but Dr. Santos said that we needed to get settled in first. We've been having some sessions with just us. Thinking of questions we want to ask you, stuff like that."

"Does Marie know you called me?"

"Well, no. She said she was going to call you later today."

Kristina sounded so insecure and uneasy, Casey rushed to reassure her. It wasn't the girls she was upset with. It was Marie. "It's fine. I'm glad you called me. As I said earlier, I'm on my way out, so I can't meet with you guys this morning. Probably not this afternoon either. Go ahead and tell Marie you talked with me and let her know I'll call her later today. Okay?"

"You're not mad?"

Casey sighed. It wasn't that she was mad, especially not at Kristina, but she was weirded out, frustrated, and pissed at Marie. She was incredibly confused about why the other woman would drag two college students halfway across the country to talk to her when that absolutely wasn't necessary at all. The whole thing was a massive red flag for Casey. Something wasn't right—and she definitely needed to talk to Marie and ask her what the fuck she was thinking.

"I'm not mad," she told Kristina. When someone knocked on the door, Casey quickly said, "I need to go. I'll see you soon."

"Thanks. Later, Dr. Shea."

Casey clicked off the phone, her mind in turmoil as she went to let her brother in. He didn't seem to notice anything off, and they were on their way to her psychologist within minutes.

Twenty minutes later, Casey was sitting in a chair in front of the man she'd been talking to for the last two weeks. Doctor Eddie Martin was a black man in his late forties, and Casey had been comfortable with him from their first meeting. He was slightly overweight and usually wore jeans and sweaters when they met. He was as nonthreatening as anyone she'd ever known and had a calming presence about him. His hairline was receding slightly and he had a habit of stroking his goatee when he spoke. He'd demanded she call him Eddie, and had let her talk to him at her own speed, not insisting she recount every detail of her ordeal.

She'd kept a lot of the specifics to herself, but ultimately, Eddie reassured her, he didn't need to know them to help her.

After a bit of small talk, Casey got down to what was bothering her. "I got a call the other day from a colleague back in Florida. She's a psychologist as well. She was super interested in what happened to me, even flat-out asked if I had been raped. She's counseling two of the women who were kidnapped with me and wanted to do a group session. I was okay with talking with them over the phone in a group session. But this morning, I got a phone call from one of my students, and she said that they were here in Texas, in Killeen, and that Dr. Santos brought them here so we could all meet in person."

"And you're not okay with that," Eddie said.

"I am and I'm not. It's just weird. I don't understand what she's doing."

"You're right. It does sound unorthodox. Have you asked her?"

Casey shook her head. "No. I told Kristina I'd call Marie later today."

"I'm happy to sit in on the session if you want me to."

"Thanks. I appreciate that. I'll tell Marie that I'd like you to join us."

Eddie leaned forward in his chair and rested his elbows on his knees. "Other than being stressed about your colleague's impromptu trip, you seem more settled than the last time I saw you."

Casey knew she was blushing, but smiled. Eddie had a way of asking questions without actually asking them. "Yeah. You know, Beatle...the soldier who's been staying with me? Helping me feel safe at night?"

When Eddie nodded, she went on. "He and I...well...let's just say we're not just *sleeping* together anymore."

"And you're happy about this."

"Yeah. Extremely so. But I'm worried that our entire relationship is a result of what we went through together. It was pretty intense."

"We talked about this, Casey. As long as you keep the communication channels open and that possibility is on the table, I think you'll both know pretty soon if that's all there is between you. But you've been living together since you got back in the States, right?"

"Right."

"And have your feelings changed about him? Or do you think his have changed toward you?"

Casey shook her head.

"So, my advice is to just go with it. Of course things are good now, the relationship is new. The sex is new and presumably good?"

Casey blushed harder, but nodded.

"Relationships are easy in the beginning, but as you get to know each other better, things will become clearer. It's not how you started the relationship, but what you do when you've been together for a while that matters. Just like every relationship. Maybe it'll work, maybe it won't, but as long as you communicate with each other, you have just as much of a chance of it working out than anyone else."

Casey thought about that. Eddie was right. Just because they'd met while she'd been kidnapped didn't mean they wouldn't make it. She certainly fell hard and fast for Beatle, just as he had for her. And her feelings hadn't diminished since they'd gotten back to Texas and had settled into a more normal life. Of course, she wasn't working and he felt as if she was still in danger, but still.

They shared dishwashing duties, had argued over

who was going to pay for the things she needed beyond what Kassie had already given to her. They liked way different television shows, and he could be up and ready to go in minutes while she took a lot longer. But they were both morning people, weren't picky eaters, she loved his friends, and they were definitely compatible in bed.

"You're right."

"Of course I am," Eddie said, sounding pleased with himself.

Casey chuckled.

"Now...you said last time that you thought there was something you were forgetting about your kidnapping...do you still feel that way."

She nodded. "Yeah. And interestingly, Marie, my colleague, said something about blocking out important details because of the trauma."

"It's definitely possible," Eddie agreed. "Do you want to try to go through it again? I know we tried the hypnotizing route and found out that you're one of the twenty-five percent of my patients that can't be put under, but maybe if you aren't trying so hard, you can relax enough to remember something else."

"I'm willing to try if you are." Casey felt bad that she couldn't be hypnotized. It would make remembering whatever the hell her brain was trying to hide much easier. She moved over to the couch and lay back, getting comfortable.

Thirty minutes later, Casey was just as frustrated as she'd been before she'd gotten to Eddie's office. She'd remembered more about the day she and her students had been taken, but there was still something missing.

She remembered yelling, and a voice that sounded different from the native Spanish speakers around her but couldn't bring the voice or the words that were spoken into focus.

Eddie reassured her that they'd keep working together and he was confident she'd eventually remember. The fact that she'd been as successful as she had been in remembering things so far was a good sign.

Casey left with a promise to contact Eddie later about the session with Marie and the girls.

Blade drove her home and they arrived at the same time as Beatle. He'd come home early for lunch because he wanted to see how her session had gone. Annie was zooming around the yard in her new tank. She'd made some sort of obstacle course, and was currently driving over piles of sticks, logs, and even a few bricks.

"She's gonna break that thing," Blade muttered.

"Yup," Beatle agreed. "And Fletch'll just get really good at fixing it for her. Hell, Annie will probably be just as interested in seeing how the thing works and fixing it as she is in driving it."

"That's true. I'm out of here," he told them. "Case,

you good?"

"I'm good. Thanks for the ride today."

"Anytime. See you back at post?" he asked Beatle.

"Yup. I'll be there in a bit."

Casey watched her brother stride to his car and back out of the driveway, waving at her and Annie as he left. Emily was sitting on the front porch talking to someone on the phone, and she gave them a distracted wave as they headed up to the apartment. Annie didn't seem interested in joining them, and Casey couldn't help but be relieved she'd have Beatle all to herself for a while.

Beatle put his hand on the small of her back as they walked and Casey couldn't stop the small shiver that ran through her body at the feel of his hand on her. She always felt safe with him around her.

They went up to the apartment over the garage and she and Beatle made a quick lunch. They'd just finished eating when Casey opened her mouth to tell him about Marie being in town, and that she'd brought Kristina and Jaylyn with her, when Beatle's phone rang.

"Sorry, Case. It's work."

"It's okay."

She listened to his short conversation with Ghost, and her stomach clenched when she realized that he had to go back to the post now. The videos had finally been analyzed by the techs, and Ghost wanted the entire team back now so they could review them once more.

"You seem tense," Beatle said as he hugged her in the doorway.

Casey tried to relax. "I'm okay."

"I'm sorry we didn't get to talk. Tonight, when I get home, I'm making that a priority. Okay? No more excuses on either of our parts."

"Thanks. I'd like that."

Beatle kissed her gently on the lips, then brought her into his embrace once more. "Me too," he said into her hair before pulling back. "See you later."

"Bye, Beatle," she said, then watched him go down the stairs, get into his car, and back down the driveway. She had the odd thought that she'd made a mistake in not telling him everything about Marie during lunch. For not insisting that they take five minutes to talk about it. "Tonight," she whispered to herself. "As soon as he gets home."

Then she shut the door and went back into the kitchen to deal with their dishes from lunch.

Chapter Twenty

BEATLE FROWNED AT the screen of the iPad in front of him. He'd been back at work for a while. He'd been ignoring the good-natured jibes and teasing from his friends. They'd all been in his shoes, and he didn't give a shit if they knew he'd rushed home to be with Casey. She was amazing, and he couldn't get enough of her. He loved everything about her. Her generosity, her strength, even things she considered to be faults…being scared of the dark, a messy cook, and indecisive when it came to what she should wear each day.

But now his mind was completely occupied by what he was watching. The tapes from their arrival in the Costa Rican village had come back from tech and had been enhanced. The team had already watched them once, but they were re-reviewing them. They'd spent the morning going over the audio and nothing in particular had stood out. It was only their own voices and the natural sounds of the forest.

It had been difficult to see the video of Casey's rescue again, to see her back down in that hole, but ever since he'd watched it that morning, the hair on the back of his neck was standing up.

"What are we missing?" Beatle asked rhetorically as he scrolled the video back to the moment when he saw the faint trail leading to where Casey had been stashed.

"Wait. Go back," Truck ordered. He was leaning over his shoulder, watching the video from behind Beatle. "What did you pick up there?"

Beatle scrolled back a little bit and they watched as he walked down a path and leaned to look into the abandoned well. It was empty, with just a bit of water at the bottom. They watched on the video as Beatle picked up the piece of green hose that was leading from the well into the jungle. Beatle tugged on the hose then dropped it and started back the way he'd come.

"Play it in slow motion from here," Truck ordered.

Beatle didn't even hesitate. If his teammate was onto something, he would do whatever he wanted.

The two men watched in silence as Beatle discovered the slight path and walked down it. They watched as he called for assistance and began to remove the vines.

Truck brushed Beatle's hands away from the controls and scrolled back once more. When the video got to a specific point, Truck stopped it and pointed at the screen. "What's that?"

Beatle leaned forward and squinted at the screen.

Suddenly everything clicked into place.

"Holy shit." He looked up at his friend. "Is that possible?"

Truck nodded. "Yeah, unfortunately, I think so." He clicked play, and they watched as the video resumed in slow motion. Truck gestured to the screen in a couple more spots, pointing out things they'd all missed the first couple of times they'd seen the tape.

"We were so focused on Casey, we missed it," Truck said.

"I'll get Ghost and the commander in here. See if you can get this on the big screen," Beatle told his friend. "We need to make sure what we're seeing is really what we're seeing, or if we're simply projecting what we *want* to see."

Within ten minutes, the rest of the team was assembled in the meeting room and Beatle was playing the video once more. He let it play once at normal speed, then slowed it down. Without him or Truck pointing out what they'd discovered, Hollywood noticed it. Then Ghost.

Within moments, all of the men had seen it and agreed with Beatle and Truck's original assessment of the situation.

"This was planned," Coach said with disgust.

"The hose from that abandoned well was delivering water to her hole," Fletch summarized. "We didn't see that hole in the board, and we thought the hose was just another vine. Casey was smart enough to create the filter out of her bra to catch the water, but without that hose, she would've been dead within days. There's no way she would've lasted as long as she did without it."

"Whoever did this wanted her to survive for as long as possible," Blade said, the anger clear in his voice. "This was mental torture at its finest. Almost as devious as those ISIS bastards."

"I bet those planks of wood at the bottom were placed there on purpose too," Hollywood surmised. "They kept her mostly out of the water, again allowing her a better chance of survival."

"But why?" Ghost asked the million-dollar question. "No one was there when we arrived. No one could see what she was doing or *how* she was doing. Why did they want to keep her alive?"

Beatle hadn't joined in the conversation because he'd seen something else the last time the video had played. "What's that?" he asked his teammates, standing up and going over to the large-screen TV. He pointed at something.

Everyone's attention swung to him.

Beatle narrowed his eyes and peered at the screen. "Right there. When we toss that second board. What's that?"

There was silence in the room for a beat before Blade said, "Goddammit, motherfucking son of a bitch!"

Beatle couldn't agree more.

He'd frozen the video at exactly the right place. One frame earlier, and it couldn't be seen. One frame later, and the board was lying on the ground.

"The bastard was watching her," Ghost said, putting to words what no one else had been willing to admit out loud. "That's a motherfucking camera."

And it was.

The video showed thin black wires hanging down from the last board. They'd all thought they were more vines, until this one frame of the video. The sun had caught the board at exactly the right angle, and the reflection of the light off a piece of glass could clearly be seen.

"That had to be a night-vision camera. It was pitch black in that hole. Bastard was keeping her alive and filming it," Coach said. "He knew the moment she was rescued because he was watching. That's how he knew to look for us in the jungle. I thought it was a bit odd that she'd been missing for as long as she was, and right after we rescued her, all of a sudden the jungle was full of people who wanted to prevent her escape."

"I can't see the camera all that well. I'll show it to tech, but I have a feeling that kind of sophisticated equipment is way over those natives' heads. If the village was any indication, they were technophobes," Hollywood told them.

Beatle looked at his friends. "So the question remains, who knew Casey and her students were in Costa Rica, and why did they want to film Casey in that hole? Was she deliberately chosen, or was she simply the unlucky one to be separated from the others?"

"It was deliberate," Truck said firmly. "Your woman is smart. She knew exactly what to do to keep herself alive. Do you honestly think a twenty-something college student would have the presence of mind to make a bra water filter?"

"I don't know," Beatle told his friend. Then he looked around the room. "Who's at the house watching her?"

"Chase, Rayne's brother. He said that he'd stop by after lunch and check on them and make sure all was well," Fletch told him.

"I need to get back there," Beatle said.

Fletch put his hand on his friend's arm. "Easy, Beatle. Call her first. Before you panic and go rushing off, see if you can reach her. I'll call Chase."

Beatle took a deep breath. "Right, okay. Yeah, give me a second." He reached into his pocket and stepped away from the table. He turned to face the wall and dialed Casey's number. It rang several times, then went to voice mail. He left a short message, then dialed again, hoping she was just doing something away from her phone and couldn't get to it in time to answer. He held his breath...then sighed in relief when she answered this time.

"Hello?"

"Hey, sweetheart. It's me. I just wanted to call and check on you."

"Hi, Troy. I'm good."

"Awesome. I'll be home around five-thirty, I think. You want to go out for dinner or did you have plans?"

"Going out sounds good," Casey said.

"Cool. You choose this time. I picked the place last time."

"Okay. Troy?"

"Yeah, sweetheart?"

"I just...I love you."

Beatle felt as if his heart was going to explode out of his chest. They hadn't said the words to each other yet, but he sure as hell had been feeling them. "I love you too," he said huskily. "I'll show you exactly how much tonight, yeah?"

"Yeah," she said softly. "You'll never know how much the last few weeks have meant to me."

"They've meant the world to me too. I gotta go. I'll see you later."

"Bye, Troy."

"Bye, Case."

Beatle hung up, and then scrunched his nose, wondering at her use of his real name. She'd almost always called him Beatle. But maybe she'd been visiting with Emily and had decided to use his real name for some reason. He turned to his friends and nodded. "She's good. Sounded a bit off, but I'm not sure why."

Proving they were way more sensitive than he'd been when *they'd* first found the women meant for them, no one gave him shit about telling Casey he loved her over the phone. He looked to Fletch, who had just hung up his own phone.

"All's well. Chase is at the house with Em. He said that Casey was in the apartment with two of the women she'd been with in Costa Rica."

Beatle's gaze whipped to Fletch. "What?"

"He was concerned at first, but made sure everything was all right before they went up to the apartment. She assured him they were good and said she'd see him later."

Beatle wasn't happy to hear that Kristina and Jaylyn were at their apartment with Casey while he wasn't there.

"He also said there was another woman there too. A Doctor Someone-or-other."

"Doctor Santos?" Beatle asked.

Fletch shrugged. "I guess. Casey told Chase that they were going to all talk for a while. He said he pushed a bit, trying to make sure everything was good, and she reassured him it was."

"I'm not sure I like this…" Beatle said.

"All right, everyone. We need to figure out who's behind this kidnapping, pronto," Ghost said in a no-nonsense voice. He'd stepped out to talk to someone about the videos, and had just re-entered the room. "Fletch and Blade, you guys go talk with tech and see if they can't sharpen up this image even more. Coach, you call Ambassador Jepsen. See if his daughter can shed any light on this. Truck, you and Beatle talk and try to remember everything Casey said when you were in the jungle that could be a clue to this shitshow. Hollywood, get ahold of the officers down in Costa Rica and tell them what we suspect and see what they know. They know more about corruption and shit in their country than we do. I'm going to meet with the commander and bring him up to speed. Any questions?"

Everyone shook their heads and got to work.

Beatle clenched his teeth. He wanted to head home and make sure Casey was all right, but he also wanted to dissect every second the team was in the jungle with Casey. Wanted to talk to Truck about the time they'd spent with Casey fleeing the village. Someone hadn't wanted Casey to die right away, but they sure as shit hadn't done anything to make sure she survived either. Not to mention, they'd sent the natives after her. He'd do what he could to make sure she never had to worry about going through something like that ever again.

Putting aside his worries for the moment, deciding that she'd be okay with Chase at the house, Beatle got to work.

Chapter Twenty-One

An Hour Earlier

CASEY WAS SITTING on the front porch of Emily's house with both Emily and Chase Jackson. She hadn't talked to the man very much the other night at the party, but she definitely liked him.

Rayne was older than her brother by a year, but you'd never know that by listening to Chase. He was a captain in the Army, having been promoted sometime in the last couple of months, and was in counterterrorism. He didn't talk about what it was he did specifically, but Casey got the impression it was some pretty serious shit. Rayne had mentioned that she didn't get to see her brother as much as she thought she would when she'd moved to the area, because he was constantly traveling with one unit or another.

They'd been watching Annie zoom around the yard—okay, zoom wasn't exactly the right word, the tank wasn't all that fast, but she made zooming noises with her mouth when she drove around—when a car pulled into the driveway and came toward them.

Chase immediately stood, ready to protect them all. Emily did as well. She yelled one word to her daughter, "red," and Annie immediately climbed out of the tank and ran to her mother.

The car stopped in front of the garage—and Casey gaped when she saw who got out.

Marie, Jaylyn, and Kristina.

What in the world were they doing *there*? She was going to talk to Marie about meeting at Doctor Martin's office in the next day or so. And more importantly, how had they known where she was?

"It's okay. I know them," she told Chase, who looked like he was about ready to pull out a gun and shoot them right there.

"You sure?" he asked.

Casey nodded. "Yeah, the girls were with me down in Costa Rica."

"And the woman?"

"That's Doctor Santos, a colleague from home. She's a psychologist and has been counseling Jaylyn and Kristina."

"I'm not sure it's a good idea to meet with them without Beatle. You want me to come with you?"

Casey shook her head. She wasn't happy with what Marie had done, but she didn't want to upset the girls. And they definitely looked uncomfortable. "We're just going to talk for a bit, not get into anything heavy. I'll be fine."

Chase's expression changed. He looked more sympathetic than alarmed now.

"I'm sorry about the interruption," Casey told Emily.

"If you need us, just call," Emily told her.

"I will." Casey smiled at her new friends. She was upset about Marie and the entire situation, but she didn't want to worry anyone.

She waved at Annie as she ran back to her tank to play. Her students and Marie were standing by the car, waiting for her to approach.

The first thing Casey did was hold out her arms to Jaylyn and Kristina. Both women threw themselves into her arms and they stood there in the Texas sun, embracing for a long moment.

"It's so good to see you guys," Casey told them.

"You too! We thought you were long gone, back home, then when the soldiers came and found us and told us that you'd disappeared, we were so worried!" Kristina said, her words all running together.

"I'm okay," Casey soothed.

Jaylyn didn't say anything, but hugged her tighter in response.

"Is it okay if we visit for a while?" Marie asked.

Casey had the snarky thought that it was about time the other woman actually *asked* rather than just doing whatever the hell she wanted, but she sighed and nodded. She dug into her pocket and pulled out her keys. She handed them to Jaylyn and said, "Above the garage. Go on up, guys. Get yourselves a drink or something. We'll be up in a sec."

Without protest, Jaylyn took the keys and the two women turned to the stairs.

Casey waited until they were inside before turning to Marie. "What the *hell*, Marie? I can't believe you flew all the way out here with them! Are you crazy?"

Marie didn't look affronted by her outburst. She merely tucked a strand of brown hair behind her ear and smiled at Casey. She was impeccably dressed, as usual. She was wearing a knee-length gray skirt with a pair of high-heeled open-toe shoes. Casey had the thought that the long-sleeve suit jacket she was wearing had to be warm in the Texas heat, but Marie didn't look like she was uncomfortable in the least.

Marie was almost thirty years older than Casey, but she didn't look it. She didn't have any gray in her hair and her makeup hid any stray wrinkles that might indicate she was older than she looked. All in all, Marie Santos looked and acted like she was an important person who had everything going for her. Casey had always admired her; she seemed to be a part of the most influential groups on campus and had served on more dissertation committees than Casey could begin to count. She had tenure, which meant she couldn't be fired unless she did something completely out of line.

Like dragging two students who had been through hell across the country for no reason whatsoever.

Casey was suddenly really uneasy. She didn't want to be alone with Marie, not even with her students there. She wanted nothing more than to tell the woman to go back to Florida, and refuse to cooperate with her group session. But she also didn't want to do anything that would harm the two women waiting for them upstairs.

"There's no need to get upset," Marie said calmly. "I brought this for you."

Casey looked down at the piece of paper Marie was holding out.

Feeling as though it was a bad idea, she reached for the paper. It both looked and felt weird, like it was some sort of absorbent material, not a regular piece of paper. She looked down and saw a picture of Astrid with an older man Casey assumed was her father.

"She's doing really well. But the other girls truly did need to see you for themselves. To make sure that you're all right. You did say that you'd do a group session with us."

"Yeah, but I was going to call or Skype in. I didn't think you'd show up on my doorstep. How'd you know where I was, anyway?"

"I asked the dean."

Casey was going to have a long talk with the dean when she got back to Florida. "I'm not sure this is a good idea. I'm worried about Jaylyn and Kristina. They don't need to be tromping around the country like this. They should be home with their families."

"They've got me," Marie said calmly. "I'm their counselor, and I'm helping them get through this awful experience. But they need your help. You were there with them. You're the only one who truly knows what they went through."

"Maybe, but—"

As if she knew Casey was caving, Marie continued quickly, "Jaylyn said that she was scared, but you kept her feeling positive. She trusted you one hundred percent, Casey. And Kristina told me that when you were taken away, she felt lost. She'd begun to think of you as a mother figure, and it physically hurt when you left."

Casey put a hand on her heart. She ached, thinking about how terrified and confused the girls had to have been when she was taken away.

"They were desperate to see you," Marie pushed. "But after I talked to you, and you indicated you weren't coming back to Florida anytime soon, they were afraid you didn't ever want to see them again. That you were ashamed of them and their behavior in that hut after you left."

"No, I'd never feel that way," Casey protested, shocked that Jaylyn and Kristina would ever think that.

"Talk to them. Please?" Marie asked. "I really do think it'll do everyone a world of good."

Casey sighed. She knew she was being manipulated, but she capitulated anyway. "Okay. But just for a little bit. I don't want to do an entire session. I talked to my own counselor, and he thinks it would be best if he was there when we all do sit down and talk about everything."

Marie smiled huge then nodded. "Great. No problem. I'd appreciate his input as well."

Casey folded the paper Marie had given to her and put it in her back pocket, then turned toward the steps and looked back at the front porch one more time. She could see Chase watching her. She gave him a small wave and got a chin lift in return. Then she led Dr. Marie Santos up the stairs and into her apartment.

Casey tried to control her impatience as she got everyone settled in the apartment. Jaylyn and Kristina sat on the couch and Casey pulled up one of the chairs from the dining room table. Marie sat on another chair on the other side of the couch.

Once they were all settled, Marie said, "Girls, you agreed that today was going to be the day that you tried hypnosis, right?"

Casey blinked. It wasn't out the realm of possibility that a psychologist would use hypnosis; heck, she and Eddie had tried it today. But it did seem weird to fly across the country and *then* decide to do it for the first time. She'd also told Marie downstairs that she didn't want to do a full-blown session. "Maybe we should just talk first," Casey said.

"Why, are you afraid?" Marie asked a little belligerently. "Maybe you'll remember something that will help. You're afraid of the dark now, aren't you? Maybe a little claustrophobic?"

Casey frowned at the harsh words from the older woman. "Well, yeah, but—"

"But nothing. I can help you with that. Unless you like being the weak little woman to your new boyfriend. Maybe you're milking it to get attention?"

"No, of course not, but—"

"Then why are you fighting this? Jaylyn and Kristina said they'd do it if you would too. You told me yourself that you can't remember everything that happened to you. If this would help, why wouldn't you do it?"

Casey had been about to tell Marie that she'd already tried hypnosis with Dr. Martin, and it hadn't worked, when Jaylyn spoke up.

"Dr. Shea?"

Casey took a deep breath to control her anger. She wanted to tell Marie to go fuck herself, but she absolutely didn't want to do anything that would damage the two young women currently looking at her with wide, worried eyes. "Yes, Jaylyn?"

"Will you try? For us?"

Casey wanted to say no. Wanted to call Marie out on her unethical behavior. But more than that, she just wanted this to be done. She nodded at Jaylyn. "Okay, sweetie."

The relief on both Jaylyn and Kristina's faces let Casey know she'd made the right decision, even though it wasn't the easy one.

Just then, Casey's phone rang. It was sitting on the counter in the kitchen. She got up to go answer it, needing some space between her and Marie for a moment.

But the older woman followed her, and before Casey could answer the phone, grabbed her, digging her nails into her upper arm.

She winced, and her eyes widened as Marie leaned in. "Don't tell him we're here," she threatened, obviously having seen Beatle's name on the screen. "I mean it. You need this, Casey. You're obviously suffering and having a mental breakdown because of whatever you can't remember. I need to know what you remember about that day. Get rid of him then come back. Jaylyn and Kristina's mental health is depending on you."

The tone Marie used was part whisper, part growl—

and Casey was immediately thrown back to her time in the jungle. She'd heard that same half whisper, half growl after they'd been blindfolded and before the truck had driven off.

"Take them to the village, but make sure no one interacts with them. Only give them enough food for two people, not four. I'll be there in a couple of days."

Marie had been there.

It was *Marie* who'd arranged for them to be taken.

Casey knew the things her colleague had been saying were off, but she never would've guessed that *she* was behind their ordeal.

But why?

Casey vaguely heard the phone quit ringing, but she couldn't stop remembering. When she was in the hole and it was being covered, she'd heard Marie again.

"If she's still alive in a week, you and the others can do what you want with her. But remember, I'm watching. She has to stay down there the entire seven days for it to be useful."

The phone started ringing again, and Casey blinked as she looked down at the device in her hand.

"Answer it," Marie said in that distinctive growl.

Casey slid the bar to the side of the screen and brought the phone up to her ear.

She wanted so badly to tell Beatle to get his ass home and save her once more, but she had no idea what Marie would do to the girls if she did. It didn't seem like she realized Casey had finally remembered what she'd so desperately been trying to recall. Yet. But Casey didn't know what Jaylyn and Kristina had heard. If they were hypnotized and admitted to hearing Doctor Santos in Costa Rica, they were all in big trouble.

She couldn't help jerking her arm out of Marie's grip and glaring at her before she answered the phone.

"Hello?"

"Hey, sweetheart. It's me. I just wanted to call and check on you."

"Hi, Troy. I'm good," she told him, hoping like hell he'd figure out that she hardly ever called him by his given name...and maybe there was a good reason she was doing so now.

"Good. I'll be home around five-thirty, I think. You want to go out for dinner or did you have plans?"

"Going out sounds good," Casey said, more than aware of Marie's eyes on her.

"Cool. You choose this time. I picked the place last time."

"Okay. Troy?"

"Yeah, sweetheart?"

"I just...I love you." Casey suddenly knew that Marie wasn't going to let them simply walk out of the apartment. If the other girls said something about knowing their doctor had been in Costa Rica, they'd all be in danger. If Casey couldn't convincingly pretend she was hypnotized when she wasn't, they'd all be in danger. She didn't think any of them would get out of this unscathed, and the thought of Beatle never knowing how much she loved him if Marie succeeded here where she'd failed in the jungle was abhorrent.

"I love you too," he told her. "I'll show you exactly how much tonight, yeah?"

Casey could hear the emotion clear in his tone. It sucked that the first time they'd said the words to each other were under these circumstances, but it didn't diminish them in any way.

"Yeah," she said softly. "You'll never know how much the last few weeks have meant to me."

"They've meant the world to me too. I gotta go. I'll see you later."

"Bye, Troy."

"Bye, Case."

Casey hung up the phone and managed not to break down in tears. *God, please let him wonder why I'm suddenly calling him Troy instead of Beatle, and please let him come home to check on me.*

Marie grabbed the phone out of her hand and held the button down to turn it off. Then she threw it onto the counter and steered Casey back toward the living room.

The kitchen wasn't that far from the sofa, and Casey knew the girls had probably heard her conversation with

Beatle. She wasn't convinced they'd heard Marie's words to her though. She was sure they hadn't when they looked trustingly up at the doctor and waited for her to start.

Marie slowly sat back down on the chair and tried to control her breathing. She had no idea what would happen, but she had to be ready for anything. She'd survived that hole, she could survive this.

Come home, Beatle. Please. I need you.

Chapter Twenty-Two

BEATLE HAD BEEN talking to Truck for twenty minutes when he stopped mid-sentence.

"What? Did you remember something?" Truck asked.

They'd been discussing the situation with the natives and how they'd found them in the jungle when Beatle had suddenly clammed up.

"It's... I thought about this earlier and dismissed it...but something isn't sitting right," Beatle said slowly. He pulled out his phone and dialed Casey's number once more. He waited for it to ring, but instead immediately heard her message in his ear. Her phone had been turned off because it went straight to voicemail.

He turned to Truck. "How many times have you heard Casey call me Troy?"

Truck looked surprised. "Maybe once? Why?"

"When I talked to her earlier, she said my name..." He paused, trying to remember their conversation. "Three times. 'Hi, Troy,' then my name before she told me she loved me, and again when she was saying goodbye."

Beatle turned to Fletch, who had just hung up with someone from the Army's tech department who he'd asked to sharpen the section of film with the hose and the camera. "When you talked to Chase, did he sound...off?"

"Off?" Fletch asked. "No. Why?"

"I'm not sure, but I think something's wrong at the house."

By now, Beatle had the attention of the entire room.

"Talk to us," Ghost ordered.

"You guys know I talked to Casey earlier, and I thought everything was fine, but the more I think about it, the more I think she was trying to warn me about something but I didn't catch on at the time. She called me Troy. Several times."

"And she doesn't do that?" Hollywood asked. "Kassie mostly calls me by my nick, unless she's feeling emotional."

"Casey has always called me Beatle. She knows my first name, of course, but literally has only used it a couple of times. But today in our minute-and-a-half conversation, she called me Troy three times."

"I'll call Chase again," Fletch said immediately, already picking up his phone. He put it on speaker and the entire team listened intently as it rang.

Chase picked it up after only two rings. "Man,

you're worse than a girl, Fletch. What now?" the other man teased.

"Is everything all right there?"

"Yeah, why?" The light and airy tone was gone from the Army captain's voice. "What's wrong?"

"We're not sure. Beatle called Casey and everything seemed okay at first, but now he's not so sure. Did you see her recently?"

"We were all watching Annie play earlier and a car pulled in. I was on alert at first, but Casey said she knew the women who got out. She said two were students who were kidnapped with her, and the other one was a psychologist." Chase told them what he'd already relayed to Fletch earlier.

The Deltas all looked to Beatle. He sucked his lips between his teeth, deep in thought. Finally, he shook his head. "I don't know. But something doesn't seem right about this."

"Casey didn't say they would be visiting?" Ghost asked.

"No. But she didn't say they wouldn't be, either. She did get a phone call the other day that bothered her, but we haven't gotten a chance to talk about it. I know she seemed worried about it, but typical Casey, I have a feeling she didn't want to seem paranoid."

"You think it was one of the girls or the psychologist?" Coach asked.

"Who else could it have been?" Beatle asked. "She's talked to her parents several times, and had no problem with me being right there. The officials down in Costa Rica don't have her number, so it couldn't have been them. It might've been her boss at the university, but we've been talking about her job, so she had the perfect opportunity to bring it up. I honestly don't know who else it could've been."

"You haven't known each other that long," Chase said. "Maybe it was a man she'd been seeing before she got kidnapped, and she felt weird about telling you she was dating someone."

"It wasn't," Beatle snapped, then took a deep breath to control his temper. "Look, I get it, there's a lot we don't know about each other, but I absolutely do *not* think the call that bothered her was from an ex."

"You want me to go up there?" Chase asked.

Beatle ran his hand through his short hair in agitation. "Yeah, but I think you should wait until we get there. It's a catch-22. If you go up there now and knock on the door and something *is* wrong, the shit could hit the fan, and with three unknowns versus Casey, it could get ugly fast. But if you wait, every second we don't get eyes on her could mean a greater chance of her being hurt."

Ghost gestured to Beatle to head out. Fletch picked up the phone and the team walked out of the room while still talking to Chase.

"Get Annie and Emily to the safe room," Fletch ordered. "The last thing we need is more civilians involved if something is wrong."

"I will. I'll wait to make contact, but I'll do some reconnaissance and see if I can find out anything more for you guys when you get here," Chase reassured them.

"Appreciate it. We should be there in twenty minutes or less," Ghost told the other man. "Call if you have more intel."

"Ten-four," Chase said, all business.

Fletch clicked off the phone without saying goodbye.

"Is everyone carrying?" Ghost asked quietly as they made their way out of the building toward the parking lot.

When everyone confirmed, Ghost nodded. "Okay, let's take two cars. Fletch, you and Beatle come with me after you stop at your cars to get your pieces. Hollywood, Coach, and Blade, you guys go with Truck. We're goin' in as quiet as possible on this one. Just like Chase said, we don't want to cause drama where none exists. When we get there, Beatle will go up first, use his key so as not to frighten anyone if nothing is wrong." He looked at Truck. "You, Coach, and Hollywood take the perimeter. Blade, you'll be behind Beatle with me. Fletch, you head to your house and make sure your family is safe. Any questions?"

Everyone shook their head. They were used to working together and knew the plan almost before Ghost had spoken.

Within moments, the two vehicles were pulling out of the parking lot and headed for Fletch's house, unsure as to what they'd find.

CASEY SAT ON the chair with her head down, her hair hiding her face from Marie. She was scared out of her mind, and pissed, but was biding her time. She didn't want to do anything that would traumatize Jaylyn and Kristina more than they already were. It wasn't their fault their doctor was bat-shit fucking crazy.

Fortunately—or unfortunately—both young women were susceptible to being hypnotized. Marie had them in an altered state within ten minutes. Casey pretended to also have been put under.

She hoped like hell Beatle had figured out that something was wrong, but it had been a long time since their phone call, and he hadn't arrived, so she had little hope. She obviously hadn't been clear enough in their conversation that she needed him. Casey kicked herself for that.

"Hold out your hands," Marie told her enthralled

audience. Casey did as requested, and saw out of the corner of her eye that Kristina and Jaylyn had done the same.

Doctor Santos stood and fiddled with something in her purse for a moment, before stepping up to Jaylyn. She placed a marble in both of her palms, then did the same with Kristina. She went back to her purse and got something else, then stood in front of Casey.

Casey tried to keep her eyes unfocused and blank and managed not to flinch when something hard was placed in her own hands. It also looked like a marble, but seemed to be coated with something.

"Close your hands into fists and hold on to what I put in your palms. Do not drop it under any circumstances. If you do, you'll feel intense pain. The most pain you've ever felt in your life."

Casey closed her hand around the marble-like thing Marie had given her and wanted to scrunch her nose at the slimy feel of the object, but refrained.

"Are you holding on?" Marie asked.

Casey dutifully answered in the affirmative along with Jaylyn and Kristina.

"Good. Now, Kristina, tell me what you were thinking when you took all the food for yourself that last day. You said that one of your kidnappers opened the door to your hut and placed one serving of food inside, and that you got to it before Jaylyn and Astrid. Be specific."

Casey kept her breathing slow and even, but what she really wanted to do was stand up and berate Marie for what she was doing. What she was asking the other women was invasive and damaging. She wasn't a psychologist, but even Casey knew that.

She thought about jumping up and bum-rushing the older woman while she was preoccupied, but was worried about Jaylyn and Kristina getting hurt in the melee that was sure to follow. Maybe she'd wait a little bit longer. Make Marie feel safer that all three of them were all the way under, then pick up her chair and brain the little bitch.

As minutes went by and Marie continued to ask the other women questions, Casey began to feel extremely weird. She no longer thought about hurting Marie, concentrating intensely instead on what she was seeing and hearing. The light in the room was bright, but when she closed her eyes, swirls of orange, yellow, and red were all she could see. The colors undulated as if they had a mind of their own. They were hypnotizing in their own right, and Casey found herself getting lost in the swirling, twirling colors.

"Casey, your turn. Why don't you tell us how you felt when you were told you were going home and your ransom was paid?"

Casey tried to concentrate on the question, but when she opened her eyes and looked at the psychologist, she was appalled to see the words Marie had spoken floating in the air around her.

"Casey? You were happy to be leaving, weren't you?" Marie asked. "You didn't care that you were leaving the others behind, did you?"

"No, I was worried, I—" Casey stopped speaking because the five words *she'd* just spoken were now floating around her head. Big black letters that cut through the yellow and red swirls like a knife cutting through butter. As she watched in fascination, they turned toward her and seemed to grow. They changed colors too. From black to dark purple, then a bright fuchsia. Casey closed her eyes in confusion, but all that did was make the colors behind her eyelids swirl faster.

"And when you were brought to the edge of that hole, what were you thinking? That you were going to die?"

Casey swayed in her chair to the colors. No, she swayed to the music...but there wasn't any playing, it was the colors making noise now. A part of her knew that what was happening wasn't normal, but she couldn't get her mind to focus. "I didn't want to die," she managed to say, before the words started pushing against her eyelids to get back inside her head.

"Yet, when you were in that hole with no way out, you still didn't give up. Why?"

Casey couldn't answer. She was suddenly back in the

hole once more. She looked up and all she saw were the swirling colors.

"Casey!" Marie shouted. "Why didn't you give up? What made you fight to survive when anyone else would've given up and just died in that fucking jungle? I need to know. It's vital you tell me!"

At the word "jungle," suddenly the nice colors she'd been seeing changed from the light, happy orange and yellows, to dark green and maroon. Casey looked at Marie, but she wasn't Marie anymore. In her place sat a giant bullet ant. The antennae coming out of her head twitched in her direction. Its mouth opened and the biting jaws came closer and closer to Casey, poison dripping from the fangs, ready to inject her with its extremely painful venom.

Casey stood and immediately fell to the ground. Her hands opened as she fell and she dropped whatever it was Marie had given her to hold, but Casey was so far gone, in the midst of a trip so bad, she saw danger everywhere she looked and didn't even notice.

The fringe of the rug brushed against her palms, and Casey looked down to see that she'd fallen right into a nest of bullet ants. They were biting her. Hurting her. She frantically tried to get them off her hands, but the more she smacked at herself, the more ants appeared.

Fully in the grip of a bad LSD trip, Casey screamed.

Everything looked normal when the cars holding the deadly Delta team pulled down Fletch's driveway. Ghost and Truck stopped just beyond the clearing around the house and garage, and all seven men slipped out of the vehicles without a sound.

Chase met them at the edge of the trees.

"I haven't heard or seen anything abnormal," he informed the group. "I went to the front door and heard voices, but they weren't raised in agitation or anything. I couldn't hear what was being said, and the door was locked."

Everyone nodded, but Beatle was already on the move toward the stairs. Ghost gestured to the others and everyone fanned out. Fletch slipped away to the back of his house, and Ghost and Blade were right on Beatle's heels.

Beatle silently climbed the stairs with his heart in his throat. He didn't like this feeling at all. It was one thing to know what the danger was that you were walking into, it was another thing altogether to have no idea what would be on the other side of the door. It was a hundred times worse because it was *Casey* who might be in danger.

He held up his hand and the men behind him stopped. Everyone had their pistols drawn and were ready for anything. Beatle slipped the key into the lock and slowly turned it, not making a sound.

He had the key in the deadbolt when he heard raised voices from inside the apartment. He unbolted the door, and was slowly and carefully pushing the door open when he heard Casey scream.

And it wasn't a normal sound. Not in the slightest. It was high-pitched and panicked.

Beatle's blood went cold.

Without thought, he shoved the door open and it slammed against the wall behind it. He was inside the apartment with his gun drawn before he'd even thought about what he was doing.

He strode into the small apartment, expecting to see Casey being held at gunpoint or otherwise being assaulted, but what met his eyes was hard to comprehend.

There were two young women, he assumed they were Jaylyn and Kristina, sitting stock still on the couch. Their hands were resting in fists on their knees and they were staring straight ahead. An older woman with long brown hair was standing against the wall, looking at him with a satisfied smirk on her face.

And Casey. God.

She was on her hands and knees, frantically slapping at her arms. And the inhuman sounds coming out of her mouth were heartbreaking and horrifying at the same time.

Ghost and Blade moved to either side of the couch and held their guns on the older woman while Beatle went straight to Casey. He reached for her, but as soon as he did, she looked up, saw him, and screamed even louder. She was absolutely terrified. Of *him*.

Beatle's attention went from Casey, who was writhing on the floor, to the woman against the wall. She was smiling…and actually laughing.

"You bitch," he bit out. "What did you do to her?"

"I really only wanted her relaxed and mellow, but I wasn't sure how much to dose her with. The blotter paper I used when I first got here didn't seem to be working, so I gave her more. I guess I misjudged though, because this was not the result I'd anticipated. But I have to admit, seeing the high-and-mighty Doctor Casey Shea on a bad trip is fucking priceless."

Ghost reached the woman before Blade could. He grabbed her arms and wrenched them behind her back. "What'd you give her?"

"Fuck you!" she replied.

Ghost wrenched her arms higher and Marie screeched in pain.

"I asked what you gave her. If you think I'm fucking around, you're insane. You see any cops here, bitch? No. It's just us. And right now, I'm thinking my friend, Beatle, really, *really* wants a chance to make you talk."

She blanched, and Beatle didn't feel in the least bit bad that Ghost had threatened her. They wouldn't hurt her, of course, but she didn't know that.

"Just a little LSD, jeez, relax. People take it all the time."

Casey moaned and scooted closer to the wall on the other side of the room. She was holding her hands out in front of her, staring at them and whimpering.

Marie continued. "She handled that hole in the ground so well, I thought she'd be fine with the drugs. All she had to do was tell me what she was thinking in that hole. How she'd realized the water was there for her and what made her fight to live. Is that too much to ask?"

Beatle divided his time between Casey and the doctor. She wasn't talking to Ghost anymore, she was rambling more to herself than anyone else.

"I can still finish my research. She'll come down, then she'll tell me what I need to know so I can write my conclusion. The paper's not done without it."

"What paper?" Blade asked. He hadn't lowered his gun, and the anger on his face worried Beatle.

"*My* paper! My research. *The Effects of Terror on Kidnapping Victims; Why Some Completely Break and Others Get Stronger.* I'm going to be famous—but I need that conclusion!"

"Oh my God. You had my sister kidnapped for a

fucking human *experiment*?" Blade asked, and Beatle saw his hand tighten on the gun.

"Blade, put it down," Ghost ordered, having also seen that Blade was at the edge of his rope.

"She was doing an experiment, and tortured my sister in order to get data," Blade bit out.

"I know. And she's going to pay for it. Put. Down. The. Weapon," Ghost enunciated carefully.

"They wouldn't approve me! I had to do it! It was easy to organize. She and the others were down there all by themselves. If she'd just died in that hole, it would've been so easy!" Marie cried.

Suddenly, Casey lunged for her brother.

Because no one was expecting it, all of them distracted by the doctor's mutterings, Casey surprised him. She grabbed for the knife he had in a holster at his hip and managed to get it out before he could stop her.

She retreated back to the edge of the room, holding the knife in front of her, her eyes wild as her head swung from one person to another.

"Get her out of here," Ghost said, shoving the doctor at Chase, who'd been standing guard on the other side of the sofa.

"Noooo!" the woman wailed. "I need more information! Jaylyn, why were you such a crybaby? Kristina, what were you feeling when you hit Astrid when she tried to take the food from you? I have to know!

Waaaaaait!"

As Chase dragged the babbling woman out of the room, everyone was surprised when the young women on the couch began to answer the questions that had been posed to them. They were talking over each other, but seemed to have no idea. In fact, they didn't even seem to notice the men who were in the room either.

"What's wrong with them?" Blade asked.

"Hypnotized," Ghost said succinctly. "And we have no idea what triggers that she-bitch might've placed in them while they were under, or how to bring them out of it."

"Casey was seeing a psychologist. Said he tried to put her under once but it didn't work. He might be able to help. His name is Eddie Martin," Beatle told his team leader.

"We'll call him," Ghost said. "They're okay where they are for now. First, we need to calm your girlfriend down. She's making me really nervous with that knife."

Beatle had already turned his attention back to Casey.

She was using the knife to stab at the air. She was obviously seeing something they couldn't. It was as horrifying as it was heartbreaking.

"Casey," he said softly, taking a step closer to her. "You've been drugged. You're just reacting badly to whatever you were given. Drop the knife and we'll get you some help. You're safe now. The doctor is gone."

Instead of calming her down, his words seemed to agitate her more and because he was worried, he got a little too close to her. She managed to nick his arm with the knife before he stepped back out of her reach.

Beatle didn't want to make any sudden moves or do anything that would terrorize the woman who meant the world to him any more than she already was. He could easily disarm her—he'd faced down much meaner and bigger foes—but he didn't want to scare the shit out of her. This was Casey. *His* Casey.

He made the decision to simply stand right where he was and watch over her until she either came down off the trip or she calmed—but she blew that decision out of the water when she turned to the window and tried to dive right through it.

CASEY HUDDLED ON the far side of the room, away from the giant bugs. They were all standing on two legs, but had faces of insects. The bullet ant had been taken away by a giant snake thing, but there were two scorpions still sitting on the couch, staring at her and hissing. She'd attacked one of the friendlier looking creatures— he only had drool coming out of his mouth rather than acid—and had managed to grab his weapon.

The ants were still crawling on her arms, but more bothersome at the moment were the flying cockroaches. They were hissing at her and trying to eat her eyeballs. They were her pets, and they were screaming her name as they flew around her head. The colors in the room were swirling constantly now. Blacks, browns, reds.

A part of her knew that there weren't any such things as walking, talking bugs, but Casey couldn't control her terror that they'd get ahold of her and eat her alive.

One of the half human, half bugs was talking to her now. She could see his words swirling around his head as he spoke, but none of them made any sense. He took a step toward her with one of his tentacles stretched out.

As if.

She heard the bug men hissing and chattering behind her, so she turned and thrust the knife at them. It felt as if she got one, so she continued to blindly stab at the creatures with her weapon. The cockroaches were laughing now, hissing happily, but somehow staying out of the way of her knife.

Knowing she had only one chance to get out alive and away from the bugs who wanted to eat her, Casey dropped the knife, happy to see for some reason that made the giant insects stop advancing toward her. Words were filling the room now, making it hard for her to breathe. They were sucking all the oxygen from the room. Using it all up. She had to get out.

Without warning, so the bug men couldn't stop her, Casey dove for the window. She laughed when she realized that it wasn't made of glass, but water instead. She almost made it away from the monster bugs, but at the last second, something caught her legs. As she hung dangling over the water, so close to escape, Casey gasped.

Below her was a giant Hercules beetle. His horns opened and closed obscenely as he reached tentacles up toward her. Casey squirmed as hard as she could, but the bug men in the room had a tight hold on her.

She began to scream and thrash as the bullet ants that had been crawling on her before decided to start biting her again. Her hands throbbed with pain from hitting the water so hard.

Even as she screamed, she watched the Hercules beetle get smaller and smaller as the bug men reeled her back into their lair.

"JESUS CHRIST!" GHOST swore as he struggled to hold on to one of Casey's legs. "Blade, call nine-one-one! Tell them your sister has been drugged against her will and she's experiencing a mother of a bad trip. She needs to be sedated."

"Already done, dammit!" Blade yelled back.

Beatle blocked everything out that was happening around him, all his concentration on Casey. He'd never seen anything as terrifying as what was happening to the woman he loved. He had no idea what was going on in her head, but she definitely wasn't seeing him or her apartment.

She'd slashed out at him with the knife, and when he got too close trying to comfort her, had actually cut his arm. The slice hurt like a mother but he ignored it, as her next step was to dive headfirst out the fucking window. And she'd almost made it, but he'd caught her feet at the last second.

He heard Truck yelling from under the window that he was there and could catch her if she fell, but it didn't make him feel any better. The window was made with some sort of safety glass, so she hadn't been sliced to ribbons, thank God. It had spider-webbed upon impact, and probably would've held, if the frame around the window hadn't given way. Fletch had obviously made sure the apartment was safe for Annie, and any other child who might stay or play there. But the frame was no match for an adult's weight.

He and Ghost managed to haul Casey back inside the window, but she was still fighting them as if her life depended on it. Nothing he said was getting through.

Beatle had never been as scared as he was right this

moment. He and Ghost manhandled Casey away from the gaping window, and then Beatle sat on the floor with her in his lap. Her back to him, his arms around her like a straightjacket. She couldn't move except to writhe and jerk against him.

Blade and Ghost held his body still so he could keep control of the crazed Casey.

The room quickly filled with the rest of the team, and Beatle vaguely heard Ghost ordering Fletch to keep Emily and Annie in the safe room. They didn't need to see Casey like this.

All they could do was watch Casey remain lost in the nightmare of her mind as they waited for the ambulance.

Chapter Twenty-Three

I T TOOK ANOTHER six hours for the worst of Casey's bad trip to finally wane. The doctor said it had taken about an hour for the drug to start working, and she probably would've been okay with the initial dose, but the additional drug-coated marble in her hand, combined with the stressful situation, had triggered the bad trip.

And it had been one hell of a trip.

Casey had screamed for hours about giant bugs coming for her. She constantly saw ants on her body that weren't there, and she had absolutely no idea who anyone was around her. After she was sedated, she was less violent, but she'd still had to be held down for her own safety, and that of everyone around her.

It was the most heartbreaking thing Beatle had ever witnessed. He hadn't ever really thought one way or another about recreational drugs. He'd smoked some pot in high school, but nothing more than that.

Seeing Casey go through what she had made him vow right then and there that he'd never, *ever* put any kind of recreational drug in his body again. Ever. He wasn't sure he even wanted to take another drink of alcohol in the near future either.

He'd been allowed to stay in Casey's room at the hospital, and now that her vitals all seemed normal and she'd been sleeping for a few hours, he felt confident that the drug had finally run its course through her body.

Beatle eased onto the mattress next to her and gathered her carefully into his arms. The doctor had stitched up the wound on his arm. He'd also gotten Casey fixed up with an IV in the last hour, now that she wasn't constantly trying to pull it out. Beatle hadn't showered or eaten since they'd arrived at the hospital, but the last thing he was thinking about was himself.

The second he put his arms around Casey, she murmured something he couldn't understand and Beatle held his breath, hoping like hell she wasn't still under the influence. But instead of pushing him away and ranting about how he had a giant ant's head, she merely snuggled as close to him as she could get.

The small mattress reminded Beatle of the times they'd slept in the hammock like this back in Costa Rica. Plastered to each other, both their bodies sweaty and dirty.

He kissed her forehead lightly, and as if his lips had touched a magic button, her eyes popped open.

Beatle held her gaze, waiting to see what, if anything, she remembered.

CASEY LICKED HER lips and looked into Beatle's concerned face. His brow was drawn down and his lips were pressed together in a tight line. She brought her hand up to run her thumb over his brow to smooth away the lines, but was stopped short by the IV in her arm.

She looked at her arm, and a bunch of confusing images burst into her brain. She closed her eyes again.

"Case?"

"Hmmm?" she mumbled.

"Can you open your eyes and say my name?"

Confused as to why he wanted her to say his name, she opened her eyes into slits and looked at him and obediently did as she was told. "Beatle."

"Fuck."

That was a weird thing to say. The more she thought, the more awake she became. "What's going on? Don't you have to be up for PT by now?" she asked quietly. "What time is it?"

Beatle lifted her chin with a finger and asked, "What do you remember about yesterday?"

It was her turn to furrow her brow. But now that she thought about it, things did seem a bit fuzzy.

"Ummm, Annie was playing in her tank?"

"Yeah. Anything else?"

Casey shook her head back and forth. She had a headache and felt kinda floaty.

"Do you remember your friend from Florida coming by the apartment with Jaylyn and Kristina?"

She started to shake her head, but then more random images started to flicker in her brain. Marie sitting in a chair in front of her. Jaylyn and Kristina hugging her. Giant ants and flying cockroaches. It was all so confusing. "Beatle? What's wrong with me?"

"Shhhhh. Nothing. You're okay now."

"*Now?*"

When he didn't say anything else, Casey took a deep breath and awkwardly propped herself up on an elbow. "Tell me," she demanded.

Beatle didn't look happy at all, but he acquiesced. "Marie Santos came to the apartment, and you apparently agreed to meet with her and the other girls. She drugged you, and hypnotized Jaylyn and Kristina. You flipped out, she was arrested, and Doctor Martin dealt with your students. Everyone's okay."

Well. That was certainly a short and succinct description of what Casey instinctively knew wasn't as simple as he made it sound. "Everyone's okay?" she asked, deciding that was the important part.

"Yes."

"All right then."

"Sleep. I need to go meet with Ghost and the others, but I'll be back later to take you home."

"Umm hmmm." It was more a random sound than actual words, but Beatle seemed to understand her anyway.

"Love you, Casey Shea. You have no idea how much."

"Love you too, Beatle."

She felt him kiss her forehead, and smiled. She loved when he did that. Then she was asleep once more.

"SHE REALLY DOESN'T remember any of it?" Blade asked Beatle an hour and a half later. All the Deltas were meeting with their commander and going over what had happened.

"Not much. Yet. The doctor says that the higher the intake of the drug, the less memory the person usually has of the incident. She may remember snatches of things here and there, but probably never all of what happened."

"I hate that fucking bitch," Truck said under his breath, obviously referring to Doctor Santos. He hadn't been in the room for most of what happened, but he'd seen the absolute look of terror on Casey's face as she'd hung above him out the window. "Not once had Casey ever looked at my ugly mug and been scared. Until yesterday. Even in Costa Rica in the fucking jungle, she was never scared of me."

"If it makes you feel better, she wasn't seeing *you*," Beatle soothed. "From what I could understand in her ramblings, she thought you were a Hercules beetle."

"Now *those* are ugly fuckers," Hollywood said with a shiver. "We came across one in the jungle and we didn't have Casey there to reassure us they were harmless. I thought I was gonna shit my pants."

Everyone laughed, and Beatle appreciated his friend's attempt at lightening the tense atmosphere. He gave Hollywood a slight chin lift and got one in return.

"Where is that bitch now?" Coach asked, referring again to Marie.

"Cops took her downtown, but she was so out of it, rambling on and on about her research, that they ended up having to take her to mental," Beatle said.

"But she's going to be charged, right?" Fletch asked.

"Yeah. I'm not sure with what yet, but I have a feeling the DA is going to do what he can to pile on as much as possible."

"Anyone call the university to give them a head's up?" Chase asked. He'd been included in the meeting since he'd been there when everything had gone down.

"I called this morning, right when they opened,"

Ghost said. "I told the dean what happened, that one of her instructors is bat-shit crazy. Told her that she essentially kidnapped two students, drugged another professor, and all of this after arranging the kidnapping and attempted murder down in Costa Rica. She was so shocked, she didn't even try to keep anything from me, informing me that Marie's latest request for research had been denied, but she didn't say what she had proposed."

"Yeah, because she wanted to fucking kidnap people and observe their reactions," Blade groused, leaning back in his chair with his arms crossed on his chest. "I'd deny that fucking research request too."

"I also talked to the officials down in Costa Rica," Ghost continued. "They confirmed that Marie Santos entered the country two days after Casey and her students. Then she left the day after we did. They're going to interview some of the people in Guacalito and see if they remember Marie hanging around, and I have a feeling they will."

"So, it's over?" Blade asked.

Beatle tensed. He sure as hell hoped so.

"I'm thinking, yes. As long as the officials down in Central America don't come back with any information saying otherwise, it's over. I'm guessing the villagers probably left after the Huntsmen rescued the other women because they were afraid of more retaliation. I'm not sure though. I wouldn't be surprised if the Costa

Rican government never finds out what exactly happened to that village or why they just up and left. The important thing is that Marie hired locals who don't have the resources, or any real reason, to come to the States to try to find Casey. She's safe and can go back to her normal life," Ghost reassured the team.

The words were a relief, but at the same time, they created more stress in Beatle. He didn't want Casey to go back to Florida. He wanted her to stay in Texas with him. She said she would, but she might change her mind now that she was safe. She was a grown woman with a career and a life. The last thing he wanted to do was hold her back. She'd told him she'd been working toward tenure. That was a big deal. If she quit and changed universities, she'd have to start from scratch, working her way back up with a new administration. It wasn't a decision either of them could take lightly.

"How are Emily and Annie?" Beatle asked Fletch, not wanting to think about Casey leaving.

"They're good. I'm so proud of Annie. She did exactly what we taught her. When Emily said the code word, red, she did just as we'd trained her and didn't ask any questions. They went to the safe room and locked themselves in. They watched what was going on via the cameras, but didn't come out until I went and got them."

"No residual bad memories from the wedding reception?" It was Chase who asked that time.

Fletch smiled. "Em is planning on redecorating the garage apartment, says that it's seen too much sadness. And Annie has been driving that tank all over the place, chasing away the bad guys. I'm going to have to replace the motor sooner rather than later, I think."

"So, they're doing okay," Coach concluded.

"They're absolutely fine," Fletch reassured everyone.

"Anyone talked to Jaylyn or Kristina?" Hollywood asked.

"I did," Ghost said. "I called their parents, and they arrived home this morning. Both girls are fine. Doctor Martin was amazing with them. Beatle, you were already gone with Casey, but he was able to talk to them while they were still under, and was able to ascertain that Marie hadn't put any weird triggers on them. They were confused when the doctor brought them out of their hypnotic state, but not panicked. He actually thinks they'll heal much faster now that Marie isn't constantly harping on the way they fell apart when Casey was separated from them."

Everyone nodded in relief. The last thing the college students needed was more trauma after what they'd already been though.

"Anyone else have anything they need or want to add?" Ghost asked, looking at each of the men in turn.

Everyone shook their heads, but Blade spoke up.

"Thank you all for having my sister's back. I know I don't need to say it, but I'm saying it all the same."

"You're right," Coach said quietly. "You don't need to say it. We've all been there. I don't know what it is about us and finding women who seem to get into extreme situations, but I'm glad we've been there for them."

"Definitely," Ghost said.

"Agreed," Hollywood piped in.

Blade turned to Beatle then. "I told you once, but I'll say it again, I couldn't imagine a better man with my sister. You've shown time and time again that you'll do whatever is necessary to keep her safe. She deserves a man like you, one who will always have her back and put her first in your life. We all know being married to a Delta isn't easy, but I have absolutely no concerns when it comes to the two of you. I just have one request..."

When he paused, Beatle raised an eyebrow at his friend.

"Just don't run off and get married in some bullshit secret ceremony. My mom would have a heart attack. And I really want to see her dad walk her down the aisle."

"I'm not sure we'll ever get there, man," Beatle said honestly. "We have a lot of hurdles to jump."

"Fuck jumping them," Truck said. "Knock those fuckers down and plow right through them. Life is short. Really fucking short. Don't wait. If you love her, and she loves you, it's stupid to wait."

Beatle eyed his friend for a long moment, having the feeling Truck wasn't talking about him and Casey. When Truck didn't elaborate, Beatle nodded at him then turned back to Blake. "I promise not to run off to Vegas to get married."

"Make him promise not to do a quickie civil ceremony downtown either," Coach added.

"Only assholes like you would do something like that," Beatle shot back.

Everyone chuckled.

"If we're done here, I need to go and get some real work done." The commander spoke up for the first time. By his grin, it was obvious he was kidding. He'd been just as concerned and relieved that Casey was all right as the rest of the team. "Beatle, you have the next two weeks off. Get Casey settled. Figure your shit out so you can come back ready to work. I expect you not to have your head up your ass on the next mission. Got it?"

"Yes, Sir," Beatle responded immediately.

Everyone stood and shook hands with the commander before he left.

Fletch slapped Beatle on the back. "Ready to go get your woman?"

"Hell yeah. Ghost?" The other man turned on his way out of the room. "You'll let me know when you hear from the officers in Costa Rica?"

"Of course. But I honestly think this is done and over, Beatle. Take Casey home and help her heal. Don't worry about anything unless you have a reason to. Okay?"

"Sounds good." He then turned to Chase and held out his hand. When the other man took it and they shook, Beatle said, "Thank you for being there."

"I didn't do anything," Chase said, shoving his hands in his pockets. "Hell, I was sitting across the yard and had no idea anything was wrong."

"Don't feel bad," Beatle told the officer. "You didn't know. None of us did. If Casey hadn't clued me in by using my real name, I would've still been sitting here on post when she was tripping. You might not be a Delta, but you're just as important to all of us. You need us, we're there, and not just because you're Rayne's brother. Got it?"

Beatle wasn't sure what was going through the other man's head, but after a beat, he nodded. "Got it. But I'll leave the wooing to you guys. I'm not in the market for a woman."

Everyone chuckled.

"That's what we all said too," Hollywood replied.

"You never know when love'll hit. You'll be going about your business, then *bam*, there she'll be," Fletch told his friend.

"Ain't that the truth," Coach murmured.

Chase shrugged. "Whatever. Now, if you pansies are done here, like the commander, I've got real work to do."

No one took offense, they just laughed as the man shook his head at them and left the room.

"You need help getting Casey home?" Truck asked.

"Nah, I think we're good," Beatle said.

"Think she'd be up for company later? I'd love to see her if you think it wouldn't freak her out," Truck said.

"She'd love that. I'll give you a yell when we're settled."

"You going back to Fletch's?"

Beatle shook his head. "No, I don't want to risk any bad memories from being there yet. I'll take her to my place."

"You clean since the last time I saw it?" Truck asked with one brow raised skeptically.

Beatle leaned over and picked up a pen off the table and threw it at his friend. "Shut it."

They smiled at each other. "Let me know when she's ready, and I'll come over," Truck said.

"Will do. Later."

"Later."

Beatle barely heard his friend. He was on his way out the door to get back to Casey. She was going to be fine. If she could get through her ordeal in the jungle, this would be a piece of cake. It wasn't her recovery he was worried about. It was the decisions they had in front of them about their relationship that scared the shit out of him.

Epilogue

CASEY COULDN'T WAIT to get home. She'd just completed her first day back teaching and it had gone really well. She'd been nervous—who wasn't for the first day?—and she wanted to talk to Beatle.

But then again, she always wanted to talk to him. It wasn't the same talking on the phone, but it was something.

When her phone rang, Casey saw it was Jaylyn.

"Hey, Jaylyn. How are you?"

"I'm good."

"How were your classes today?"

"They were okay. It's not the same without you here, you know?"

Casey smiled and wiped her sweaty forehead as she walked to her car. She'd been in Texas for a couple months and didn't think she'd ever get used to the heat. Florida had been hot, but Texas was hot on a whole new level. "You get your paper finished?"

Casey had insisted that all three students finish their research papers they'd been working on in Costa Rica. It had been a tough road for all four of them. No one really had enthusiasm any longer for the ant species they'd been researching before the kidnapping, but the university had been really good about granting an extension, and Casey had worked with each of the women to help them get their papers done.

"Yeah. I should know my grade next week," Jaylyn said. "But you know what?"

"What?"

"I don't really care anymore. I could fail the stupid thing and it wouldn't matter. We went through something awful, but I learned a lot about myself in the process. And my new counselor says that as long as I'm growing and learning, it doesn't matter how others grade me."

"She sounds very smart," Casey said with a smile, twisting the key in the ignition. The air that blasted out of the vents was hot, but she knew it would cool off soon. "But be that as it may, don't throw away your education because of what happened."

"I'm not," Jaylyn assured her. "But I might be changing my major."

"As long as it's not to psychology, I'm okay with that," Casey said dryly.

The young woman on the other end of the line laughed. "Hell no. I was thinking education. I'd like to teach elementary school, I think."

"That sounds wonderful," Casey told her former student, and meant it. "How are my babies doing?"

She didn't remember a lot of the bad trip she'd had as a result of the LSD Marie had forced on her, but one thing she *had* remembered were the flying cockroaches she thought were trying to eat her eyeballs. As a result, when she and Beatle had gone to Florida to empty out her apartment and pack up her stuff to send to Texas, she'd taken one look at her pets, and had immediately rushed to the bathroom to puke. She'd had to rehome them—much to Beatle's relief, since he wouldn't be living with the cockroaches—and luckily, Jaylyn said she'd love to have them.

"They're good. You know they're going to outlive us both."

"True. I appreciate you taking them. Beatle was super happy he wasn't going to have to share his space with my babies."

"But he would've," Jaylyn said with confidence.

"Yeah, he would've," Casey said with a smile. She still thought it was hilarious that a woman with a PhD in entomology ended up with a man who couldn't stand bugs, but she'd gladly overlook that flaw in him because everything else was amazing.

"Anyway, I just wanted to call and say thank you for all you've done for me. I know things weren't easy for you either," Jaylyn told her.

"You're welcome," Casey said softly. "I wish you all the best. Call anytime."

"I will. I gotta go. Later, Doctor Shea."

"Later, Jaylyn."

Casey hung up and looked at her phone, lost in her own thoughts. When she felt the air cool down enough to make her more comfortable, she shook her head and put down the phone. She had shit to do. Namely, get home to her boyfriend, so they could talk about their workdays together.

It was one of her favorite things about living with Beatle. Regardless of how late it was, they always talked about how their days had gone.

BEATLE CHECKED THE app on his phone to see where Casey was. They both had the locator apps installed on their phones so they could keep track of each other. Since Casey was driving back and forth to Baylor University every day, he wanted to make sure she was safe.

He'd rented a nice townhouse in northern Temple, to cut down on her commute a little. His old apartment in Killeen had been small, and he'd wanted to do whatever he could to make sure Casey never regretted her decision to give up her job and move to Texas.

He still couldn't believe she'd done it. She'd told him that he was way more important than a job, but he was still in awe that she'd changed her entire life for an Army guy like him. He didn't deserve her, but he sure as hell wasn't going to be a martyr and give her up.

The university dean in Florida hadn't been surprised when Casey told her she was quitting. She'd admitted that after the kidnapping, she had a hunch Casey wouldn't be back. But she'd gone a step further and called a colleague at Baylor, and told him that Casey would be moving to the area and would make an excellent addition to his team.

Beatle'd had no doubt she'd get the job, and after a couple interviews, he'd been proven right. The transition had been fairly easy, and she'd managed to be ready to go for the fall semester. Everything had fallen into place so easily, it was as if it was meant to be.

Seeing that Casey was almost home, Beatle hurried to put the finishing touches on the special dinner he had planned. Not only were they celebrating her first day at her new job, but he'd gotten good news from the commander that day. He couldn't wait to share it with Casey.

Within five minutes, Beatle heard Casey's key in the lock. He waited in the kitchen for her, and the first thing he saw when she came around the corner was her bright smile.

He relaxed. He'd been nervous for her. He wanted her to like Baylor and her new job. Apparently, she did.

She came right to him, dropping her bag on the floor as she did so. Throwing her arms around him, she stood on her tiptoes and tilted her head back.

Beatle gave her what she wanted. He kissed her long and hard, only pulling back when he felt his control slipping. It didn't matter how much time went by and how often they made love. Every time he was around her, he wanted her as badly as he had the first time.

"Have a good day?" he asked.

"Yup. I didn't think I'd like teaching that freshman biology resource seminar, but surprisingly, the kids all seemed really interested in finding out what they could do with a degree in biology."

"And your entomology class? How'd that go?"

"You know I loved it. Even though I have no desire to travel outside the US to study bugs again, it was really nice to informally chat with my students about my experience in Costa Rica...the experience of studying bugs, that is." She grinned. "Although I'm sure the students will become less enamored of their seemingly down-to-earth teacher when they have their first test. Back in Florida, the students knew I was tough. This new batch of kids will have to learn that the hard way."

Beatle smiled down at Casey. He loved listening to her talk about teaching. It was obvious she loved it, and that she was good at what she did. Maybe if he'd had a few more teachers like her, he would've made it further along in his education than he had. But then he might not be here with her now. "I love you," he said.

"I love you too. What'd you make for dinner?"

Beatle suppressed the chuckle. He loved how nonchalant she was about telling him she loved him. It wasn't a big deal for her. It just was.

"Steak. They're resting now and should be done in a minute or two."

"Yum. Steak," Casey said, pulling away from him to lift the lid off a pan on the stove. "And rice? Excellent."

Casey helped him dish up their supper and he carried their plates to the table. "Sit, I'll get you a glass of wine."

They shared general conversation throughout the meal, and Beatle mused again about how different his life was now compared to a few months ago. He never thought he'd be the one making sure dinner was ready for his woman when she got home from work. He wasn't an asshole, but he'd always pictured himself in a traditional man-woman type relationship. Where he worked and made the bulk of the money for the household, and his girlfriend would clean and have dinner ready for *him* when he got home.

Casey blew that stereotype out of the water. She made way more money than he ever would in the Army, and many nights, she got home after him. Their house wasn't exactly clean, but it didn't bother either of them. They were together and happy, that was all that mattered.

They were still getting to know each other, and every morning, Beatle woke up wondering what he'd learn about Casey that day. He couldn't imagine ever being bored with her.

When they were finished, he brought the dishes to the sink and left them there; he'd put them in the dishwasher later. He took Casey's hand and led her to the couch. He sat, pulling her onto his lap as he did.

"I talked to the commander today," Beatle said.

"And?"

"The police down in Costa Rica found that guy from the jungle the other day."

Her eyes widened. "The one I pushed into the bullet ant mound?"

"Yeah. That one."

"He's alive?" Casey asked.

Beatle could see the hope in her eyes. He didn't know she was worried about the asshole's fate, but he should've realized it. She wasn't a soldier. She wasn't used to violence. She sure as hell wouldn't want the death of another human resting on her shoulders. "Yeah, sweetheart. He's alive." The relief in her eyes was confirmation that he should've talked to her about this before now.

"Good. What'd he say?"

"He confirmed what we thought all along. Marie paid him and the others in his village to kidnap you and the girls. When they were rescued, and she found out that you were too, she said she'd double what she had offered them if they tracked you down for her then killed you."

Casey's shoulders slumped. Beatle hurried on to tell her the good news.

"It's over, Case. He confirmed that no one was looking for you. When Marie left Costa Rica without paying them, and after so many of them were killed in the jungle, no one had any desire, or the funds, to chase you all the way back to the States."

"So I don't have to worry about anyone tracking me down and trying to kidnap me again?" she asked hopefully.

"No."

Every muscle in her body relaxed against him, and Beatle was thrilled he could do that for her.

"And Marie? Have you heard anything more about her lately?"

This was the not-so-fun part of the new information he had for her. "She'd dead, Case."

Casey sat up on Beatle's lap. "*What*? I thought she was getting help?"

"She was. Her trial wasn't set to start for another couple of months, and the Florida DA ordered that she remain in the mental health facility. But I guess she fooled people into believing she was more stable than she was. After she received word that her research was morally reprehensible and would never see the light of day, she hung herself in her room, between the nightly welfare checks by the guards."

Casey sagged back against him, and Beatle waited for her to process what he'd told her.

"I'm not sure what to feel about it," she admitted after a minute or two.

"Feel however you want, sweetheart. I'm not going to condemn you if you're happy she's dead and you don't have to testify. I have to admit, I wasn't all that thrilled about you having to relive what you went through at her trial."

"Well, me neither, but I'm not exactly thrilled she's dead."

Beatle put his finger under her chin and turned her face toward his. He gazed into her eyes for a long moment, trying to figure out where her head was at. When he didn't see guilt, he was satisfied. "You wouldn't be the woman I loved more than life itself if you were happy she was gone. But, I'll tell you, I am ecstatic she's dead. She kidnapped you. Tortured you. Hired men to rape then kill you. Then she tried to fuck with your head some more—and *laughed* when you were so out of it, you thought me and the others were giant bugs. I'm not sorry she's no longer living."

"Well, jeez, Beatle. Why don't you tell me how you really feel?" Casey mumbled.

Beatle let her break eye contact and he gathered her against his chest. "I won't pretend to be sad she's gone, Case. I've killed more people than I can even remember in my lifetime, all of them bad. I didn't get to kill Marie Santos, but I'm not sorry she's gone. I'm just sorry she didn't have to suffer like you did. If I had my way, she would've died by being thrown into a hole in the ground and left to die."

"You're a little bloodthirsty, Beatle," Casey informed him.

He couldn't help it. He smiled. "When it comes to you, yeah, I am. You have a problem with that?"

She didn't answer for a beat, and just when Beatle was getting concerned he'd gone too far, she shook her head. "Nah. I'm okay with you going all he-man on someone's ass if they try to hurt me. As long as you're okay if I do the same."

"Case, you couldn't hurt anyone."

"I hurt *you*," she informed him, running her fingers over the scar on his arm where she'd sliced him with the knife when she'd been tripping.

He chuckled. "I didn't even feel it," he reassured her

for the millionth time.

"Huh," she huffed. "Liar. But yeah, you're right. Violence isn't really my thing. But I *do* have access to lots and lots of creepy-crawlies. I can get my revenge without having to resort to violence."

Beatle shuddered. "God. I don't even want to *think* of what you could do with all those bugs in the lab at the university."

Casey giggled. Then she looked up at him, her gaze intense. "I'm happy."

Beatle ran his hand up and down her back. "I'm glad. I am too."

"As much as what happened sucked, it led you to me. I can't be sorry about that."

Beatle took a deep breath and nodded. "Love you, Case. You'll never know how much."

"I do know how much, because I love you the same way."

Beatle stood then with Casey in his arms. She didn't protest, simply held on to him as he moved.

He went down the hall to their bedroom. Without saying a word, he put her down on the bed and reached for the hem of her shirt. Beatle needed to be inside her. Now.

An hour later, they lay snuggled together on the king-size bed, the covers in disarray around them, but neither made a move to pull the sheet up and over themselves. A light sheen of sweat covered their bodies and their breathing wasn't yet back to normal after their enthusiastic lovemaking.

"Beatle?" Casey asked.

"Yeah, sweetheart?"

"Do you think we could maybe hang a hammock in the corner of the room?"

Beatle threw his head back and laughed. He had a feeling Casey would always keep him on his toes. "I'll go online tomorrow and order one," he told her when he had himself under control.

Her fingers absently traced patterns on his chest, and he felt her smile against his shoulder. "When I was in that hole, I wanted to live so badly," she said softly. "I didn't know why; all I knew was that I couldn't give up because something great was right around the corner waiting for me. Then you appeared. I looked up and knew with one glance, *you* were that great thing waiting for me."

Beatle's throat closed up and he couldn't speak. All he could do was tighten his hold around her. As if she understood, Casey leaned up, kissed his jawline, and settled her head back against him.

Later, after Beatle had pulled up the covers to keep their cooling bodies warm, and when he heard Casey snoring lightly, Beatle found the words he hadn't been able to call forth earlier.

"I had no idea I'd find the other half of my soul in the jungles of Costa Rica."

TRUCK LET HIMSELF into his house, closing the door silently behind him. He didn't know if Mary was sleeping, and if so, he didn't want to wake her. She didn't sleep well as it was. He put down his bag in the front hall and went into the family room.

She was fast asleep on the couch, a cooking show playing on the television. Truck kneeled down next to her and simply stared at her for several minutes, soaking in all that was Mary.

Her hair had grown back enough that she no longer looked sick. The fact of the matter was that she *was* no longer sick. She'd beaten cancer...twice. But this last time had been close. She'd worn a wig until her hair had grown back enough that she could style it. No one had noticed because she went out of her way to avoid Rayne and the others as much as possible.

Despite being closed now, Truck remembered how her beautiful brown eyes had been dulled by pain and suffering. The chemo this last round was tough, but it was the radiation that had almost done her in. The skin on her chest had literally been burnt because of the treatments. It had been painful to the touch, and she hadn't been able to lift anything. The doctor had prescribed several different highly potent painkillers, and she'd used at least three different types of creams to try to both relieve the pain and heal her skin.

But that was behind her...*them*...now. All they were dealing with was the lingering numbness and tingling in her fingers as a result of the chemo. But the doctor had said that too should fade with time.

Giving in to temptation, Truck ran one of his hands over the soft, short hair on her head. She'd had beautiful, thick brown hair before she'd lost it, and it had grown in fine and gray. She'd gone to her hairdresser and had her put in pink and purple stripes and highlights, much as she'd worn it the first time he'd seen her.

Even though his touch was light, Mary's eyes opened. "You're back," she said sleepily.

"Yeah, babe. I'm back."

"You good?" she asked.

"I'm good," Truck told her with a small smile. Then he stood and easily picked her up. She didn't protest, simply snuggled into his chest and wrapped her arms around his neck.

Truck loved that Mary was never afraid to speak her mind. If she was tired, she admitted it. If she was pissed at him, or anyone else, she had no problem letting him know. He understood her, probably better than anyone. To others, she seemed like a bitch. Hard. Unbending.

But it was times like this, when she relaxed and let him care for her, that Truck loved the best.

He carried her into the master bedroom and placed her gently on the huge California king-size bed. She immediately turned on her side and fell back to sleep. Truck wanted to climb in next to her, but had a few things to do first.

Reluctantly, he stepped away from the bed toward the door. His eyes were drawn to the framed photo on the wall just inside the door. It had been taken a couple months ago, on their wedding day. It was the day his friend, Fish, had needed him and the team out in Idaho, but Truck had finally convinced Mary to marry him, so he hadn't been able to go.

Truck had loved Mary practically since the first time he'd seen her. She'd been super snarky to him, all in defense of her best friend, Rayne. Their wedding day had been one of the best days of his life.

Truck ran a hand over the glass-covered picture and smiled. Mary thought after she was better, they'd get a divorce and no one would ever have to know they'd been married. Mary still had her apartment, but more often than not she ended up sleeping at his house. When she was sick she went out of her way to talk to Rayne on the phone instead of seeing her as much as possible, but when they did meet, she made sure to have Rayne pick her up at *her* apartment.

But there was no way he was letting her go. Not after he'd been sleeping next to her most nights for the last couple of months. Not after he'd held her when she felt like shit after chemo. Not when she'd been in so much pain from the radiation burns on her chest that she'd let him put the salve on her skin.

He closed his bedroom door quietly and headed back to the living room. Nope, Mary Weston was his. Period. Forever.

BLADE SAT ON his couch and picked half-heartedly at his meal. He'd made a microwave dinner because he was too tired for anything else. No, that was a lie. He was simply too depressed to make anything else.

He was happy for his sister. Casey and Beatle were deliriously content, and Blade was glad. But he'd realized earlier that now he was the last man on the team who didn't have a woman of his own. The rest of the guys were home with their wives and girlfriends now, happier than pigs in shit. And here he was, pathetically sitting on his couch, looking at a blank TV screen, wondering if he'd ever find someone who could put up with him.

His phone rang. The house phone. The one he never answered and only had because it was cheaper to get the cable and Internet package if he threw in the phone line too. It periodically rang, but he never picked it up. But tonight, he was bored. And restless. And…jealous. Jealous of the happiness his teammates had because he wanted it for himself.

"Hello?"

"Hi! My name is Wendy. How are you?"

"Uh…good."

"Awesome. I'm calling tonight to ask if you've thought about your future."

"My future?" Blade asked. He knew he wasn't going to buy anything from someone who'd cold called him, but the woman's voice on the other end of the phone was melodious and soothing. How pathetic was he that he was prolonging the conversation because he liked the sound of her voice?

"Yes, your future. Are you married?"

"No."

"Kids?"

"No again."

"Right, well, you must have family."

Blade could tell that she was getting desperate. "Yeah, Wendy. I have family."

"Great!" Her voice was perky again. "If anything happens to you, you'll want to make sure your family doesn't have any burdens. You'll want to take care of them. I can help you do that. Did you know that term life insurance is way cheaper than whole life? It is. And for only about twenty bucks a month, you can get a sizable policy that will allow your loved ones to give you the funeral you deserve, and give them closure and peace of mind at the same time. Also, when you—"

Blade tuned out the actual words she was saying, and concentrated once again on the sound of her voice. He closed his eyes and imagined that she was sitting next to him on his couch and talking about her day. Pathetic, but it made him feel less lonely.

"Sir?"

Blade blinked and opened his eyes. He realized that she'd stopped talking and was waiting for his response.

"Yeah, Wendy?"

"What do you think?"

"I'm in the Army."

"Oh...uh...okay?"

He chuckled. "I've got life insurance. I don't need any more."

"Oh." Now she sounded defeated. "I understand."

For some reason, Blade didn't want the conversation to end. "How are *you* doing tonight, Wendy?"

"Me? Um...I'm okay, I guess."

"You don't sound okay," Blade observed.

"Well, you're the eighty-third person I've called tonight and I haven't sold even one policy."

"That sucks," he commiserated, not sure if she was

trying to make him feel bad so he'd order a life insurance policy he didn't need, or want.

"Yeah." Her voice perked up. "But at least you didn't hang up on me. Or call me names. Or swear at me."

"That happens?"

"All the time," she told him.

"I can't imagine making cold calls is all that fun," he observed.

"It sucks," she whispered.

"Then why do you do it?" Blade honestly wanted to know.

"Because I need the extra income. I've got a day job, but working here a few hours each night gives me enough extra that I can keep my head above water."

Blade understood that. When he'd joined the Army, he'd been flat broke. Even ketchup sandwiches were too expensive some days. "I've been there," he told her.

"Can I...can I ask you a question?"

"I think you just did," Blade said dryly.

She giggled, and the girly sound went straight to his cock. Blade blinked in surprise. He hadn't been thinking about the woman on the other end of the phone in a sexual way, but the second she laughed...all of a sudden, he wanted her. Had no idea what she looked like, or anything about her other than her name, but that quiet, sweet sound was like nothing he'd heard before.

"What's your name?"

"Aspen," Blade said without hesitation.

"Really? Like the tree?"

It was his turn to chuckle. "Yeah, like the tree."

"I like it. It's unusual. Aspen?"

"Yeah, babe?"

"Thanks for being nice. I've had a rough day, and while I didn't really expect you to buy any insurance from me, I appreciate you being nice about turning me down."

The thought of someone being *not* nice to her struck Blade hard. "You're welcome. So...do you do this every night?"

"What?"

"Call strangers and talk to them?"

"Well, no. I only work a few days a week, and as I told you before, most people hang up on me or cuss me out."

"If you call me again, I won't hang up or cuss you out," Blade told her.

She was silent for a moment, then asked, "Are you saying you wouldn't mind if I called again?"

"That's what I'm saying," Blade confirmed, wondering if he was out of his mind. The guys would give him all sorts of hell if they knew he was so hard up for companionship that he was practically begging a stranger to call him. Hell, she could be decades older than him, or hideously ugly, but he didn't think either was true.

"I...I'd like that," she said softly. "But you should know, I don't always sell insurance. Every night it's something different."

"Then I'll look forward to seeing what you're selling next time. It'll be a surprise."

She giggled again, and Blade closed his eyes, taking it in.

"I'm not sure it'll be anything you need."

"I need a lot of things," Blade said cryptically. "You have my number?"

He heard papers shuffling, and then she said, "Yeah."

"I'll look forward to hearing from you soon then."

"Okay. Aspen?"

"Yeah?"

"You said you're in the Army. Thank you for your service. I don't know what you do, but whatever it is, I'm sure it's important. You'll be safe...right?"

And just like that, Blade was gone. It had been a long time since anyone, other than his sister, had worried about him. "Thanks, sweetheart. Yeah, I'll be safe."

"Good. Okay, I gotta go. My boss is giving me the side eye. I think he knows that I'm just shooting the shit and wasting time. Thanks again for not being a dick."

"You're welcome. Later."

"Bye."

Blade clicked off the phone and sat on the couch for several minutes, deep in thought, trying to decide if he was pathetic, crazy, or simply a sucker. Finally, he got up and dropped his half-eaten dinner in the garbage. He went down the hall to his room and got ready for bed.

As he laid there and tried to shut down his mind long enough to fall asleep, he couldn't help but wonder if Wendy would call again. He hoped so...he really did.

"HOW'S SADIE?"

Chase kept his voice down, as he knew the woman Sean Taggart was asking about was asleep in the other room.

"She's good."

"Any sight of that prick, Jonathan Jones?"

"No."

"I'm going to come down again this weekend."

Chase silently sighed. Sean had been coming down to the Fort Hood area—with his blessing—to check on his niece every Saturday since Chase had brought her to his apartment to keep an eye on her. Jonathan Jones was a pedophile who had somehow become obsessed with Sadie, and was still on the loose. Chase had volunteered to keep watch over Sadie until the asshole had been found.

"Sounds good. I have another meeting with the detective who's been in contact with the FBI down in San Antonio on Saturday. You want to meet us at the station?"

"That'll work. Grace packed another huge bag of her stuff that I'll bring with me too. You really okay with all this?" Sean asked. "It's been a month, and Sadie can be a handful at the best of times. I still think she's safer there with you because Jonathan could easily find out her connection to us and come up here looking for her, but if she's cramping your style, I'll make it work."

"No," Chase said quickly. "It's not a hardship having her here."

Sean must've heard something in Chase's tone, because his voice lowered and he said threateningly, "Don't mess with my niece, Jackson."

"I'm not. She's safe with me. In every sense."

There was silence on the phone for a moment before Sean said, "She'd better be. I'll see you Saturday." Then he hung up.

Chase clicked off the phone and listened for a second to see if his conversation had woken Sadie. When he didn't hear anything from the guest bedroom, he sighed in relief.

He'd been drawn to Sadie from the moment he'd

seen her picture, but having her living with him, sharing his space, had only solidified his attraction. She was tough, didn't take shit from anyone, and was quick with a smartass comeback. But more than that, she was compassionate, generous, and had a beautiful soul.

The thought of Jonathan Jones getting his hands on her—again—was abhorrent. She'd handled what had happened to her amazingly well, but Chase didn't want that asshole to ever touch her again.

Sadie's uncles were more than qualified to keep her safe, but the caveman inside of Chase wanted her with him. *He* wanted to protect her. He'd do whatever it took to not only ensure she could live her life how she wanted, but to earn her love as well.

Look for the next book in the *Delta Force Heroes* Series, *Rescuing Sadie*.

To sign up for Susan's Newsletter go to:
www.stokeraces.com/contact-1.html

Or text: STOKER to 24587 for text alerts on your mobile device

Discover other titles by Susan Stoker

Delta Force Heroes Series

Rescuing Rayne

Assisting Aimee – Loosely related to DF

Rescuing Emily

Rescuing Harley

Marrying Emily

Rescuing Kassie

Rescuing Bryn

Rescuing Casey

Rescuing Sadie (April 2018)

Rescuing Wendy (May 2018)

Rescuing Mary (Oct 2018)

Badge of Honor: Texas Heroes Series

Justice for Mackenzie

Justice for Mickie

Justice for Corrie

Justice for Laine (novella)

Shelter for Elizabeth

Justice for Boone

Shelter for Adeline

Shelter for Sophie

Justice for Erin

Justice for Milena (Mar 2018)

Shelter for Blythe (June 2018)

Justice for Hope (Sept 2018)

Shelter for Quinn (TBA)
Shelter for Koren (TBA)
Shelter for Penelope (TBA)

Ace Security Series

Claiming Grace
Claiming Alexis
Claiming Bailey
Claiming Felicity (Feb 2018)

Mountain Mercenaries Series

Defending Allye (Aug 2018)
Defending Raven (Dec 2018)
With lots more to come!

SEAL of Protection Series

Protecting Caroline
Protecting Alabama
Protecting Fiona
Marrying Caroline (novella)
Protecting Summer
Protecting Cheyenne
Protecting Jessyka
Protecting Julie (novella)
Protecting Melody
Protecting the Future
Protecting Alabama's Kids (novella)
Protecting Kiera (novella)
Protecting Dakota

Stand Alone

The Guardian Mist
Nature's Rift
A Princess for Cale

Special Operations Fan Fiction

www.stokeraces.com/kindle-worlds.html

Beyond Reality Series

Outback Hearts
Flaming Hearts
Frozen Hearts

Writing as Annie George:

Stepbrother Virgin (erotic novella)

Connect with Susan Online

Susan's Facebook Profile and Page:
www.facebook.com/authorsstoker
www.facebook.com/authorsusanstoker

Follow Susan on Twitter:
www.twitter.com/Susan_Stoker

Find Susan's Books on Goodreads:
www.goodreads.com/SusanStoker

Email: Susan@StokerAces.com

Website: www.StokerAces.com

To sign up for Susan's Newsletter go to:
www.stokeraces.com/contact-1.html

Or text: STOKER to 24587 for text alerts on your mobile device